WARRIOR REVEALED

With deliberate movements, he removed his long-sleeved black T-shirt. His breath gave off little puffs of air, but he seemed immune to the cold. He had his back to her and his eyes facing skyward, so she could see a second tattoo—this one of a lion—where it sat high on his right shoulder.

Unable to tear her gaze away, she drank in the perfection of his body. Broad shoulders gleamed in the moonlight as the tight play of muscles along his back responded to his every movement. His torso grew narrow as it descended to his stomach and formed into lean hips. A small network of scars crisscrossed his lower back.

Where had they come from? The scars were faded white with age, faint on his skin, but visible nonetheless.

He shifted slightly and extended his arm. An intricately designed tattoo decorated his exposed left arm. The ink had interlocking circles with a zodiac symbol she couldn't identify clearly visible in the center of the pattern.

Brody tossed her a glance over his shoulder, a broad smile on his lips. "Ready?"

WARRIOR ASCENDED

THE SONS OF THE ZODIAC

ADDISON FOX

A SIGNET ECLIPSE BOOK

SIGNET ECLIPSE
Published by New American Library, a division of
Penguin Group (USA) Inc., 375 Hudson Street,
New York, New York 10014, USA
Penguin Group (Canada), 90 Eglinton Avenue East, Suite 700, Toronto,
Ontario M4P 2Y3, Canada (a division of Pearson Penguin Canada Inc.)
Penguin Books Ltd., 80 Strand, London WC2R 0RL, England
Penguin Ireland, 25 St. Stephen's Green, Dublin 2,
Ireland (a division of Penguin Books Ltd.)
Penguin Group (Australia), 250 Camberwell Road, Camberwell, Victoria 3124,
Australia (a division of Pearson Australia Group Pty. Ltd.)
Penguin Books India Pvt. Ltd., 11 Community Centre, Panchsheel Park,
New Delhi - 110 017, India
Penguin Group (NZ), 67 Apollo Drive, Rosedale, North Shore 0632,
New Zealand (a division of Pearson New Zealand Ltd.)
Penguin Books (South Africa) (Pty.) Ltd., 24 Sturdee Avenue,
Rosebank, Johannesburg 2196, South Africa

Penguin Books Ltd., Registered Offices:
80 Strand, London WC2R 0RL, England

First published by Signet Eclipse, an imprint of New American Library,
a division of Penguin Group (USA) Inc.

First Printing, March 2010
10 9 8 7 6 5 4 3 2 1

PUBLISHER'S NOTE
This is a work of fiction. Names, characters, places, and incidents either are the product
of the author's imagination or are used fictitiously, and any resemblance to actual per-
sons, living or dead, business establishments, events, or locales is entirely coincidental.
    The publisher does not have any control over and does not assume any responsi-
bility for author or third-party Web sites or their content.

For Mom and Dad.

You have given me so many gifts, but one stands out as I type this—the courage to believe in myself.

Thank you for believing in me.

Thank you for your love and affection, your sense of humor, and your willingness to always guide with compassionate honesty.

Thank you for keeping the waters of our safe harbor ever calm.

And thank you for saying no to space camp and diving lessons. Being an author is way more fun.

I love you and I am so blessed to call you mine.

ACKNOWLEDGMENTS

My deepest thanks to:

Becky Vinter, editor extraordinaire. Your belief in this book and your dedication to making it shine have been a gift beyond measure.

Holly Root, agent extraordinaire. Your warmth, talent, and absolute classiness make you such a joy to be around. Your belief in my work means so much to me and I am so happy to be on this publishing journey with you. (The fact you love red wine is really only a small side benefit.)

My family—every single crazy branch—the Karkosaks, the Foxes, the Milardos, the DeMarios, the Krafts, the Deorias, the Tabarrinis, the Naradkos, and the Freeses (and if I go into married surnames the lovely and wonderful people at NAL will likely ask me to pay for extra pages). Most especially to my beautiful, awesome sister, Beth, who bit her nails right along with me the day "the Call" came and who this past year gave our family my beautiful, awesome niece, Amelia.

The Writer Foxes—Alice Fairbanks-Burton, Lorraine Heath, Jo Davis, Tracy Garrett, Kay Thomas, Suzanne Welsh, Julie Benson, Sandy Blair, and Jane Graves. You ladies are my writing rocks and I love you all. (And the fact you all *also* love red wine is really only a small side benefit.)

An extraspecial thank-you to Alice Fairbanks-Burton, critique partner and cheerleader beyond measure.

To my peeps—the many wonderful people who make up my cheering section each and every day—you know who you are. And extraspecial thanks to the sisters of my heart—Christine, Carley, Roxane, Gregory, Beth G., Heather, Ellen, Margaret, Karen, Meridith, and Mary. Most are lucky enough to have one or two deep friendships to sustain them, but my cup of friendship overflows—with red wine, of course!

Finally, those of you well versed in Egyptology will no doubt notice I've taken some liberties with the tomb of Thutmose III. Any errors are admittedly mine, in the hopes of putting an intriguing spin on the lives of the ancients and their potential to influence our lives, even today. . . .

Leo Warrior

Proud and passionate, my Leo Warriors will guard their pride with fierce devotion.

Those they love will never be left unprotected and their enemies they will hunt to the ends of the earth.

Generous and loyal, my alluring and enigmatic Leo will charm the most distant of women with born ease.

But when he falls in love . . .

—The Diaries of Themis, goddess of justice

Prologue

The Fifth Age of Man

Zeus cast a look at the woman he'd once loved with mad abandon. Prim stature, back arrow-straight, auburn hair curling down that slim back in luscious waves.

It was the hair. It'd always been the hair. He'd seen her on Mount Olympus with her Titan sisters and the rest had faded away until only she remained.

Only Themis.

Clearing his throat, as if the action could clear the memories, he kept his voice purposely gruff. "Why did you drag me from the comfort of my bed?"

They stood before the Mirror of Truth—a large viewing screen in Themis's lodgings. She still refused to live in the grand home he'd left her, preferring instead this one-room servant's lodging. The mirror—the only possession she took with her after their separation—stood proudly in the center of the room so she could maintain her ability to monitor justice day and night.

Zeus glanced around him, the quality of her living quarters leaving a pool of acid churning in his stomach. "I should have banished this hovel years ago. I gave you a palace to live in and you chose this."

Themis lifted her chin. "I will not live in splendor when my brothers and sisters live, century after century, imprisoned in Tartarus."

"They betrayed me."

"We see it differently."

Unwilling to battle with her on this subject yet again, Zeus turned his attention toward the viewing screen. An empty vista spread out before them, a broad clearing amidst a forest of trees. The daylight was fading, the afternoon hues of gold creating pockets of color on the barren soil.

"What am I looking at?"

"You never did have any patience." A slight air of amusement threaded her words.

"A god doesn't need patience."

The small smile that ghosted her lips faded completely. "Then you wear the mantle well since you have never had any." Her blue gaze was pointed as she delivered that barb. "Or any other virtue, for that matter."

"What is this about?" He waved a hand, gold rings making a satisfying flash in the sun's dying rays. The newest one—a large gold circle encrusted with gems—particularly caught the light; a most suitable gift from his wife, Hera. "This is nothing but an empty field."

"Oh, how I wish." She exhaled a soft sigh just as the sound of hoofbeats broke the silence and a band of peasants broke through the forest into the vast clearing.

Within moments, the field before them filled with death and mass destruction, war cries intermingled with the screaming of the disheveled peasants as a band of soldiers tore them to pieces.

Fire rained down on two peasants who carried a bloody

third between them. Their clothes caught fire, dropping all three to their knees to writhe in agony in the dirt.

A young woman ran across the field, her skirt flying in her wake as tears of pure panic flooded her eyes—eyes that stared lifelessly at the sky moments later as one of the soldiers pulled his sword from her heart.

A small man, attempting to change direction and move away from the battling soldiers, veered in a zigzagging pattern as he ran while an angry rider bore down on him, trampling him in a burst of speed.

Zeus watched the display, the action on the field over nearly as fast as it had begun. Small fires continued to smolder as the sound of hoofbeats faded, the riders dispersing back into the forest from which they'd just come. Lifeless bodies littered the ground.

"You call me here to look at this? To what end, Themis? You think I find joy watching a band of peasants?"

"A band of peasants who were just murdered because they've no ability to defend themselves."

"So now the world is free of a dozen suffering souls. What of it?"

"You can fix this."

Zeus turned toward Themis, the sense she'd planned this conversation for some time taking hold. "Fix what?"

She flung a hand toward the screen. "This. This death and destruction. This vast wasteland humanity has become. It doesn't have to be this way. It isn't right."

"Right? What of right? They're humans."

"But there is no reason for it. There was a time, when we first created them, when humans lived in a golden age of peace. Now it is the strong versus the weak; the powerful few oppressing the vast, miserable masses."

"Ah. That's the root of it, now, isn't it? The injustice of it all. Even though these humans make their choices freely and live their lives as they see fit."

"I can't bear it." Without warning, the ever-stoic, ever-strong woman at his side fell into a fit of weeping that was so deep—so real—it took his breath away.

Could she really care for them? For these silly humans who did nothing but toil away their days in miserable, work-filled pursuits? These humans who had nothing but the gall of living hard lives, full of work and pain, only to die at the end?

Could they really matter to her?

"They've done this to themselves. Changed through the ages. Turned on one another."

She looked up at him, large tears rimming her eyes, wet, spiky lashes framing the irises of pale blue. "To themselves? How? They have no protection. No recourse from pain and suffering."

"They are mere humans. Mortals. They're not worthy of your tears. Why are you wasting my time with this?" The gruff anger was back; the bruised pride he didn't want to acknowledge but couldn't ignore. She had watched him walk away without so much as a tear; yet she cried for these weak humans as if the very fiber of her soul were being rent apart.

"But I can't let them stay like this. I have the power to help them if you'd only allow it."

"To what end? So you can prolong their miserable lives so they still die in the end? What benefit is that? What kindness do you do them if they still perish?"

"It's not simply about death in the end. They can have lives. Experiences. I can give them that. Make their lives better. Worth living."

"This is a waste of time. Mine, certainly, but yours as well. Human lives are brief. Meaningless."

"You owe this to me, Zeus."

He should have known it would come to this. There was nothing to be gained by seeing her again, only further castigation for something he had no control over—a love for Hera that simply consumed him. "I owe you nothing."

"You know I can't do this on my own. You must help me."

The pleading in her eyes—coupled with millennia of lingering guilt—weighed him down. "Help you do what?"

"I know a way to help them. I have a solution to all this." She waved a hand at the field still visible before them, even though they were in another dimension, watching from Mount Olympus. "A way to help them."

He might crave Hera with a passion that defied logic, but he could never deny Themis. His Themis. His partner for so many ages. "Tell me how you think to fix this."

"Not fix it. You know I am bound to maintain the great scales of balance. Justice must always be served."

"So let them figure it out on their own."

"But they can't. They can't do it on their own. I can balance the horrors for them. Provide them with help."

Despite himself, he was intrigued. The eager light that had come into her eyes was proof she'd thought this through long before calling him to her side. "You can't give them immortality."

She nodded, that riot of curls that ran the length of her back an enticing flash of flame. "Of course. But I wish to give them protectors—from the evil that lives in the world."

"What do you propose?"

"Warriors. Warriors to protect them through the ages, to help them rise above the muck of their lives, to protect them from the weakness of their natures."

"Isn't it true balance to let them deal with the consequences of their nature? Besides, if they know they have helpers, they will not be motivated to better their world."

Her hands clenched, but that was the only outward sign of her frustration. "But they're not all like this. I wish to provide a light in their darkness. And if my warriors must work in secrecy, then so be it."

"And who will you name to this? Who can possibly give them the protection you so desire?"

She glanced up at the rapidly darkening sky. "The inspiration is in the heavens."

The heavens? She'd put someone above them? "No one will rule above me. No one."

That small, castigating smile was back. "Cool your ire, former beloved. I wasn't suggesting anything that would usurp—either now or in the future—your precious power."

"What then?" He heard the petulance in his own voice, yet couldn't stop it. He'd fought his very own father for his position and he'd never let it go. "I won't allow others who can rise above us. I won't even consider those who might find a way."

"I was suggesting the heavens as inspiration. Nothing more."

"Inspiration?"

Night had fully fallen on the field as stars twinkled. Themis turned back toward the screen, pointing heavenward. "The beauty of the stars. The balance there."

"Balance?"

"Look." She pointed to the vast sky, stars blanketing the top of her viewing screen. "The zodiac, in all its glory, Zeus. It is innately balanced; no matter where you start, you always complete the circle."

He watched her as she named off various constellations. He followed her hand as she pointed out the entire circumference of the skies, twelve equal houses that completed a full circle.

Themis sighed, wiping the lingering tears from her cheeks. "Perfect balance."

"And you think twelve warriors are enough to protect your humans?"

"Twelve times twelve. They will cover the entirety of the globe, protecting man no matter where he roams."

He had to admit, her plans had merit. He could give her this indulgence and alleviate the horrible guilt that wracked him every time he thought of her. Each moment he spent with their children—the Fates, the Hours and assorted others—only reminded him of his great failure to her: his inability to deny his great love for Hera, no matter what it cost others.

But could he capitulate that easily?

And what if Hera found out as she surely would? There was no end to the price he'd pay for granting Themis this request.

A *no* formed on his lips, nearly put to voice when the image in his mind's eye of his wife changed, morphing into the visage of their daughter Enyo, goddess of war and his wife's favorite child. As the image of his daughter took shape, an idea swiftly followed.

"I require an additional form of balance in order to grant you this."

"Ah. The price. I knew there would be one."

"Not a price." He lifted his eyebrows. *"Balance."*

Her eyes narrowed. "What do you propose?"

"My daughter Enyo. She will be empowered to fight you."

"You can't be serious. Her power is broad enough. Give her any more and she'll destroy all humanity."

Oh yes, this plan had merit. Despite his love for his

youngest child, he recognized that Enyo had become a bit of a problem. This would get her out of his hair, while protecting his pride when Hera found out about his deal with Themis.

"Enyo will provide balance to your warriors. Take it or leave it."

"Then grant me three things."

A thunderbolt resounded as a sharp flash of lightning struck outside her door. The dark, dangerous smell of ozone wafted in through the open windows of her servant's cottage. He narrowed his eyes, barely holding back the second bolt. "You'd do well to remember who is in charge."

Her eyes stayed level on him, her spine straight as an arrow. "Three things."

"Give me your list."

"I require twelve more warriors." At his raised eyebrows, she continued. "Gemini must have his twin."

He quirked a brow. "An oversight in your grand plan?"

A slim shoulder shrug gave away nothing. "Additional resources, nothing more."

"Second?"

"They are bound by common rules. Enyo is a goddess; my warriors are simply immortal. She can have no oversight into their plans. She will learn information like any other. She will have to ferret it out as others would. And if they must operate in secrecy, so must she."

Although he knew this second rule would limit his beloved daughter's fun, he had to admit it was a fair one. "Done. And third?"

"For every battle she loses, her power will diminish."

Zeus ignored the sinking feeling in his gut that when Hera found out about his deal, he would have more than a few nights on the couch. He was too far along to give up his bluff now. "Then it is only fair that for every one she wins, her power will grow."

Themis nodded. "Of course."

"How many battles will she be given?"

"One for each of my warriors."

"One hundred fifty-six battles? For all eternity?"

"Then she'll have to select the ones that really matter."

"And when these battles are over?"

"My humans will be left to their own devices. Either they will have learned how to live in the world in harmony, or they will deserve what the Fates have procured for them."

"And what of my daughter?"

Themis's eyebrows shot up. "What of her?"

"Upon the completion of these battles, will she be banished back here, to Mount Olympus, potentially in shame? Her mother would never allow it."

"Her mother shouldn't have birthed such a demon. Not only did she do so, but she proudly calls her the goddess of war."

"She is still her child."

"Well then, I'll leave it up to you to tell Hera you don't believe Enyo can succeed."

Another thunderbolt dropped as the skillful trap Themis had laid snapped closed over his ankle.

His pride would not allow him to back out; nor would it allow him to truly acknowledge his concern that his daughter might not succeed.

"Make it so."

The mirror winked out to darkness. He moved for the door, unwilling to engage in any more debate that might lead him even farther down a path he'd regret.

As he approached the door, a question came to mind. Why he'd even care, he couldn't quite say. "And what of your warriors? Will there be no joy for them? No reward? The love of humans is *your* domain, not necessarily theirs."

She leveled her gaze on him, the directness of her stare jolting another twist to his stomach. "Love, you mean? The joy of love?"

"Yes. Everyone seeks it. Even your beleaguered humans"—he tossed a hand at the now-dark viewing panel—"seek love."

"I won't stop it."

"But you won't encourage it, either?"

"Why should I? My warriors have a job to do and I want them to be strong."

Zeus thought of Hera and the glorious need he felt for her that beat in his veins. "There is strength with love, Themis."

Her gaze never wavered, but an odd darkness came into those glorious blue orbs. A death, of sorts. "There is only pain with love of an equal. Yet there is no love with anyone other than an equal. If my warriors can find a way past that dilemma, I will not stand in their way."

Zeus wasn't sure how long he stood outside her door, absorbing the bright sunshine of Mount Olympus. He knew only that long after he returned to the mansion he shared with Hera, long after joy illuminated Enyo's face as he told her of her new challenge, long after the days had faded into years and years into millennia, he would never forget the look in Themis's eyes—the darkness that had descended into them at the mention of love.

It was a death that rested solely with him.

Chapter One

Two Months Ago, the Tomb of Thutmose III, Egypt

Brody Talbot hit the desert floor with a thud and a muttered oath.

He hadn't been this clumsy since his turning, millennia ago. While he didn't love porting, he knew how to arrive without making an announcement of it. If he hadn't flipped his body backward just as his molecules reassembled, he'd have landed on a napping dig worker.

As much as it galled him to admit, Quinn's berating lecture had gotten to him. Damn their Taurus and his self-appointed, dictatorial approach to everything. Even now, the Bull's words echoed in his ears. *Get your head in the game, Talbot. You've been in Egypt for two fucking weeks and you haven't found it yet.*

Brody got to his feet, his gaze on the back of the still-sleeping form of the hired help—help he recognized from memory from the oh-so-catchy phrase LEAVE THEM WET emblazoned on the back of the man's T-shirt.

Help, Brody admitted reflectively, was a subjective term;

this guy had spent far more time ogling the bare-legged female archaeologists than doing his job of carrying waste and already-panned dirt from the tomb.

The temptation to shake the lazy shit awake nearly overtook him, but Brody fought the urge, instead moving toward the man to wake him up with a bit more finesse. After all, if he weren't such a sound sleeper, the worker would already have been running for the hills, screaming in all his superstitious glory about a man who had appeared out of thin air.

Brody reached the man's side, a knife-edge of awareness skating up his spine. What exactly was this guy doing asleep back here behind the pyramid? And . . . shit.

Shit. Shit. Shit.

Dark red colored the sand underneath the man's chest. As Brody rolled him over, a low, breathy moan and the sight of a large gunshot wound greeted him. The wound was gaping, with congealed blood and clumped sand over the words emblazoned on the front of the guy's ratty old T-shirt, FIND THEM HOT.

It was an old fireman's joke the scrawny punk probably barely understood; his body did not scream *I rescue people from burning buildings* and his English wasn't good enough to get the language's odd nuances.

"Who did this to you?" Brody spoke in rapid Arabic, assessing the man's injuries and seeking as much information as he could.

The man let out another low moan, his words coming in fits and starts. "The prophecy . . . has been . . . put . . . into motion."

"How did you get back here? Who did you meet?"

Another gasp of air. Another keening wail. "They will not lose."

They?

Brody knew he needed to go for help, but he also knew from the worker's gurgled breathing he wasn't long for this world.

"Who won't lose?" The name Enyo was on the tip of his tongue, but he held back. "Or do you mean *she*?"

Brody accepted that the question was rhetorical as the dig worker exhaled his last breath. The brown depths of the man's gaze, so full of pain mere moments before, grew peaceful in death, their sightless focus now on the blazing sun above.

As Brody stood to alert the others, he had to give Quinn his due. Their Taurean Bull might be a stubborn pain in the ass, but he sure as shit knew how to call them. Quinn had an eerie sixth sense when something was brewing.

What that something *was* exactly, they were all racing to figure out.

The bigger question at the moment, however, was who'd put a bullet in this guy. As a Warrior, Brody had been trained to suspect Enyo's influence in every act of evil he encountered. But something was off. The goddess of war enjoyed the weapons of her own making far too much to put her stock in modern firearms.

Brody eyed the gaping chest wound again.

Nope. Not the bitch's style.

What could this guy possibly know that got him killed? Brody did a quick scan of the area for something—anything—to give him a clue to what had happened. The weight of his Xiphos, concealed on his calf, provided a small measure of reassurance as his gaze swept the base of the pyramid.

Damn it, nothing.

The attack had to be recent. Brody had ported no more than thirty minutes before from this very spot. But desert winds had already eradicated any footprints, leaving no clues to who had accompanied the dig worker.

Another shot of awareness hit the base of Brody's spine.

How could this guy have found his way to the back of the pyramid, engaged in something, got shot and already had a seriously congealed chest wound, all in under a half hour?

Brody lifted his gaze from the body to the endless stretch of the pyramid's perimeter. He knew violence could wreak horrific damage incredibly quickly, but this murder smacked of a deal gone bad.

But how?

Neither he nor his Warrior brothers put a lot of faith in coincidence, but Brody's predatory leonine senses screamed on high alert. Even without his predator's sixth sense, it didn't take a blinking sign to put the timeline together.

The worker must have followed him when he snuck off the dig, and then been followed by someone else.

Or maybe he was *met* by someone else—someone who possessed the same powers of interdimensional travel Brody did.

But who?

After thousands of years spent battling Enyo, he knew the rhythm, the feel of her influence. The execution was all wrong. The worker's death was too clumsy, too . . . male. Someone had used an actual weapon on the scrawny mark, not the violent electrical current that pointed to Enyo's Destroyers.

But why?

Brody leaned down and lifted the dead guy's wallet. With one final glance at the body, he took off for the team assembled on the dig site. If he was lucky, the stolen wallet would throw everyone off the scent of what had really happened and give him a few extra days to continue his investigation.

He just hoped like hell he figured it out first.

Although the dig site buzzed with the news of the worker's death, things returned to normal relatively quickly. Ahmet hadn't been an integral part of the dig. Add to that his lazy attitude and barely there attendance, and few—if anyone—actually missed him.

The stolen wallet had helped. Although anyone who thought hard enough would know pickpockets weren't exactly haunting the back sides of pyramids looking for random, easy marks to stumble upon them, it diverted everyone else's attention and bought him a bit of time to investigate the real culprit.

But twenty-four hours later he wasn't any closer to an answer.

Brody wiped his face on a rag and looked around at the assembled team, running again through a mental checklist of who might have had the motive to put a bullet in the team slacker. Just as with the last twenty times he'd gone through the exercise, he came up empty.

Add to that his being dog-tired from pulling an allnighter, roaming the slums of Luxor and then porting to ask more questions in the even shittier slums of Cairo, and frustration was ramping up faster than he'd like to admit.

The dig team members were deep inside the pyramid of Thutmose III, and all were engaged in their work. Some took photographs; others used the finest brushes to move thousands of years' worth of earth; still a few others had pedestaled pieces they were working on, moving dirt away from the artifacts they wanted to study.

The luscious Marguerite, the chief graduate student on

the dig, caught his eye over her brush and pail. He'd heard the rumors she'd broken up with her boyfriend. The hot stare and come-hither smile ghosting her lips confirmed it.

He smiled back, the response as natural as breathing. He might not have been Brody the Meek for the last ten thousand years, but the memories of his first eighteen years of life haunted him still.

He never turned down a willing woman.

Ever.

Even if he'd been enjoying the loveless interludes less and less of late.

As the promise of a very enjoyable evening shaped up, he shifted his attention to his work. His own pedestal had come together in the last twenty-four hours, a piece of funeral text coming into focus as he slowly brought it to full visibility out of the detritus of age.

He was actually enjoying himself. Every one of the Warriors contributed differently in their quest to save humanity. Brody knew his contribution—seeking out and dismantling the power of the tools of the ancients—had real value.

Relics had power. In times gone by, the command of the elements and the ability to channel their power had ruled the world. As superstition increasingly gave way to science and technology, those influences had waned, to the point that the average person no longer believed in the power of inanimate objects.

But he knew better.

The power that had been channeled into those inanimate objects wasn't simply reversed by lack of belief.

Only by finding them and destroying them—as the equivalent of supernatural land mines—would he fulfill his role as a protector of humanity.

So what paranormal land mine were they currently sitting on?

Brody refocused his attention on the chamber. The undiscovered chamber had been missed during the tomb's original discovery in the late nineteenth century.

"Dr. Talbot, as always, your work is excellent."

Brody glanced up from the funeral text, directly into the dull brown eyes of Dr. Wyatt Harrison. As the resident patron of their dig site, Wyatt made sure everyone knew it was *his* money funding their discovery efforts. The little toady roamed the dig, playing the charming, old-world scientist, encouraging everyone and building up the team, but Brody wasn't buying the bullshit the doctor was peddling.

Something about the doctor rang entirely too false.

His pudgy body was out of place among the lithe forms of the dig team. Long days of hard labor had created sculpted bodies, well used to the work. Wyatt Harrison looked as out of place as a candy bar garnishing a salad.

"Thank you, Dr. Harrison. I should have it fully removed by later this afternoon."

"Your assistance on this dig has been invaluable. I am so glad you managed to fit us in."

I'll just bet you are.

Brody had nearly missed the opportunity to join the dig, his lack of published papers almost losing him a spot on the team. It was only because of Quinn's quick thinking—and a sizable donation to the other entity funding the dig—that Brody had managed to land a position. "I'm honored to be a part of history."

Wyatt gave a small sigh as he made a production of looking around the room, mopping at the beads of sweat on his forehead. "I feel my brother when I'm in this tomb. He loved his work, but this tomb held a special place in his heart."

"Your brother's reputation and his work here are the stuff of legend."

"I'm only sad he had but one season here at the tomb." Wyatt's dishwater gaze roamed the cavernous chamber. "Clearly, there would have been enough work to keep him busy for years."

"His death has left a hole in the field that still hasn't been replaced." While Wyatt Harrison was the epitome of slime, his late brother had been his polar opposite. A refined scholar with a passion for archaeology, Russell Harrison was gone before his time.

"My niece tries, but her fieldwork is sorely lacking. Sadly, she doesn't have her father's gifts. She's much better suited to her work at the museum."

Brody tried to conjure up an image of the renowned archaeologist's equally renowned daughter but failed. Anna? Amy?

Harrison wiped his forehead again. "Yes, Ava's calling is definitely more scholarly."

With every ounce of willpower, Brody held his tongue at the not-so-subtle insinuation his own work wasn't scholarly. Before he could change his mind and say anything further, a shout rang out from the adjoining burial chamber.

Brody was on his feet and running toward the entrance. A shout like that meant one of two things—a discovery or an injury—and he was determined to be in the thick of either one.

What he hadn't expected was the sight that greeted him as he cleared the outer chamber and moved into the burial chamber.

A long section of wall was exposed, pulling his attention immediately. The team had trained as much light on the wall as they could, line after line of hieroglyphics clearly visible, even from across the room.

Brody's gaze had barely moved through the first two lines when the truth of the matter became crystal clear.

The team had just discovered the Great Prophecy of Thutmose III. As he looked around at the jubilant faces of his fellow archaeologists, a whisper of truth skated down his spine.

They had no idea what ungodly hell they'd just unleashed.

Stomach twisting with each successive glyph he translated, Brody read through the rest of the hieroglyphics engraved on the tomb wall.

The Prophecy of Thutmose III was not just any prophecy. Although humans had transcribed their musings for thousands of years, convinced their prescient writings had the power to foretell the future, most were nothing more than mental scribbling.

Unlike those diabolical few who'd sought to channel power through the use of sacred objects, the vast majority of humans had no problems believing the tales they made up in their own minds.

These writings, however, were vastly different. Rather than incoherent, mad scribblings of an odd dream or two, these hieroglyphics had a very specific purpose. Carved by Thutmose's high priest, they foretold of the power of the famed Summoning Stones of Egypt.

While the world had become enamored of the stones more than twenty years ago when Russell Harrison had first discovered them, no one—least of all Russell—had any idea of the true power the stones held.

Hell, all the Warriors had was a boatload of speculation

and millennia of experience that suggested five matched, inanimate objects discovered in the tomb of an Egyptian pharaoh couldn't possibly lead to anything good.

So they'd watched and waited, with Quinn keeping tabs on the stones just as he did with a variety of other discoveries from all over the world. Brody understood only roughly half of what their Taurus mumbled about his computer programs and algorithms and the time-space continuum, but it really wouldn't have mattered if he understood each and every word. Their six-foot-five resident geek kept tabs on all of it.

Then, two months ago, all that monitoring paid off. Quinn's computer programs started going ape-shit and Brody found himself heading for Egypt.

But now, it was all clear.

Brody read the prophecy again, but the meaning was still the same. The prophecy explained how to use the stones and how to channel their power. These writings were the missing puzzle piece for which the world had been searching for two decades.

Now that they'd found it, Brody could only hope he and his brothers could dismantle the stones' power in time to avert disaster.

Ava Harrison shot up in bed, a scream reverberating through her chest. Cold sweat ran a line down the center of her back and her sheets tangled around her legs like a mummy's funeral wrappings.

Her breath caught in her tight throat and vague colors— swirling reds and blacks—hazed her vision. Her fingers scrabbled at her windpipe as if the useless motion could force her body to breathe again.

Through sheer will, she held herself still, desperately waiting until the air circulated through her chest.

Seconds felt like hours as her chest cavity calmed, as air slowly trickled its way down her throat.

Panic receded into the darkness, along with the swirling haze of shapes in front of her eyes. The vague outline of her room came into focus as her pupils adjusted to the lack of light.

She slowly took in the outline of her sturdy dresser under the window; the hulking shape of her armoire as it stood sentinel by the bedroom door; the small glow that illuminated the open doorway from the kitchen light she always left on when she went to bed.

As the familiar returned, with it came the memory of her dream: images of her father, so robust and healthy, so full of life as he grinned at her and wrapped her in his strong arms; smiles just for her; smiles that told her she was the most important thing in the entire world to him.

The dream always started that way; something so warm—so special—that let her know once upon a time she was loved.

Deeply.

The image of his smiling face changed then, moving her from the warm cocoon of sleep to the horror of terrifying memories.

The images came to her. His large body—the body of a man who spent more of his life outdoors than behind a desk—lying in a pool of blood. Those warm brown eyes, so like her own, boring into hers as he begged her to keep his secrets as he gasped for life. The horrifying knowledge that he was well and truly gone when the ambulance medics pronounced him dead at the scene.

Ava wrapped her arms around herself, willing the shivers away and the memories back to the place that lay heavily guarded inside her heart. What made this nightmare different from all the others she'd had over the last twenty-three years?

As she rolled over, sleep taking the corners of her mind, an image of a large, oversized Egyptian relief flitted through the edges of her consciousness.

As large as a wall, the piece pulsed with life. With promise. With prediction.

Did she know this piece? Had she studied it somewhere? She closed her eyes, hoping the effort would help her to see the piece more clearly in her memories.

Before she could pull the piece into full focus and translate the rows of hieroglyphics, sleep had claimed her once again.

Brody watched the swishing hips of one very annoyed woman as Marguerite sashayed off to her tent. He wondered why he wasn't more upset at his ruined evening. It certainly wasn't for lack of interest.

Or was it?

As the team worked the prophecy from its resting place in Thutmose's tomb, the details of his mission grew increasingly clear. And his interest in banging yet another willing woman faded in the rush of adrenaline and professional curiosity.

The prophecy pointed to *someone* who had the power to use the Summoning Stones, so now all he had to do was find the one person in the world who fit the description: a Chosen One, predestined with the innate knowledge of how to use the Summoning Stones.

One person in a sea of six billion? Sure . . . easy.

Dr. Peter Dryson dropped down next to him, in the lawn chair Marguerite had recently vacated. The man held out a fresh beer in offering. Brody took it, settling himself in for one of the polite nuances of his job.

Small talk.

"What'd you do to piss her off, Talbot?"

Brody couldn't stop the wry grin that creased his cheeks. "Passed on the merchandise."

"Careful with that one. She won't forget it."

He watched as Marguerite ducked into her tent and let out a small sigh. "I suppose not."

They sat in companionable silence, the desert air cooling around them as night descended on the Valley of the Kings. Brody spoke first. "You do realize you made your career today, don't you?"

"I don't fucking believe it, Talbot. To think that's been here all along."

"It's quite an accomplishment, Peter. This will ensure your dig next year in the valley."

"To hell with next year. I'm so damn excited about this year."

Peter practically vibrated as he drank his beer, the enthusiasm emanating off the man in waves. Just muscled enough—and well-rounded enough—not to reek of geek, Dryson had led the team to the goal of finishing the work Dr. Russell Harrison had started twenty-three years ago in his excavation of the tomb of Thutmose III.

"Harrison's brother been all over you yet?"

"Wyatt?" Peter took another large swig of beer and nodded. "White on rice, man. He's so intent on getting the relief for that damn exhibit for the Natural History Museum and we haven't even gotten it out of the tomb yet."

"Think he'll get it?"

"Definitely. Museum's got a lot of pull all by itself. Add to that the fact they've got an exhibit in progress that has artifacts from the same tomb *and* the Harrison money behind them. Slam dunk."

Brody's discussion that morning with Quinn came back to him. His quick port back to New York had proven rather interesting as Quinn got him up to speed on his latest background check of the Harrison family. Quinn's words still echoed in his ear.

"The Harrison family is in this."

"In what?"

"This whole business. The reopened dig at Thutmose's tomb in Egypt. The Summoning Stones. The upcoming exhibit at the museum. They're involved with Enyo—I know it."

Brody's initial reaction was always to underestimate Quinn's seemingly paranoid ideas. Even as his rational mind told him it was absurd—wealthy New York blue bloods up to their eyeballs in supernatural artifacts and in league with the goddess of war—Brody had to admit their Taurus wasn't off the mark very often. And to be fair, this one looked good on the surface, but it didn't take much digging to see past the smoke and mirrors the Harrison money had created.

Twenty-three years ago Russell Harrison had discovered the famed Summoning Stones of Egypt—five stones, now housed in five major cities around the world, that had captured the imaginations of people around the globe.

What was their purpose? And how did five equally perfect, flawless stones made of an iridescent material no one had ever seen before come into being?

Then Harrison had been murdered, his estate wrapped up so tightly in layers of red tape, even a Greek goddess couldn't get through. It had shut down the archaeological team and perplexed the world's scholars, who believed Harrison's work should continue.

Owing to a small loophole the ever-wily Harrison had been smart enough to write into his contract, no one had been able to touch the dig site. The world's scholars had argued for years, but the tomb had lain untouched as the courts and professional institutions and the Egyptian government worked their way through the mess.

And then, three months ago, everything had changed. The spigot opened as quickly as it had been shut off and the restrictions on the tomb's excavation were lifted. A team of scholars were assembled for the dig and they were off to the races. The same week came the announcement of the next major exhibit at the American Museum of Natural History.

Mysterious Jewels: a walk through the history of the world's most famous pieces, with the Summoning Stones of Egypt as its centerpiece.

And wouldn't you know it, Dr. Ava Harrison was its curator.

Brody was pulled from his thoughts by the pop of another can of beer and Peter's rumbling voice in the waning evening light. "Any guess what it means?"

"What what means?"

"The relief. My first assumption was that it had to be funeral text. But I'm starting to wonder about that."

It wasn't a funeral text, but Brody kept the thought to himself, curious as to what had changed Peter's mind.

"Why do you say that?"

"It's the placement. The wall isn't that far from where Harrison found the Summoning Stones. I think the prophecy's tied to the stones. Almost like instructions."

Brody kept his tone even. "Interesting theory. Do you really think Harrison would have missed the relief, though?"

"If he'd had time. But think about it, Talbot. Harrison found the stones. There was a huge outcry of interest and then less than a week later he was killed. Forget further discovery—he never even saw the tomb again."

"True."

"And you have to admit, it's weird. I always wondered what got him off the dig site and to New York."

"You think it was more than a mugging? The papers said it was just an unfortunate incident gone bad."

Peter shrugged. "Maybe. But it's awfully coincidental. Harrison's called back home to New York three days after his biggest professional achievement. And then a day later he's conveniently murdered via a mugging. It's never played well for me."

It hadn't played well for any of them.

The lion tattoo on the upper part of Brody's right shoulder swished its tail with impatience as his thoughts ran wild with Peter's speculation. Although Brody had ultimate responsibility within his team for recovery, management and, if possible, destruction of hazardous ancient artifacts, his Warrior brothers all had a take on the situation that was tied to their own areas of expertise.

It was why Quinn was keeping such a tight leash on the Harrison family via his security systems. It was also why Rafe, their cerebral Cancer, had an eye on the Harrison finances and why their stubborn Ram, Grey, had his finger on the pulse of the world's underground activity via his nightclub, Equinox. When money flowed illegally, news of it inevitably caught Grey's attention.

Nope. Coincidences were for movies. In real life, as

he'd had millennia to learn, coincidences meant connections.

And connections meant a problem, especially when the common thread was Zeus's beloved daughter Enyo, the goddess of war, the dark to his boss's light and an all-around grade A bitch.

Recognizing Peter was waiting for some degree of validation, Brody nodded. "Makes sense. Which means it probably makes sense to watch your back around Wyatt."

"Especially after what happened to Ahmet." Peter rubbed a hand over the back of his neck. "Even with the tightened security, it still freaks me out. I have a fiancée waiting for me at the end of this dig and she's going to be seriously pissed off if something happens to me."

"She's awfully understanding to let you come here."

Peter smiled, his broad grin well past love struck and heading round the bend toward sappy. "She gets me."

Brody held out his beer can and clinked it with the besotted fool. "A rare trait indeed."

"Speaking of Maggie, I need to go give her a call. I'll catch you in the morning, Talbot."

"Later."

As Brody watched Peter walk across their camp, his stride far more enthusiastic than Marguerite's had been, a small shot of envy lodged in a dark corner of his heart. It was a telling thing he didn't dare dwell on for fear of what it might actually mean.

To head off for a conversation with the person you loved. Not a one-night stand. Hell, not even sex.

Conversation.

Companionship.

Courtship.

"Fuck," he muttered to himself. "You're seriously losing it."

Annoyed at himself—for the thoughts and the gaping emptiness he didn't even want to acknowledge—Brody took off for his own tent across the camp.

By mutual agreement, the men had set up farther away from the women, placing them in the center of the camp with the men in a watch formation around them. Brody had nearly cleared his tent when a frisson of electricity snaked up his spine.

The lion tattoo on his shoulder came to life immediately, mane shaking and tail twitching. Brody bent and retrieved the Xiphos from his calf before moving at a fast clip past the rest of the tents.

As his steps took him farther and farther toward the back of the pyramid—and the same area where he'd found Ahmet—the waves of static electricity grew stronger. Brody felt it in the air, like the heaviness just before a lightning storm. But this storm portended something far more sinister—far more evil—than a simple burst of rain.

Sharp, pointed stabs of energy ran the length of his body in increasing intensity, prickling his skin and sinking into his muscles. And as Brody cleared the far side of the pyramid and moved along the back side, he saw them.

Destroyers.

Two oversized, muscle-bound assholes had Peter up against the pyramid wall, their supernatural slaps of voltage twisting his body in malevolent jerks as sharp waves of electricity rocketed through him. Although they had the form of men, Destroyers' bodies were really just shells, housing concentrated, evil, superconductive energy.

Brody leaped at the first one he could reach, his only goal to remove the Destroyer's deadly aim from his colleague. He caught sight of Peter's lolling tongue, a clear sign he didn't have much time.

Brody caught the first Destroyer unawares. Actions swift, he pulled on the Destroyer's hair, exposing the guy's neck to the swift punishment of his Xiphos. Oily ooze spewed from the wound, as the body began to disintegrate, falling to the ground like an abandoned husk.

He felt his tattoo prickling with anticipation, but he held it in check. He wanted to avoid suspicion from Peter if at all possible. *Yeah, Talbot, right on that one. He's got two guys slamming serious voltage through his tissues. He's so focused on your aura.*

Abandoning his mental argument, Brody shifted his focus from the expanding pile of oozing grease at his feet. The pounding waves of electricity had momentarily stopped as the second guy snapped to attention, his focus shifting from Peter to Brody. With that shift, the Destroyer threw a wicked fireball, the harsh wave of energy so named for its impact on the body. Brody took it full force, a grunt passing his lips before he could keep from crying out, the fire of a thousand suns singeing his nerve endings.

The force of the blast had Brody on his knees as the Destroyer let go of his hold on Peter. Char marks covered Peter's khaki shirt and his skin had a bluish tint to it as he lay lifeless next to the base of the pyramid.

Brody got to his feet, spitting a mouth of dust and sand. "Bring it on, asshole. See if you can fight someone who actually knows how to kick your sorry ass."

The Destroyer hissed at him. "Defending your weak little friends, as always. This one squealed, screaming his woman's name. See if I don't go after her next."

"I don't think so." His movements true, Brody lunged for the guy as another wave of electric fire lit up his body.

Ignoring the pain, he maintained his forward movement as the wicked edge of the Xiphos sliced through the guy's shirt and straight for his heart. Although not the killing blow, it slowed the asshole just enough to give Brody the advantage.

With quick movements, he had his blade out of the chest cavity and into the guy's throat before the Destroyer could conjure up any further heat.

The shell of the Destroyer's body went slack immediately, the limp form falling to the sandy ground to a matched fate with his partner.

Job done, Brody rushed to Peter. A slight, thready pulse pumped in the hollow of the man's neck, as his breath wheezed in and out in light pants past blue lips.

"Peter. Peter, man. Come on. Can you hear me?" When he got no response, Brody tried again. "Peter, come on. Maggie's waiting for you. She wants to talk to you."

Peter's eyelids fluttered open at the mention of his love's name. "Not . . . not gonna make it, Talbot." He exhaled a large gasp. "Mags'll be seriously pissed at me."

"Don't talk like that. You're going to be fine. We're going to get you help."

Brody was surprised by the strength of Peter's grip when he grabbed his forearm. "You gotta tell her I love her."

"I will. And so will you."

Another heavy breath wheezed out as Peter shook his head. "Need—need to tell you. The relief. It's def-definitely not funeral text."

Brody supported Peter's neck, trying to find some way to ease the horrific pain that clouded his eyes as he pushed his body. "Okay, okay. Take it easy."

"Know you tried, Talbot. Know you're not like us."

What? "Come on. I'm on your team."

"Nope." A slight smile ghosted Peter's lips, which were turning bluer by the second. "Never were. I knew. You know there's something not right. You know."

Respect for his colleague grew tenfold as Brody held Peter's body. "Yeah, I do."

"I heard those guys before they got me. Before they kn-kn-knew I was listening. You need to take care of this, Talbot. The relief is a prophecy. And they're coming for it. They're coming for her."

"No one's going to hurt Maggie."

Peter's eyelids fluttered as his eyes rolled back.

"Peter. Come on, Peter. I promise you, no one will hurt Maggie."

Another sputter of air slipped from the good doctor's lips as his eyes opened again, a soft smile playing around his lips. "Not . . . not my Maggie. Maggie's . . . safe. You have to protect *her*."

"Who?"

Peter gasped, his chest heaving as he tried to push out the words. "Har—"

Har? Her? "Who is she, Peter?"

Peter took one more strangled breath of air, his final words leaving his body on a rush of air. "Sh-she's next."

Brody felt Peter's body slacken as the last vestiges of life left him. His eyes cut from the young face to the twin pools of oily residue that lay a few feet from them as rage filled his chest, making him want to howl at something.

Anything.

Enyo had taken another good man.

And clearly she had her next victim square in her sights.

Chapter Two

Today, New York City

Brody had kept an eye on her for three days and all he had to show for it was a caffeine headache from an endless parade of Venti lattes and a raging hard-on. All of this had managed to make him feel like a cornered pit bull—tired and cranky and pissed as shit.

Because he never got headaches.

And because, if he wanted to, he got relief from a hard-on in way less than seventy-two hours.

And most of all, because in those wretched, agonizing seventy-two hours, she hadn't noticed him.

Not even once.

Fuck.

Ava Harrison smiled at the guy behind the deli counter where she'd ordered her third dinner of champions in a row—a toasted bagel with cream cheese. Brody hadn't even bothered to follow her inside this time, but had just hung out on the corner observing. On top of the fish eye he'd gotten that morning from the proprietor when the man had noticed him milling around for the third morning in a row, there was no way he could stuff down another cup of coffee.

And besides, he could see her just fine out here.

Two months.

It had taken Brody two mind-numbingly frustrating months to figure it out. Peter had given him a clue and he'd been so focused on getting an answer, he hadn't really listened.

A dying man's last breaths. *"Har—"*

Not *her. Har.* As in Harrison.

Ava Harrison.

Three nights ago, it had all come together as he sat going over Quinn's intel for what felt like the millionth time since returning from Egypt.

The copious notes on Russell Harrison's daughter, Ava. The detailed descriptions of her educational background, work experience and published works. The full report on her curation of the upcoming exhibit.

Why that time—that read-through—the pieces fell into place, he'd never know.

Brody only knew his saving grace was that Ava had been blessedly untouched by Enyo or her minions.

After three days of following her, the mystery was only murkier. What did Ava have to do with the prophecy from Thutmose's tomb? And an even bigger question, to Brody's mind, was what Enyo could possibly want with her, a mousy, scientific type who hid her body behind shapeless clothing and worked the hours of a slave?

Yep, he was still working on that one.

He'd been through the translation on the prophecy's hieroglyphics until his eyes bled and still, he had nothing to show for it—no clues that told him why Peter had been killed or what Enyo's next move would be.

He focused on Ava again, watching as her pale blond hair picked up the dingy light of the overheads as she moved to the counter.

Like a halo.

But that made absolutely no sense, since the deli's lighting was for shit and that ugly gray sweater she swathed herself in absorbed light like a funeral shroud.

His cock sprang to attention, a painful reminder that it hadn't been let off the leash in weeks—months, if he were honest, which only added another layer to the royal piss off.

Over a gray sweater a grandmother wouldn't have been caught dead in?

With another quiver, said cock confirmed it. Yep. The gray sweater had an odd sex appeal to it.

So he was in a dry spell.

And yeah, while it chafed at his famous leonine pride, he hadn't figured out a way around it. He hadn't enjoyed looking at a woman quite this much in far too long.

Maybe that was the reason for the dry spell. No one had fired his blood like this in centuries and he'd gotten sick of going through the motions. As he took in the smooth curve of her cheek as she turned away from the counter, he had to admit no woman had had him this enthralled in—well, ever.

Not even Sasha. He'd loved her in a gentle way, as though he wanted to spend his entire life protecting her.

But this—this fierce need was something else. The most primal part of him wanted to cover her, brand her with his scent and make her his mate.

And she was oblivious to him.

This seriously sucked.

Even though he had to admit he was seriously enjoying himself.

Ava pulled her cell phone from one of her pockets as she pulled money out of the other one. Her delicate shoulders moved up and down in a slight shrug as she closed the phone almost as quickly as she'd opened it. After she paid, she picked up her dinner from the counter, gave a small finger wave to the guy who'd made the bagel and headed out of the deli and toward her apartment. Keeping a good distance, a bag of cashews in hand to munch on, he followed her as he'd done the last several days.

Although the ratty sweater covered her ass, he could still see the outline of her curves through the stretch of the material—high and firm, with plenty of room to plant his hands.

His fingers itched to touch the sweet arch of her delightful bottom as her back curved straight into it. Under him. Over him. Next to him. Soaping him in the shower.

Oh man, he had it bad.

Ava turned the last corner toward her block, just barely moving out of his line of sight. He kicked up his pace, moving faster so as not to keep her out of his field of vision. Just as he rounded the corner, without warning, a ball of energy blasted him, shooting him straight on his ass and scattering what was left of the cashews across the sidewalk.

"Son of a bitch," he rumbled, a cocktail of anger and adrenaline infusing his bloodstream in a rush.

Scrambling, he moved his limbs to shake off the fireball as he moved into a run. Ava's screams assaulted his ears as he focused in their direction and found her locked in the grip of a muscle-bound Destroyer. Slabs of his forearms covered her chest and neck as the asshole traced his tongue around the rim of her left ear.

The Destroyer's dead eyes focused on his and, coupled with the fireball, ensured Brody knew exactly what he was dealing with.

Waves of static rushed off the Destroyer, the constant popping and crackle of electricity floating toward him in the darkness.

Shit. This was so not good, although the Destroyer's presence did confirm a few things. Namely, why Quinn's intel had suddenly gone off the rails three days ago, suggesting they follow the lovely Ava Harrison. Where Destroyers dared to tread meant Enyo was sure to follow.

But where was the Destroyer's second? These assholes always traveled in pairs and he was only picking up on a lot of swirling static from this one guy.

Refocusing his energy on the threat in front of him, Brody looked at the Destroyer. Six foot two and a solid one-ninety—or that's what you were supposed to think when you looked at him. The reality was far, far different. As a soldier in Enyo's army, he carried out her orders with about as much internal thought as an android.

And he was treated as equally disposable.

Brody hadn't met this one before, but that was hardly a surprise. Enyo had a ready supply of minions to do her bidding and few of them survived a skirmish with him or his Warrior brothers.

Question was, did the Destroyer know a Warrior was protecting Ava?

Forcing equal parts gym rat and oversexed cowboy into his swagger, Brody approached the pair. "Leave the woman alone."

Ava's soft brown eyes were large and wide as she struggled against the beefy arm covering her windpipe. A heavy ringing pulsed in his ears, in time to the pumping of his blood. The very thought of the panic she must be feeling shot wave after wave of anger through him as he continued stalking toward them.

The Destroyer stopped curling his tongue around Ava's ear long enough to look up with a menacing stare. "Get out of here, asshole. This doesn't concern you."

"It does now."

Brody began to charge when, without warning, Ava shifted her stance, stepping on the Destroyer's foot and knocking him just enough off balance to free her arms. With swift movements, she spun around, then extended her hands toward the Destroyer's neck, hitting both sides with a large, chopping movement.

A heavy, inhuman growl went up as the Destroyer's eyes went wide. Although her movements weren't hard enough to deliver the death blow, Ava had done a damn fine job of stunning the Destroyer and forcing him to regroup. Wild waves of static flew through the air, forcing Ava's hair into an untamed pattern as the guy stumbled back on the sidewalk, staggering like a drunk.

Moving on instinct, Brody wrapped Ava in his arms, dragging her down the street. The need to move her away from the Destroyer was overwhelming, and his muscles braced for an attack from behind once the Destroyer regained his equilibrium.

In all his years in service to Themis, he'd never felt such a primal urge to defend.

To protect.

To shelter.

His lion tattoo was restless with the need to move, but similar to the night in the desert two months ago, he kept it on a tight leash, unwilling to expose himself to Ava in that way if he could help it.

He glanced down at the gloriously disheveled mess of woman pressed against his chest. Her blond hair still stood out from the Destroyer's static electricity and he felt the heavy pumping of her heart where she pressed against him. With his free hand, he tilted her chin up to him, concerned to see flat eyes and a dazed look that suggested she was near shock.

Fierce tenderness rose in his chest in great, syrupy waves. His need to protect went so deep, he didn't know where his own needs started and his job as a Warrior of Themis ended. His instincts, normally razor sharp and honed to a definite point, were all over the board. Finish the job and kill the Destroyer or take care of her.

The tender side was putting up a hell of a fight.

And winning.

It was insanity—mind-numbing, wonderful, glorious insanity.

He squeezed her shoulder, even as he picked up their pace once more. "Come on, sweetheart. We have to keep moving."

He headed for Columbus Avenue, a more heavily traveled street, so he could put both of them in a cab. He'd get her back to the museum, try to explain what was going on and then try to convince her that she needed protecting.

Neat. Clean. Orderly.

His Warrior brothers liked to rib him for his impulsive approach to life. To hell with that. He wasn't taking impulsive chances with Ava.

"Who are you?"

He glanced back down at her as her whispered words penetrated his thoughts. "I'm a friend."

An eyebrow quirked over one brown eye that was rapidly losing its sightless, fearful gaze. "And you expect me to buy that?"

She pushed at his waist and he had to keep a firm grip on her upper shoulder before she could squirm out of his grasp. "Excuse me?"

Her voice grew breathless as she continued to struggle under the heavy weight of his arm. "A friend. Yeah. Right. You and *your* friend back there. You're tag teaming me?"

He let go of her so quickly, she nearly stumbled as her words penetrated.

She thought he wanted to hurt her?

Before he could question her, she took off down the sidewalk.

"Wait!"

She ignored him as she kept running. His longer strides closed the distance in short order, even as he cursed himself with each footfall.

Damn it, but he was off his game. First, he hadn't anticipated the Destroyer attack.

He saw Ava round the corner and added a burst of speed, continuing the mental tirade. Second, he was so surprised by this slip of a woman that he'd dropped his hold on her.

And third . . .

Shit.

His biggest mistake of all.

Unless his ten thousand years of training had been for naught, they'd just found the second greaseball. And there wasn't a damn thing he could do as he watched Ava run headlong into the other half of her worst nightmare.

Oh God. OhGod. OhGodohGodohGod.

What was she in the middle of? Who were these people? And when had her quiet little West Side neighborhood turned into a war zone?

Panic flooded her in hot waves as her stomach cramped. A scream lodged in her throat as her attacker's heavy arms wrapped around her, pressing her face into his chest. She faintly registered the garish print of his Hawaiian shirt.

Where was his coat? It was November.

And you'd be worrying he's going to catch cold, Ava Marie?

Idiot.

More weird waves of static hit her, making her limbs quake with pinpricks of activity.

Where was someone—anyone—to help?

She'd run toward Columbus on purpose, hoping the additional level of activity on a busy avenue would attract attention. Of course, she'd worked late—again—and damn it if now she wasn't paying for it with no one around to help.

What kind of scam were these guys running? Three of them? And all of them using bodily attacks? Didn't they just want money so they could go get their next hit?

The big one didn't look like a drug addict. He looked like a fashion model—one of those large, hot, nonmetrosexual ones who knew how to wear an old T-shirt just as well as Armani.

He had broad shoulders and an acre of chest that narrowed down to a taut stomach and slender waist; blond hair that would have been girlish if not for the harsh planes and angles of his face; a sharp jaw, firm nose and a pair of killer cheekbones.

And the most incredible, sky blue eyes she'd ever seen.

Damn it, Ava. Focus.

Determination renewed, she struggled against the prison

of hands and arms, her self-defense classes coming back at her in a rush as she used her elbow to jam a harsh blow to Hawaiian Shirt's midsection. Although his grip didn't lessen, he did grunt in pain.

Guess that self-defense instructor at the Y really did know what he was talking about.

Continuing to struggle like a she-cat, she slammed her foot down on his instep. More of that weird static shot through her, but she'd made enough of an impact that his grip lessened, enabling her to slide through his arms, the silky material of his shirt helping to ease her way. Scrambling, she pushed herself across the sidewalk, trying simultaneously to escape while attempting to get her footing.

Which meant she did neither well.

Those horrible hands reached for her again, plucking her up and dragging her to her feet. A scream lodged in her throat, desperate as she was to alert someone to her predicament.

Before she could let out another scream, the other guy was back.

Mr. GQ.

The grip around her tightened, her back to his chest, and even without being able to see him, she felt her captor's movements. His head lifted away from her neck and in the direction of the large man who stood before them.

"Leave the woman alone."

The man behind her grunted, his fetid breath skating across her cheek and forcing goose bumps down her spine.

The blond continued toward them, his long hair reminding her of a lion's mane as he stalked toward them.

Stalking his prey?

"Maybe you didn't hear me. Move your limp little dick

away from the woman." Ava caught sight of a wicked-looking blade in the guy's hand, light from the overhead streetlamps shining off it.

Oh. My. God.

The sight of the weapon and the fact that it was clearly intended for the man behind her gave her a small measure of hope that she might get out of this alive.

But—*oh, shit*—that was a nasty-looking knife.

Although weaponry wasn't her strong point, she'd worked in the museum long enough to have a basic, working knowledge, and that thing looked very old and very lethal, the point no doubt able to slice through her captor's chest with a flick of the wrist.

The need to struggle infused every single fiber of her being, but she held still, even as the air in her lungs whooshed out with heavy pants. Her gaze followed the blade again, the flash of lights along its shaft nearly hypnotic in its sheer malevolence.

Was she going to get out of this alive?

And then there were no thoughts—only feelings—as everything happened at once. Her blue-eyed hottie let out a war cry as he leaped.

Something—a taser?—flared off the end of her captor's hands, slamming into the guy fast shaping up as her protector. His large body stopped in midattack as an invisible wave seemed to knock him backward to the sidewalk, his long, blond hair stiff with static.

Her captor's focus on the other man gave her the opening she needed and, again, she used the silky smoothness of his shirt to slide out of his arms. The need to flee pounded through her, while a strange compassion for her felled blond hero gave her the mad urge to stay.

Stay?

Had she finally gone over the edge?

She had put quite a few yards between herself and the two men when the prick of her conscience had her turning around to check that GQ had gotten to his feet.

He still lay on the ground, but he definitely had movement. She could see him struggling to stand, looking as if his limbs weighed a thousand pounds.

Ava edged back a few steps, that odd need to debate the situation still holding her back from a full-on run when she caught a whiff of something on the air. What was that? Ozone? Like during a lightning storm?

Ignoring the large man lying on the sidewalk as if he no longer posed a threat, the Hawaiian-shirted stalker fixed his gaze on her. His movements were measured.

Deliberate.

And filled with pure menace.

Her hesitation firmly gone, one thought pounded through Ava's mind, signaling her muscles into action. *Run!*

Only she couldn't, as a strange, restless energy seemed to drift toward her, like the shimmering waves of heat that floated off the sidewalk on a hot summer day. As the slow-moving waves came straight at her, she felt prickles of static slamming into her body, which made no sense, but she could feel them as they ran up and down her body. Sharp pricks, just like when she tried to make her arm wake up after sleeping on it wrong.

Ava shuddered as another wave of prickly energy ran through her. What was this? It felt like sleep numbness, but instead of her limbs waking up, it happened in reverse.

The tingles grew worse, morphing into hot, sharp spikes of pain as she tried to shake some movement into her limbs.

Even focusing all her attention, she could barely move. Small, uneven twitches were the only response to her focused efforts.

The stalker moved closer as the roar of adrenaline rushed her veins.

She had to get away from this. Had to move faster. Hell, had to move at all. She looked down to her frozen body. She tried to lift a foot, but nothing moved and the smell of lightning got closer.

Her windpipe tightened as panic filled her chest cavity.

If she could have moved her arms, her hands would already be at her neck, scratching, clawing. Desperate for air as the panic took over. Drowning without water. No escape.

In the midst of it all, one single image kept floating to the top, past the madness of fear, beyond the paralyzing terror.

Last guy . . . Neck . . . Disabled him . . .

She had to get to his neck.

But she couldn't move.

And then Hawaiian Shirt was on top of her and a weird roaring noise filled the air, so loud it drowned out the heavy thuds of her racing heartbeat. And then he wasn't on top of her because her hottie had come to her rescue again, locked on the sidewalk with the stalker in a death grip.

Loud grunts wafted up to her as she tried to shake herself free of the paralysis. Waves of pain ran through her nerve endings as her limbs fought to wake up. There was more of that sharp, prickly pain as skin and nerves and muscle came back to life.

The moment she felt enough strength in her feet to move, she leaped aside as the two men rolled over the hard concrete of the sidewalk.

With screaming insistence, her mind pressed her to act, to run, to *survive*.

"Ava!"

Her hottie grunted her name as he pinned the stalker's arms over his head on the ground.

"I need you!"

The urge to flee nearly overwhelmed her. Then she saw the appeal in those sapphire orbs and ran over.

"The head," her protector grunted, pressing harder on the stalker's arms as his legs pinned the lower half of the struggling body.

More grunts. "You need . . . to snap . . . the head."

Like a small piece of kindling setting fire in a cold fireplace, the fear that hummed perpetually under her skin was squashed, killed by the desire that somewhere inside of herself there was a woman who was bigger than the fear.

Ava understood his terse orders and the moment she saw a chance—the moment her hottie had rolled the guy over in a show of pure strength advantage—she took her shot.

With a loud, feral scream, she ran to them and locked one foot firmly on the stalker's neck. He twisted so that she nearly lost her balance, but she managed to keep it by planting her back foot. Strength she didn't know she had kept him from moving, but it couldn't stop the movement of his eyes as they locked with hers while a hand snaked out and grabbed her ankle.

Her own movements quick, she lifted her other foot and came down on his head. Where she'd expected a loud crack, all she heard was a soft pop as the man's body went limp.

And then a wave of electricity went through her as though she'd stuck a knife in a light socket. Great waves of pain lasered into each and every nerve ending, like her body was on the verge of exploding into a million pieces.

It slammed through her so hard, she went sailing through the air. The last thing she felt as she hit unforgiving concrete was a sense of wonderment.

How did her hottie know her name?

Chapter Three

Enyo shot her nephews a glance as she refreshed her lipstick. "Read it to me again."

Although Phobos and Deimos normally engaged her with their seemingly endless supply of ideas to cause fear and dread, the last few weeks she just hadn't been in the mood.

It all started the night she learned of the prophecy.

What the hell good did it do to have a series of minions, ready and willing to do your bidding, if none of them could keep current with the times?

And damn Wyatt Harrison's black soul; he'd kept the news from her. Oh, he'd done his fair share of groveling— even pretended he had no idea what the hieroglyphics meant— but she knew better. She smelled the lie on him like it was cologne.

Even her lover's most *strident* attempts to distract her hadn't abolished the anger, or her raw fury, at Wyatt's lie.

The prophecy had been found two months before in the very same chamber where Wyatt's brother made the discovery of the Summoning Stones. And he'd kept the information to himself and told her about it only two weeks ago.

He might offer a wealth of contacts and connections, but the man had outlived his usefulness. He'd grown far too cocky, too sure of himself.

Well, she could fix that. She'd managed many a similar situation before. Men and those dicks of theirs. Always getting themselves in over their heads, thinking no one could touch them.

But later for that.

Despite her raging anger at being so ill informed, the prophecy had gone a long way toward explaining some things.

She recognized the Summoning Stones had power. She had always felt it. She even knew of their existence during Thutmose's reign, but had been prevented from gaining a full understanding of their use. Thutmose's damn high priest— he'd known just how to block her.

After the rediscovery of the stones two decades ago, she'd returned her attention to them, but no matter how hard she'd searched for a link, nothing presented itself—no supernatural force she could detect on a higher plain of reasoning; no extraordinary reaction when put together. Not even a whisper of power emanated off their surfaces.

But now. Ah yes, now it all made sense. The prophecy explained it all.

Deimos smacked Phobos on the head. "You got ketchup on it."

Phobos struck back, the blade he wore on the underside of his ring, slashing his brother across the cheek. "I've told you not to hit me. And the ketchup was an accident."

At the best of times, her nephews had the energy of puppies. The fact they hadn't been let off the leash in months had only made the problem worse. "Read it again!"

"Yes, Aunt Enyo," came the matched replies.

Deimos's voice rose above his brother's, the macabre undertones resonating through Enyo's residence on Mount Olympus. "Once in every age, a Chosen One, selected by the great god Ra, will harness the Great Summoning Stones of Egypt. The five stones grant the Chosen One dominion over everything. Death. Life. Love. Sexuality. Infinity."

Phobos's voice overtook his brother's. "The Chosen One—the Key—will bind the power of the stones under its command. The Key will rule over all the earth and no portal will be immune to its influence. No god can rule above the Chosen One when he commands the power of the stones."

The stones *did* have power.

And she needed every drop she could wring out of them to replenish her own.

Hell, once she had the stones, her own power was immaterial.

Take that, dearest father of mine.

And yeah, okay, fine. The rules had been laid out for her before she said yes to this little contest with Themis—everything must be done fair and square in the hallowed, rarified air of Mount Olympus, after all—but she'd barely paid attention in her eagerness to get started.

Admittedly, she'd caught on quickly when reality came crashing in.

Every battle she lost diminished her powers.

When she'd begun so many ages ago, her eagerness had rivaled that of Deimos and Phobos, her enthusiasm for her task a bright, shiny object of joy. The truth, though, had become evident during her tenth loss. She'd weakened to a point where she required aid to execute her plans against Themis's damn Warriors because she could no longer handle it all on her own. And this, when added to the insult of the loss, was a special sort of punishment all in itself.

Oh, her father would never call it punishment. He simply called it *balance*. A necessary requirement in the bargain that got her this gig in the first place.

He was so fucking old-school sometimes.

Who needed balance? They were gods. They needed power and nothing more. Seeing as how that reasoning regularly fell on the deaf ears of everyone but her mother, whining about it got her nowhere.

The die was already cast and each loss weakened her. Each minion she created to help her weakened her more. Like some cosmic wheel of balance, her power had finite limits. If she used it and didn't replenish it with wins, it was spent. And if she wanted more minions to help her battle Themis's damn zodiac assholes, she had to give up a little more power to get them.

Not that it mattered in this case. When she could get the stones under her control, there'd be no more lost battles. She'd have all the power she needed, all the power she could ever use.

Maybe it would assuage some of her ire about that whole World War II thing, which *still* pissed her off. Of course, it had taught her a valuable lesson. That was the first— and last—time she'd pinned her hopes fully on a human. Adolf had talked a good game, but he'd still failed her in the end.

Brushing the thought away, she stood and walked around her study, her focus on the weaponry table in the corner. She really shouldn't complain. There *were* perks to her situation. Themis might have believed humanity needed protectors from some giant, evil forces beyond their control. What they really needed was protection from themselves.

They were so easy to manipulate.

So easy to turn.

Drugs. Sex. Money.

They were such willing pawns, she almost didn't miss operating at full power.

Almost.

Enyo took stock of her arsenal, the various toys she kept lying around the house an avant-garde form of self-expression. A guillotine sat in the corner, sadly out of fashion. She'd so enjoyed that delightful reign of terror.

Her gaze shifted to her antique sideboard, the top littered with the most fascinating items. Crossing to her collection, she couldn't stop the rush of pride at what she'd amassed over the years. Brass knuckles, a tomahawk, throwing stars—all winked brightly back at her under the lights.

She ran a finger over the wicked end of a ten-blade, images of the disease she could paint on the edges of the blade buoying her thoughts.

Ah, hope really did spring eternal. And if there was one trait she had in spades, it was an innate belief in her own power.

She would prevail.

Always.

Because she had one great advantage people always forgot. Her brethren on Mount Olympus forgot it. Themis in all her justice bullshit always forgot it. Even the dumb humans always forgot it.

She was the goddess of *war*. And everyone who went to war believed in what they were doing, both sides fiercely willing to sacrifice for their goals.

As long as that held true, she'd never be out of a job—sort of like her own personal insurance policy. Even if she never conjured up another battle on her own again, Themis's beloved humans would never cease to provide her with entertainment.

Of course, the problems she generated were so much more *interesting* than puny human concerns, but, still, a good battle was a good battle.

Period.

With another glance at Deimos and Phobos, she decided to bump up her recruitment schedule. She had Wyatt in line, which meant she'd have the stones soon enough, so what did a few extra shots of power drain hurt?

And the task would have the added benefit of getting Deimos and Phobos out of her hair.

After a quick outline of what she required for the next job, she watched them run for the door in excitement.

"Boys. Remember what I said! Find the drug *dealers*, not the addicts. The dealers can be motivated. The addicts are useless, even by human standards."

The door slammed in the twins' wake as Enyo reached for her cherry red nail polish. Unscrewing the bottle, satisfaction hummed through every pore. Once she got her hands on those stones, Themis's little puppets were never going to know what hit their oh-so-fine asses.

Brody cradled Ava in his arms, willing her to open her eyes. A litany of anger ran through his head on a loop.

If only he'd thought to find the second Destroyer before he found them; if only he'd found a way to keep her out of harm's way instead of simply following her. If only he'd been quicker, he could have ported and caught her before she landed.

If only . . .

He drew her closer as the mental tongue-lashing continued. Why had he been so distracted around her, like a moronic teenager dealing with his first hard-on? Why hadn't he taken care of her as he should have, keeping her away from the danger that, while not expected, wasn't a complete surprise, either?

"Ava." Her breath came out in light gasps as he continued to rock her. He'd tried to feel her body for broken bones, but the impatience to have her in his arms overrode the good sense to leave her on the ground. "Ava," he whispered, his voice more insistent.

Her eyelids fluttered and she mumbled something unintelligible, but the fact that she mumbled anything at all gave him hope. His voice louder, he purposely made his tone harsh to get her attention. "Ava!"

Her lids fluttered back to reveal the dark, chocolate brown of her eyes. Even in the darkened light of the street he could see her pupils respond normally. A good sign. "What?"

His grip tightened, willing her to stay conscious. "Do you remember what happened to you?"

"Mmm." The lids fluttered, but she fought to keep them open. "Mugged."

Is that what she wanted to call this? That explanation would make it a lot easier for him in the long run, so he went with it. "That's right." He gentled his voice, but kept it at an insistent tone to keep her awake. "And do you know what they were after?"

"Purse, I s'pose."

"Why did you try to fight them?"

"I didn't fight them. I couldn't fight them."

"Why not?"

"Too 'fraid."

Too afraid? The librarian-turned-goddess act he'd just witnessed suggested otherwise. "You didn't look afraid to me. You fought those guys like a sexy little Amazon."

She shook her head, but the movement clearly caused her pain, because she stopped almost instantly, clamping her eyes shut again. After a few moments, she took a deep breath. "Wasn't me. I don't act like that."

What was she talking about? She'd just kicked serious Destroyer ass.

"You just did act like that. You were amazing."

"Had to help you. Had to be bigger . . ." Her voice trailed off and he hugged her closer, the movement forcing her eyes open again. "Had to be bigger than the fear."

Relishing the feel of her body in his arms, he reached for the hair at her temple. Smoothing her hair away from her face, he continued to pepper her with questions to keep her awake. "Is there someone I can call for you?"

She reached up, her fingers tracing a light pattern down his jawline. The look in her eyes—trust mingled with the smoky hints of desire—humbled him and turned him on all at the same time. "No one to call. 'Cept work."

"Okay. We'll call work."

"No!" With sudden movements, her hand dropped from his face as her eyes widened and she struggled to sit up.

"Whoa! Okay. Stop. Slow down!" He held on to her, trying to keep her head from jostling as much as possible. She might not have a concussion, but she had to be working on the headache of the century. "I won't call your work."

She settled down again, her eyes going droopy as her head flopped against his shoulder. "Big project. Don't want them to know about this."

Well, this was interesting. "You mean your job at the museum?" He shifted their bodies, cradling her closer to minimize any jerky motions as he regained his feet.

"Mmm-hmmm. Big project. They won't let me work on

it if I don't show up; if I show weakness. I have to be strong. Like you."

"What weakness are you afraid of, sweetheart?"

Her eyes fluttered open again, going a wide, rich chocolate brown. "The stone."

As in the Summoning Stones?

What could she be afraid of? And why? And if she *was* afraid of them, what the hell was she doing curating an exhibit full of them?

Damn it, he needed to talk to Quinn.

He carried her the short walk back to her apartment. At the front stoop of her building—an Upper West Side converted brownstone—he did a quick glance up and down the street for any potential witnesses. A few days prior, on his recon of her building, he'd confirmed the lack of a video camera, but a nosy neighbor could do a hell of a lot more damage than a grainy videotape.

"Shhh. Don't worry about any of that. Close your eyes." Her fluttering eyelids dropped closed as her already-limp body slackened further.

He took stock of his own energy level, the post-adrenaline burn of the fight still coursing through his veins. He visualized her apartment, the recognizance photos Quinn had pulled providing the image of her bright, yellow kitchen. Did he have enough energy to port into her apartment?

The answer was a resounding yes as his surroundings shimmered. Air rushed at him from all sides, a crushing weight wrapping around his body like a lead blanket. Willing as much soothing energy into her as he could, he hunched his body around her, hoping to take the brunt of the jump from the sidewalk to her apartment.

It was over barely before it had begun. A glance down

at Ava's sleeping form confirmed she'd missed the entire thing.

Other than wall-to-ceiling bookcases, the apartment was sparsely furnished, but neat as a pin. He transferred her to the couch and leaned over her, brushing the hair away from her face again.

Brody debated the wisdom of questioning her further. On one hand, he wanted the information she held and her memory was just fuzzy enough to forget their conversation, which would make their next few weeks a lot easier. But based on her mumbled answers so far, the likelihood of getting useful information was slim.

The fact that he wanted to talk to her and have those luscious brown eyes on his again had absolutely nothing to do with it.

Nothing at all.

Decision made, he dropped a lingering kiss on her forehead and rose from her side. He'd get his answers soon enough.

"You're a mystery, Dr. Harrison."

With a last glance at her, he walked to the front of her apartment and took a seat on the floor on a pastel-colored rag rug, his back to the door. He pulled another bag of cashews out of his pocket and glanced at the box of graham crackers on the counter. She'd never know if he nicked a few.

When she did stir, he'd have enough energy to port himself away before she even realized he was there. He needed to find his Warrior brothers and get their take on what had happened.

In a little while.

After he made sure the apartment was secure and she didn't need anything else.

In the meantime, he leaned his head back against the

door as he worked his way through a sleeve of graham crackers. He wasn't going anywhere for a while.

Brody felt the harsh thumping bass of Grey's nightclub as his molecules reassembled. He ported into a private area of the basement used for just that purpose and marveled that the place didn't actually crumble from the constant throb of ear-shattering music.

Equinox was humming tonight. And it was only a Tuesday. Course, Equinox hummed every night. Their Aries Warrior had the hottest spot in all of New York.

Hell, all the East Coast.

His gut still churned at the idea that he'd left Ava behind, alone, but he had to talk to his brothers—needed to get them the latest intel and get their take on the situation. He'd be in and out in fifteen minutes.

Brody walked into a private bar area reserved for the Warriors. Although its current iteration was Equinox, Grey had owned this plot of land since New York's colonial days. He changed it up every few years, ensuring the good members of their growing metropolis had a place to go to let off steam or see and be seen. He'd even beaten prohibition.

And he'd managed to keep everyone blind to the fact that the place hadn't changed ownership in more than two hundred years; nor had the proprietor aged a single day in all that time.

It was a tricky business, but Themis had been kind with her gifts, anticipating the challenges immortality might force, no matter how clever the Warrior or how glib his tongue.

A slight mind trick here or there; the ability to erase even the most deliberate thoughts—when used wisely, those gifts ensured all her Warriors could function in society with society being none the wiser about its protectors.

Grey occupied the corner seat at the small, sleek private bar in the back of the room, his white button-down shirt and pressed black slacks conveying more the after-hours suave businessman than bartender. "I don't let ugly assholes into my club. Didn't you get the memo?"

Brody took a seat across from his oldest friend. "Fuck you, Aries. Your club sucks."

"Tell the DA that. He's been entertaining his merry band of ADAs all evening. His office won the Pritchard case and they're out celebrating." Grey whistled. "And man, there is just nothing sexier than a prim little lawyer in one of those black pencil skirts."

"And you wouldn't have anything to do with the last arrest that tied up that case, now would you?" Brody reached for a handful of salted nuts. "And when did you start getting all hot and bothered for lawyers? Always thought you had a greater appreciation for the sort of women they were likely to throw the book at."

Grey slapped him in the head as he walked around the back of the bar. As he reached for a bottle of Vox, the ram's broad smile couldn't be missed in the dim lighting of the bar. "The ADAs tied up the case, Leo. A whole little contingent of them. Young, nubile and smart."

It didn't escape Brody's notice Grey avoided the direct question. What the Aries did with his free time, he'd made clear—on more than one occasion—didn't affect the rest of them.

Yeah, right.

But Brody left it alone. As the jovial member of their little contingent, he worked to keep peace on this subject, not egg it on. Reaching for another handful of nuts, he aimed his gaze toward the back staircase. "Maybe I should go upstairs. Check out all those skirts, then."

"Stick to what you can handle, Talbot. Besides, clearly you're here to talk. Quinn's on his way." Grey handed him a glass of vodka and club soda, then poured one of his own. "Lay it on me."

Brody glanced around the club. The area they were in was roped off and far enough away from anyone else to ensure privacy. It still bothered him, though, as he looked down the long length of the basement, that there were others close by.

Although the street level of the club entertained the city's finest, the basement was reserved for any number of unusuals and immortals who made Manhattan their home.

Or their workplace.

He recognized Themis's daughters, the three Fates, at the end of the big bar that dominated the majority of the basement. A few seats away from them a buxom nymph and a clearly besotted incubus seemed to be getting acquainted with each other. In a small conversation alcove, a band of Argonauts were clearly letting off steam, their hollers for more pitchers echoing all the way down the room.

Brody jerked his head. "What has them so wound up?"

Grey shrugged. "No idea. But they tip well—even better when they're lit—so my waitresses are happy and keep bringing the rounds."

Quinn walked out of the back office, with a puss on that would rival a two-year-old in a temper tantrum.

"Swallow something?"

"Fuck you, Talbot. I've had a shitty day and an even shittier night so far."

"Join the club."

Grey deposited a scotch in front of Quinn and gave him a pointed stare. "You're scaring my customers."

"The Fates love me."

"Actually, they hate you since you fucked Clotho and then didn't call," Grey added, the soul of diplomacy.

"She wanted a bounce, nothing more."

Brody tossed a glance over his shoulder to take a look at the offended sister. One look at the death mark in her eyes and Brody started to laugh as he turned back toward his brothers. "Oh yeah. You'd better be damn glad you're an immortal, or her sister would be cutting the string of your life prematurely."

Quinn didn't even turn to look at the woman; he just downed his scotch and nodded at Grey behind the bar. "You summoned us here for something, Talbot. Get to it."

"You first. Something has happened to get your panties all bunched up. What is it?"

Quinn pointed his empty at Grey for a refill. "Where's the woman?"

"Safe at home."

Quinn's gaze was laser sharp. "She wasn't safe earlier. Why'd you leave her?"

A distinct itch settled in the center of Brody's back and it had nothing to do with his lion tattoo currently flicking its tail. "You want to watch that insulting tone?"

"Why'd you leave the woman alone and unattended?"

"So I could spend ten fucking minutes getting intel from you and then I'm heading back."

Grey nodded his head in the direction of the offices. "Let's take this somewhere else. You two morons are drawing attention."

In Grey's office, leather couches took up the far side of the office, creating a conversation area. Highly polished chrome and glass took up the business end of the room, the Aries's standard office furniture of desk, chair and credenza oozing command and control with panache.

Grey shut the door, turning on the two of them. "Whatever little lovers' spat you two have going on can stop right here. Quinn—fill me in on whatever the hell's got you in a mood worse than your usual congenial self."

"Talbot's got one job. Follow Ava Harrison, since the air around her apartment has suddenly become electricity central. Neighbors complaining about random power outages. Activity's too concentrated. Too controlled. Enyo's got Destroyers on her."

The itch in the center of Brody's back was quickly morphing into an irrepressible need to pick a fight, his laid-back, easygoing self nowhere in evidence tonight. "No. Enyo *had* Destroyers on her. Took care of two of them tonight."

"And then you go and leave her alone to come here."

Grey slammed his feet on an oversized coffee table. Whether the move was done out of annoyance or to serve as the bell at the end of round one, Brody couldn't tell. "What can possibly be so important about this that Enyo will risk going to war with us? She's lost quite a few rounds lately."

Brody gave Grey the *Reader's Digest* version of the prophecy and its content. He had to give their Aries credit—the guy might have been absent lately, but his sharp mind missed nothing.

"So of course, Queen Bitch wants the stones. They're her ticket to mass destruction and big wins on every remaining battle left to fight."

Brody nodded, the itch to port back to Ava's raging through him like a river in a flood. "Exactly." Every time Enyo went up against them and lost, she lost some of her powers, too. 'Course, that little tidbit worked in reverse, but that's why they trained the way they did and stayed as vigilant as they did. Even Quinn, with his nonstop, paranoid surveillance, did a huge service to their team by ensuring they had a constant stream of information.

They avoided surprises as often as possible and were always prepared. Hell, they were really just modern-day Boy Scouts—with immortality and weapons.

Always one to love giving a lecture, Quinn took over the conversation. "If the prophecy is to be accepted, the stones have a phenomenal amount of power. Until further notice, I suggest we consider it a real threat."

Grey leaned forward as he continued probing to get up to speed. "And Harrison? Why's that name familiar?"

"If you'd bother to come to a meeting every now and again, I wouldn't have to explain it."

Brody saw the fight brewing and jumped in. While he'd have loved nothing more than getting Grey's help in pounding Quinn's ass, he didn't have the time. Every second spent arguing was another moment Ava spent alone. "Russell Harrison discovered the Summoning Stones more than two decades ago. His daughter is a museum curator at the Natural History Museum and is currently preparing an exhibit with the same stones—stones that haven't been all together since they were discovered."

Grey reached for his own glass, curiosity quickly replacing his scowl of annoyance. "So where are they now?"

"Scattered across the world at five different museums. The exhibit at the Natural History Museum is bringing them all back together." An image of Ava's reaction to the suggestion he call her work and tell them she couldn't come in filled Brody's mind. Even through the haze of fear and a Destroyer attack, panic had filled her at the thought he'd call her boss. "The museum is clearly banking a lot on this."

Quinn took another sip of his scotch. "Of course they

are. No one is immune to the lure of technology. Museums are as much a victim of that as any other old-school environment. A pile of old dinosaur bones just isn't interesting anymore. Everyone needs a hook and an angle. The lure of these stones—and the potential curse they represent—has the museum's brass salivating."

Despite his having missed their last several team meetings, Grey caught on quickly. "What's your angle, Quinn? And why's Brody following her? You think Ava is being set up? The daughter of the cursed discoverer and all that."

"It's either that or she's responsible," Quinn added dryly.

Grey pressed on, his stubborn Aries nature forcing them back on point. "Regardless whether she is or she isn't, what does any of this have to do with Enyo?"

"It all goes back to the dig I was on in Egypt and the explanation in the prophecy. How a 'Chosen One' can harness the stones."

Grey leaned forward again as he continued to press his points. "So even if she gets the stones, where is Enyo going to find one of these Chosen Ones? 'Chosen,' by default, suggests there aren't a hell of a lot of them."

"Because calm and rational are her defining characteristics," Quinn muttered.

"Doesn't matter. Seems like she's betting a hell of a lot on very little information and supposition. Does she even know about the prophecy?"

"Of course she does. I had to fight off Destroyers behind the tomb."

"Yeah, but the prophecy was discovered on the dig. She's not Cassandra. How'd she know in advance?"

Chapter Four

"**W**hat happened to you? And since when do you walk in an hour and a half late? You've got a meeting with Dr. Martin and his new security guy in less than thirty minutes and you have a ton of things to approve before you leave for London tonight."

Ava juggled an oversized latte, her purse, her workbag and a roll-aboard as she turned the fish eye on her assistant, Suzy. "Good morning to you, too."

Suzy clamped a hand on her ample chest. "Praise the Lord, it's finally happened. You went on a bender and had wild, monkey sex with a hot man you picked up at Crazy Eights."

The urge to shake her head had almost traveled the sluggish path from thought to action when Ava caught herself at the last minute. The pounding in her head was threatening to actually jackhammer her face off. "While I recognize you are desperate for me to pick up the pool hall owner in that place so you can get free games for life, that's not what happened."

"What did happen? You look like you've been run over."

The banter felt good. Human. Until a bucket of tears welled up, prickly wet heat at the back of her eyes. "A man followed me home last night."

"Ava. Oh, Ava!" Suzy leaped up from her desk and had her in a warm embrace in less than it took to blink. "Are you okay?"

More tears at the show of sisterhood pricked the backs of Ava's eyes. With a large sniff, she caught her breath. "No. No, I'm fine. It didn't happen in my apartment. He didn't even get near my apartment. It happened on the way home."

"Oh, sweetie. Tell me about it."

As Ava took a deep breath, the truth of the situation ran cold fingers of panic up and down her spine. A woman by herself in the city, alone and vulnerable. It happened all the time. People got mugged all the time and now it was her turn.

"How'd you get away?"

"What?"

Something at the edge of her consciousness hovered, like a name you couldn't remember. *How did I get away?* And why was it so hard to remember? And then—triumph!— as another memory filtered through the ooze of her fuzzy head. "I hit him in the neck."

"Oooh. Good one. Their Adam's apple is almost as vulnerable as their balls."

The bloodlust in her friend's voice made her smile as she recounted the night before—or what she could remember of the night before.

Why couldn't she remember?

"Are you going to call the cops?"

"And tell them what? That two big guys held me up and I got away?"

Suzy shrieked at her, the sound reigniting the headache from dull throb to roaring attention. "*Two* guys? You didn't tell me there were two guys."

"Well . . . yeah." Ava blew out a deep breath. There were two, right? Or three? "I'm sure all they wanted was money."

Suzy gave her a quick once-over. "You've got your purse, thank goodness."

Ava looked down at her bag. So she did.

"I guess I got lucky. I forgot it yesterday." An increasing occurrence in her absent-minded worry about the upcoming exhibit. "I had my keys when I walked out and forgot the rest."

"And the twenty you always keep buried in that sweater pocket"—Suzy pointed at her—"ensured you never missed it." The small woman whistled through lips perpetually painted fire-engine red. "You got so lucky, girlfriend. Although why they targeted you, I don't even want to think about. Do you think they were after your grandmother's money?"

"What?"

"Seriously. People know your pedigree. It's not hard to tie you to the Harrison fortune, even if you do prefer Goodwill to Bergdorf's for your outfits."

"Hey!"

Suzy held up a hand. "I don't mean to nag. At least not this morning. But why would someone randomly attack you on the street to mug you when you don't have any visible items to mug? These guys are into quick hits—grab it and go."

Quick hits.

Quick.

Hits.

Ava's stomach dropped as bile rose in her throat. Her mind filled to bursting with images of landing a blow to her attacker's neck. A death blow? *Oh God, did I actually kill someone last night?*

Making a polite excuse, she fumbled to right her workbag on top of the small suitcase. "Um, look. Why don't I finish telling you the rest over lunch? I need to get to my desk and get caught up for the morning."

It was Suzy's turn to give her the fish eye. "Assuming you take lunch today."

The not-so-subtle censure wasn't lost on her. "Yes, yes, yes. I won't blow you off today. We'll grab a bite in the cafeteria."

Suzy pulled her close and wrapped her in a hug. Ava felt some of the chaos of the morning fade under the warm mantle of friendship. "Okay. You've got a deal. Love you, girlfriend."

"Love you back."

As Ava walked down the corridor to her office, the shakes she'd hid from Suzy came back in full force. She flipped her light, dropped her bags on the closest chair and closed the door behind her. She clutched the oversized paper cup of coffee in her hands, desperate for the little warmth that seeped into her palms.

Back against the door, she sank to the floor, teeth chattering. Cold sweat ran down under her arms and a flat, metallic taste covered her tongue. Her body quivering from the darkest fear she'd ever known—even darker than the day Daddy died—she looked around her office.

Her breath caught on a sob as she acknowledged the truth, the memories undeniable. She really was a murderer.

Dr. Lorna MacIntyre's heels clicked as she walked briskly through the Great Court of the British Museum. Although it was celebrated as an architectural marvel, she hated the

Great Court. Hated its great, cavernous echo. Hated the bright light that spilled into what should have been a somber place of learning. Most of all, she hated the way she felt so *on display* whenever she walked through it.

There were too many brightly lit square feet for onlookers to watch and gaze and draw their conclusions about the people they watched.

And people did watch.

And that was how *they* knew about her—and about the dark, desperate need for money that drove her every action. Jason would die if she couldn't afford his treatments.

Her status as a well-respected scientist allowed her access to others in the scientific community. The physicians who were developing new, experimental drugs; the research labs where they did their work; and the sordid few who were willing to take payment for their work not yet approved for patient treatment.

The steady supply of money she provided ensured her connection would continue to steal the drugs Jason so desperately needed to survive.

Clack, clack, clack. Her heels tapped the last few feet before the bright light faded to a more respectable level as she moved into room 4.

Egyptian antiquities.

Or one antiquity in particular.

With deliberate movements, she walked through the now-empty room, the daily throng of tourists long since gone for the day.

Oh, how they loved this room.

No one missed the Egyptian room on a visit to the British Museum. All day long, large groups pressed around various exhibits—the piece of the Great Sphinx's beard, the never-ending cluster of people around the Rosetta Stone and the horde that was drawn, without even understanding why, toward the Great Summoning Stone of Egypt.

She walked through the now-quiet room and knew the timing was essential. She had exactly ninety seconds in the Egyptian room until the cameras would go back on and the security would be restored to full power.

Her skin crawled as she imagined the normal throng of people. She could imagine the press of their bodies, the fetid smell of their breath, the sheer joy of their comments as they oohed and aahed.

They enjoyed while her own son suffered day after day.

With that injustice clamoring in her head, she bent under the exhibit case that held the Summoning Stone and removed the panel that covered a recessed keyboard. The simple removal of the keypad cover would normally send an alarm, so she kept her movements quick, forcing the images of Jason to the back of her mind as she worked.

She keyed in the new codes she'd received as her short, dull fingernails caught the light of the overheads. Three more codes and she'd be done.

Tap. Tap. Tap.

She reset the alarm so the lights shifted from red to green.

Then replaced the keypad cover.

Then walked from the room, through the Great Court and back to the office.

As Dr. MacIntyre took the seat behind her desk, she lifted the day planner on the left side of her desk blotter. The plain white envelope containing her payment sat underneath, exactly as promised.

Politics.

From ancient Rome to the French Revolution to right

this very minute inside the American Museum of Natural History, Brody was convinced politics were the most loathsome part of human existence. Hell, he'd bet a lost battle to Enyo that human politics could be traced all the way back to the Garden of Eden.

"I've been told your security firm is top-notch, Dr. Talbot. Perhaps you can tell me why I'm just now meeting you face-to-face."

Brody walked the length of the exhibit hall with the head of the museum, Dr. William Martin. The man's slight frame and distinguished gray hair gave him the look of the elder statesman, but his sharp comments suggested a man in his prime. They'd spoken several times on the phone since the discovery of the prophecy, and Brody had deduced the esteemed Dr. Martin was a scientist with the highest degree of wit, charm and decency.

The last ten minutes in his company had shot that theory to hell and back. Martin was a spiteful little fucker who showed very little evidence he even had a clue how the museum ran.

"I thought our previous conversations had cleared that issue up, Dr. Martin. My fieldwork concluded only last week. That's why I've worked so hard to provide you with thoughts over the phone. But I'm here now and we've got plenty of time to finalize all the details."

"Yes, well, still, I don't know that you'll be ready to take on this challenge. We're two weeks out from our opening and we're still waiting on the stones from our partner museums. I've scheduled Dr. Harrison to go in your place."

"Dr. Harrison? The curator?"

"Yes. She's more than qualified and her pedigree"—Martin's gaze roved the length of Brody's body, clearly unimpressed with the standard adventurer's outfit of khaki pants, black T-shirt and work boots—"is excellent. Her father discovered the Summoning Stones, you know."

"Yes, I am familiar with both generations of Harrisons and their work. What I'm not understanding is why there is suddenly a problem with my involvement in the project. Or why Dr. Harrison needs to divert her precious time from last-minute preparations on the exhibit."

"I've changed my mind. I think Dr. Harrison will be a welcome replacement and will ensure the proper relations are maintained with our partner museums."

Brody bit down on a quick retort.

Why was there suddenly a problem?

And wasn't it an odd coincidence the timing fell right in line with the attack on Ava?

Coincidence, my ass.

Although he couldn't pinpoint the cause of the bug that had crawled up Martin's ass, Brody figured the best course of action was to keep him talking.

"I thought you made it clear to Quinn this project required the highest level of security detail. The investment your partner museums are making—allowing the transport of their stones for the exhibit—requires significant expertise."

"I'm simply questioning, Dr. Talbot, whether Emerald Securities is up to the task."

A little late to question it now, asshole.

Upon the discovery of the prophecy, and its subsequent award to the museum as an added piece of the Summoning Stones exhibit, Quinn quickly moved to put Brody in place as an expert "consultant." His role as security specialist with an archaeological background had made him the perfect choice. Add his role on the recent dig at Thutmose's tomb and he'd been a shoo-in for the plum assignment of finalizing the security for the exhibit and overseeing the transportation of the stones.

Through a series of conversations, it had been evident to Brody that he and Dr. Martin had comparable philosophies on the removal and display of artifacts, his respect for the scholar growing with each call.

And now—when they were finally meeting face-to-face—Martin wanted him out of there?

The sound of tapping heels interrupted the debate as both men turned their attention toward whoever had come to pay them a visit.

Brody had exactly two seconds to clear the expression of primal hunger that crossed his face as Ava Harrison came into view. Gorgeous calves flowed in feminine glory from the bottom of one of those black pencil skirts Grey was so fond of. A thin white blouse was buttoned over full, perfect breasts. Even that hideous gray sweater she covered herself up with couldn't hide the perfection of her hips or the hourglass detail of her figure.

Dr. Martin put out his hands in a welcome gesture as Ava crossed the room toward them. "Ah, Dr. Harrison. I'm so glad you're here. I'd like to introduce you to someone."

His heart thudded in his chest as if he were a schoolboy waiting for his first date as his gaze drank in her perfection. Her scent—the raw, raspy smell of the hot desert as it descended into cool moonlight—hit him with full force.

He knew she wouldn't remember him—his mind alterations as she slept ensured that—but he could wish, couldn't he?

Ava's eyes took him in as she extended a hand in greeting. As the words formed on his lips to give her his name, he saw that flicker.

A spark that flamed to life as her eyes widened and her mouth dropped into a delightfully surprised little *o*.

Ava Harrison knew exactly who he was.

Ava clutched at her stomach, praying whatever was left of its contents would stay down.

What was *he* doing here?

The hottie who had saved her from the attackers. The one who had gotten her back to her apartment somehow. The one who'd told her to murder the other man.

Her stomach turned over.

There it was again, that horrible awful truth she couldn't forget and couldn't escape. She'd murdered someone.

Would she never feel clean again?

Whole?

And just who, exactly, was this man? Why had he followed her? And, if he wasn't working in tandem with the two guys who tried to jump her, which, from what her fast-restoring memory could piece together he was *not*, then what the hell did he want?

Pushing every ounce of personal theater she'd learned over many years of interacting with her grandmother, she painted on a pleasant demeanor for her boss. "Good morning, Dr. Martin." With a nod, she accepted her boss's introductions and smiled when she addressed the other man by name. Like the last tumbler falling into a lock, she realized why she knew him. Or his reputation, more specifically.

"Dr. Talbot. You were part of the team that removed the

prophecy from Thutmose's tomb? It's quite the accomplishment."

"Thank you. It was Dr. Dryson's work. I feel privileged to have been part of the team."

It was another death at the hands of that tomb—first her father and then Dr. Peter Dryson. Maybe the curse the media wouldn't stop clamoring about had more elements of truth than her scientific mind wanted to accept.

An involuntary shudder ran the length of Ava's back. She was almost getting used to the sensation as her central nervous system attempted to deal with the chaos going on around her. Shaking it off, the reality of the situation—curse or just plain rotten luck—was sobering. "I'm so sorry for the loss of your colleague."

"Thank you. So am I. The world has lost an amazing archaeologist and an incredible man."

It was the sincerity in his words that got her first. She'd spent her life reading people, the majority of her social interaction spent in observation rather than action. And Dr. Talbot seemed genuinely sad and hurt by the loss of his colleague.

With a slightly altered outlook on the large adventurer, she risked another glance into his eyes. The heat of that sky blue gaze shot a ribbon of desire curling through her bloodstream. It felt good. Real. Raw.

And it sent a torrent of heat crashing through her system, a welcome change to the cold numbness that had taken up residence in the marrow of her bones that morning. Even her forty-five-minute pruning session in the shower, the water steaming hot, had done nothing to warm her up.

"Dr. Talbot and I were just discussing the security and transportation of the stones."

She and Dr. Martin had already been through this, but she put on a patient smile and tried to look interested. She wanted to add travel to London, Paris, Sydney and Alexandria to her workload about as much as she wanted to take a vacation with her grandmother.

Not bloody ever.

But, like the surprise trips he'd sprung on her the other day, she smiled and went with it. Dr. Martin had been seriously off his game lately. She adored the fatherlike figure he had been to her since she joined the museum straight out of college. Sadly, in the last few weeks he'd started to show his age.

She supposed it was the natural order of things—if her parents had lived into their later years, she suspected she'd have dealt with it as her friends did. Suzy certainly did, regaling her with tales of lost car keys, misplaced bills and snits at the drugstore.

But knowing it was the natural order of things didn't make it any easier to watch—or any easier to accept the speed with which it happened.

Of course, her conscience taunted, Grandmother hadn't shown a bit of slowing down in her old age. A few misplaced memories or forgotten tasks would actually be quite welcome.

Good grief, what's wrong with you? Ava gave herself a mental head shake, dragging her mind back from the ether. From missing memories to scattered thoughts, she was a freaking mess this morning. Painting on another big smile and nodding her head, she hoped she didn't come off like the village idiot.

Murdering village idiot, her still-taunting conscience added for good measure.

"I'm all packed and ready to leave this evening."

"Dr. Talbot will be joining you for the trip to London."

"Excuse me?" The words flew out before she could stop them. At least she had the small comfort of seeing her surprise match Brody's, whose wide eyes and open mouth reinforced her own shock.

"Dr. Talbot has just convinced me these trips require a security expert. He will be going with you."

Old age be damned, this was too much. She laid a hand on his arm. "William, may I speak with you for a moment? Please?" She almost dropped her hand at the darkness she saw in his eyes, but when she blinked to look again, whatever she thought she'd seen was gone.

William?

Or is that darkness a reflection of yourself, Ava Marie?

Brody walked off with the quick excuse that he wanted to study the layout of the exhibit. "William. You can't be serious about my traveling with Dr. Talbot."

"Dead serious."

"Yes, but why? If you want him to go, then send him. It's his area of expertise. I could use the time here at the museum, anyway."

"Delegate it. I've told you more than once you need to share the responsibility. Lighten your load a bit. I need you on those trips, Ava. I need someone to follow him. I don't feel good about him."

"You've been raving about him for weeks."

A tight, mulish expression flattened Martin's lips. "I hadn't met him yet."

"What changed your mind?" *And why are you sending me off alone with him, then?*

"This is your exhibit. I suggest you get your work requirements in order so things can progress in your absence."

"Of course, William."

"Oh, and Dr. Harrison, keep an eye on Talbot. There's something in that cocky demeanor I just don't trust."

Before she could come up with any other argument that might change his mind, William was gone, marching across the wide expanse of the exhibit hall, expertly weaving his way around glass cases still to be built and oversized printed reliefs that still needed to be hung on the walls, educating their visitors as they walked the route of the exhibit's story arc.

Brody walked back over to her, a smile on his lips. Damn, but the man was too attractive for his own good.

And why did she have the overwhelming urge to kiss him?

It would be so easy, really, to just reach up, grab a handful of that black T-shirt and hang on for dear life as his mouth ravished hers, over and over and over. . . .

Oh God, she'd done it again. More jumbled thoughts, like an incoherent mishmash in her brain, tumbled like clothes in the dryer.

Had it finally happened? Was she just having the nervous breakdown her grandmother had predicted years ago?

Of course, a nervous breakdown didn't change the fact this man standing in front of her had saved her from two thugs last night. Nor did it change his having told her how to kill one of those thugs.

Now he was here?

At the museum?

Traveling overseas with her?

The mushy, soupy haze of her thoughts cleared as, with surprising speed, clarity descended.

Was she really so desperate she was blindsided by sexy

bedroom eyes and a bit of kind regard for a dead colleague?

Forcing the tone she lovingly referred to as her "Haughty
Harrison" demeanor, she stared down her nose at him.

"Who the *fuck* are you? And what are you really doing
here?"

Chapter Five

Enyo listened to the report with half an ear, the shade of her new manicure far more interesting than the increasingly whiny tale being spun before her. No one had managed to truly capture bloodred, but this new shade from OPI came close.

She had to admit—only to herself, of course—that while humans had minimal uses, their ability to manufacture cosmetics did elevate a rare few.

This human standing before her, on the other hand, was no permanent use to her whatsoever.

Temporarily, however . . . Wyatt Harrison was spewing more information than Mount Vesuvius on a good day.

"Get to the point, darling. I'm aging here."

"You never age, my Queen."

Ah . . . another point she'd admit to no one. Flattery did get you somewhere. If nothing else than a stay of execution.

"Don't avoid the question. Get to the point and tell me why it took you almost two months to tell me about the prophecy."

His gaze immediately dropped to the floor, a gesture that

irritated her despite her requiring it. "As I told you, my Queen, I wanted to make sure it was something truly tangible before wasting a minute of your precious time."

One perfectly arched brow shot skyward in a move more reminiscent of her mother than she'd prefer to acknowledge. "And you expect me to buy that?"

"Well, yes, your Highness. It made no sense to drag you into it if there was nothing worthy of your attention."

"I believe I made my wishes very clear when you first contacted me, claiming you had information I'd value. I will decide what is and what isn't important. Did I not?"

He bowed his head in supplication. "Yes, you did."

"So, let's begin with your niece. Did you tip her off to our discussions?"

Wyatt's head shot up, his eyes going wide. "No, I did not!"

"Well then, how did she manage to secure protection from my Destroyers last evening?"

"Protection?"

"Yes. I had two of my best men ready and waiting to bring her to me and she had protection." Wyatt didn't need to know that his niece's protector was likely one of Enyo's immortal enemies. He didn't need to know there was anyone who could possibly challenge her for dominance and superiority.

Themis and her damn Warriors. She'd bet every last drop of power she possessed Ava's defender was a Warrior.

"Yes, protection. There was a man with her."

A loud snort passed through his quivering lips. "My spinster niece hasn't had a man . . . well, ever, if I were to guess."

"She's a young woman. Single, from what you've told me."

"As if that matters. She's a workaholic in drab clothes,

with no personality and no spark. And besides, if she was seeing someone, my mother would have shared the news."

"Well, *someone* is protecting her." Even though she knew he wasn't nearly as well connected as he claimed, Enyo couldn't resist playing with Wyatt for a bit. At best, she'd get some new information and at worst, she'd have a bit of sport—sort of like burning ants under a magnifying glass.

It had been one of her most favorite games as a child.

"Truly, my Queen, it isn't me. How could you think that?"

"You did keep the news of the prophecy from me. How am I to know I can trust you?" Without warning, she shifted, moved up so close she could smell the fear that layered over him in a thin layer of sweat and laid a finger on his neck. Heavy, pounding waves of static shot through her limbs, out one long fingernail into his neck.

She watched his pudgy body shake under the assault; watched as his eyes bulged, his nervous system unable to respond to the attack.

Without warning, the current stopped as she lifted her finger from his neck. His body convulsed into a heap at her feet, his cheek on the ground as he huddled into fetal position.

With the toe of one high-heeled foot, she lifted his downward-facing cheek until he looked up at her. "Now perhaps you'd care to review your story?"

Spittle formed at the corners of his mouth as he huddled and shivered at her feet. "My Queen. She doesn't know. My niece doesn't know."

"Doesn't know what?"

"Ava doesn't know she's the answer to the prophecy. It was in my brother's writings, but my niece has no idea. No knowledge."

The answer?

Ava Harrison was the Key to the prophecy?

Oh, this was rich. And so unexpected. Who knew Wyatt would break so quickly? She should have started the torture weeks ago.

Enyo processed his words, the ramification of them so delicious she could barely stand it. Since learning of the prophecy, she'd simply wanted to get her hands on the stones, and she knew Wyatt's niece was the quickest path to them. She'd assumed finding the Key to the prophecy would have to come later.

But this. Well, this news changed the game. Changed the strategy. Created a completely different method of handling it.

"She really has no idea?"

Wyatt struggled to sit up, nearly there when a wracking cough rattled through him, dropping him back at her feet. "None . . . none at all."

"How can she not know?"

Wyatt shook his head as he managed a sitting position this time. "Russell was killed before he could tell her. Even if he'd lived, I'm quite sure my brother would never have told her."

"So what does she think about the stones?"

"She thinks they're the subject of myth. Nothing more."

Oh, this was just too rich; the mad irony of it was the best part.

Almost.

With a tender caress, she reached down and laid a hand on Wyatt's back. Bright, soothing waves of energy filled him, the pain filling his face shifting to ecstasy in mere moments.

"Darling. Forgive the outburst."

A bright smile spread across his face as he stood up to his full height, facing her. "Yes, my Queen."

"Now then. I want you to help your niece. Be the supportive uncle who is oh so excited for her success. Once the stones are all here, in New York, we'll put our new plan in place."

"Plan? What do you need me to do?"

"I need you to know Ava's plans. All of them. And I need you to give them to me."

The light of rebellion—or was it remorse?—filled his eyes; a silent "but" that she immediately wanted to squash.

Eyes on the prize. Eyes. On. The. Prize.

With a sigh, she tamped down on the anger and closed the deal.

"Only you can do this, Wyatt." She glanced again at the red polish, then lifted a finger to trail it down his chest, her nail making a raspy noise as it dragged across the fabric of his thin shirt. "You're the only one who can handle this."

His chest puffed higher under the pad of her index finger; the mutiny in his eyes vanished as if it had never been. "If it pleases you."

She flicked the edge of her fingernail over the tip of his nipple in one harsh scrape. "It pleases me."

A flash of desire glazed his eyes at her motion, so she did it again, adding a static charge to the movement. As if on cue, the fabric of his pants—just visible past his doughy stomach—showed a noticeable growth.

"Then—then it pl-pleases"—his eyes closed as she shot one more charge straight through his nipple in a harsh burst the fat little pervert clearly enjoyed—"pl-pleases me."

She leaned in and whispered in his ear. "Then make it so."

Without waiting for his response, she disappeared from the man's office to her dining room on Mount Olympus. Without missing a beat, she reached for the always-full bowl of ambrosia on her table and helped herself to a generous scoop. With a small chuckle, she glanced at the perfection of her manicure as she gripped the spoon.

Men really were so easy.

"I love it when you get that smug expression," a male voice spoke from behind her.

Enyo held the shriek back, but barely. Leaping from her chair, she assumed a battle stance and faced her intruder.

The large, bare-chested figure moved toward her, his firm pecs, rippled abs and long, long legs far more appetizing than the sweetest ambrosia.

Ajax.

Her Warrior.

Dropping her raised fists, she pasted on her best sneer. "I gave you a job to do, and since the subject of said job is likely under the protection of one of Themis's little boys, I suggest you get out of my sight."

Ajax shrugged. "So the Destroyers fucked up. We'll get her."

"My, my, aren't we the cocky one." Enyo's eyes grazed over the firm bulge in the front of his jeans. "In more ways than one."

"I've got it under control."

"Yes, well, it seems we're at an impasse there. I'd like you to take a more personal interest in this situation. Get your head in the game, Ajax. You've been flitting in and out. I've barely seen you since this whole prophecy thing started. Are you even interested in the stones?"

While he was a delicious sight for the eyes, that she even needed his help at all still chafed at her. Damn the bargain her idiot father had struck with Themis and this weakened state of hers.

Thank the gods Ajax had no idea just how much she

really needed him and no idea her power was growing weaker by the day.

"Of course I'm interested. Enyo darling, this is the chance we've been waiting for. You get these stones and you'll be invincible."

"She's the one." At his raised eyebrows, she continued. "Ava Harrison is the answer to the prophecy. She's the Chosen One."

Ajax moved closer, his sky blue eyes narrowed. "Who told you?"

"Her oh-so-loyal uncle. Nothing like a bit of familial greed to expose all sorts of delicious information." She took her gaze off him to reach for the ambrosia. "What are you doing here, anyway?"

"I figured you were in need of a fix."

Enyo let out a small sniff as she swallowed the mouthful of ambrosia. Relaxing into her favorite pose—arrogant, pampered goddess—she glanced back at her manicure. "I can fix myself, if I need to. Those vibrators the humans are so fond of do a rather nice job."

With a flash, he had her back flattened against the far wall of her dining room. Heavy, gilt-framed paintings rattled at the force of their landing. "Are you sure you really mean that?" He ground his hips into her, the proof of his erection far more enticing than a piece of plastic.

She let out a small sniff, her pretend pique something she'd picked up watching *Gone with the Wind*. "You think that impresses me?"

In one smooth move, he had her gown up and a jean-clad leg pressed against her clitoris. His movements were harsh, punishing, as one clever hand slammed down between them, rubbing the small center of her sex into immediate frenzy. The tight bud throbbed with need as a delicious quiver settled in her muscles. His teeth scraped against her jaw as his voice penetrated the haze of lust like a sharp razor. "Since your eyes are already dark with passion and I can feel your wetness covering my palm, I suggest you provide me with an answer if you'd like to come, my sweet."

"Never." She fought him, fought the insistent tug of her body. He really was too full of himself for this to continue. She wouldn't—couldn't—let anyone have this much power over her. "I don't need you."

"But you want me."

"I have my vibrator."

"Fuck the vibrator." His hand pressed harder, his fingers so far in her sex she could feel all her muscles clenching around him. "You will come for me."

Her breath came out in pants as her muscles fought for release, but she held on. "You first, darling."

With speed that rivaled Hermes, she had her hands at his waist and his jeans pulled down over his hard buttocks. She dragged her long nails along his sex, satisfied when the movement caused him to jerk, slipping slightly away from her as his eyes closed on a wave of need. Without giving him time to regain any leverage, she squeezed the base of his cock with one hand as her other reached for the pleasure-pain vulnerability of his twin sacs.

She dimly registered the harsh scrape of his day-old beard on her cheek; she felt his balls tightening as her other hand continued to drag on his cock. She knew the moment she'd won, his breath heaving out on a long, low groan as his body shifted into the defenselessness of release.

Only when she knew she'd won did she allow her body its own release. Eyes closed, she leaned her head against the wall as Ajax covered her, his head drooping at her neck as he exhaled deeply into her collarbone.

Men really were so easy.

Brody had seen Ava's eyes go wide as they were introduced and at that moment, knew he was sunk. The woo-woo mind shit that worked on every other freaking human being on the planet—including heads of state and corporate raiders—hadn't held.

Not one fucking bit.

"I'm your new travel companion, sweetheart. That's who I am."

"You can wipe the cocky cowboy routine. You were there. Last night when I got mugged. You followed me. And you made me kill that guy." Ava's stony gaze blew ice at him, but it was the shaking of her hands that suggested all wasn't as it appeared.

She remembered everything.

"Are you okay?"

"Why'd you follow me?" Her stormy gaze didn't let up, but the softening of her voice suggested he may have gotten through.

"I didn't follow you. I was protecting you. Big difference."

"Protecting me? From what?"

"The nasty assholes who attacked you on the street, for starters."

What the hell was he doing? He needed to calm her down, not rile her up. If he could get her calm, he could try the soothing vibes again. She was agitated last night. No wonder they hadn't fully taken.

Arms folded against her chest, she stared up at him with

mutiny shining brightly in those chocolate brown depths. "Beyond my better judgment, I'm giving you exactly two minutes to explain who you are before I call security."

"I *am* security. Security detail for the exhibit."

"So your whole archaeology background is a fake?"

He couldn't stop the words before they were out, the vehemence he felt at the idea he hadn't been responsible for his own accomplishments coming out in a burst. "No!"

"Well, how did you get to be an archaeologist-slash-bodyguard?"

"My archaeology background makes me perfect for this job. I understand the exhibit and I can also manage security needs. My employer is very progressive. We're not just hired muscle. We're experts in our field."

He saw her gaze dart across his shoulders and down his arms and couldn't hold back the grin.

"I can see you agree on the muscle."

A small grimace edged her lips as her eyes snapped back up to his.

The same feeling he'd had the night before, standing outside the deli, came back to him.

He was enjoying himself.

If she'd had any lingering confusion earlier, it was gone as she rapid-fired questions at him like an attorney. "And why would a well-respected archaeologist want to come out of the field to run security detail on a museum exhibit?"

"Money."

"Of course. How silly of me. You're a mercenary archaeologist."

Ava settled back on the edge of a makeshift table, plywood stretched over two sawhorses. Before he could protest the mercenary part, that ugly gray sweater went flying through the air as she tumbled off the edge of the unsteady desk.

He reached for her just as she shifted to sit up, the two of them barely avoiding slamming their heads into each other. Instead, the air between them stilled as their foreheads, then cheeks, then mouths, came into close proximity with each other.

Damn, she smelled good.

He took a deep breath, the urge to press his lips against hers nearly overwhelming. Instead, he extended a hand to touch her, unable to stop himself even if he wanted to.

And he didn't want to.

The pads of his fingers met the soft yarn of her sweater— that gods-awful ugly sweater.

"Dr. Talbot?"

"Hmmm?" He dragged a fingertip down the length of one arm, then back up, his finger shifting to trace her collarbone at the open neckline of her blouse. With slow, deliberate strokes, he traced the curve of her neck, marveling at how small she was and how delicate.

As his palm covered the length of her neck, he used the pad of his thumb to brush over the soft edge of her jaw. Where had this come from? This insane need to simply touch her?

To memorize the feel of her?

To simply *be* with her?

He shifted his gaze to her chocolate brown eyes, their stormy depths hitting him square in the gut. He saw desire— thank the gods, yes, he saw desire—but underneath was something else.

Fear.

Of him?

He stilled the sweep of his thumb to look closer.

"Are you really okay?"

And when she nodded, he took an easy breath. She

might fear what was happening around her, but she didn't fear him.

The husky whisper of her voice coated his senses. "Why can't I remember all of last night?"

He stepped back and put his hands on his hips. He had to get down to business and to do that, he needed distance from her. The longer she remembered, the harder it would be to make her *un*-remember. "Stress?"

She let out a bark of laughter, full of dark undertones and secrets. "Trust me. I've lived with stress my whole life."

He filed that one away and volleyed a new one at her. "Muggers, then?"

"I didn't have my purse. And I did something to that guy. The second one in the Hawaiian shirt. You told me to go after his neck and I did."

Shit. She really, truly remembered last night.

"It's complicated."

"Complicated?" Her hands bunched at her sides as she leaned in closer, her voice an angry hiss. "I killed someone!"

"No, you didn't."

"One minute he was there, struggling with you. Then you told me to step on his neck and the next minute he was gone."

Shamelessly, he poured on his legendary Leo charm. It was a gift that didn't require any mind erasing, just his trademark smile and standard, cocky attitude. "You only think that. You passed out. Remember?"

"Why'd I pass out?"

"Which takes me right back to door number one. Stress?"

He was oddly sorry when she didn't take the bait. "I didn't kill that guy?"

"No, you didn't." You couldn't kill something that was already dead.

"And you let him get away?"

"I couldn't leave you there alone." When she didn't say anything, he leaned forward and took her hand in his, a new idea taking root. If he could get her distracted, maybe he could get her out of the trip to London. "You took a nasty hit to the head. Are you sure you're ready to fly?"

Her gaze caught with his, tangled as the moment stretched out between them. "Dr. Martin is insistent I go."

"I'm sure we can—"

The ringing of her cell phone broke whatever was between them, pulling her attention back to the present. "Excuse me. It's my assistant."

He watched her walk across the room, her steps comfortable as she wove her way through construction debris and saw-horses. The curve of her cheek was the only part of her face visible as she turned away to take the call. Gods help him, he couldn't look away, the soft sweep of her hair as it framed her jawline as enticing a sight as he'd ever seen.

"Thanks, Suzy. I'll be right up."

She closed the phone and turned back to him. "I'm sorry, but I have to go. I have some more questions, but our biggest contributor just arrived and I need to speak with her."

"Can't Martin handle her?"

Ava gave him a wry grin as she tucked her phone back into a cavernous gray sweater pocket. "Seeing as how the contributor is also my grandmother, I can't avoid the summons. Suzy confirmed the car service to the airport will be here at five. I'll see you then."

"Ava, if you're not up to it, you shouldn't have to go. I can handle the retrieval and be back tomorrow."

A small smile hovered at the corners of her mouth. "I'm actually a lot better than I was before."

"What changed?"

"I'm not a murderer anymore."

"No." Brody shook his head. "You're not."

As he watched her walk away, he couldn't stop the sense of foreboding. She might not be a killer, but she was a target.

The sounds of the TV greeted Lorna MacIntyre as she walked into her house. Hands full of mail, she dropped it all on the counter. "I'm home!"

She walked through the small kitchen nook into the family room to find her son's day nurse, Sheila, with a soft smile and a finger to her lips as she pointed to Jason's sleeping form on the couch.

Lorna nodded to show she understood as great waves of pain assaulted her. Her Jason. Her baby. He was so small— so little, curled there on the couch with his arms wrapped around his stuffed tiger. And it was so unfair.

So fucking unfair that he suffered like this.

Sheila stood and followed her into the kitchen.

"Good evening, Dr. MacIntyre, ma'am. Jason had a good day today." These were the words Lorna desperately longed to hear each day.

"It was good? No coughing? None of the side effects we were watching for?"

"Yes, ma'am. He took all his medicine and felt pretty good. He fell asleep only about a half hour ago. The new medicine is working wonders so far. You are so blessed by the doctors you're working with."

Lorna questioned the blessings part, but didn't dare tell that to Sheila, the devout-believer. "I'm so pleased the medicine is working."

Sheila set an empty mug on the counter, its surface littered with medical equipment and pill vials. "I'd best be on my way. I'll see you bright and early tomorrow, ma'am."

"I'll see you then."

Lorna put the kettle on for tea and waited until the headlights of Sheila's car had faded from view.

Only then did she pull out the letter that had been placed in its usual spot under her day planner along with the payment for resetting the security system.

Tomorrow is the day for action. You know what to do.

She read through the note several times, the knowledge of what she was partner to a sickening void in the pit of her stomach.

As the kettle boiled, she added water to her tea and left it to steep, moving into the family room.

As her gaze roved over her son, she thought about the note—thought about the expensive, illegal medicines it bought and thought about the opportunity it gave her for more time with her son.

With careful movements so as not to wake him, she lay down on the couch, wrapping Jason's frail body up in her arms.

And as she lay listening to her child's even breathing, she knew she was doing only what had to be done.

She was fighting for her child's life. And she'd do anything—*anything*—if it meant keeping Jason alive.

Chapter Six

Ava hit Send on her last e-mail of the afternoon, comfortable, if not completely satisfied, that preparations would continue moving ahead with the exhibit.

Grandmother's visit certainly hadn't helped.

"Ava Marie, why are they sending you to London like a common worker?"

"Do you really think the exhibit will be ready in two weeks, Ava? There is so much still to be done without your flitting off to London."

"I've told all my friends about this exhibit, Ava, and if you don't deliver on this and honor your father and the Harrison name properly, I don't know what I will do."

Ava rubbed her stomach around the sick ball of fear that lodged there. And she thought the possibility of being a murderer was bad?

Ava leaned forward, and laid her head in her hands. Did she actually think she could do this? Pull it off? How was she going to go to London? And Paris? And Sydney and Alexandria?

To actually touch the stones?

Retrieve them and carry them back home?

She could barely walk the museum corridors to *look* at the New York stone, she was so sick with fear.

She supposed there was an odd, fitting sort of justice to it all. She hated the stones, but she saw them as her father's legacy. So she'd studied them; she had made herself an expert on them.

Even though she'd never even laid eyes on the other four.

Way to keep that one to yourself, Ava Marie. Think Dr. Martin would have even considered you for the exhibit if he knew you'd never studied the stones face-to-face?

The stone she had seen, she kept at a very comfortable distance—like across the room or from another room entirely where she could look at photographs of it. Her books and her father's notes had provided far more information and knowledge than studying it in person.

Or that's what she'd told herself.

At the same time, she'd begged Dr. Martin for years to put her in charge of an exhibit. And now the joke was on her, her first major exhibit being for a museum piece she'd always hated with a passion.

And to think the New York stone had four pieces that matched it—four other pieces that matched the seething rock of evil nestled in velvet and pulsing in a case in this very museum.

Oh God, how had she gotten herself into this one? And vastly more important, how was she going to get herself out?

Not for the first time she wondered why she was so compelled to bring her father's greatest success to life—the very accomplishment that had served to get him murdered.

Because it venerates his status as a great contributor to the world's collection of archeological finds.

And because maybe if you do this, you can finally—
finally—*lay his ghost to rest.*

Unbidden, images of those quiet moments with Dr.
Talbot—Brody—came back to her. She reached up to touch
her neck, to trace her fingers over the line of her jaw, where
he'd caressed her and stroked her skin with the most delicate care. Even now, a few hours later, her pulse still fluttered under the skin of her neckline as she remembered.

Had she ever been looked at like that before? As if she
were . . . precious? Special?

Desired?

Determination came back to her in a rush. Damn her
grandmother and her undermining, biting ways.

She could do this.

With a quiet sigh, Ava left her office and headed for the
one place in the museum she usually avoided like the very
plague. With a smile, she passed Joe, one of their longest-
employed members of the security team. His ready smile
and warm, rheumy brown eyes boosted her spirits.

"Afternoon, Dr. Harrison. Museum's quiet today."

Ava wasn't sure if that was good or bad. Fewer people
meant fewer potential witnesses should she have a melt-
down. On the other hand, she always felt safer with others
around.

Less alone.

"Enjoy it while you can. The holidays and kids' vaca-
tions will be here sooner than you think, Joe. You'll have so
many people in here, you'll be wishing for a quiet day."

The older man chuckled good-naturedly, his still-straight
back shaking with laughter. "True enough, Doc. True enough."

Ava saw it the moment she crossed the threshold. The
stone was one of the centerpieces of the museum's collection and the lighting had been rigged for dramatic effect.

An oversized glass case with viewing capabilities on all four sides; muted lighting around the room's perimeter so that the key lighting on the case stood out; a crushed-velvet resting place to hold the stone.

She risked a head-on glance at the stone and marveled that no one else ever seemed to notice how evil it was. The moment she got within five feet of it, the stone was *all* she could notice.

Smooth and round, a little larger than the size of her fist, the indigo blue stone lay nestled against a bed of velvet. She knew it was an inanimate object—understood it really couldn't move—but God help her if she believed that.

During college, she'd attended a medical lecture and the speaker had held up a jar with a preserved heart in it. The image of that heart had immediately made her think of the stone and now, as she stood before it, she couldn't stop thinking of how creepy that disembodied heart had looked, preserved in a jar of formaldehyde.

As if it just waited to beat again.

Ava swallowed hard, more of the inadequacy her grandmother had heaped on earlier rearing up. Nasty tentacles of self-doubt that worked to squash any sense of accomplishment she strove so hard for—fought for, really—on a daily basis, reached out.

She knew she was better than that. She knew she could do it. But like the preserved heart, the sense of impending doom weighed down on her.

You seriously think you're going to be able to fly all over the world. With these stones. With the delectable archaeologist?

Yeah, right.

She risked another glance at the glass case, but still, she held back. The few stragglers at the museum on a random

Tuesday morning had other exhibits to see. Excited talk of dinosaurs hovered over them as they left the room.

The stones were shrouded in mystery. What was their purpose? How was it they were perfectly intact—with absolutely no visible wear or tear—upon their discovery? Unlike other Egyptian antiquities discovered in the last century, nothing like this had ever been seen.

Add to it the perceived curse of the stones that began to circulate upon the death of her father, and the public's fascination stayed strong. In fact, now that there was so much information available online—along with about two hundred different conspiracy theories—the stone had experienced a resurgence in popularity and public attention.

Rumor around the museum was that the relief discovered in the tomb and going up on display with the Mysterious Jewels exhibit would explain it all, but the scholars working on the translation hadn't completed it yet. Their working assumption was the relief provided some explanation or definition related to the stones.

Sighing, she added that to her running checklist of things she still needed to complete before the exhibit went live. *Talk to Egyptian scholar to get full definition.*

Ava pulled her attention from her mental to-do list and looked at the descriptions of the stones from the various reliefs posted around the exhibit room. The posters talked about her father's discovery, that there were five stones, how they were excavated and where they were all housed.

When she couldn't put it off any longer, she pulled her attention from the last poster she'd reread three times and turned toward the glass.

She could do this.

She would do this.

She—

Snakes with bared fangs danced before her eyes and heavy drumbeats stuck in her ears. A pit of fire held writhing people, screaming as they fought the pull of death, as even more snakes rained down on their bodies. A sweet, metallic scent hit her nose as she saw blood drip down the glass panes of the case.

A wave of nausea flooded her stomach as her mouth began to water with sickness.

Pushing away, she clutched at her stomach as she drew deep breaths into her lungs. Frantic, she turned to call for help, when the reality of the situation hit her.

The room was just as it had been moments before. No blood. No snakes. Nothing.

Nothing except a raging headache and a desperate sense of loneliness. No matter how hard she tried to tell herself she could do this—could handle the stone—she couldn't. There was something wrong with her. Something so deeply broken, she didn't even know what it was to be right.

To be whole.

Pushing through a new group of museum-goers who had entered the room, she nearly stumbled over a young mother with a baby stroller.

The tension lessened as she escaped the room, but a vague sense of disorientation filled her as she moved through the museum. Avoiding another group of people milling around at the elevators, she took a back set of stairs that brought her right back to her office.

With a deep breath, she walked into the center of the room and took a seat behind her desk, the familiar surroundings soothing her nerves. Safe. Secure.

What a joke.

*   *   *

Brody buckled his seat belt and marveled at the various
rituals going on around him. Several people dithered with
their bags, above the head, below the feet, on the seat next
to them, back into the overhead. Others played with iPods.
Still a few more fiddled on BlackBerrys. No matter what
the action, everyone prepared themselves to sit in a large
metal tube and be propelled across the Atlantic Ocean.

A strange panic filled his chest and he felt the unpleas-
ant urge to shove his head between his knees.

He glanced at the hard tray in front of him, eyeing the
distance between his chest and the seat, then mentally cal-
culated the size of his body.

Nope. That one wouldn't work. And these seats had
way more legroom than the ones behind them. He'd already
eyed the seats in the back of the plane as he'd done some
recognizance.

How the *hell* did people sit in *those*?

He and his Warrior brothers might be tasked to protect
humanity, but if Themis *really* cared about humans, she'd
do something about airplanes. This was barbaric.

Ava turned toward him, the quizzical look in her eyes
adding to his need to fidget. "Are you okay?"

"Sure. Why?"

"You look nervous."

"I'm not nervous."

"You sure?"

"Positive."

"Have you flown before?"

Brody feigned annoyance and bit back the odd slither of
embarrassment that worked its way under his skin. "Of
course I have. I've worked on digs all over the world." And
I've *flown* to them, in a sense, if having your body flung

into the time-space continuum after disintegrating to a molecular level counts as flying.

"Of course. I'm being silly." Ava laid her head back against the seat, giving him a chance to really look at her. It had the added benefit of taking his mind off their impending hurtle through the atmosphere.

In a large metal tube. Powered by explosive chemicals.

Dark circles framed the undersides of her eyes, circles that hadn't been quite as prominent earlier. The paper-thin skin of her eyelids was pale, the blue of her veins standing out in sharp relief.

Clearly, something had happened since she'd walked away from him in the exhibit hall.

And even more clearly, it had taken its toll.

Brody started to wake her when the captain's voice filled the cabin yet again, his British accent instructing them on flying time and their expected altitude. The odd, stick-thin woman in front of him got up to get something from her carry-on bag for the *fifth* time since they'd boarded, and a semidrunk businessman stumbled out of the lavatory and to his seat.

And then the whole show got under way.

"You can thank my grandmother for the first-class seats."

"What?" Brody shifted to find Ava's eyes open again and a small smile at the corner of her lips. Although the corners of her mouth were turned up, the smile didn't reach the sad depths of her chocolate brown eyes.

"These seats. We were supposed to sit back there." She pointed toward those foul, evil seats that must have been designed by Zeus's bitch-wife Hera, and Brody felt an involuntary shudder. "We're in first class thanks to the Harrison money. It makes a flight like this easier to handle."

"My sincere thanks to her, then."

"You can fully recline in these seats. Even sleep in them."

You could recline? Brody eyed the other passengers, none of whom were reclining. "No one else is."

"Once we're airborne, you can do it. They like everyone sitting upright for takeoff."

As if on cue, the plane began to lumber down the runway. The heavy, rumbling feeling made him think of the giants who used to roam the forest near his childhood home. Their overly large bodies made the same thudding sounds as they ran through the forest after their prey.

Ava's voice was low and he had to lean closer to hear her over the sounds of the plane as it picked up speed down the runway. "Isn't it funny, really, how we're all afraid of something?"

"What are you afraid of?"

"Hold my hand and I'll tell you."

He glanced down at the long, tapered fingers capped off by softly buffed nails. Her hand was lovely. Elegant. He laid his own large one over hers and watched as their fingers intertwined, as if of their own accord.

When he pulled his gaze away from their hands and to her face, her eyes were already closed. Squeezing lightly, he waited for her eyes to open.

"What?"

"You didn't tell me what you were afraid of."

She smiled again and this time it reached her eyes. "Nothing worth mentioning. I just wanted you to feel better as we took off."

Ava smiled at her father, his large, oversized presence reassuring. She always felt safe with Daddy. Protected. He'd been away traveling for so many weeks, it was wonderful to have him home. He promised they'd have daddy-daughter day when he got back and now, after all those weeks of waiting, here they were.

"I can't wait to see your special stones that you discovered. And the rubies like the one in Fergie's ring. You'll let me take you to the rubies, too. Right?"

He smiled down at her, his eyes so warm and golden with crinkly edges when he smiled at her. "Yes, sweetie, we'll go see your rubies."

Ava danced down the street next to him, her hand enfolded in his big one.

They walked up to the front entrance of the Natural History Museum and Ava could feel her excitement growing even bigger—sort of like her tummy, but in a good way.

Fergie was her new most favorite person-she-didn't-actually-know, ever since she married Prince Andrew. Ava remembered how beautiful the wedding was, watching the videotape of the news coverage at least six times since Daddy had left on his trip. It was one of the few things Grandmother deemed acceptable. Ava had watched it so many times, she could even recite their vows by heart.

With a skip, she walked through the doors of the museum, no longer frightened by the humongous dinosaur in the front hall. She wasn't a baby anymore. No way.

Now she wanted to be a duchess. And an archaeologist, like Daddy. With a shrug as they passed the large dinosaur skeleton she'd named Fifi when she was little, she decided she'd be both.

An archaeologist duchess.

They walked toward Daddy's office and she gave a little tug on his hand. "Don't you want to see the rubies first?"

He smiled down at her, but there was something funny

in his voice. "Come with me, Ava. I said we'd go look at my new stones first."

"Okay."

They walked into his office and she ran over to his leather jacket, hanging on the back of his chair. She loved that jacket. It smelled so good, like leather and like the outside and the way it got at night after a hot day where you could still smell the sun.

And it smelled like Daddy.

Her hero.

She looked up from the coat, a sleeve still wrapped in her arms. "You know what? I think I'd like to have a ruby engagement ring like Fergie."

"What?" Daddy was bent over a worktable on the other side of his office, looking down at something.

"The Duchess of York, Daddy. The one I've been telling you about. The pretty red-haired lady."

What was the matter with him today? He wasn't listening to anything, as if he had earphones in his ears. Daddy always gave her his full attention. Not in that mean, teasing way like everyone at school, or in that focused way like Grandmother, but in that wonderful Daddy way that meant she mattered.

"Daddy!" She walked over and tugged on his hand. "What's wrong today? You're not listening and I'm trying to tell you all about Fergie and Prince Andrew and their wonderful wedding."

"What?" He pulled away, but his attention and his eyes stayed on the case in front of him.

A small kernel of unease rumbled in her belly. It felt like that horrible Halloween movie Cousin Brett tricked her into watching over the summer.

"Will you shut up about that stupid woman, Ava? I am sick to death of hearing about her wedding."

Tears threatened, but she held them in. "Oh. Okay."

"I told you, I wanted you to see my work. Well, here it is." He reached for her hand, but when she didn't move fast enough, he tugged harder, pulling her closer, then picking her up. His movements were jerky as he struggled with her weight.

He hadn't picked her up in a long time.

She used to be sad about that, but now, with his arms pressed in the roly part of her tummy, it was hard to breathe. Maybe she didn't want to be carried around like a baby anymore.

His arms jostled her as he held her up over the table. "Look at it!"

There was only one stone, even though he'd told her he'd found five of them. She was glad there was only the one. The blue stone was more than enough. It was about the size of her Walkman, but rounded like an egg. The moment she stopped thinking about how big her belly was and actually looked at the stone, the scared feeling in her tummy rolled completely over, just like when she watched Freddie Krueger jump into kids' dreams.

A wave of heat swamped her and she thought she was going to throw up right there on the table. Her mouth started to water and horrible images, way worse than Freddie Krueger, hit her. Some flashed in front of her eyes while others felt like they lived in her head, slithering through her mind so that she couldn't stop seeing them even when she closed her eyes.

Snakes with bared fangs danced before her eyes and heavy drumbeats stuck in her ears while an icky, metally *smell hit her nose. A pit of fire held writhing people she somehow knew were dying as more snakes fell on their naked bodies.*

Stark terror crawled down her spine as something that had the body of a man and the head of a wild animal started dancing around the pit. "Daddy!"

She screamed it, trying to make him let go of her; trying to get them away from the case and whatever horrible thing was pulsing behind the glass.

"Daddy!"

Chapter Seven

"Ava!" Brody gripped her shoulders, trying to wake her from whatever nightmare had her in its hold. Her eyes were open, but the blank stare let him know she was still locked in the hell she'd visited in her sleep.

Ava whimpered her father's name one more time before the haze in her eyes began to clear. He saw the moment the dream winked out and recognition of her surroundings took its place as those deep brown orbs drank him in.

"Shhh. You're safe here." He brushed at her hair, frustrated when he couldn't pull her limp form onto his lap over the privacy divider between their extended seats.

With impatient movements, he pressed the controls to close up his own seat so that he could reach her. Lifting her, he folded Ava in his arms. Her body trembled with cold and her clammy skin was icy to the touch.

With soft, soothing words he held her as she calmed down. The beat of her heart pressed against his chest, the rapid count slowing along with her breath as his words slowly penetrated the last vestiges of the nightmare.

"Are you okay?"

"Yeah," she whispered, her voice coming out as a scratchy sound from the back of her throat.

"Want to talk about it?"

She whispered again, but her tone gained strength. "I don't know."

"It was a dream about your father?"

She gripped a fistful of T-shirt as she curled farther into his arms. "How did you know?"

"You were moaning his name. Have you had it before?"

She struggled, her eyes going wide. "Did anyone hear me?"

"No. Shhh. Come here." He pulled her close again. "Tell me about it."

"I used to have it every night. It stopped when I got older. I haven't had this dream in years."

He was tempted to push some soothing thoughts toward her, pressing them into the recesses of her mind where fear of the dream still lingered, but he held himself back. No matter how well-intentioned it was, the more time he spent with her, the less he felt it was a fair thing to do. He'd done it last night without reservation, hoping the calming thoughts would replace the nightmare she'd experienced with the Destroyers, but now, well, it just felt wrong.

Pulling her closer, he whispered, "Tell me about it. Telling it will get it out of your head. Make it less real."

"I can't talk about it."

"Why not?"

"I never talk about it. It's too real. It *was* real."

Fear dripped off the end of her words like blood. This was something more than just a bad dream, conjured by her subconscious mind. A memory?

"Did something happen to you?"

She was silent for a while, her fingers running over the duvet. "Yes."

"Did someone hurt you?" The mere thought of someone laying a finger on her filled him with rage, awakening the lion tattoo on his back as adrenaline spiked through his system.

"Not exactly." He thought she would go silent again, but she took a deep breath and began to tell him. "It happened a couple of days before my father died."

"Why don't you want to talk about it? What are you afraid of? It obviously happened a long time ago. Whatever it is, it can't hurt you now."

"But it makes my father sound like a horrible man."

Something dark unfurled in his stomach. Had the man hurt her? Abused her? "Did he touch you, Ava?"

Catching the thread under his words, she immediately struggled to sit up straight again. "Oh no. Nothing like that. He was a wonderful father."

"What is it, then?"

"It's just that this story makes him sound like he's not a great father. And he was. He was the best."

"Why don't you just tell me and I promise to give him a fair hearing."

She sighed, the sound heavy between them. "The first time I saw the stone in New York, I was with my father. We'd gone because I wanted to see the Burmese ruby collection the museum is so known for, and he was so excited to show me the stones he found on his dig, so we made a day of it." He listened as she explained their visit and how she had always loved spending time with her father. They were clearly the words of someone who had loved her parent very much—not someone trying to hide flaws.

"So we went to his office first and I was immediately

obsessed with telling him all about the rubies and imagining myself as Fergie."

"The singer?"

She smiled, the first real smile he'd seen in a while. "No, silly. This was more than twenty years ago. I'm talking about the duchess. Of York."

An image of a beautiful red-haired woman came to mind and he nodded. "Got it."

"So I was dancing around his office and smelling his leather jacket and imagining myself as a duchess and all of a sudden my father called me over. And he was gone."

"What do you mean, gone? He disappeared from the room?"

"His body might have been there, but his soul most certainly wasn't. I can't explain it, but I've never forgotten it, even though I've desperately wanted to. To the depths of my toes, I know the man I stood in that room with was not my father. Something happened to him when he looked at the stone."

"Ava. You were a child. Did something else happen? Maybe he yelled at you for touching it and you misinterpreted his actions." Brody felt stupid even saying the words. From the prophecy, they knew what the stones were capable of; knew they needed a conduit to bring out their potential.

But he wanted to draw out the story. He knew there were answers in there, buried somewhere in her memories.

Was Russell Harrison that conduit?

"No. I know what I saw. I know it wasn't him. And—" She grew quiet as another round of shivers wracked her body.

Brody pulled her closer, rubbing her back in an effort to restore some warmth to her system.

"And what?"

"The stone makes me sick when I look at it."

Oh shit. A funny feeling hit him low in the gut. He'd studied ancient artifacts long enough to understand how they worked. And one truism was that families had connections. And where one family member had a reaction, their child had a greater likelihood of the same thing.

If Russell was a chosen channel for the stones, was it possible Ava was, too?

"Sick how?"

"I see visions. And the visions make me so nauseated I get sick. It's worse if I look at the stone when I'm running low on energy. I had to go look at it a few weeks ago for the exhibit. It was right before lunch and I hadn't eaten breakfast. Waves of images assaulted me and I thought I was going to pass out."

"What are the images like?"

"There are snakes—so many snakes you can't believe it. And loud chanting and fire and naked people. Victims. They're being sacrificed in some way."

"For what?"

"I can't tell. I've never been able to look at the stone long enough to understand what it is."

"Do you know where these things are happening?"

"I assume Egypt."

"You said your father's soul disappeared. Does the same happen to you?"

She shook her head. "No, I don't think so. It doesn't feel like that's happening, but what do I really know?"

They sat there in silence. Brody stroked the soft waves of her hair, helpless to do anything else.

"Brody?" She looked up at him, those dark circles under her eyes dragging a wave of empathy through him so strong he felt dizzy. "I went to look at the stone today. After lunch and on a full stomach."

"And?"

"It was no different."

Brody pulled her close, pressing kisses to her forehead. "Shhh. Just relax. I promise I'll take care of you."

She might not know what was going on, but it was quickly becoming clear he knew exactly what was happening.

And in order to take care of her and get her out of this mess, she'd have to face her most horrific nightmares.

The Destroyer huddled in his coat, wrapped up against the biting November cold.

"You had a simple job last night: Remove the woman."

He shrugged, memories of his former life—and this sector of the park—coming back to him. "She had protection."

"Not an excuse I ever want to hear. You act. You take down anything in your way. Hence the name, Destroyer."

Destroyer. Yeah, right. His name was Bill. *Bill, you motherfuckers!* he wanted to scream. "What the fuck do you want me to tell you? Me and Paulie ran up against the guy. I got away. Paulie wasn't so lucky."

"You left a man behind?"

"Behind? Damn, I told him he needed to regroup. Didn't pay any attention. I wasn't going down just cuz Paulie was stupid."

Bill saw the assessing gleam in the guy's eyes. He knew that look. He had used it himself on several occasions when he was sizing up his dealer crew, trying to figure out which ones would get the job done and which ones would just take his blow for themselves.

Dealing was hard business. *Underappreciated work,* he chuckled to himself.

Course, this gig was better by far. He had so much power

in his little finger, he'd started working his magic back in the park. He figured he could do double duty—jobs for Queenie and back to his old business to line his coffers.

He looked at the guy in front of him. Blond hair. Chiseled jaw. He knew this one. Right-hand guy to Queenie. Didn't take a leak unless she told him it was okay.

"I've got a situation I need your help with. Consider it a chance to redeem yourself."

"Fuck off. I got nothing to redeem."

The asshole was on him before he had time to take another breath. Hot waves of electricity lit up his insides like the Fourth of July.

What was this shit?

Hot, molten pain filled his head as a great, horrible pressure built at his temples.

Holy shit!

Bill looked down at his hands as his eyes bulged in their sockets. His fingers looked bigger. Plumper. Was this asshole going to blow him up?

"Now are you ready to listen?"

Bill nodded, his body paralyzed.

"That woman. The sweet piece you couldn't manage to handle last night? I'm going to give you a second chance. She's on her way to London, and you're going to help me capture her and the asshole she's traveling with."

Bill took a great gulp of air as the pressure eased slightly. "Man, I think that guy was a Warrior. He didn't act like no standard boyfriend."

A malevolent smile spread across Queenie's man's face. "He *is* a Warrior. So nice of you to finally show up to the party."

"Fuck man, so what do you want me to do? They're not easy to kill."

"Then you're not doing the job properly." The asshole sent another shock wave of pain ricocheting through his system.

He would not scream. Bill allowed the weird-as-shit body he still hadn't grown accustomed to to absorb the pain. No, siree. He would not scream.

"Now, are you ready for a chance to redeem yourself?"

As the last shock faded, he turned toward Blondie. "Tell me what you want me to do."

"First, you tell no one. You're in this with me and you're taking orders from me now. Not a word to Enyo. Got it?"

So maybe this guy *could* take a leak without Queenie's involvement. And although he had no desire to go up against the bitch, Bill knew all about a bird in the hand and all that crap. Alive and working for this schmuck was better than dead waiting for orders from the lady. "Yeah."

"You ever been to London, my fine man?"

"Shit, no."

"Well then, consider this your lucky day. We're porting there now."

"Port? I can't do that shit, man."

"No, but I can."

Brody felt Ava's deep, even breathing where she lay against his chest and finally allowed himself a moment to relax. Against his better judgment, he'd grown accustomed to the noises of the plane in flight and, in the face of Ava's raw fear at the nightmare, his earlier discomfort seemed foolish.

The quiet also gave him a chance to puzzle through all he'd learned in the last day and a half.

He'd gotten updates from both Quinn and Grey via texts before they took off. Quinn was digging deeper into Wyatt Harrison's financial records and Grey was working his network of contacts to find out about any underground dealings, while the rest of his brothers were taking shifts keeping an eye on the museum.

The texts weren't all that surprising.

An infusion of cash had recently made its way into Wyatt Harrison's bank account in the sum of twenty million dollars. Add to that the news that Wyatt was asking around for places he could purchase a firearm in Egypt, and a few more pieces of the puzzle slipped into place.

So the likelihood was high Wyatt had killed the site worker. But it still didn't explain the Destroyers who killed Peter—or why it took almost two months for an attack on Ava.

Brody pulled her closer, enjoying the feel of her in his arms. Was it just last night he'd imagined what it would be like to hold her? Last night, when he'd stood guard over her, watching and waiting.

Protecting.

Through it all, he'd been utterly captivated by her. The soft sweep of her cheek, the light rise and fall of her chest as she exhaled the simple, even breaths of sleep. Even her hands drew his interest with their long, tapered fingers and lightly polished nails.

As the long hours of night faded into dawn, he'd grown more fascinated with each passing second.

On first glance, her apartment had offered few clues to who she was. But as he'd sat in his spot on the rug by the front door, he'd come to realize that very sparseness told a different story.

Her bookshelf held stacks of books, yet none of them were the educational or literary tomes he'd have expected of a woman who held a PhD and worked in a museum. No, instead he found the latest thrillers, row upon row of romances, a jumble of Westerns and a good, healthy dose of mysteries to boot.

The woman was a beach-read addict and his fascination had grown a little more for it.

The minimal pictures scattered around her house indicated there was no one to stand for her, to stand by her. Other than a few framed photographs on the bookshelf—one of her and her father, one that was clearly her as a baby in the arms of a woman, standing with the same man and the last, a stoic, cold picture of her and an old woman—that was it.

That was all she had to show for her life?

The thought saddened him in that place way down deep where he'd buried his old loneliness, his old inadequacies, his old life.

Now, as angry as his Warrior brothers made him, they still had one another. And yeah, they fought, but it was more than that.

They were a family—an odd one at best, but a family all the same.

Other than a creepy uncle and a cold-fish grandmother, Ava had no one.

As she burrowed herself deeper into his arms, the shudders that had wracked her for so long finally having faded, Brody wondered, again, what it would be like to kiss her.

Kane Montague groaned as the most delectable tongue ever to rove over his body licked the edges of his scorpion tattoo. The incredible Ilsa—if that was even her name—had offered him the perfect distraction to while away a few days as he waited for Brody to arrive in London.

He'd been collaborating with MI6 for almost a decade now. Although a perpetual free agent, he was well-known throughout the organization for his assassin's abilities. Couple that with discretion that rivaled a vault, and his private number rang regularly with work.

He knew he didn't have a lot of years left with MI6—people tended to notice when their secret agents didn't age—but damn it if he wasn't going to miss the work. And damn it even more if that thought hadn't been an increasingly frequent companion of late.

Shifting his attention to a far more scintillating companion, he rolled under Ilsa, pulling her long, lithe body over on top of his. Dark chestnut hair cascaded over him, covering his head as she rained kisses over his face and down his neck.

He'd wanted her from the first moment he saw her—long legs and toned arms shown to perfection in a little black dress and all that luscious hair pulled up into a sexy twist. She'd walked into his debriefing at headquarters exactly one week ago and every thought in his head—every single question he needed to ask about his mission—fell out along with his tongue.

What was it about this woman?

One week and he was as starry-eyed as Zeus for Hera—more so, if you considered he'd never felt this degree of attraction to anyone.

He'd certainly enjoyed his fair share of companions over the centuries. From peasants to royalty, he'd tried them all. But this woman—she'd managed to twist his insides and drive his body into overdrive with barely a glance.

Her tongue darted over the top of his pecs as she shifted, then moved lower, running wet circles around one of his nipples. The sensation shot straight to his cock, pressing even more proudly against her flat stomach.

While she used one hand to support herself, the other moved down to stroke his straining erection. With firm move-

ments, she took the wetness at the tip, painting his shaft with
deft movements. Base to tip and back, her expert strokes
had his balls curling up against his body with fierce need.

"Whoa, darling." He reached for her shoulders, the dim
realization that if he didn't slow her down he was going to
embarrass himself before his mouth even touched her.

Pulling her up toward him, he forced his mind toward
reciting the Greek alphabet backward—anything to stop the
madness clenching his stomach muscles as he fought to
keep himself in control.

Her voice, husky with dark desires, whispered against
his lips. "This one's for you, lover. Don't ask me to stop.
Just go with it." She shifted again, using her thighs to squeeze
his engorged shaft. He released her immediately as pleasure
shot the length of his spinal cord, allowing her to slip from
his grip.

Somewhere in the back of his mind, some small voice
tried to warn him that something wasn't right. Even the
most devoted lover shared the pleasure, touching and stroking as those gestures were given in return.

This—oh gods, what letter came before Omicron?—was
like an assault of pleasure. A fight for—Xi, yes, Xi, that
was it—for sexual control. A battle to draw—he gritted his
teeth as the symbol for Nu wavered at the edge of his
consciousness—an orgasm as if it somehow admitted defeat.

The edge of her fingernail scraped the sensitive underside of his sac and he knew defeat was imminent. He opened
his eyes, as if that small measure of control could counterbalance the fact that she was about to unman him three
days into some serious marathon sex.

"Good. Your eyes are open. I like that in a man. Makes
the victory that much sweeter."

Her words lodged dimly in the back of his mind as

great, heaving spasms overtook his body. As he spilled himself over her belly and breasts, he barely registered the swift movement, almost didn't feel the quick, stinging prick through the mind-numbing pleasure of his orgasm.

Her sky blue eyes—absolutely unwavering on his— were the last thing he saw before his entire world blacked out.

The nonstop excitement of Heathrow Airport greeted them the moment they stepped off the plane. Complaints about baggage checks, pages for gate changes and several businessmen running to catch their flight were a few of the sounds that made up the airport's raging cacophony.

"I'd like to go straight there, if you don't mind."

"I think that's a good idea," Brody muttered as he played with his phone. Where the hell was Kane?

"Who do you keep calling?"

"My firm arranged for a London-based agent to meet us as well. I can't seem to get a hold of him." Brody rubbed his stomach as he listened to the sound of Kane's voice mail for the fifth time. Where the hell was he?

"Are you okay?" The silky tone of Ava's voice shot straight through him, despite his rising discomfort at their situation.

Brody glanced up from his phone midtext. "I'm just a little hungry."

"Airplane food is hardly filling." She rooted around in her carry-on, several small tendrils of hair falling around her cheeks as she dug in the cavernous bag. "Here's a granola bar."

He had the wrapper off and the bar half devoured before she'd even gotten her bag zipped up. "Do you have any more of those?"

"No, last one. And it's the middle of rush hour. He could have gotten stuck in traffic."

Their lethal Scorpio, who could get himself in and out of any situation . . . stuck in traffic? Even if he couldn't port for some unknown reason, he should have been here. Kane never missed a meet. Never.

Brody swallowed the last bite of the granola bar, his spirits lifted ever so slightly with the food. It wouldn't last long, but he'd take what he could get until they hit the city.

He tried Kane again as they moved through the arrivals area. Ava kept up his pace, her bright-eyed expression as she took in everything in the terminal warming his heart.

"Come on, we'll get a cab."

"No need. Grandmother insisted on car service at the same time she was forcing first class down my throat."

"Rough life."

"Don't I know it." She grinned at him, and a small knot of tension loosened in his gut at her carefree expression. The dream had upset her, but clearly she'd gotten some good sleep on the rest of the flight.

"Look." Ava pointed to a man holding a large white sign. "There he is."

Brody didn't like giving up control to another driver, but he wasn't interested in arousing suspicion, either. He'd have preferred to simply port them to Kane's flat, but since he couldn't very well knock Ava unconscious, they were stuck with the town car.

The driver kept his head down and his cap over his eyes as he took care of their bags. Brody felt a stray wisp of something touch his subconscious, but turned toward Ava to help her into the backseat of the car. As he reached for the metal door handle, he felt it.

The damn driver was a Destroyer—and the cap and hunched shoulders were hiding something else.

Stray wisps of energy and a distinct zap of stray voltage came off the handle.

Shit.

"Ava," he whispered against her ear, "turn toward me and giggle."

"Wha—" He didn't get the giggle, but he did get an armful of woman. Pressing his mouth to hers, Brody pulled her against his chest, his back against the frame of the car to absorb the increasing streams of electricity.

After a few, brief seconds of initial surprise, Ava responded, her body molding to his. Their tongues met, insistent and seeking. Fire raged through him as the insane urge to brand her as his gripped him.

Brody knew he had a job to do—knew there wasn't time for this—but damn it if he didn't want to stay like this for real. Take his time. Learn her secrets.

Make her moan.

Opening one eye, he got a clean look at the driver.

The guy from the other night.

Shit, shit, shit. It was the one he let get away; the one who attacked Ava.

Pulling his mouth back, Brody made a show of working his way down her neck, then back up toward her ear. With a low whisper, he murmured in her ear, "You need to get ready to run. The driver is a setup."

He felt her body tighten as she went fully alert in his arms.

"Do you understand me?"

At the subtle nod of her head, he reached for her hand. "Now!" he hissed, and pulled her along, threading their way through the throngs of tired travelers heading out into the London morning.

Brody heard the shout behind them as he and Ava made a run for it. A glance over his shoulder showed the arrival of the airport police, who made quick work of their driver.

"Is he following us?"

Brody gave one last look before they got too far away to see anything and was satisfied to see their captor still hadn't gotten himself away from the police.

"He's a bit tied up. Airport police won't let him leave his vehicle." He grabbed the bag she still carried on her shoulder—what the hell did she have in here?—shifting it to his own. "Come on. Let's head for the Underground. It's actually above ground for quite a few stops until we hit London. If we have to jump off, we will."

They wove through Heathrow and toward the airport's Underground station. As they submersed themselves in the throngs of travelers, he kept a watchful eye behind them.

Just what the hell was going on here? Even if the driver was deployed by Enyo, where the hell was Kane?

Ticketing proved uneventful, as did their wait on the platform. It shouldn't have surprised him when, twenty minutes later, Ava hissed at him from their standing-only spots on the packed train. "Do you mind telling me what's going on?"

Brody watched the doors close as they cleared Osterley station. He really did need to relax. "Nothing's wrong."

She kept a broad smile on her face as if to broadcast to anyone watching them that they were a happy couple, traveling on vacation. Her words, however, were razor sharp as she delivered them in calm undertones. "Let's try that again. You know, where you don't underestimate my powers of intuition."

He felt his mouth drop as her words penetrated. "Excuse me?"

"You heard me. I didn't finish questioning you about what happened on my way home the other night because I got distracted at work. Then I was going to ask you about it on the plane and I had the nightmare. But you need to spill it. Who are these people and who are you? Really? You just happen to show up the night I get mugged on my block and then you show up at the museum, all ready to protect me. I'm not buying it."

He was Leo Warrior. He was a protector. He was a fighter.

And he couldn't very well tell her that. He could see the conversation now. *"Oh sorry, Ava, you mean I didn't tell you? I'm an immortal Warrior, working in service to the Greek goddess of justice."*

Yeah, right.

Add to it the fact they'd all taken an oath to keep their roles quiet. What had started out as a necessary step to keep humans unaware of their protectors—and therefore engaged in their own self-preservation—had morphed into something else entirely in the last fifty years.

As humans developed ever-more modern technologies and devices that allowed them greater understanding of the world around them, no one, not even the powerful Greek gods, would benefit if they were found out. Either revered as deities, harangued as celebrities or sought after so humans could use technology to replicate their abilities, no one wanted discovery.

If there was one thing they all agreed on—Enyo included—it was that no one benefited if humankind knew who was protecting them.

"I'm your bodyguard and, right now"—he eyed the Tube

map over her left shoulder, seeking the stop they needed to change lines—"I need you to listen to me and follow my lead."

"Is this tied to my father?"

"Why do you think that?"

"His murder was ruled a random act of violence, but I've never believed it."

As several people got off at the next stop, Brody saw an opportunity to shift their position, placing Ava in a more sheltered area behind him, two hard walls of the train protecting her back. "You think he was murdered?"

"I know he was."

Chapter Eight

"Murdered? But why?" He knew the intel, knew the rumors and knew the damn unusual coincidence that was Russell Harrison's death.

But the idea his daughter knew it, too? If she believed it, why hadn't she pressed for justice? Pushed the police to keep working the case?

"I was there with him when the guy came out of the park and assaulted us on our way home."

Brody ran a finger down her cheek, imagining the horror of it. To experience death at all was a tragedy, but to see it at such a young age and to have it happen in front of you—well, that was something many people would never have recovered from.

He held his initial harsh thoughts in check as he let her explain herself. "Go on."

"It wasn't random. For starters, it was broad daylight when it happened. I realize we're from New York, but contrary to the tales told the world over, most people don't get murdered in broad daylight. And certainly not on Central Park West."

"That's true." Unless they're targeted for a hit, that is.

"Add to that the fact that my father had a child with him. Further add to it that he wasn't exactly dressed like a rich man, in his usual archaeologist uniform of ratty khakis and a T-shirt. It just never felt, well, arbitrary."

"So why was the case dropped and called a random act of violence?"

"It was my grandmother. She made a big stink of it at the time. She suggested the only reason the media was putting on their circus was because of our money. She found a way to squelch it—it wouldn't do, after all, to have such a scandal befall our family. But I've always known."

The grandmother was a serious piece of work, that was for sure. "Her will was enough to evade the police?"

"Her iron-clad will can evade anything."

They both fell into their own thoughts as they pulled into the next station, then switched train lines with no issue. It wasn't until they were nearing their final stop, Westminster station, when Ava grabbed his arm.

"Do you feel it?"

Brody scanned the train yet again, unable to identify a Destroyer in their midst. "I don't see him."

"I feel it. That weird electricity. It's across my back. Does he have a taser or something?"

Brody gathered her closer, pulling her away from the metal handrail that hit her at waist level. "Our stop is next. Are you ready to run for it? Our hotel is on the other side of the river. We just need to get inside."

Was it their driver who'd managed to get himself free or a new threat? Brody figured he'd know soon enough who'd targeted them when the guy gave chase in the station.

Although he kept his voice calm and level, Brody's lion had opened up, his tail flicking in annoyance at the stray wisps of electricity that kept hitting him in the back as he shielded Ava from the Destroyer's view. He kept the tattoo in line, knowing that a lion popping from his aura on a morning rush hour train would go over about as well as a cockroach in a five-star restaurant.

Likely even worse.

"We're next. Ready to run?" When she nodded, he conjured up a vague memory of the station from a hit he had helped Kane with several years before. "When we get to the top of the stairs, we need to get out on the street. There's a bridge across the Thames. Head that way, in the direction of the London Eye."

Ava's pupils had dilated in huge orbs, drowning out the brown of her eyes to small circles. He leaned in, pressing his lips to hers in a quick kiss, damning his earlier vow and pushing some warm, soothing, encouraging energy toward her. "You can do this, Ava."

While he wasn't sure he'd had nearly enough time to make an impression, the stiff set of her shoulders eased.

"Ready?"

She nodded her head. "Yep."

The doors swooshed open and he pushed her. "Go now!"

Her long, lithe body darted from the train and he followed, ignoring the pain that shot through his muscle fibers. He ignored the signs that his strength wasn't at one hundred percent as they ran up the station steps toward fresh morning air.

Rain greeted them as they hit the exit of the station, and Ava nearly slipped on a slick spot on the floor. He grabbed her arm, steadying her, but the quick stop gave the Destroyer time to close the distance and launch a fireball at them at close range. With a hairsbreadth of time, Brody shoved

Ava away from him and took the hit, the strength of the electricity doubled by the puddle of water he stood in.

He pitched forward, his hands heading for the floor, when Ava grabbed his arm. His weight nearly toppled both of them to the ground, until she planted her feet at the last minute in a wide stance, providing much-needed balance. "You got your feet?"

He nodded, holding firm to her hand as they started moving. "Yep. Come on."

They cleared the station, the morning throng of people again helping to keep the Destroyer at a good distance. Ava's feet flew toward the bridge and he followed, his lungs burning with the exertion.

The London Eye rose up in front of them as they ran across the bridge, over the Thames. Although it looked like a large Ferris wheel from a distance, the Eye was actually an observation wheel, with individual, closed viewing bays. He briefly toyed with the idea of hiding in one of them, then discarded it. The Destroyer might keep himself in check in a throng of people where he would draw undue attention, but the structure of the Eye would offer too much temptation to simply dismantle it, making it look like a very violent accident.

Ava looked back over her shoulder, whatever fear she'd had on the train now spurring her into action. "Brody! He's gaining on us."

"You go. I'll deal with him."

"Absolutely not."

He kept pace with her, his mind reeling for some course of action that would get them out of this without a public display.

And even if they managed to get into a more discreet location, there was no way Ava wouldn't see.

No way she wouldn't know what he was.

Did he dare?

They'd nearly cleared the end of the bridge when Brody felt another fireball as it passed him. The shock of it dropped Ava to her knees, just far enough out of his range that he couldn't quite grasp her as she fell.

As he watched, Ava tumbled down a set of stairs that led toward the riverbank, her screams reverberating in the cold morning air. The need to go to her fought with the blazing rage that welled up inside of him. When he saw her stand, helped to her feet by a morning jogger, he shifted, his body taut with tension as rage beat a rapt staccato under his skin.

The asshole stood a few feet away, the distance just far enough to make a neck-shot impossible as he leered at Brody. It was their driver. Although Brody had remembered his face, the disheveled uniform confirmed it. He'd obviously made quick work of the police.

The Destroyer licked his lips. "I'll give you a minute to look, seeing as how it's the last time you're going to see her. The woman dies today. Right after I rip you apart."

Brody launched himself at the Destroyer, ignoring the smacks of electricity the asshole started throwing immediately. His lion was feral, desperate to get out, but still, he held him back.

He'd let the lion go postal on the Destroyer's ass after he'd had his fun.

With swift kicks he worked on the guy, forcing him against the ages-old stone of the bridge. Brody was barely aware of the passersby who gave them a wide berth, their fight looking for all those who observed it like a bar brawl gone bad.

A bar brawl one greasy-ass Destroyer wasn't walking away from.

Brody reached for his ankle, his movement toward his Xiphos as natural as breathing, before he forgot it wasn't there. *Fuck! Damn airline regulations.*

That split second was all the asshole needed to press his advantage, taking them both tumbling the last few feet toward the stairs, then down them.

Brody caught sight of Ava, huddled under the bridge, her eyes wide with fear as she watched them. She was alone, the jogger who'd helped her nowhere in sight. Every instinct he possessed wanted to draw their fight away from her, but . . . if he could only drag the Destroyer under the bridge, he had a real shot of taking care of him without an audience.

He dodged another fireball—this one weaker than the last—then responded with another roundhouse kick to the guy's midsection. Tired or not, the Destroyer's footwork kept him out of range for Brody to get to the neck to land the death blow.

Impatience warred with strategy as his lion quivered in barely leashed fury.

Three more steps until they'd cleared the bridge and any pairs of prying eyes.

Two . . . Brody grunted as he took a fireball—more like a sparkler—to the shoulder.

One!

His lion leaped from his aura, clamping its powerful jaws on the Destroyer's neck as its equally lethal paw scraped at the guy's midsection.

Brody watched with bone-deep satisfaction as the Destroyer immediately began to disintegrate. Dark, inky black oil oozed from the neck as the skin shriveled to a husk. His lion shook its head, more of the oil flicking off in small spatters from the edges of its mane.

It was then that he heard Ava's screams.

Whirling, realization flooded his veins at what, exactly, she was screaming about.

His lion.

Although contained within the frame of his aura—a connection that tethered them to each other with roughly three to four feet to spare—when fully engaged a full-grown lion fought right next to him. The lion watched his back, having complete range of motion as well as an ability to turn around.

And, of course, the lion also had an ability to shred his enemies to pieces should they dare to get too close to his back.

In the great balancing act that was the gods' playground, everyone had something. The Destroyers got electricity out of their life force.

Themis's Warriors got really kick-ass tattoos.

He'd actually bitched a hailstorm about it at first, the concept so ludicrous he'd let his leonine pride run his mouth. Words he'd ended up eating many times over seeing as how it didn't even take one full battle before he'd come to appreciate the merits of something that could watch his back.

He had his lion. Kane his scorpion. Grey his ram. Their Aquarius, Aidan, could actually create flood waters against his enemies.

Why had he ever doubted Themis's wisdom? Brody still wondered from time to time.

Ava's screams echoed off the old stones of the bridge and he moved forward to soothe her—until another round of ear-piercing shrieks stopped him in his tracks.

With deep, calming breaths, he willed the lion back into tattoo form, the large beast folding up on itself as Brody kept his face firmly toward Ava.

"Where'd it go?" Her eyes were wild in her face as she focused her attention on the air behind him.

"Away." He reached out to put a hand on her arm, but she snatched it from him.

"You saw it, didn't you? You had to have seen it. It was . . . was . . . *attached* to you."

"Ava."

"What are you?"

Without waiting any longer to consider all the angles—and damning common sense and discretion to hell—he reached out and grabbed her, whirling them both headfirst into a jump to the one place the Destroyers could not go.

The home of a Warrior of the Zodiac.

Chapter Nine

Ava heard the loud whistle of air, then nothing, and then a loud whistle again as her body felt as if it were flying apart. Muscle-deep pain gripped her before she hit a very soft surface.

Her muscles no longer hurt and that high-pitched whistle was gone.

Where was she?

She heard a groan and then a very large, very naked man rolled on top of her, pinning her to what her rapidly-assembling senses realized was a bed.

And who was this man?

The scent of sex was heavy in the room as her senses sparked to life with a vengeance.

"Get off my woman." Ava heard Brody's growl before she saw him. Felt the pulsing violence before she registered his movements as he bodily lifted the naked man off her.

The naked guy might have a body the size of a small truck and a six-pack of abs she could have played a tune on, but his actions were anything but lethal as he slumped, semiconscious, against the wall. He seemed as out of it as a drunk after a wedding, but the broad width of his chest suggested someone who shouldn't be messed with.

Who were these people?

What were she and Brody doing landing in someone's bedroom? A very sleek, modern bedroom, with chrome-edged furniture and a mile-wide bed covered in black sheets.

Egyptian cotton, if she wasn't mistaken.

And why, oh why, had she put her trust in Brody? She hadn't been able to empty her memory of the image of his big arms around her, holding her through the night as she'd slept after the nightmare. The feel of his arms was practically imprinted into her skin.

But was that a reason to abandon common sense?

And where had that lion come from? There was no way that was a hallucination.

As the big naked guy on the floor registered his surroundings, Ava watched him leap up at Brody, the slight stagger to his walk the only indication he'd been passed out cold less than a minute before. Unable to help herself, she took in the sleek lines of his very impressive—and very naked—body, sculpted to perfection.

Brody held him off. "Don't fuck with me, Kane. You missed the meet, you had yourself wrapped around my woman and you're buck naked. Get the fuck out of here and get dressed."

The big man—Kane—glanced over and offered up a small "Sorry" before he disappeared.

Vanished.

And then the fear she supposed she should have felt morphed into real fear—honest-to-goodness get-me-the-fuck-out-of-here fear.

Panic rode Ava in hard, galloping waves as she gasped for air. Her heart was pounding so hard, she couldn't imagine how she wasn't having a heart attack.

For the nine-hundredth time since she was attacked and pulled out of her quiet little life the night before last, she tried desperately to make sense of what was going on.

Even in all the mind-numbing shock of those days after Daddy died, it was never like this—surreal to the point of a horror film.

Where were they?

Who were these men? And how were they any different from the ones who attacked her at home and in the airport?

She clutched her stomach, hysterical pants clogging in her throat.

"Ava, you have to calm down." Brody held her arm as he gently sat down next to her on the bed.

"Don't touch me!" She pulled her arm away as more breaths caught in her throat. With crablike motions, she scrabbled to the head of the bed, putting as much distance as possible between herself and Brody.

And then he was moved closer, reaching out toward her with seeking fingers and soft, murmured words. She shifted again and nearly fell off the bed before he caught her, then pulled her close, rubbing soothing circles on her back with his large, warm palm.

And God help her, she liked it.

"That's better. Shhh, now. I promise you're safe here." They sat like that until her breathing returned to normal; until she was ready to talk to him.

"Where are we?"

"Kane's home. The security specialist I told you about. The one who was supposed to meet us at Heathrow."

"But where are we? How did we get here? One minute we're standing on the banks of the Thames and the next we're here." She turned to look at him, her gaze roving the strong sweep of his jaw and the firm lines of his neck where she could almost swear she saw his pulse.

He was human. He had to be. She'd *know* if he wasn't.

Wouldn't she?

"I'll explain to you what I can."

He'd explain what he could? "Oh no, buddy. You dragged me here. You can damn well tell me who you are and how you did that . . . that . . . little trick."

"I can't tell you. It's for your protection."

"Bullshit."

Her panic twisted into hard, jagged spikes of adrenaline that pummeled her nervous system.

"I am not fragile. I don't need to be coddled or taken care of."

"Could have fooled me."

Words spilled from her, frustration and anger seething in every word—every thought—she'd been desperate to get out for years. "You're the one who dragged me here. What do you expect me to think? I'm not some whimpering coward who needs protecting."

"Oh really?" His words spewed out through gritted teeth. "You really don't think you need protection? That's rich."

"Where do you think you can get off—"

"I've watched you for four days and I can see it. See you hide. From life. From men. From yourself." He ran a hand down the sleeve of her sweater. "This, for example. This awful, ugly sweater an eighty-year-old woman wouldn't be caught dead in. You wear it like a freaking mantle of protection—the impenetrable fortress of Ava Harrison."

Shocked to her core, she couldn't believe what she was hearing. The sheer insult of it was enough to bring tears to her eyes, but she wasn't crying.

Quivering in frustration and anger and need and raw fury, yes.

Crying? No.

"You know nothing about me."

"I know you're kind and hardworking and warm and passionate. And I know you hide it under ninety-hour work weeks and drab clothes."

"I don't know what I'm doing here, but since my spinster wardrobe and I are clearly such a burden, show me to the door and you're rid of me."

She leaped off the bed and headed for the doorway. Although larger than most city apartments, it was still an apartment. It wouldn't be that hard to find the door and get on her way.

They had to be in London—she hoped. She'd find a cab, get to the hotel and get cleaned up for her meeting at the museum.

Except, of course, that all her clothes were sitting in the trunk of some disintegrated felon's car.

Her feet sank into heavy, plush carpet as she crossed the room. A long hallway greeted her, suspended over a large loft to serve as the walkway to the second story.

She'd barely passed the second bedroom when she felt Brody's hand on her arm.

"Please give me a chance to explain a few things."

"Why? So you can insult me again?"

"Are you going to make me jealous by jumping into bed with another one of my friends, then ogling his naked ass?"

A small snort escaped her. While it wasn't the most lady-like gesture, it sure beat quivering panic. "As your prisoner, no doubt."

"You're not a prisoner. But you also don't need to be stupid. In the last eighteen hours you've been attacked twice. And neither time by me. Don't you think you may want to channel a wee bit of that rage at your situation and away from me?"

"You'd go a long way toward making me feel better if you told me a few things."

He nodded. "That's fair."

"And maybe let me call Dr. MacIntyre to reschedule our visit today. Assuming you have a phone."

He smiled and nodded. "Fair again."

"Okay, then. Let's talk."

As she waited for him to say something, the moment spun out in silence. His blue eyes locked on hers as her senses heightened, sharpened, *expanded*.

And then they exploded.

"First things first." Brody's husky whisper washed over her as he wrapped her in his arms and . . . *oooh*.

Oh my.

His mouth pressed to hers and with lips and teeth and tongue, they played a guessing game of what came next.

The hot press of his lips shot sparks to every region of her body as his tongue teased the seam of her lips. Helpless to resist the heady seduction, she opened for him, eager to learn the taste of him.

With powerful thrusts, his tongue swept through her mouth, drawing a low, deep moan from the back of her throat. With drugging tenderness, his teeth scraped against her lips as they tenderly drew her bottom lip into his mouth.

Hot suction pulled at her lower lip, the erotic tugs at her mouth shooting arousal throughout her body—arousal that pooled between her thighs; arousal she was helpless to resist.

Her mind might still be confused by who he was and what he'd brought into her life. But this—this was unmistakable.

He lifted his mouth from hers to look down at her, his lazy-lidded blue eyes searing into hers. "Now, I believe you said you had a few questions?"

Questions?

Right. Questions. What did she want to know? Something. Some things. What things? And then she focused on the lazy grin he had aimed in her direction and she sobered up quickly. "You did that on purpose."

"Yes. Because I wanted to. Because I've wanted to for four days. It wasn't to divert you from asking your questions. So shoot."

Ava took a deep breath. "Where are we?"

"London."

"How'd we get here?"

"I'll explain it only if you promise to believe me."

"Explain it first."

"Promise first."

"Okay. Fine. I promise."

"We ported here. As in teleported. Telepathically transformed all our molecules and moved them through time and space."

All the air left her body in a rush. "You did that?"

"Yes."

"How?"

"I don't know *how*; I just know it works. Anything in my life force, such as clothing, or anything I touch, comes with me in the port."

She wanted to scream. Wanted to rage that it wasn't possible and that people just didn't do that. But the evidence was overwhelming. A few minutes ago she'd heard Big Ben ringing from across the water and now they were here.

Maybe her molecules hadn't all reassembled correctly if she was actually buying this.

But it did make an odd sort of sense.

Of course, maybe it was just further proof of what her grandmother had always predicted: that some day her mind would—once and for all—snap.

"Where is that lion?"

"Can I get back to you on that one?"

"So there was a lion."

"I'm not going to argue with what you saw."

"Is it a pet?"

"Not really."

"Brody. Come on."

He smiled again. "No. Give me an easier one. I'll explain the lion later."

"Fine. Who was that man you tried to throw across the room?"

"I told you. His name is Kane and this is his apartment."

"And Kane's just a little ole security expert?"

"He is."

"Then how come he can 'port,' too?"

"It's a special gift we each have."

A deep sigh rumbled up from the depths of her stomach. "The fact I am even sitting here buying *any* of this means you might as well tell me everything. And if you won't, I'll go down and try to pull it out of Mr. Sex-on-a-Stick."

Her comment about Kane hit the mark she aimed for.

"I'll tell you."

"Are you sure? You've lied to me since you met me."

"I haven't lied."

"You've misrepresented yourself at every turn."

"I've answered almost all your questions. And tell me, Ava. Is this a misrepresentation?"

She sensed what he was going to do before his lips actually made contact with hers. Knew it wasn't a good idea to enjoy this too much. Oh yes, she knew it, even as she responded to the soft caress of his mouth.

And the heavens help her, she didn't care.

Didn't care that she'd watched yet another man get killed—or something that looked like a man—less than an hour ago.

Didn't care that she'd stared down a very large lion that somehow seemed to fit with Brody.

Didn't even care that she actually, maybe, kinda sorta, believed she'd disintegrated to the molecular level and moved across space and time.

With that thought came another. She pulled her lips from his. "Are you a real man?"

"Flesh and blood."

Her mind fought for some semblance of sanity through the haze of pleasure. But the other men? The ones who attacked her and the one who just died. "Are you positive?"

The light tone of his laughter rumbled through his chest as he ground his hips into hers as tangible proof. "What do you think, sweetheart?"

Shaking off the flood of warm shivers at the endearment, she pressed on, determined to get at least this answer from him. "But those men who held me up outside my apartment— they looked real. The one felt real, too, as his arms came around me. And then . . ."

He nodded. "And then what?"

"And his body just shriveled up and disintegrated. And he became this oily ooze."

"That one falls in the same category as the lion. Can I take a message and get back to you?"

"Not if you expect me to kiss you again."

Ava saw the light register in Brody's eyes, the small crinkles that framed the corners of those cornflower blue orbs, when a loud thud reverberated through the loft.

Ava looked in the direction of the noise and saw a large man with shoulders like a highland warrior and dark, close-cut hair that stood up in spikes staring up toward the landing from the loft's living room. He looked furious. "What the fuck is going on, Talbot? And why, for the love of Themis, are you porting fully conscious mortals?"

Brody disengaged himself from Ava and raced down the stairs. "Get in the kitchen. I'll discuss it with you there."

For once, Quinn didn't argue, but just turned on his heel and disappeared as fast as he had appeared.

The knowledge he needed to deal with Quinn immediately had him staring back up at Ava. She hadn't moved from the spot where he'd kissed her; a slightly dazed expression still covered her face in the form of a half-quirked lip and wide eyes.

"Why don't you make that call to Dr. MacIntyre? There's a phone in Kane's room. Can I trust you not to call anyone else? I promise you're safe here. I need to keep you that way."

Although Ava didn't say anything, she did nod, which Brody took as a good sign. He wouldn't blame her if she still tried to make a run for the door, as he'd done nothing to earn the trust he so desperately wanted her to offer.

"I'll come back and get you when I'm done with Quinn."

He headed for Kane's kitchen, throwing one last glance

at Ava's retreating back as she returned to the bedroom. Stark black appliances, black marble counters and black marble tile greeted him as he walked into the kitchen.

"Who's your decorator, Kane? The Grim Reaper?"

Their Scorpio had managed to rustle up a pair of jeans and he leaned against the far counter, a cup of coffee in hand. "I like black."

"Obviously."

Quinn interrupted, his always-thin patience now nonexistent. "Talbot, what are you doing bringing her here?"

"I didn't have a choice."

"Wrong answer." Fury snapped its sharp teeth in Brody's direction as Quinn paced the kitchen.

Brody gritted his teeth, absolutely unwilling to lose his temper with Quinn, their round less than forty-eight hours ago at Equinox more than enough. As Fixed signs, the two of them thrived on constant rounds of head butting and today he flat-out wasn't in the mood.

Besides. He wanted to get back to Ava.

"My job is to keep her safe. That's what I'm doing."

"And opening the rest of us up to exposure in the process? No one gets into our lives and into our homes, Brody. No one. The rules don't change. And you agreed to them, all those many centuries ago."

"Yeah, well, I didn't have a choice. You know about the two Destroyers who attacked her outside her apartment. Another one came after us at the airport." He'd leave out the fact the one at the airport was part of the New York duo until he could puzzle it out himself.

"So deal with them, Talbot; then erase her memories. It's your job."

"Yes, but she's the first person I've stumbled on who I *can't* make forget."

Kane pushed himself off the counter. "She remembers everything?"

"Yep. I even erased her memories while she slept. It didn't work."

Quinn slammed his coffee cup on the counter, the movement so harsh it was a wonder he didn't break the mug. "So bringing her here was an even shittier idea than I first thought."

"You know, Quinn, I'm not sure when you started thinking of this little gig as yours to run, but we're all in this together. I made a choice and I'll live with the consequences. I couldn't leave her exposed."

Quinn nodded. "So what's the next move?"

The tension lining Brody's shoulder eased slightly. "We get the second stone and get out of London. And now that Ava knows we can port her home, we're *not* flying the friendly skies back to New York."

Ava paced around the small room. She'd called Dr. Mac-Intyre to reconfirm their late-afternoon appointment.

That had taken a whole minute, the woman's impatience to get off the call clear, even through the phone lines. Brody had been gone nineteen more.

Was she insane to be here still? Just preparing to be another statistic in some crime log? And now that she was separated from the heady, sensual feast that was Brody's mouth, the lack of a sexual haze was producing a good bit of clarity.

What was really going on?

Who was that very large man who had interrupted them? And why could he just order Brody around? And why didn't he want her there?

Were they doing something illegal?

And again, what was wrong with her? Why wasn't she running for the door? She wanted to trust her instincts; she wanted to believe that, no matter how large they looked, these men and this situation wouldn't harm her.

Willing some order out of the chaos that coursed through her mind, she tried to line up what she *did* know.

Something—human or otherwise—had come into her life. She'd been a scientist too long not to accept that there were still many things outside the realm of human understanding. She could even go so far as to accept that life existed beyond their planet.

But men who disintegrated into pools of grease?

No way.

Okay. Put that in the what-I-don't-know column. Next.

Although she couldn't get a handle on who—or what—Brody was, he *felt* like a man. And he didn't seem as if he'd hurt her.

No. Correct that.

He *wouldn't* hurt her. She knew that to the depths of her toes. Whatever else he was, he wasn't the enemy.

A light knock sounded on the door frame before Brody stepped into the room. "Make your call?"

"Yep. We're now on for three."

He inclined his head toward the hallway. "Sorry about that."

"Who was that?"

"That was Quinn."

When Brody wasn't forthcoming with anything else, she pressed on. "And Quinn would be?"

"Um. Well, that's where it gets a bit tricky."

"How so?"

"It's complicated." At his closed-mouthed stare, she knew she wouldn't get any further details. His lack of faith in her hurt, especially as she was the injured party.

"You ask me not to run out of here and I don't. Now I ask you for some degree of explanation and you won't give it to me."

"Ava. It's not like that." He paced, his large body appearing even larger in the small room, reminding her of a caged animal.

That image brought her back to the question of the lion.

And that only pissed her off all over again.

"Then what's it like?"

"Please don't ask for what I can't tell you."

As from a balloon with a small pinprick in its base, some of the air deflated from her anger. She didn't know how to answer his plea, but, if she were really honest with herself, she couldn't exactly fault him, either. There were things she didn't tell anybody—ever.

It still didn't mean she liked being kept in the dark.

"You're more than an archaeologist."

He reached over, placing a hand under her chin. With slow, soft movements, he turned her face toward his and leaned in. With a small sigh, he pressed a chaste kiss to her lips, then laid his forehead against hers. "Yes."

"But you can't tell me what *more* means."

"I can't give you specifics."

"What about broad strokes?"

Ava couldn't hold back a small smile at his sigh. She'd always been persistent and it was nice to see it finally pay off. "All right. In broad strokes, I've devoted my life to protecting humanity from the evil that lives in the world."

Humanity's protector?

"And those other men? The naked one and the ogre who just stormed in? Are they the same as you?"

"More or less, yes. I mean, we're all different people, but they have sworn the same oath as I have."

Images of their time on the plane came back to her and she recognized, in that brief instant, why she trusted he wouldn't hurt her. For all his muscle—all his apparent supernatural abilities—there was a very real man inside.

"Does it bother you? To be different? Separate from people? This protector thing that you are. Doesn't it get tiring?"

He pulled back slightly to look at her. "What?"

"I know what it is. To be separate from others. It gets lonely. Much of it's been my fault, but I've isolated myself from others, some of it by circumstance and sometimes by choice. I rarely connect with others. Rarely match with anyone. Family. Friend. Lover. And I guess I just see something in you that reminds me of that."

He hesitated and for a moment she thought she overplayed her hand, had said too much. What had made her even start down this path? Was it simply a tactic to get him to open up, or had she actually been the one to open up?

And then he nodded and laid his forehead back against hers, and Ava knew it didn't matter.

She'd shared something of herself with someone else.

And *that* mattered.

A lot.

"You want me to play this how?" Ava glanced at the three large, powerful men standing in front of her as they shoveled Chinese food into their mouths, and she marveled at how far she'd come. A year ago—heck, a week ago—she'd never have dreamed of questioning their authority.

Now, butterflies filled her stomach, but she was speaking up, using her voice, asking questions.

Why she trusted them, she couldn't quite say. And well, if she were honest, it was Brody she trusted. The other two she continued to eye cautiously, as one would a great big guard dog. Yeah, the animal acted as a protector, but you also knew better than to turn your back.

Clearly, this strange foray into the supernatural would ultimately be good for her.

Unless you get yourself killed by some stray voltage, Ava Marie.

Ava took a quick gulp of her warm Diet Coke. *Don't go there. Do. Not. Go. There.*

Brody interrupted her thoughts as he took the lead on the briefing. Still, she could tell it wasn't easy for either Kane or Quinn to keep their mouths shut. The neon blinking sign of narrowed eyes and stiff postures said it all. "Kane and I worked it out this morning. We want you to go in and play the brainless bimbo scientist with attitude with Dr. Lorna MacIntyre."

"And why should I do that? I've spoken to the woman several times. I've been a competent colleague with her as we've worked on this project. I can't just turn into a moron. Oh, excuse me, a bimbo moron with attitude."

Kane let out a discreet cough, but she could see the light in his dark gray eyes. "I think the term we originally came up with was 'flighty scientist.'"

Her suspicion those eyes didn't crinkle up in that über-sexy way very often only added to her concern about this little plan the boys had cooked up. "Oh, that makes me feel so much better about it."

Quinn offered up a helpful smile. "And with attitude is

just, you know, giving it the whole *I'm a big, badass New Yorker and I can handle anything*."

"I still don't understand why you think this is the right approach."

Brody sighed as he reached for his Egg Foo Young. "Because either MacIntyre's aboveboard and will just think you're a"—he had the decency to wince—"flighty bimbo or, she's actually working for someone else and will underestimate you."

"Why would you think she's working for anyone?"

At raised eyebrows from all three men, she narrowed her eyes in response. "What has you all so suspicious?"

Quinn laid his empty container on the counter. "Very little has gone smoothly on this project from the get-go. From the discovery of the stones to the deaths during the discovery of the prophecy to the attacks on you. We can't be too careful."

"And you think another museum's involved in this? That someone *internally* at the museum is involved in this?" Ava's stomach clenched at the very thought.

Brody's voice was gentle. Soothing. "We can't be too careful."

Ava laid her half-eaten meal on the counter. "Before I do this, there's something I want you all to answer for me."

She kept her gaze leveled on Quinn—waited until he nodded his head. "What's that?"

"You owe me an explanation of what I'm walking into. I want to know who these people are. And who are those men who keep disintegrating into pools of grease? Does that happen to you if you get hurt?"

Kane snorted and uttered, "Not bloody likely," before all three men looked at one another.

Ava saw the looks that passed among all three of them. She saw the pointed look Brody leveled on Quinn. Finally, the man nodded. "I suppose you're in this pretty deep already. Fair enough."

Quinn laid his half-eaten egg roll on the counter and wiped his hands on a napkin. "You sure you want to know?"

"Positive."

"Okay." He nodded. "We're immortal Warriors, granted our powers by the Greek goddess of justice, Themis. The men who disintegrated into piles of ooze work for our mortal enemy, Enyo, the goddess of war."

Chapter Ten

Enyo circled the cell where one Dr. William Martin was now spending his days. The delicate little man had proven a greater challenge than she'd expected, but she was delighted to see the days of imprisonment were wearing him down.

The normally fastidious man had several weeks' growth of beard covering his face. Although she'd held out so far, she was seriously considering giving Deimos his head to play with Martin, using a few of his favorite torture devices.

While she'd like nothing more than to see the good doctor suffer a bit for his stubbornness, she'd allowed her nephew to play with her prisoners before. His zeal for his craft had cost her some good information and she wasn't about to repeat that mistake.

"So, Dr. Martin, enjoying your day?"

"What can you possibly be keeping me alive for? I won't give you the information you seek. Kill me and get it over with."

"Tsk, tsk, tsk, Dr. Martin. Surely you can't believe I find you that expendable."

"I know you do. I'm an old man and I can't take much more of this. End this misery and be done with me."

"Yes, you would like that, wouldn't you?" She heard scurrying in the walls of the abandoned subway tunnel they currently occupied and briefly pondered adding a few enticements to the good doctor's cell to lure the rats.

Or something even more interesting, perhaps . . .

"I'd like that very much."

"Well then, I guess it's just not your lucky day. You have something I want and since you refuse to share it"—she plastered a moue of pique on her features—"it looks like we're at an impasse."

He leaned on the bars, his weakened spirit painting his features with a grayish pall. "We've been through this several times. I don't have anything for you. I'm a man of learning. What could you possibly want from me?"

Just for fun, she touched a long, red fingernail to the bars, inciting an electric shock that raced through the metal, forcing him back with an agonized scream.

"As a man of learning, you should know about shock therapy, Dr. Martin. And as someone who has spent years and years around some very important artifacts in the Museum of Natural History, you do have the information I'm seeking. It's my job to part you from the information before you are parted from your earthly life."

"I don't have it. We've been through this before."

"Of course you have it. You've had it in your head for years and years. I want to know about the Summoning Stones of Egypt. I know they have power when used together and I want you to tell me what your dear, late friend, the esteemed Dr. Russell Harrison, knew about them."

"This is madness. Absolute madness. I don't know what you're talking about."

She shot another beam of electricity at the bars, even though the old man was already huddled on the floor. The satisfying pop and hiss of static arcing through the air took a slight edge off her increasing irritation with the conversation.

The scratching she heard in the walls got louder, then turned into a light scurrying as a large, emaciated rat crawled into the room. She watched the twitch of its nose as it scoured the floor, an idea taking root.

It was time to set an example, and she didn't need Deimos to do it.

"You know, Dr. Martin, I actually think I've been rather patient with you. I've given you endless hours to sit here and think about your situation. I can't imagine a high-ranking academic has an abundance of that."

At his blank stare, she added, "Time, you know. Such a precious resource, especially when the days you're given on Earth are numbered, unlike my own." She scooped the rat up, cradling it in her hands, her grip firm on the creature so it could do little more than sit there.

The man huddled in the corner, his eyes following the slow sweep of her fingernail as it ran over the animal's quivering back.

"Since you have proven to me that you don't appreciate the gift I've given you, I'm afraid it's time to set an example— to actually leave you with something to think about so that when I come back, you might have rethought your decision to tell me about the Summoning Stones."

Although he kept his gaze as blank as possible, she couldn't miss the frissons of fear that spiked off his person.

She allowed the animal to dangle as a shiver of power ran through her as she sensed the older man's fear.

Fear was such an aphrodisiac.

"You must be always running here and there. Working on the next paper. Leading the preparations for the next major exhibit, designed to knock the socks off your bene-factors. Such a tiring life and so like this little creature here. Always scurrying to and fro, never finding time to sit still."

She walked over to Martin's discarded food bowl, still full from the evening before. With a swift kick, she sent the dish flying toward the bars of the old man's cell, tossing food across the floor and over his huddled form.

"But if this rodent had a better life—a life only *I* could give it—what more could it accomplish? How much more could it be?"

Extending her hand, she placed a finger on the back of the rat, shooting great rays of life-affirming energy into its gaunt body.

One beat. Two beats. Three beats. She watched Martin's eyes as the creature grew in her hand, its proportions ex-panding until it was comparable to a medium-sized dog. With another flick of her wrist, a ridge of spikes grew out of its tail.

"Now, Dr. Martin, I believe it was you who mentioned madness mere moments ago." Setting the rodent in front of the bars, she watched as it scrambled forward. The animal squeezed its now-large body through the cell bars and shot toward the first piece of food it could find, giddy in its move-ments as it attacked the food. The animal scurried over and around the contents, eagerly gobbling up as much food as it could manage.

Enyo kept her voice low, the sound echoing off the walls around them as she maintained her gaze on the old doctor. Stubborn fool, he really had no idea whom he was dealing with. "Such simple creatures. Nourishment and shelter are all they really want. And, even as low on the food chain as it is, it can clearly appreciate the need for sustenance, unlike yourself."

As the animal scurried around the discarded food, a heavier sound reverberated off the walls. As the sound got louder, Dr. Martin huddled into the corner of the cell, doing his level best to shrink into the corner.

As the thundering sound got even louder, the hungry rat stopped to watch the door, wary at its potential loss of food. Enyo felt a wave of deep satisfaction wash over her as a Chimera burst into the room. Body and head of a lion, tail of a full-grown snake, with a second head of a large goat that extended from its back, the creature leaped through the door she'd left slightly ajar. The lion portion of its body shook its head and roared, eyes wild as it caught the ripe scents in the room.

Dr. Martin moaned as the animal scrambled around the room. "I don't believe it. It's not possible."

Enyo stepped aside as the animal rushed the bars. "Believe it, Dr. Martin. It's very possible."

With its paw, the Chimera brushed at the rat, cornering it until it had no choice but to leave the food and race outside the bars to escape the seeking claws. As soon as it cleared them, the snake wrapped around the large, oversized body of the rodent, squeezing the life from it. Flicking its spoils to its other two mouths, the goat and the lion ripped the animal apart as blood sprayed in a pattern across the cell.

Deimos and Phobos had clearly not been feeding their beloved pet.

Satisfied her little experiment was moving along nicely, Enyo sashayed across the room to the exit. "Enjoy your visitor, Dr. Martin."

As the door swung closed behind her, she heard the satisfying thump of the Chimera as it threw itself against the bars of the good doctor's prison. As she walked down the hall, the last thing she heard was the long, low moan of Dr. William Martin as his new friend paid him a visit.

Brody thought through his approach as the seconds ticked away between them in Kane's kitchen. He'd expected screams, a faint, possibly even a few punches thrown in a haze of panic and fear.

What he didn't expect was somber quiet and the waiting, expectant look in Ava's eyes.

Or her calm, even voice as she nodded at the three of them. "Go on. I'm listening."

More time ticked by. Explain, explain, explain.

How do you condense millennia of information into a brief, concise explanation?

And how do you explain to one extraordinary woman that she very possibly had an extraordinary set of paranormal gifts that could rule the world and everything in it?

Kane and Quinn left the room, the only sound their heavy footfalls as they passed through the kitchen's swinging doors.

"So is it true? What Quinn just said?" She sighed and ran a hand through her hair, the soft blond locks falling into a neat frame around her face.

"It's true. And, while there are a few more details, Quinn pretty much gave you the *Reader's Digest* version."

"So what does this have to do with me? You think I'm the target of this Enyo person?"

"I know you are. She's the only one who can send Destroyers. Those are the guys who work for her. The ones filled with the oily ooze."

His heart turned over at her scared-rabbit expression.

Gods, how did he explain this to her? It wasn't as if he walked around every day giving out his life story. Matter of fact, he actively worked to hide his life story from the real world.

As he fought to find the words, another thought took root. He could show her.

"Hold my hand. I think I know a way to make sense of this."

He extended his hand and watched as those long, slim fingers folded against his.

"Are you porting us again?"

"Yep. Hang on."

A rush of air pulled them out of the kitchen, London receding far behind them.

Brody's arm tightened around her as they landed in the center of a large, marble foyer. Her body responded to the feel of him, the large hand that held hers so tightly while his opposite arm wrapped around her waist.

Traitorous thing, her body.

Seeking some measure of equilibrium—and much-needed composure that flew out the window when he touched her—she looked around. "Where are we?"

"Back in Manhattan. At my home."

"What you want to show me is here?"

"It's a start. Plus, I figured if we ported here, you'd have to believe at least some of what I'm about to tell you."

"How do I know I'm really in Manhattan?"

He nodded toward the front door. "Open it."

Was this a test? A test to see if she would run? Or a test to see if she would stay?

And which did she want to do?

With tentative steps, she walked to the door and opened

it, only to be greeted by the loud cacophony of Manhattan traffic.

"You really flung us back home?"

"Yep."

The sheer, overwhelming truth of it stared her in the face. The sun wasn't yet up because it was still only about four thirty in the morning, but the city that never slept lived up to its name.

Okay. Check one box. They really were in Manhattan.

"I'd like to show you more, if you'd like to come with me."

Whether for good or against every bit of judgment she'd been given, Ava closed the door—and followed Brody as he began a path through his home.

They walked through the house, giving her the opportunity to see more of her surroundings. The house was positively palatial. Had they just passed a room that held an Olympic-sized pool?

In Manhattan?

As they walked through the house, they passed by an impossible number of rooms, and more artwork and sculpture than was found in most museums. "Brody, where *are* we? I mean, I know you said your home, but where in Manhattan are we?"

"The Upper West Side."

"But this place is huge. There aren't any homes like this on the Upper West Side. I've lived here my whole life. I'd know."

They came to a doorway and Brody reached for the doorknob. "I'll tell you about those men first. The ones who attacked you on your block and the one who followed us from the airport. Then I'll explain the house."

"You said before they're not men."

"Not technically." He flipped a switch and they started down a large staircase into the basement. "They were once, but not anymore."

A large crater opened in the pit of her stomach, images of standing on the man's neck filling her mind's eye. She'd managed to put it aside—forget about what had happened based on the assumption he wasn't human. "You mean I really did kill someone?"

"No, Ava. He's been well and truly dead a very long time."

"He didn't loo—" Her breath caught as the basement spread out before them.

Floor-to-ceiling bookshelves stood against one wall. In the center of the basement was a fountain—an honest-to-God running, working, *functioning* fountain—that looked like a depiction of Mount Olympus.

As they moved farther into the basement, past the fountain and toward the books, they came upon an alcove she hadn't been able to see from the stairs. The same rich tapestries she'd seen covering the walls upstairs covered the floors. The alcove held two large leather sectional sofas. One wall was taken up by an enormous, large-screen TV and another by floor-to-ceiling bookshelves, filled with scrolls in place of books. The final wall held an enormous tapestry, woven with all twelve signs of the zodiac, the gold thread that made the symbols in stark relief on a deep blue background.

"The tapestry over there—the symbology on it. I saw that upstairs, too. On pillows on the couch and several paintings in the hallway."

"Yes, it does. We have it throughout the house." He gestured to one of the large couches. "Let's sit down. I need to show you some things and I want you to be comfortable."

She sighed, still not sure how she was believing all this,

yet not sure she *couldn't* believe it. It was far too elaborate to be made up or to be a figment of her imagination. "Tell me about these Destroyers."

"They're dead men who have been reanimated to hurt and kill humans."

"That guy didn't look dead when he attacked me. And the two last night on the sidewalk didn't look dead, either."

"And that's their true deception. The average person can't tell the difference. Quinn has spent years trying to figure out exactly what they are, but he hasn't had any success yet. So, even though we don't know all the specifics, as best we can tell, the ooze that fills them is some sort of superconductor of electricity."

And if she followed through to a logical conclusion— no matter *how* illogical it sounded—the next natural leap was simple. "The head's the key to killing them."

"Exactly."

Maybe it was all that had happened in the last twenty-four hours or maybe it was the overarching abnormalcy that had ruled her personal life for so long, but his revelation about the hired killers wasn't nearly as startling as it should have been. "Why the head? You'd think it would be the heart."

"It's balance."

"Balance of what?"

"That's the only way I can be killed. Removal of my head will destroy my human form. Otherwise, I'm immortal, along with my fellow Warriors, like Quinn and Kane. The fact that the Destroyers can only be killed at the head is a sort of balance between them and us."

Brody took a deep breath. "What Quinn told you is true. I am an immortal Warrior of the great goddess of justice, Themis. I am a Warrior of the Zodiac."

Thoughts slammed into one another, all fighting to be heard first. Beyond any confusion she'd felt yet, this was like sensory overload, only on the mental plane.

Human form?

Immortal?

Warriors?

The same words Quinn had used.

"Zodiac? Really and truly? As in astrology? As in what's your sign and the Age of Aquarius and all that? Come on, Brody. You can't be serious."

"But I am. Themis used the balance of the heavens—the perfect proportions of the zodiac—to create us. I've taken up her battle for justice and balance here on Earth."

Back to the balance stuff.

Ava scoured her mind, remembering a school course on myth and society. The story of the Titans worked its way forward from the depths of her memories and with it, an image of Themis. Scales. Lady Justice. Mother of the three Fates.

And slowly the balance stuff started to make a bit more sense. The zodiac, on the other hand—what was going on around here and what the hell had she fallen into? A cult of some sort? People did it every day, worshipping things they *believed* had power, and astrology likely had more followers than any other pagan practice. Heck, just open a newspaper on any given day. The whole world paid attention to it, even if for most it was a haphazard sort of appreciation.

"So this Greek goddess?"

He nodded. "Yes. Our patroness, Themis?"

"Scales of justice and all that?"

"Among other things, yes. She is also the mother of a race of warriors. She selected me for her service and in the Fifth Age of Man—the age I was born in—I accepted."

Service? Acceptance? Ava's stomach flipped over. "Oh my God. This can't be real and the fact I'm even sitting here listening to you means I must be as insane as you are!"

"I'm not, Ava, and neither are you."

"There's no other explanation, because there is no way I can believe this. Any of this."

Brody's mouth was a grim line. "I'm telling you the truth."

"Your truth, maybe."

"I don't know how to make you understand this."

"You can't. Because it's completely nuts."

His blue eyes alighted on one of the framed paintings in the room, an ancient star chart depicting the world as the artist knew it then. "I know. Come with me."

She felt a moment of calm when he didn't reach for her, instead allowing her to follow on her own.

They left the basement and wound their way back through the house—back to the oversized staircase that seemed to be the center of this palace and up three flights of stairs. Finally, he led her to a door at the end of the third floor.

"Where are you taking me? And what is this place? You can't actually expect me to believe we're in New York?"

"We are and we're not."

"What?"

"You are in New York. In a building that, to the common observer, is a brownstone on the Upper West Side. If I gave you my address, you'd come in my front door. If you walked out my front door, you'd be on a Manhattan street."

Reality warred with his description. "But this place is huge!"

"You'll see. As Warriors, we exist in both the human world and the world of Mount Olympus."

This just couldn't be. It just . . . couldn't.

"I know it's hard to process. Leave it for now and come with me. I have something I want to show you."

Brody opened the door at the end of the third-floor hall and she followed him up a small spiral staircase. His large body moved with immeasurable grace as he took the twists and turns that led to the roof.

"Where are we now?"

A small smile ghosted his lips. "Our original command center."

Cold November air greeted her as the lights of Manhattan spread out before them. Above them, the sky looked ready to burst, it was so full of stars.

Unable to tear her gaze away, she mumbled to Brody as she looked to the skies. "I've never seen New York like this. Usually the city lights drown out the sky."

"Up here, it's a little different."

She tore her gaze away, shifting to look at him—into those magnetic blue eyes that looked so sincere, even though she wanted to rage and call him a liar and a fraud.

But how could she?

She saw this; she was looking at it with her own two eyes. Belief without faith, but it was something.

"What did you mean by 'original command center'?"

"I can communicate with my Warrior brothers from here."

And then there were no questions as he showed her.

With deliberate movements, he removed his long-sleeved black T-shirt. His breath gave off little puffs of air, but he seemed immune to the cold. He had his back to her and his eyes facing skyward, so she could see a tattoo—this one of a lion—where it sat high on his right shoulder blade.

Unable to tear her gaze away, she drank in the perfection of his body. Broad shoulders gleamed in the moonlight as the tight play of muscles along his back responded to his every movement. His torso grew narrow as it descended to his stomach and formed into lean hips. A small network of scars crisscrossed his lower back.

Where had they come from? The scars were faded white with age, faint on his skin, but visible nonetheless.

He shifted slightly and extended his arm. An intricately designed tattoo decorated his exposed left arm. The ink had interlocking circles with a zodiac symbol she couldn't identify clearly visible in the center of the pattern.

Brody tossed her a glance over his shoulder, a broad smile on his lips. "Ready?"

"For what?"

He pressed his fingers to the tattoo and light shot toward the stars from the symbol. The night sky made a dome around them like the ceiling of a planetarium. Ava couldn't hear any noise except for the distant sounds of Manhattan traffic, but she could see various parts of the sky light up, blinking on and off.

"Are you talking to them?"

"Yep."

"But how?"

"It's a combination of light from the tattoo, telepathy and a bit of old-world Morse code thrown in."

"Prehistoric text messages?"

He leveled her with another grin and Ava responded without thinking. Something carefree and wild landed in her chest as her knees quivered under the impact of that *GQ* smile. "I'm not quite that old."

That response only added more questions. "How old are you, then?"

"I was born roughly ten thousand years ago."

"Oh."

More sections of the dome lit up as he continued to shift his arm, the light dancing across the sky as it projected from his forearm.

Ava moved closer, unable to contain her wonder at what he was doing. "Does it hurt?"

"Not at all."

Yet another question spilled from her lips, her natural curiosity getting the better of her. "So, if you do this all telepathically, can you read minds?"

"No." Brody broke the link, reaching for his T-shirt and pulling it back over his head. "The telepathy is tied to our link to one another through the night sky. Nothing more. One of my brothers is telepathic, but as the rest of us aren't, outside of this realm we can't communicate that way."

She watched in fascination as the T-shirt slid over his washboard stomach. *Check, Ava Marie. You were right on that guess. Those abs are to die for.*

"Although it can be useful, it really is a primitive way to communicate. It's why I called it our original command center. Nowadays, we do everything on highly encrypted computers. Warriors move within the normal dimensions of time, so modern technology has made our communication much easier. And instantaneous."

"Same as for humans."

That wry grin was back. "That would be because we *are* humans." He moved up close to her and took her hand in his, laying it against his chest. Despite his recent bare-chested stint in the cold, all she felt was delicious warmth through the fabric of his shirt. "Feel me, Ava. I'm as human as you."

His heart beat firm and strong under her palm. "With some exceptions."

"I'm human."

Ava searched the depths of that gorgeous, sky blue gaze. She *wanted* to believe him—wanted to believe *in* him.

But . . .

Look, Ava Marie. With your own two eyes. Look at this man. Look at his world.

Feel it.

Believe it.

Shaking it off, she stepped back to put some distance between them while the pesky scientist in her continued to pepper him with questions. "So what happens to those who are in different parts of the globe in daylight?"

"They can respond later."

"Did you have any, um, messages when you logged on just now?"

Brody reached down to tuck his T-shirt into his jeans. "No. As I said, we do pretty much everything on computer right now. Besides, I knew there wouldn't be anything. My tattoo pulses when there's something to go find."

"Like cosmic voice mail."

His bark of laughter echoed around in the cold observatory. "I guess you could call it that."

"So how many of you are there?"

"When Themis first created us, we were twelve bands of thirteen, tasked to roam the earth as humanity's protectors."

"Were?"

"We've lost a few Warriors. Some to death. More to Enyo."

"Brody, I want to believe you—honest, I do. I'm looking at you and I'm feeling"—she broke off, glancing around the observatory—"this. But Enyo? Themis? They're just myths."

"Myths were born of something."

"Yes. Idle imaginations trying to make sense of a world

they didn't understand. Hesiod and Homer. They didn't have the tools to understand their world the way we do, so they made up the myths."

"No, Ava." Brody shook his head. "They were whispered to them so the truth would be written somewhere."

"But it defies everything I know as a scientist."

He took her hand as he led them back toward the door. "But you feel it?"

She sighed. Every rational thought she possessed screamed that this couldn't be, but heaven help her, she did believe him. She understood there were things happening that went beyond normal human understanding. "I do."

He opened the door for her and she walked through, descending back down the narrow, spiral staircase.

She felt his heavy footfalls on the stairs behind her, his tone open and giving as he said, "Is there anything else?"

As she took the last twist and stepped off the bottom step, Ava's gaze alighted on yet another tapestry hanging in the hallway. "Actually, yes. What *are* you? You know. What's your sign, baby?"

"I am Leo Warrior."

The last piece of the puzzle fell into place: the bossy personality that acted decisively and wanted to do things his own way; the mane of hair, just shy of vain on a man; the pompous, know-it-all, I-can-handle-anything attitude.

Suddenly, she knew exactly why she'd seen a lion roaming the streets of London.

He was standing right in front of her.

Chapter Eleven

Brody loved watching her. The expressions on her face. The movements of her body as new thoughts struck her. The rapid questions as she worked to process new information.

Innate beauty. Bone-deep intelligence. Endless curiosity.

She was a wonder.

He took her hand and led her down the hall. They needed to get back to London and he wanted to eat again before expending all the energy required to port. They had no idea what awaited them at the British Museum and he didn't want anything to threaten his strength. "You seem a little calmer. Is this starting to make sense?"

She quirked an eyebrow at the calmer comment, but her voice stayed level. "So you're a lion?"

"No. I'm a man. An immortal one, but a man all the same."

"But the lion. The one I saw. It's a part of you. It fits you, you know. I'd already thought your long blond hair seemed like a mane and there is a fierceness to your features that reminds me of a predator."

"I'm not a lion."

"But you have one. As a pet?"

"Not exactly."

"You might as well bring it on. You can't shock me any more than you already have."

He doubted that but kept the observation to himself. She'd started to relax and he was loath to do anything to remind her that she'd wanted to leave fifteen minutes before. But she had asked. And seeing as how he'd scared the shit out of her with his tattoo during the fight under the bridge, he figured she had a right to know.

Reaching down, he grabbed fistfuls of his T-shirt again and pulled it back over his head. Turning, he presented his back to her, his lion tattoo high on his upper-right shoulder blade.

A wave of need rushed him as Ava's small fingers brushed the top of his shoulder blades as she pushed his hair aside to get a better look.

Soft, tentative fingers stroked over the tattoo, and he could feel the rumbling purr in the lion's chest at her touch.

"What is it?"

Her fingers continued tracing the lion's shape, the movements sending shock waves through his body. His stomach muscles tightened at the sensual torture of her touch and his erection—the semihard state he'd spent the last four days in around her—climbed to full strength. "It's a tattoo."

"But it's not."

"No, really. That's all it is. It's part of my aura. It can't be separated, but it can come to my aid and protection."

The lion shook his head and flicked its mane under her stroking touch, and Brody felt an answering roar rise up in his own chest.

"It's moving." The wonder in her voice shot another round

of sparks through his system. Although rarely in doubt, he had debated whether or not to show her his tattoo yet. Inked images that moved didn't exactly incite waves of calm in people, but her reaction was much more controlled than he ever could have expected.

It was . . . sweet.

"It likes you."

"It's almost like in the Harry Potter movies. Where their photos move. I'm looking at this and it shouldn't be moving, but it is."

He closed his eyes, welcoming her touch—taking it in and warming the places that had been closed off for so long.

Separate, she'd called them.

And now, as her fingers brushed the lion's mane, not separate. Connection. They were connected.

Ava watched as Brody doused his third stack of pancakes in syrup. The man had the eating habits of a gangly, growing teenager. Thankfully, his manners were those of an adult. His napkin was firmly in his lap and his lips stayed closed as he ate.

"Hungry?"

"I have to keep my strength up."

"For what? You just had Chinese food about an hour ago. At least I think it was an hour ago."

He glanced at his watch. "Yep. We haven't been here that long. And I need my energy for porting."

"That depletes energy?"

He nodded, then swallowed his latest bite before responding. "A hell of a lot, as a matter of fact."

"Will you die if you run out of energy?"

"No, not at all. But the weaker I get, the more vulnerable

I am to attack. My brothers and I stay on our game. That means taking care of the body."

Made sense. Food fueled the body. "Anything else besides lack of food?"

"Sleep and sex."

Sex? As in a lot or none at all? "I get the sleep part. But sex? Are you allowed to have it?"

A wicked grin answered *that* question and Ava could feel hot waves of heat creep up her neck to flush her cheeks. "I'll take that as a yes."

"Orgasm returns us to one hundred percent."

"Even without food? Or sleep?"

"Yep. It's like an automatic get-out-of-jail-free card."

"Well, there goes all your hard work in getting me to buy into the idea you're human."

A frown crossed his mouth as he swallowed his last bite. "Why's that?"

"Most men need food and sleep after sex. You are clearly *not* a human male."

Great waves of laughter greeted her across the table and Ava couldn't stop the answering laugh in return. It felt good to laugh—a moment of normal, in the midst of all they were dealing with.

Now . . . if she could only get the idea of him as a human equivalent to the Energizer Bunny out of her head, maybe she could stem the arousal threading through her body in great, warm waves of need.

An orgasm to regain strength. Who knew?

"Are you a Gemini?"

"What?" The change in topic caught her off guard. The fact he guessed correctly on the first try was even more surprising. "How'd you know?"

"You're incredibly curious. Even when you're not asking questions, I can see them etched across your face."

Ava wasn't sure why that embarrassed her, but a light flush crept up her cheeks as one of her grandmother's ever-vigilant philosophies came to mind. *Girls who talk like walking encyclopedias need to remember reference books don't get taken out.* "Occupational hazard, I guess."

"It's adorable."

"Hardly."

At that he snorted. "Darlin', I've got far too much pride to make shit up. If I say it, I mean it."

"So why does it matter if I'm a Gemini?"

"It doesn't matter as in good or bad. It's a point of definition. Of who you are. Of the forces that shaped you."

"Modern science disproved astrology quite a few centuries ago. And genetics has a heck of a lot more to do with who we are than anything else. Again, science's contribution to our understanding of ourselves."

"Just because science has proven things about us doesn't mean there aren't grains of truth in the things we can feel. Do you think I'm a fake?"

It was getting harder and harder to think of him as anything but one hundred percent real. "No."

"Ah, but I still see the skepticism. And here I thought you wanted answers to your questions."

"I do."

"Then why do you find it so hard to believe what I'm telling you? My Warrior brothers and I, we really do have the traits of our signs."

Where had her brain gone? She was a learned scholar. A PhD, for cripes' sake! Why was she listening to this? Encouraging it?

Ah hell, why start questioning your sanity now, Ava Marie? Go along for the ride. You know you want to.

"Okay, fine. Look, even if I can buy into the rest of it— the whole Themis-made-you-Warriors thing—you can't possibly believe the idea that you think the way you do and act the way you do just because of your sign."

"I don't just believe it. I know it. It's the very definition of who I am."

"Right. You are Leo; therefore it dictates every action you have?"

The corner of his eyes crinkled up and he ran his fingers over his chin like a detective. "What was your first thought when you looked at me?"

Oh my God, my panties have just exploded into flames. "He's cute and I think he may be trying to kill me."

The crinkles at his eyes spread farther as his lips turned up in a smile. "I mean when you met me at the museum."

"Why has this cute jerk followed me to work?"

"Nope. Wrong answer, Dr. Harrison." He leaned forward, his blue eyes full of good-natured merriment. "Try again."

She wasn't sure what did it. The light teasing between them that felt more natural than breathing or the sheer pleasure of being the sole focus of his attention. But something— maybe a combination of both—had her sharing the truth. "I'd like to climb on top of him and take him for a ride."

"Exactly."

Her jaw dropped at his audacity—and at her own. "What do you mean, 'exactly'?"

"Leos are known for their sensuality."

She snorted. "Vanity in there, too?"

A satisfied smile spread across his face. "Absolutely."

"I guess we can add stubborn and immovable in one's beliefs."

"Yep."

"Hedonistic?"

"Right again."

"So, I've acknowledged I believe you about Themis and the Warriors and flinging yourself through the time-space continuum. But you still seriously expect me to believe 'your sign made you do it' is a viable reason."

He held up his hands. "I rest my case, Counselor."

As her silent agreement hung between them across the table, his smile grew even broader and his tone took on a distinctly scholarly note. "Which brings us right back to where we started this conversation. As with most everything in life, your belief or disbelief in something doesn't make it any less true."

The sensual haze zapped, she fought for the mental equilibrium to parry back. "Nor does your belief in it make it fact."

"Touché." He waited a beat, his gaze like a caress over her cheeks as the word hung between them. "But I'm still right."

She couldn't help it. A small burst of laughter gripped her and wouldn't let go. "You really are full of yourself."

"Quinn says so all the time. And Kane. And Pierce. And"—he stopped his list to stare at the ceiling, then drew his gaze back to her—"well, pretty much everybody."

"I get it now."

"Get what?"

"Your role among the other Warriors. You're the naughty little boy."

Before he could press her further, her cell phone rang. Following a quick glance down at the readout, she couldn't bite back the sigh rising in her throat. "Hello, Grandmother.

"Yes, I'm fine."

Brody wiggled his eyebrows at her and crossed his eyes, and she couldn't stop the small giggle from escaping on an exhaled breath.

"No, Grandmother. I am listening to you. I'm just, um, diverted by the sights—of London."

Her grandmother blathered on for a few more seconds about the high tea at some old hotel and then she said her good-byes.

Ava breathed an inward sigh of relief when the call ended. "That was close."

"Close for what? A coma?"

"No, I almost blurted out I was back in New York. I'd have an easy time explaining that one."

"That's the second time in my presence you've had to cater to her. Any chance you could just let it roll to voice mail? You *are* supposed to be out of the country."

Ava pressed down on her rising embarrassment and pulled her sweater tighter across her chest. "You don't say no to Grandmother."

His voice was soft, but the message was clear. "What about saying yes to Ava?"

Where did he get off? "I'm not some little martyr who needs a pat on the back."

"No?"

"What, Brody? Is psychotherapist part of your job description? Outgoing Leo, available for individual or group appointments?"

"No, I'm more than willing to dispense the advice for free."

"Well then, save it for someone else. We have to get

back to London." She pushed back her chair, a clear signal the conversation was over and it was time to leave.

She'd already crossed the oversized formal dining room but didn't feel his familiar presence behind her. Turning, she saw Brody still standing at the table, slowly pushing in his seat.

"Life's short, you know."

Despite her rising embarrassment at how close he'd come to hitting a wound, she couldn't stop the wry smile. Didn't even try. "Strange observation, coming from you."

"Sometimes it's easy to be the observer. You see what the other person is too close to see for themselves. You see what they're missing."

Her shoulders drooped on a small sigh. "Sometimes you just accept the way things are. Live with them."

And then he was around the table, stalking toward her in all his leonine fierceness. He took one hand as the other settled at her waist, his forehead pressed against hers as he'd done back in Kane's flat.

"You don't have to accept it. Live with it. There's so much more to you, Ava. All you need to do is reach out and take it."

What could he possibly know about her? What could he possibly understand? He was an immortal Warrior, empowered by a Greek god and tasked to save the world.

Freaking *save the world*. How's that for empowering?

And then there was her. Little Ava Marie Harrison. Poor little fat girl. Then poor little orphaned girl. And now poor little lonely spinster head case.

Oh man, this was a bad conversation. She *hated* playing the martyr. Hated feeling like that. Hated thinking of herself that way. If she wanted a different life, she needed to do something about it.

Up until now, she'd been content with safe.

Up until now, she'd never had a reason why.

And now she did.

The last few days had shown her that safe was an illusion, anyway. Even if you didn't have immortal beings jumping in and out of your life, you still couldn't control what happened to you.

Couldn't live your life in a safe little bubble.

And in that moment, the clarity she'd sought came crashing down in waves around her.

Empower yourself, Ava.

Reach for what you want.

She didn't need to look far. What she wanted was right in front of her.

"Show me," Ava whispered. "Show me how to take it."

That was all he needed to hear. Instantaneously, he ported them to his bedroom, the soft light of dusk just breaking through the curtains.

Brody watched the play of expressions on her face, muted in the dim light of the room. Oh gods, she really was beautiful. Heartbreakingly so.

And then there wasn't any time to think—there was only time to feel as her arms came around him and her body pressed to his.

The internal protests—those that told him she was fragile and needed protecting—were quickly drowned out by the acknowledgment that she needed him as much as he needed her.

He hadn't *needed* someone in so long, it took his breath away. Wanted, yes. Needed?

Never.

And because it was Ava who offered him that precious

gift, he'd give her one in return—something that belonged only to her.

Walking her backward through the dim room, he took her on an unerring path toward the bed. The moment the backs of her legs hit the side of the mattress, he took them in an easy slide down onto the bed and covered her body with his.

He groaned against her neck as his hands fisted in the heavy cable-knit that covered her. "This sweater. Why does it drive me so crazy?"

"What?"

"Bat-shit, insane-with-need crazy. It's drab and ugly and a bag lady wouldn't be caught wearing it."

She lifted herself onto her elbows. "Thanks for the vote of confidence, Brody."

Her frown and narrowed eyes were so amusing—so absolutely adorable—he couldn't stop the great, gusty laugh that welled up from his chest. "Aren't you listening to me? You're gorgeous. And this damn thing"—he pushed the sweater off her shoulders—"drives me wild." He whispered the last word in her ear, delighted when a wave of shivers ran the length of her torso.

With long, smooth strokes, he glided his hand down her body, reaching for the waistband of her slacks. In seconds, he had them unbuttoned and unzipped and sliding down over her hips. He then made quick work of her blouse, lifting it over her head. Nothing but a silky bra and panties remained to cover her gorgeous curves.

"You are so beautiful."

His mouth enveloped hers again, his tongue mingling with hers in a warm, wet tangle of need. He could feel her smile under his mouth and laughed when she whispered against him. "Now this is what I'm talking about. Flattery will get you everywhere, Brody."

He loved the sound of his name on her lips.

He loved the small moans coming from the back of her throat as he ran his hands over her.

He shifted himself slightly, pulling up on his forearms as he held his weight above her.

With one finger he traced lazy circles over her abdomen, narrowing the loops smaller and smaller until he traced the outline of her belly button. "Now this is what I'm talking about. These sexy little panties are way better than that sweater." He flicked a finger at the top of the silk, using that single finger to brush against her mons. "But am I correct in assuming these have been underneath that ugly gray wool all along?"

Her breath came in heavy pants as he continued to move his finger in small, sweeping movements. "I think I'll leave you guessing on that one."

"Good thing I'm a man with much imagination."

Her voice was husky, like the finest whiskey, when she wrapped her arms around his shoulders and lifted herself up for a kiss. "I really do like that sweater."

"Knowing these are underneath," he said, wiggling his fingers and managing to shift the panties halfway down her hips, "I'll find a way to like it, too."

And then he got serious about the panties, shifting so he could pull them all the way down her body, tossing them to the side of the bed. She reached for him, lifting his T-shirt off so there was nothing between them.

Refocusing his attentions, he pressed her back against the pillows and leaned toward her breasts. She gasped as he licked a warm, wet circle around her nipple, over the silky material of her bra. Her responsiveness to his touch pushed his body into overdrive, his undertended cock harder than it'd ever been before. And for the very first time in his very long life, he didn't care.

This wasn't about him.

This was about Ava.

He wanted this to be good for her. Wanted to make her come. Wanted her to take something purely for herself.

He felt her shift under him and knew she meant to return the pleasure as her hands drifted toward the front of his pants. Just as her fingers reached the top of his zipper, he captured both wrists with a hand and lifted them over her head. "Just enjoy," he whispered against her, then shifted his focus to lave his tongue over her other nipple. With a growl in the back of his throat, his warm mouth enveloped her, driving her farther over the edge of reason.

Shifting their bodies, he reached behind her to unclasp her bra, freeing her perfect breasts to his touch, his taste, his view.

Perfection.

He returned his attention to her breast, traced his tongue in wet circles around her hard nipple, drawing on her with deep suction. Her answering moan was all he needed. Her responsiveness was such a turn-on, he wondered how he'd ever looked at another woman before in desire.

In need.

All he needed was this woman.

His needs now nearly as fevered as her own, he probed at the opening of her thighs, pressing a finger at her slick channel and satisfied to realize how ready she was for him.

As he pressed his finger deeper into her cleft, he felt her

open for him, then felt the play of her inner muscles as her body hovered just at the precipice. . . .

Her hair fanned around her on the pillow, a goddess taking her pleasure. "Brody. Oh, Brody."

"My sweet, glorious, gorgeous Ava. So beautiful. So ripe. And so incredibly wet for me."

A soft moan of pleasure ripped from the back of her throat as he played her body. Sweet, torturous moans came from her as his finger entered her, then retracted. He pressed harder, and he knew she was close . . . so very, very close to the edge.

"Come on, baby," he whispered against her ear. "I want to see you come in my arms. Come for me."

He increased the pressure, adding another finger to his movements, then a third.

Her breaths labored, he willed her to let go. To fly in his arms.

And then she was flying, clenching around him and screaming his name. He pressed his lips to hers and let her ride the wave. He watched every glorious moment of her release.

And wondered how he was ever going to get through the rest of his life without her.

Themis watched as her dear, beloved Leo pulled his woman close into the curve of his arm, the sun covering them in a rosy, early-morning glow. Tears made twin tracks down her own face as she watched this sweet, generous woman emotionally awaken and come alive to all life could offer her.

She'd watched Ava over the years. Had known the secret strength wrapped up in that delicate package. Had known—when the time was right—that Ava's inner strength would come to the surface.

Themis also knew she'd be lying to herself if she didn't

admit just how much fun she was having, watching Brody process it all.

They really were a matched pair, her Leo Warrior and the woman who would be the Key. But only time would tell if they had a future together.

Or if forces beyond their control would tear them apart.

Chapter Twelve

"Are you sure you don't mind doing this?"

"For the fourth time, Ava, I really don't mind."

"Then I'm ready." She smoothed her hair behind her ear. "But how do you know no one will see us on the other end?"

"Ava, I've done this before. You've told me where we're going. We'll be fine."

She shrugged and figured he knew way more about porting than she ever would. But still. What if they landed on someone?

Brody settled his hand on her lower back and kissed her temple. "The Marble Cemetery, Ava. I know where it is. I'll land us behind a vault."

"Okay. Let's go."

That whistling sensation, then the rush of air, then a hard landing. Brody kept her upright, but it didn't stop the rush of gravity or the sting that ran up her calves as her feet hit the ground.

True to his word, Brody positioned them so they landed behind a large vault. Luckily, there were only about two rows between them and the Harrison family plot.

Orgasms to cemetery plots. You're quite a gal, Ava Marie.

"You really don't mind?"

Brody leaned in and pressed a hard kiss to her lips. "If you ask me one more time, I'm calling your grandmother on you."

Her jaw snapped closed as she held up a hand. "Say no more."

Brody took her hand and their fingers entwined, the move as natural as breathing.

Where had this come from? So sudden and so . . . easy. Comfortable.

"I didn't get a chance to come here yesterday afternoon and I like to make sure I see my dad before I go out of town."

"Lead the way."

They walked the two rows toward the Harrison vault, the family name visible at the top of the large, ornate slab of granite. Generations of Harrisons were buried here, their rich corpses some of the few that lay beneath Manhattan soil.

"Where did your family get all their money, anyway?"

"Railroads. My great-great-grandfather made the family fortune, which my great-grandfather managed to double and which my grandfather managed to squander significantly before he died."

A fall wind whipped Brody's blond hair around his face, and Ava was reminded more than ever of a lion's mane. "But I thought your family was wealthy?"

Drawing her attention from the remembered silky feel of those locks, she focused on his question. "Oh, there's still plenty of money. When I say squander, I mean from a high of about a billion down to roughly one hundred million."

"Oh."

"Yeah. Rough life, I know." One of her ever-present questions where Brody was concerned sprang up. "Does money even matter to you?"

"Sure. We need it to function in modern-day society. One of my brothers, Rafe, is our financial whiz. He takes care of us. Makes sure we have what we need financially to accomplish our tasks."

They stopped in front of the Harrison crypt, and Ava could see the writing that indicated the timeline of her father's life.

The comfortable banter vanished as the sobering reality of her visit hit her, as it always did.

She stood before the grave of her father.

A lone tear worked its way down her cheek, the whip of wind cooling it on its journey toward the ground.

"So why'd your father become an archaeologist? It's not exactly the family business, after all."

On a deep breath, she inhaled fresh air past the constriction in her throat. "He always said that for him it was a calling."

Brody's hand tightened on hers, drawing her attention from the lettering etched in granite.

"Ava. I don't believe I didn't tell you this. In all that happened, in all my explanations, I forgot to tell you this."

"Forgot to tell me what?"

"The prophecy. Has anyone told you what it says? The one that was discovered a few months ago?"

"They haven't finished the translation yet. We were hoping to have it complete by the opening of the exhibit but—"

"I've already translated it."

Her eyes grew wide at that news. "You know how to read the hieroglyphics?"

"I read them the day the prophecy was uncovered."

Would she ever get used to this? This odd mix of competence and easy grace? He translated ancient Egyptian hieroglyphics. He ported from place to place at will. He spent his days saving the world.

He gave mind-blowing orgasms, her conscience added.

"What did it say?"

"It talks about the power of the stones. How they work. How they can be harnessed."

"Brody. This is amazing." Her gaze darted toward the dates of her father's life and death, then shifted back to him. "My father's work can finally be explained."

"So can his death."

The flat tone of his words squelched her excitement. "But what does this have to do with the prophecy?"

"According to the writings of Thutmose the Third's high priest, the stones carry great power for the chosen few who can harness them. One in every age, is the core message of the prophecy."

"And you think my father was chosen somehow?"

Her words hung heavy in the air, as if their weight could actually be seen.

"Yes, he was. And someone clearly wanted to stop him before he fully understood that power."

"But who? Enyo?"

Small frown lines worked their way across his forehead. "We're still working on that. Presumably, Enyo didn't know about the stones' power when your father was still alive. None of us did. So it's likely a different threat."

"But she knows about it now. Knows about me."

"Yes."

"But what does it mean? To be a Chosen One?"

"It's why you see visions when you see the stones."

The lovely equilibrium that had infused her limbs since

letting herself go in Brody's arms vanished, replaced by the harsh reality that was her life.

That was always her life.

"Chosen One? Were you planning on telling me? Planning on letting me in on yet another little secret?"

"It wasn't a secret, Ava. And I wasn't trying to keep it from you. Hell, I just pieced it together late yesterday myself."

"This is why those Destroyers are after me? Because Enyo knows who I am?"

"Yes."

"So I'll never be free of it? Because something like this isn't about putting a few stones together or getting a museum exhibit off the ground. This is about my life."

"I'll take care of you, Ava. We all will. We'll find a way to keep you safe."

She heard the words and wanted to believe them. She wanted to believe the safety she felt in Brody's arms could exist in the real world and could be a real, *present* part of her life.

With a strangled cry, she moved away from him, needing some distance to think. She crossed one row of graves, then a second, when the sudden sound of gunshots rang out.

With a scream, Ava dropped to the ground, then turned immediately to find Brody.

Her large, powerful Leo lay on the ground in front of her family's crypt, blood pouring from his shoulder.

Chapter Thirteen

Brody reached for his shoulder, trying to hold the wound closed to speed up the healing process. As another bullet slammed into the crypt, barely missing his head, he realized he had bigger things to worry about.

Someone wanted him dead.

He had to get to Ava and get them out of here.

Heavy footfalls and the rustling of winter coats echoed off the walls of granite in erratic patterns as their attackers stalked closer.

"Ava! We need to get together." Brody belly-crawled toward her, his progress slowed as another bullet ricocheted off the crypt next to the Harrisons'.

Her screams lit up the cold morning air, adding to the echoes of battle.

Who were these people? He hadn't felt any wisps of stray electricity. No, this had a very real, very human feel to it, with modern-day weaponry and modern-day thugs.

How had they found them? And how did they know to keep them apart, eliminating his and Ava's chances to port together?

And how did they know to go for his head?

Brody reached for his Xiphos, grateful he'd remembered to put it on before they'd left the house. The friendly skies might abhor personal weaponry, but he'd flown for the first and last time. From now on, Air Talbot was his only mode of international travel.

All the carry-ons he wanted and no lines in customs.

Ava motioned at him, her gestures indicating the closest man was nearly in range. Every instinct he possessed urged him to keep moving toward her, but he held himself still and waited.

Wait . . .

Her gaze focused on the attacker, she kept a hand up as though waiting to launch cars off a finish line.

Wait . . .

Taut lines of tension rode her beautiful face as her hand stayed still.

Now!

Ava's hand dropped as Brody saw a large thug turn the corner. The heavy steel of the Xiphos whistled through the air as it flipped end over end in the early-morning cold.

The force of the blade threw their lead attacker to the ground, where he landed on his back about five feet from where Ava lay. Brody leaped across the remaining space, covering Ava's body and ignoring the potential threat from the other two guys moving through the clearing.

He reached for the hilt of his weapon, pulling it from a very-human chest that hadn't shrunk at all. The moment he had the Xiphos free of their attacker, Brody sent them into the ether, headed for London.

"Where have you—" Kane stopped midsentence as Brody held Ava close to his chest, absorbing their fall into the loft.

"Shit!" Quinn dropped his BlackBerry and in less time than it took her to blink, Ava felt his gentle hands lifting her off Brody and cradling her in his arms as he moved her to the couch.

"I'm fine. Fine. It's Brody. He's the one who's shot."

Quinn loomed over her, his large frame blocking out all light as well as her view of Brody. As she struggled to sit up, he kept his hands on her shoulders, holding her down.

"Shhh. Hold still. Just hold still for a minute."

"I have to get to him."

"I know. Shhh. Let Kane look at him."

Ava calmed down under the continued restraint of Quinn's hands. Despite his overwhelming size, his hold was gentle and his voice soothing as she watched Kane minister to Brody's wounds.

"What the hell did you do, Talbot?"

"We were ambushed," Brody grunted.

"By who? Where?"

"In a cemetery. And I'm not sure who it was. At least one of them was human."

Quinn's fingers flexed as his grip tightened. She reached for him. "I promise. I'll stay put."

The big man glanced down at his hands, an embarrassed flush creeping up his neck. "Sorry." Before she could say anything, he was up and pacing around the apartment. "What the fuck were you doing at a cemetery?"

"I wanted to go see my father."

Quinn's retort was fast and unapologetic. "Hell of a time for that, Ava."

She stood, cold fury and raw fear driving her to act. "It was a cemetery at seven o'clock in the morning. In a city where neither of us is supposed to be."

"So how the hell did someone know to find you?"

Air knocked out of her, she sat back down on the couch. "I don't know."

Brody waited until Quinn had ported to New York to try and figure out who was responsible for their attack. Ava had already gone up to shower, the distant hum of running water assuring him they wouldn't be overheard.

Damn it, but his shoulder still hurt like a bitch and he was shoveling in another carton of their earlier Chinese feast in the hope of speeding up the healing. Even the softness of the leather cushion behind his back wasn't doing much to ease the discomfort. He turned to Kane. "I need to know what happened to you this morning. Why'd you miss the meet?"

"You think it's relevant?"

"Seems like a hell of a coincidence that you're prevented from joining us, and Ava and I are ambushed in a place no one expected us to be."

"Although I'm usually more than willing to agree with your theory that there are no coincidences, I think this one may be the exception."

Brody saw the tired, bloodshot eyes of his friend and asked his question again. "So why'd you miss the meet?"

"I was played. Royally."

"How'd it happen?"

Kane's bloodshot eyes told part of the tale, but it was the frustrated swipe of his fingers through his four-hundred-dollar haircut that clued Brody in.

"I swore she was legit. I knew she was probably undercover and I figured her name was bogus, but she's MI6. No way I expected her to burn me like that."

"Do you think they're trying to get rid of you?"

Kane leaned his head back against one of the couch cushions. "MI6?"

"Yeah."

"How the hell should I know? I've gone over it in my mind since I finally regained the ability to put a coherent thought together. Damn, but she nailed me good. It's insulting."

"Any jobs gone bad?"

"Nope. Every one's gone flawlessly. Got in, got out and got the job done."

"Maybe you're too good. Ever think maybe they've started to wonder why?"

Kane dropped his head in his hands as he stared down at the floor. "I haven't fucked up like this in a long time. It chaps the ass, ya know."

Did he know? The timing of Kane's question was uncanny, coming on the heels of the shoot-out he'd just been in with Ava. Every moment was burned in his brain, tattooed in each neurofiber in indelible ink.

His very identity was wrapped up in his ability to protect people. And here was the one woman he wanted to see safe above all others and he'd nearly gotten her killed. Almost left her vulnerable to gods knew what.

Talk about an ass chapping.

Unbidden, a question popped to mind. "Do you ever think about before?"

"Before what?"

"Before Themis. Before we became her Warriors. Just . . . before."

"Not often."

Where had this come from? Maybe it was all Ava's questions from earlier. Or maybe it was just a sense that they kept going around in circles without ever really getting anywhere. One battle ended and another began. "No, me either."

"On the rare occasion I do think about it, I'm grateful she saved me from that hellish life."

"She saved all of us. Different reasons, I'm sure, but the end result's the same." He grew quiet, glancing around Kane's ultramodern apartment as his thoughts took root.

"Ever wonder why?"

Brody shifted his gaze from the plate of half-eaten food, back to the Scorpio. "Why we weren't each left to die in our own miserable little lives?"

"Yeah."

"Maybe she has a sense of humor."

Kane's bloodshot eyes bored into his. "You don't really believe that, do you?"

"No. No, I don't." Brody stood and headed for the second floor. The ultramodern loft, decked out in chrome, exposed walls and enough concrete to lay a parking lot, always left him slightly ill at ease. There was a coldness here he'd always associated with Kane, as if the Scorpio's living space had absorbed his personality and then reflected it back at him.

Cold. Unyielding. Deadly.

Kane had always been their loner, but in the last decade he'd spent with MI6 he'd changed—grown darker, more desperate, somehow, as though he crawled along the edge of a precipice and wasn't sure he wanted to keep himself from falling.

Are the rest of us that far behind him?

"Don't move too fast and open that wound."

"There's not enough time to wait for it to fully heal. We have to get ready for the meet at the museum. I'm borrowing some clothes."

Kane's voice reverberated off the acres of chrome and concrete. "You're not touching my shit."

"I don't want your fucking Armani. I need a pair of jeans and a T-shirt. Preferably something that didn't fall off a designer rack."

"Port your ass to Rafe's and raid his wardrobe. The Cancer has no style and more T-shirts than he knows what to do with."

"I'm here. I'm taking clothes. Either you pick 'em or I'll choose them myself. Get over it."

Brody rifled through a rack of clothes, the fine silks and designer labels barely registering as he hunted up something that looked designed for comfort. Projecting his voice in the general direction of the stairs, he bellowed at Kane. "All I want is a damn pair of jeans and a T-shirt!"

"Bottom drawer!" The response came flying back at him, echoing through the loft.

As Brody turned toward the dresser, his eyes caught on something on the floor, near the edge of the bed. It peeked out from under the bedspread that lay crumpled in a tangle on the floor. Intrigued, he reached for it, shocked when he realized it was bigger than he had first been able to see.

He picked up the syringe, the plunger fully depressed, the wicked, gleaming, sharp end of the needle shooting a wave of nausea through his stomach.

Port him all over the universe and he'd take that over an injection. Any day.

Muttering, he marched downstairs to a closed-eyed Kane. "What the hell is going on?"

Kane murmured a few choice expletives before opening his eyes again with a sigh. The moment his eyes alighted on the syringe, he scrambled to sit up, reaching for the plunger end of the device. "Fuck. I knew she got me, but why'd she leave the damn thing behind?"

"She?" This was getting more interesting by the moment.

"I told you I got played."

"Yeah, but you didn't mention this. She drugged you?"

Kane inspected the small syringe, holding it up to the light, then turning it over in his hand. "What the hell did she give me?"

"Save it for Quinn. He can run the tests, find out what it was." Brody watched as Kane continued to turn the syringe over in his hands. "What'd she do to you?"

"Nothing."

"Looks like a hell of a lot of nothing."

With a sigh, Kane ran a hand through his hair again. "Three days in bed and she ends it by playing me like a Gibson."

"Was it a good tune?"

Time hung suspended as the Scorpio sat there and stared at him, those bloodshot eyes unblinking as they locked on his. And then the corners wrinkled up as Kane's face broke into a broad smile.

"It was a fucking symphony."

Ava wrapped the towel tighter around her midsection and took another look at the clothes laid out on the bed. A beautiful box lay discarded next to the clothes, the box top embossed with the name of an incredibly expensive boutique usually reserved for celebrities and royalty. Kane hadn't missed anything when he'd called in this order. Clearly he was used to buying clothing for women.

When she'd opened the box before her shower, Ava couldn't help but be impressed at Kane's exquisite taste. The black, hammered silk dress and matching bolero jacket from Dolce and Gabbana was soft to the touch. The Christian Louboutin black pumps had her salivating. The La Perla black lace bra, matching panties and garters had sent her thoughts winging right back to her morning with Brody.

She'd quickly buried the underwear underneath the dress as she thought about the discussion the men had had after she and Brody returned from New York.

After she'd assured herself he'd begun to heal, she'd shifted her focus to the discussion. Their focus and discipline. Their planning and strategy. Their innate belief they'd win.

Ava fingered the edge of the bolero jacket and wondered what it must be like to be that confident.

"You ready?"

Brody's gaze assessed her from where he stood in the doorway of the bathroom, a towel riding low on his hips. Even as heat arced between their nearly naked bodies, she reveled in the fact that he looked at her face as he spoke to her. She blossomed under his care and concern.

"As ready as I'm going to be."

"I have to say this." He moved into the room, placed his arms around her and pulled her close. "You need to take this seriously. Enyo is determined to win this battle and after what happened in the cemetery, we can't afford to risk thinking this is a cakewalk."

"I'm not."

"If she gets control of those stones, she'll use the power they can harness to control everything. Forget life as you know it. Forget freedom and order and reason. Forget love and laughter. Forget everything you know. She is a soulless, heartless bitch, and she would love nothing more for all humanity to live in darkness and anarchy."

Ava felt a shiver course the length of her spine. "And this is what you fight?"

"Every day. The stones have only made it worse. Usually she incites wars and starts problems. This is different. If these stones have one tenth of the power she believes them to, we won't be able to stop her."

Ava tightened her arms around his waist, allowing the warmth of his body to seep into hers, to give her much-needed strength. "How do you do it?"

"Do what?"

"Live with this? Live with this knowledge. Fight against it, always believing you will win."

"Because I do believe I can win. With a good dose of caution and recognition of my opponent's strength thrown in."

As they stood there, Ava thought about all she'd lost, all the pain she'd already suffered because of those stones.

Her father. Her innocence. Very nearly her sanity, if she were honest.

But it brought you Brody, too, a small inner voice whispered to her.

As she stood in the circle of his arms, she couldn't help but wonder if he was as invincible as he claimed to be—or if he could survive in the face of her track record.

No one she loved lived. Her father, her mother; both were gone. She was alone.

Was immortality really a match for the undeniably bad luck that seemed to live under her skin?

Chapter Fourteen

"**Y**ou still didn't get her? I thought these Destroyer things you all were always throwing around were invincible. Is it just Enyo's Destroyers who can get the job done?"

Ajax shoveled in the Big Mac as he stared down Wyatt Harrison. Although it chafed to keep the little fucker around, Ajax knew he was playing a dangerous game. He needed all the allies he could get. "As I've told you," he mumbled around a mouthful, "your niece has some powerful protection."

Wyatt huddled into his jacket, his back against the base of Cleopatra's Needle. Erected during Thutmose III's reign in Egypt, the obelisk had been gifted to the United States in the latter half of the nineteenth century as a gesture of goodwill.

Goodwill, my ass, Ajax thought. Dumb, stupid and short-sighted was a better description.

Fuck, some people really didn't get the value of their antiques.

Since its "gifting," the obelisk had stood in Central Park, largely ignored. The latent power held inside the monument would make people shudder if they knew. This actually fit his plans nicely, because he had every intention of using all that power all by himself.

Enyo only *thought* she held all the cards. Once he had the stones, he'd be in charge. Hell, he already owned her body.

"Why'd you drag me here?"

"I think we need to speed up our plans a bit."

"I programmed my niece's cell phone like you asked. It's not my fault you can't close the deal and capture her. Frankly, I'm starting to wonder if you really have the authority you think you do."

Ajax shoveled the last bite into his mouth and threw the wrapper on the ground, his back teeth grinding through the meat and cheese.

"I've told you before, I'm handling this project."

"Poorly."

Ajax leaped across the space, picked up Wyatt's pudgy little body and slammed him against the obelisk's base. "I've got it under control."

Wyatt held up his hands, palms out. "Calm down, all right?"

"How did your conversation with Enyo go? Did you share the information with her as we discussed?"

"I've told her only what you want her to know. The bitch nearly zapped my nuts off, but I stuck to our plan."

Ajax let Wyatt drop to the ground. "What did you tell her?"

"That my niece didn't know anything."

"And she believed you?"

"Why wouldn't she? My spinster niece isn't exactly setting the world on fire, if you know what I mean. She slaves
over her job like it'll bring her happiness. Or bring back my
brother." Wyatt emitted a high-pitched giggle. "I fixed that
problem a long time ago."

"You really don't have any redeeming value, do you?"

Wyatt's grin was cocky. "Not much."

"Are you ready to implement phase two?"

"I've got my part down cold."

"Repeat it to me."

A heavy sigh escaped those enormous cheeks on a rush
of air. "I'm to go to Enyo and convince her to ambush my
niece instead of trying to steal the stones directly."

Ajax nodded. "And when Enyo balks at the suggestion,
as she inevitably will?"

"I'll tell her that my niece already has plans to show the
stones to her grandmother and me in a private viewing and
we can pluck them—and her—off then."

"Perfect."

"I need to go now. I've got breakfast with Mother. Can't
be late."

Ajax waved a hand in dismissal as he dug into his pocket
for another burger. "Yes. Go." As he sank his teeth into the
greasy meat, satisfaction surged in his chest in time with
the energy that flooded his system from the food.

Wyatt really was useful. The little toady would divert
Enyo off the scent of the hunt for the stones by letting her
think they would be easy pickings. In the meantime, he could
deal with Ava on his own, grabbing her and getting her into
a safe house until he could finish gathering the stones on
his own.

It really was a perfect double cross. And by the time

Ms. High-and-Mighty Goddess of War knew what was going on, he'd have the stones and there wouldn't be anything she could do about it.

'Bout time, too. They'd spent far too long together and he was getting sick of her.

The obelisk cast a heavy shadow in the early-morning light as he polished off the burger. Damn but he was burning through a lot of energy. Seven ports back and forth to London. The energy he kept expending to pose as Dr. Martin at the museum. And then that superior fuckup this morning at the cemetery.

Were his Destroyers inferior to Enyo's? He knew he'd had to pick off those who were least loyal to her—generally the ones who weren't quite as well versed in their art—but they were still killing machines.

As he threw another empty wrapper after the others, he ported himself back to the museum, behind the locked doors of Dr. William Martin's oh-so-stately office.

The gig wasn't so bad. Thick, plush swivel chair. State-of-the-art technology. Huge office that overlooked the park. But, thankfully for him, he'd always had a little more ambition than "not so bad."

Nope, he wasn't stopping until he was truly the badass of the universe. It was *that* image that kept him going.

As Ajax powered up Martin's computer, he worked through his next meet with Enyo. How to play that one?

Valued sidekick?

Tender, understanding lover?

Crazed, vengeful lunatic, hovering on the brink of madness—a brink only she could calm him from?

Oh yeah. Now *that* sounded like fun.

* * *

"Dr. MacIntyre. I'm Ava Harrison. This is my colleague and the head of security on this project from Emerald Securities, Dr. Brody Talbot."

"Lovely to meet you both." Dr. Lorna MacIntyre extended her hand to both of them, her pinched expression suggesting she felt anything but the polite sentiment.

"I'm sorry we're late. Had a bit of trouble finding our way over."

The dark slashes that passed for eyebrows shot upward. "You didn't take the car service arranged for you?"

Ava reached for a piece of hair lying flush against her lapel. With a quick twirl, she shot MacIntyre a surprised glance. "Car service?"

"Yes. We discussed that when you confirmed the appointment? The museum arranged car service for you from your hotel. It was part of your itinerary."

With a diffident shrug, Ava put a breathy pout in her voice. "Oh well."

At the dark look that swam in the other woman's eyes, Ava knew she'd hit the right note—dumb New York bitch. MacIntyre handed them each a visitor security badge, then began a brisk walk across the Great Hall to the museum's offices.

As Ava walked through the museum next to MacIntyre, she put a subtle swing in her hips. The Louboutins made it easy, the height of the heels naturally aiding the swing. Having Brody so near made it even easier.

Dr. MacIntyre led them into the office area of the museum. "We need to take care of some paperwork in my office first."

"I thought we'd see the stone first."

"Paperwork. Always paperwork, Dr. Harrison."

Professional interest flared as Ava compared the British Museum's offices to her own. If the moment hadn't been so serious, she'd have laughed that competition could rear its ugly head in the oddest of ways.

As they crossed the threshold of MacIntyre's office, a sudden image of her mother rose up in Ava's thoughts. Big smiles and an encouraging hug as she read the line of a book, all by herself. *Cat in the Hat*, wasn't it?

Another thought tumbled on top of it. Her mother leaning over, kissing her knee through a Band-Aid as soft, blond hair fell around her face.

"Dr. Harrison, are you all right?" Although the question should have held concern, MacIntyre's stern tone held the opposite as she stood on the other side of her desk, hands on her hips.

Ava shook her head, the memory fading at the narrow-eyed gaze from MacIntyre. "Yes, yes, fine."

"Well then, please sign the paperwork."

A quick glance down revealed all the paperwork lined up in even rows, with *X*s for where she needed to sign.

How long had she been daydreaming?

And where were these memories coming from? Although she certainly thought about her mother, and often, losing her so young had left Ava with very few tangible, specific things to remember.

She caught Brody's eye where he stood sentinel against the door, a puzzled frown on his face.

With a discreet cough, Ava reached for the pen and sought something to say as she worked her way through the bureaucratic red tape that was museum life. She was actually grateful for the mundane task—anything that might make her seem less like a lunatic. She had an important role to play, but she'd started feeling strange the minute she'd set foot in this room—like being in a dream.

"Do you have the stone here in your office?"

"Heavens, no." MacIntyre let out a small, nervous laugh. "The stone is safe in security's hands. We'll go there next."

"Of course."

Fresh out of conversation and with a stack of forms still to sign, Ava searched desperately for something—anything—to keep her focused.

And promptly found herself staring into the chocolate brown eyes of her mother as they rubbed noses in the cold winter air of Central Park after building a snowman.

Ava felt the carefree giggles welling up in her throat and slammed a hand over her mouth.

What was wrong with her? This was the most important thing she'd been asked to do in her life and she kept slipping into daydreams?

Taking a deep breath, she forced her mind back to the present.

Her gaze landed on a framed photograph of a small boy on the doctor's desk. Dr. MacIntyre was in the picture, too, holding the child tightly to her chest. Of their own accord, her eyes shifted to where the doctor sat across the desk. A penetrating, unkind stare met hers across the small, cramped space of the office, shooting sheer panic to the tips of Ava's nerve endings and back. She was suddenly very grateful Brody was standing against the door.

MacIntyre's cold gaze was at odds with the happy woman in the picture, and at even greater odds with the memories of her own mother that danced in Ava's head.

Every ounce of feminine instinct she possessed screamed there was a problem.

Shaking it off like the ethereal dreams of her own mother,

Ava again focused on the paperwork. Lorna MacIntyre's mothering skills had nothing to do with her job.

Nothing.

With a flourish, Ava signed the last page, thrilled they could finally go get the stone and get out of there. The day had been taxing enough, but now that she'd begun worrying about the parenting skills of a stranger, it was clearly time to get the job done and get out.

MacIntyre grabbed her purse from the back of her chair and came around to stand next to Ava. "Ready, Dr. Harrison?"

Unbidden, another memory of her mother swamped Ava's senses. Her mother's arms wrapped around her as they flew down a large slide at an amusement park. A half scream, half giggle erupted from her throat as their bodies undulated over the hills of the ride.

"Dr. Harrison!"

"Yes?"

"Is something bothering you?"

What *was* wrong with her? While the memories were lovely, she had no idea where they were coming from.

MacIntyre shook her head. "Let's get a move on, shall we?"

Brody expected obstacles; he was prepared for them. He braced himself for the shock of electricity as they took each twist and turn on the path toward the museum's security department.

None came.

What he hadn't expected was Ava's erratic attitude. What was wrong with her? He knew they'd told her to play the flighty scientist, but why did she keep going in and out of a trance?

"Just this way. We have two more turns and then I'll turn you both over to security." MacIntyre pushed them through a door marked PRIVATE, NO ADMITTANCE, then stopped in front of a large, heavy door. Brody saw her take a quick inhale of breath before she squared her shoulders. A flicker of unease ran through him as he and Ava followed her through the door, straight onto the museum's loading dock.

Unease morphed to the high alert of an adrenaline burn, but still he wasn't fast enough.

MacIntyre grabbed Ava before he even realized, pulling her out of his range and pushing her toward a set of stairs.

Six Destroyers surrounded the raised platform of the loading area.

And with Ava firmly behind her, MacIntyre pointed the business end of a far-too-steady gun straight at his head.

Brody's lion flicked its tail as he assessed the situation. The Destroyers were all popping with static electricity as each bounced from foot to foot, but MacIntyre was the only one with a gun.

Risk getting himself shot and potentially leaving Ava alone?

Or use the element of surprise to his advantage?

In the end, it was MacIntyre's insane calm that decided it. Nothing like ruffling a few feathers.

With an ease born of millennia of battle, Brody let the lion off its leash. Raw fury and a commanding roar echoed through the loading dock as the lion leaped from its position on his back, straight for Lorna MacIntyre's outstretched arms.

The woman let out a choked scream as the large claws dragged their way through the wool of her suit jacket. The gun clattered to the ground as a second scream followed the first.

Her purse followed the gun to land a few feet from Ava's left leg.

"Ava! Grab the gun."

His lion shook its mane and roared at MacIntyre as the woman let out yet another scream. Brody kept watch on them as his gaze kept darting out toward the Destroyers. All six worked at a stealthy pace, narrowing the space between them while ensuring any possible escape off the loading dock was blocked.

"Ava!" Brody shifted his gaze quickly toward Ava. Why was the gun still lying on the ground, where MacIntyre dropped it? "Pick up the gun, Ava."

Nope, nothing. Just a blank stare as a small smile ghosted her lips, her eyes glazed in a dreamy look.

What was wrong with her? MacIntyre had had no time to drug them. She hadn't even offered them water.

"Ava!"

If he moved close enough to get the gun, he and his lion would be too far out of range for the beast to stay on top of MacIntyre. But if he didn't move soon, the Destroyer closest to Ava would have the gun.

"Ava!"

Ava's gaze shifted from dreamy to aware just as the Destroyer stepped into range of the gun. The asshole reached down as Ava finally moved with purpose toward the weapon. MacIntyre be damned, Brody and his lion leaped toward Ava and the Destroyer as Kane and Quinn appeared on the loading dock.

The long, lethal tail of Kane's scorpion swatted at the Destroyer as his hand closed around the butt of the Glock.

The harsh, punishing arc of the powerful tail caught him off balance as the gun went flying through the air to land in the far corner of the loading dock.

Brody kicked MacIntyre's purse out of reach of the woman in the event she had another gun in it, then pushed MacIntyre toward Ava with his lion's paw. A quick glance at Ava showed clear eyes and alert features.

Thank the gods.

"You okay?"

"Of course."

Of course? "You weren't fine a minute ago."

He saw the confusion chase its way across her features, then understanding as she acknowledged wherever she'd been in her head.

Quinn tossed Ava a pair of plastic restraints as he ported across the space next to her. "Tie her up. We'll question her when we're finished here."

Satisfied Ava was safe in a small alcove, her back to the outer wall of the museum, Brody turned back to his brothers. With matched moves born out of endless battles, they charged at the same time, the beasts of their tattoos fighting right alongside of them.

Brody heard the battle cry leave his lips, the deep, guttural growl as he fought to protect his woman. Baring his teeth at the Destroyer closest to him, he snarled, "Bring it on."

Kane's scorpion had emerged as well. About six feet in length, its large tail flicked in great, menacing arcs while its claws flashed with lethal grace in the cold, blustery London afternoon.

Two more Destroyers stepped up, light on the balls of their feet. Kane flipped a discarded shovel he'd found back and forth between his hands. "These guys are tired. I haven't felt a fireball yet."

Brody focused on his body, using his nerve endings to get a sense of his surroundings. Stray wisps of energy floated around them, but Kane was right. No fireballs. Nothing hardcore.

These guys *were* tired. But why? It wasn't like Enyo to be so sloppy, sending her own minions into battle in a state that put them out of commission.

With a snarl, one half of the pair that stood opposite Brody taunted him. "Your girlfriend's next. She's quite a sweet piece, Leo. I'm going to have some fun with her, once we get rid of you and your friends."

"If you think you're gonna make it that long, you guys are even dumber than we give you credit for. And that's pretty damn hard, isn't it, Kane?"

"Impossible."

Shouts rang out as the next pair stepped up, their battle cries echoing around the loading dock. Brody swung out with a foot, catching his guy off balance. His lion was almost on him when the asshole pulled a nifty trick of his own, kicking straight out as he fell.

The solid ground beneath his feet shifted as Brody tumbled backward. Unable to catch himself, he instinctively shifted his arms to break his fall.

And cracked his head against the concrete.

A haze of pain enveloped him. He tried to open his eyes, but throbbing waves attacked him like a thousand knife points to his skull. He slammed his eyes closed, stars floating behind his eyelids as agonizing twinges ran the length of his spinal cord.

"Brody!" Kane's voice rang out just as his lion roared.

He opened his eyes in time to see the same Destroyer back on his feet and headed straight for him.

Seeing no way he could get to his feet in time, Brody imagined himself across the lot. As the instructions to port filled his system, the large claw of Kane's scorpion snapped the asshole's neck in half.

As his body reassembled, Brody hollered at Kane from across the length of the loading dock. "I owe ya one!"

Kane grunted, swung out and hit his Destroyer square in the windpipe. He used the handle of the shovel to drop the death blow, hollering as he delivered the lethal movements.

"Behind you, Brody!" Brody spun around, the swift movement causing his still-throbbing head to explode again. Although the pain had faded somewhat, he'd taken quite a hit to the head. Even his rapid powers of healing weren't quick enough to fight it off just yet.

Blinking, he pushed back on the pain, willing the haze in front of his eyes to clear. He blinked a few more times as the second half of the pair he'd fought came into focus.

Movements deliberate, the Destroyer stalked toward Ava and Lorna. Brody ran, his legs heavy and awkward. *Shit, shit, shit.* The blow to the head was fucking with his equilibrium.

Taking a deep breath, he pushed through, his lion fully extended as they both ran hell-for-leather toward the Destroyer. As they narrowed the gap, nearly on the guy, Brody pulled up short as he watched the Destroyer pass right on by the women, headed for the discarded purse.

What the *fuck* was this?

He'd taken a blow to the head, but he wasn't seeing things.

With a feral battle cry, Brody and his lion leaped, slamming the Destroyer to the ground. The lion swiped at the neck, but the asshole shifted at the last minute and the paw flew through nothing but air.

Grunting, Brody reached out for an ankle, preventing escape. As he dragged on the asshole's legs, Brody climbed the body, hands reaching for the broadest part of the torso to get some leverage and pin him down.

With a backflip, the guy pushed him off and rolled to his feet. He nearly had his freedom—and would have been on his way if he hadn't bent over for the discarded purse. With a roundhouse kick, Brody dropped him, then scissored his legs over the Destroyer's to hold him still.

His lion clamped its mouth on the exposed neck, ripping at the throat with his powerful jaws. The body went limp immediately as oil began to pool next to the purse.

A glance at Kane and Quinn showed matched oil slicks near them and not a Destroyer in sight.

Brody grabbed the purse and moved toward the huddled women.

"Now, Dr. MacIntyre, what could possibly be so important that a soulless creature with social issues decided he needed your purse?"

Lorna cried softly, sobs wracking her pointy shoulders. "What are you people?"

Brody ignored the sudden show of remorse laced with fear as he dropped to a squat and opened the purse. With one deft motion, he dumped the contents next to where Ava sat cross-legged.

Or content—as in singular.

There on the ground, next to Ava's leg, lay the only thing that fell out of the purse.

The London stone.

Round and slightly smaller than his fist, the deep indigo

blue stone had a pearlescent smoothness that showed a flaw-less surface as it caught the light.

From the corner of his eye, Brody saw Ava fall to her side. Dropping the stone, Brody reached for Ava's uncon-scious form.

"Ava!" With a gentle shake, he pulled her onto his hip. "Ava!"

Chapter Fifteen

"*H*e's a lovely man, Ava. And so handsome, too."

"*Mom?*"

"*I've wanted this for you for so long.*"

"*Wanted what?*"

A small, feminine smile washed over Marie Harrison's face as she rocked them both on a porch swing. "A sexy man, silly. And one who is strong enough to handle the real you."

"*The real me?*"

"*Of course.*"

"*But Mom.*" *Hot tears pricked the back of her eyes as her throat tightened. "I'm nothing. I've sat back, afraid of everything."*

Warm arms came around her, the soft embrace so full of love, Ava nearly cried out from the absolute sweetness.

"*You can handle it. You can handle anything. You've always been able to handle anything.*"

"*No, I can't.*" *The words ripped from her throat as memory after memory served up the reminder that she couldn't handle anything.*

The day of her eleventh birthday when she snuck away to eat her entire birthday cake, unable to stop shoveling in the rich layers and luscious frosting.

The night in college when she'd run out on the man she'd selected to lose her virginity to. Unwilling to go all the way, she'd snuck out when he'd excused himself and pretended from then on out she didn't know who he was.

The raw fear that had filled her when Dr. Martin told her she'd run the Mysterious Jewels exhibit.

Every one of those and so many others were ever-present reminders of what a failure she was. With a sob that felt pulled from the very fiber of her being, she clung to her mother. "I really can't."

"Ava!"

Then she heard it. It sounded like her name coming from very far away, but then it got louder as she felt her mother give her a strong push on her shoulders as she pulled back from her.

Shoved back to the present?

Ava stared up into Brody's clear, gentle eyes. "What happened? And where are we?"

"You passed out. And we're in the British Museum. Inside Dr. MacIntyre's office."

Office? What was she doing in Brody's lap? And why was Dr. MacIntyre tied up on a chair in the corner?

"Why did I pass out?"

Brody glanced in Kane's direction before dropping his gaze back to her. "We think the London Summoning Stone made you faint."

Ava searched her mind for the evidence it could possibly be true. "But how? We never even got to the stone."

Brody's arms tightened around her. "Ava, Dr. MacIntyre

had the stone with her when she led us outside to the Destroyer attack. Don't you remember?"

At his words, a small kernel of fear unfurled in her belly, slithering through her system in chilling waves. "No. I saw the stone?"

"She had it in her purse the whole time we were with her."

Oh God, why couldn't she remember? "But I haven't had any visions."

"Nothing at all?"

"No."

She saw Brody's eyes dart toward Quinn's, then resettle on her face. "Then why have you gone in and out of lucidity since we entered Dr. MacIntyre's office an hour ago?"

Scrambling, she held on to Brody's elbows to gain some leverage and shifted into an upright position. "I did what?"

"Off and on, you've looked like you were in a trance. It was noticeable here in the office, but got worse once we got outside."

"What happened outside?"

Brody brushed a strand of hair behind her ear. "Sweetheart, I screamed to get your attention outside on the loading dock and you ignored me."

"I don't remember any of that."

"What do you remember?"

"Following behind Lorna in the hallway on our way to what she kept calling security. That large door she led us through before we realized it was the loading dock. Your herding her and me into that corner as Quinn threw me the restraints."

Brody glanced across the room. Twisting, Ava followed his gaze and saw twin frowns spread across Kane's and Quinn's faces. "It has to be the stone, then."

"But how? I might have been out of it, but I *know* I haven't had any visions. None of the usual nightmares."

Quinn stepped forward. "You've been affected by something. Did you have *any* visions? Anything at all?"

"I have been thinking of my mother. Random memories of her I didn't even know I had."

Warm, lovely memories.

Maybe this was a good thing. Maybe it meant she really wasn't a Chosen One. She was just plain, old Ava Harrison, and really, would that be a bad thing?

"Is that all you remember?" Quinn pulled her back to the conversation.

"Well, yeah." They were just memories, weren't they? Except for that strange conversation with her mother.

About Brody.

She glanced from Brody to Quinn to Kane, then stole a glance at the huddled, weeping form of Lorna MacIntyre. "Do you have the stone?"

"We do now." Quinn's voice was grim as he moved to stand next to Lorna. "And I think Dr. MacIntyre needs to explain a few things."

Misery was etched in every facet of the woman's face and tears traced twin paths down her cheeks. Empathy rose up inside of Ava, even as she knew this woman had nearly got her killed—nearly got them all killed. Still, her tone was quiet, soothing, when she pressed the woman for answers. "Why'd you do it?"

"Who are you people? What were th-tho-those things? Outside?"

"I think you need to answer the question, Dr. MacIntyre. Why did you agree to this?"

"I'm not a bad person, Dr. Harrison. Honestly, I'm not,"

Lorna whispered as her gaze darted around the room, landing on each man in turn. Her large, green eyes filled to the brim, as more tears spilled over and down her cheeks. "I just don't know what to do. I don't know who I am anymore. Please don't hurt me."

"Why, Lorna?"

Although the men didn't have her restrained, Lorna hadn't moved from her position on a stiff-backed chair. With careful, tentative movements, she reached over and picked up the picture frame on her desk—the one Ava had noticed earlier. "My son, Jason. He has leukemia. He needs medicine. Experimental medicines."

Brody took over, his voice gentle. Ava knew the effort it cost him by the set of his shoulders and the fury that danced in his irises. "So you just abandoned your principles and went to work for madmen?"

"You don't know! You don't understand what it is to watch your child suffer."

Ava shot Brody a dirty glare. "That's right, Lorna. We don't know. We also don't know who contacted you."

"The initial conversation and all subsequent instructions have been executed anonymously."

Ava struggled to piece it all together as yet another secret revealed itself to her. The world as she knew it was just that . . . the world as she'd *believed* it to be; not the world as it was.

Brody laid a hand on her back. "You don't have to do this. We can question her."

"No. I can do this." At his probing gaze, she nodded. She *could* do this. She felt the warm strength of his hand— the small touch that spoke of true belief in her—and found the courage to go on.

"Okay, Lorna. I need you to think. Try to remember every conversation you've had with this anonymous person. Any descriptive factors you can remember."

Lorna sniffled as her gaze ran over the photo again. "But I don't know anything."

"So you get a mystery contact—presumably some strange person who doesn't tell you his name—and you didn't question it?" Quinn's deadly calm ran a shiver down her spine. Damn, but the man was a scary piece of work.

"He knew about me. Knew about Jason! Knew in detail about his medical history and the drugs that weren't working. He found me a few months ago. Told me his employer would pay me a lot of money that would allow me to get special treatments for my son. Experimental treatments. Treatments that aren't legal." She broke into another round of sobs. "I didn't have any other choice. He's my little boy."

Ava worked to keep the sympathy out of her voice, but damn, it was hard. Despite her anger and upset about the woman's choices, Lorna's desperation was real. "Did you ever meet anyone face-to-face? Get any sense of static electricity when you spoke to them? Surely, even in your grief, you didn't do all this without a face-to-face meet?"

Lorna looked down at the floor. "Yes, I did meet the man face-to-face. Once. The first time. And what do you mean, static?"

"Like fuzzy socks on carpet. Did your hair stand on end? Did you get any shocks?"

"No, not at all. Why?"

"Um. Well." Ava struggled with the right words to use, discarding phrase after phrase that didn't seem to fit. Finally, she opted for a version of the truth. "The people who have contacted you use a type of taser to keep their victims in line."

Quinn's gaze shifted toward her, a wry quirk to his mouth. Ava warmed at the approval she saw in his dark brown gaze.

Lorna kept her eyes on the photo. "About three months ago, I was approached by a man. He found me, sitting alone at lunch, but I didn't pay a lot of attention to it until you just mentioned it."

Ava kept quiet, the silence an encouragement to continue.

"He told me he knew about my personal life. About how sick my son was. About how there were some experimental therapies that would be so much better for him than his chickenshit doctors were willing to use. Even told me I knew one of these experimental doctors, from our days at university."

"That's it?"

"It's all I had to do. Instructions came in the form of typed notes, placed under my day planner."

Ava's mind whirled with the information. Pity versus anger. Disgust at such poor choices juxtaposed against a mother's desperate struggle.

And a nasty bunch of assholes who had clearly found a mark to use to their advantage.

"So what did these instructions entail?" Quinn pressed at MacIntyre, his sympathy chip nowhere in evidence.

"Different things. Plant items in various places. Make a few phone calls on deliveries. Odds and ends. Nothing that would ever raise suspicion."

Quinn didn't let up. "Yet still, you never questioned this?"

MacIntyre's gaze took on a hard, mutinous glare. "I figured it wasn't to mine or Jason's benefit to try and find out who the directions came from."

"That's all they asked you to do?"

"In the last month, the requests have gotten more complex. Get a few people on research lists so they can come

and go in the museum. Arrange for a special, private viewing as part of a sizable donation to help make it all look
legitimate. The last request came the other day."

Ava saw Lorna's eyes dart down on the last word and
braced herself. "What was it?"

"He told me it was my last job. I needed to disengage
the security system and replace the stone with a fake."

Quinn's eyebrows shot up. "You have access to that?"

Her wry laugh came out as a scratchy hiccup. "You work
somewhere long enough, especially as an upstanding em-
ployee with an impeccable record, and you'd be amazed at
what you're given privileges to."

"And who told you to steal the stone?"

Lorna's eyes darkened, the first emotion for herself she'd
exhibited since they'd returned to her office. "I wasn't meant
to steal it. I was told that we were exchanging the stone to
keep the original safe."

"And based on all the other upstanding things you were
asked to do," Quinn said, verbally slapping at her, "stealing
never crossed your mind."

The sharp set of Lorna's shoulders dropped. "It came
like all my other directives. A message appeared in my office and I was to execute it. Upon completion of the task,
another envelope appeared with money."

"Convenient." Disapproval stamped itself in Quinn's flat
tone.

Lorna nodded toward the photo. "Necessary. Do you have
any idea—any idea at all—what it's like to see your child
suffer? To watch him die a little bit every day and know
you can't take his place?"

"And would he be proud of the person you are right
now? Would he be proud there are people who will possibly
die because of what you've done?"

The urge to comfort was strong, but Ava kept her seat, allowing Quinn's words to do their job and following the expressions on Lorna's face as the ramifications of her actions began to sink in.

"This is a museum exhibit. Why would anyone be killed over a museum exhibit?"

Brody stepped up, his voice low in the cramped office. "The fact people were willing to pay you so much never raised your awareness that this actually *was* a big deal?"

"I realize I've done nothing to earn your trust, but could you at least tell me what you believe the stones are capable of? Or tell me what the people who've hired me think they're capable of?"

Brody's voice was bleak as he stared down at the frightened woman. In that moment, Ava understood the path he'd chosen, the difficulties in his task.

Compassion had its limits when it came to saving the world. "Complete and utter destruction, Dr. MacIntyre. Armageddon."

Chapter Sixteen

Ajax paced Enyo's subterranean castle—an old rail-way station in one of Manhattan's abandoned subway tunnels—his features morphing with each step he took. "Why won't you just let me kill her? And Brody, too, while I'm at it. He's had it coming for way too long."

"Patience, Ajax. Patience."

Enyo watched his features morph back and forth—from Dr. Martin to the overbearing frame of Ajax the Wild and back again—and knew the Warrior was losing control.

Well, *former* Warrior. He hadn't served under Themis since Enyo had stolen him away.

Oh, he'd been such an easy one to turn. A few promises—a few grand visions added to his subconscious to sweeten the pot—and he'd been hers.

Ajax was the first one she'd turned. No single one since had felt quite as sweet or quite so *satisfying*.

"You promised me long ago we'd have our revenge. I've been patient, Enyo. Waited. Helped you on every mission since the first one. Why can't we just take the stones?"

"Because we need the key."

"Well, let's steal it."

"It's not that easy. It's protected."

He moved up into her space and nuzzled her neck. "Everything's easy for you, baby."

How lovely he thought so. How necessary he never knew the truth.

She pressed on his shoulders to push him away. They had things to do and his inability to see the bigger picture had grown annoying. "I need you back at the museum. It's only for a short while longer."

"Do you know how hard it is to maintain my Dr. Martin masquerade?" Ajax morphed into his standard frame—six foot four, shoulder-length blond hair—and stood before her. "Do you have any idea how much energy it takes? I can barely eat enough, I'm burning through so much fuel."

"We all make our little sacrifices."

"Little? And what the hell is Wyatt doing? I barely see him. He's so far behind the scenes, he might as well be invisible. Our plan's falling apart, Enyo."

"Nothing is falling apart. I have everything under control. And you'll do well to remember who is running this show."

Although he didn't apologize, Ajax did have the decency to look contrite.

"Now, as I told you a few minutes ago, have patience. And as for Wyatt—well, Ava's uncle has his uses. He hasn't exactly been the doting uncle for thirty-two years. He needs to work his way in and make it seem plausible."

"I don't like him."

"I'm not surprised. No one likes him save that prim idiot mother of his. Couldn't see his faults with a magnifying glass. But . . . you know how mothers are with their oldest sons."

"Fine. I need to eat again and then I'll get back to the museum."

Satisfied his focus was back where it needed to be, she purred at him. "Later. Right now I find I need a bit of a diversion this afternoon. And it's got the side benefit of giving you that energy boost you're looking for."

Ajax's blue eyes shifted in an instant from stubborn and belligerent to long and lazy. "What did you have in mind, my love?"

"Over there. The chains."

His eyes darted to the manacles hanging by chains from the wall. Within moments, he was naked, heading toward the manacles without hesitation. He snapped his wrist into one, then held out his other hand for her to lock it up.

"You really are my kind of man."

He shot her a cocky grin in return. "You really are my kind of woman."

That hum that played under her skin every time she looked at him, every time she touched him, buzzed a little louder as she sashayed toward him. With a quick snap, she locked his wrist, shooting a mild bolt of electricity through it for good measure.

He didn't scream, just closed his eyes and leaned his head back against the wall. With deliberate movements, she ran one bloodred fingernail along the underside of his cock where it stood proudly against his stomach.

As his grunts and groans echoed around the chamber a few minutes later, she couldn't hold back the laughter.

The sweet, sweet laughter.

How glorious that he was hers.

How splendid that he used to be under Themis's command.

* * *

Brody's heart fisted in his chest when he found Ava in his room, weeping in a curled ball on his bed. She'd said little through their debriefing to Grey and even less during an early dinner. He couldn't honestly say the tears were a surprise after the last few days.

It was his reaction to the tears that caught him off guard.

The backs of his eye pricked with moisture and his throat grew tight. He'd been so focused on her physical safety, this evidence of her emotional distress was a sucker punch to the gut.

Without saying a word, he walked to the bed, lay down and curled himself around her, his body absorbing the shaking sobs of her much smaller one.

"Tell me why you're crying."

"I've been thinking about Lorna."

Fierce waves of anger pummeled his system, heating his bloodstream with the need for vengeance. "She set you up, Ava. She set all of us up. You could have gotten killed."

"I know. Really I do." He watched as she traced a repetitive pattern into the silk of the bedspread. "But I can't help it. Can't help feeling horrible pity at what she's dealing with in her son's illness. He's a little boy, Brody."

"But she made the wrong choice. Her son's illness is a horrible thing, but she made a terribly bad choice."

"I know." She continued with the pattern, swirl after swirl imagined in the smooth fabric. "What will happen to her?"

"Kane stayed behind to erase her mind. He's also found a resource to help her son. An above-board research facility that can help him with his illness. It doesn't change the fact that she'll have to pay for this."

"More balance."

"Yes."

They lay in silence, the moments spinning out like Clotho's thread.

Ava's voice was quiet long minutes later. "Is it really as simple as all that?"

"As what?"

"Choices. We make them every day, for good or for bad."

"I believe it is."

Choices. He'd made many in his ten thousand years of living. As his mind drifted back to earlier times, one choice stood out above all others.

"They used to call me Brody the Meek."

"Wh-when?"

"Before Themis. Before my transition to life as one of her Warriors." At her silence, he continued his story, his mind flashing through the thousands-year-old trip in a matter of moments.

He shoveled straw from the corner of their hovel, the action useless as a cleaning technique. All it did was churn up dust and move dirt around their small cottage.

"Brody, dear, help me knead this dough."

His mother's tired eyes pleaded with him as she placed a hand on her lower back.

She was pregnant again. He'd long stopped believing the babes would survive. It was as if they knew there would be no joy for them in this life. Except for him and his older brother, none of the other seven children his mother had brought into this miserable world had lived.

He had no doubt the next season would find the eighth who chose the same path.

Yet year after year, his father forced himself on her along with any number of women in their village, both willing and unwilling.

His mother touched the sensitive area around his eye as he moved to the table to help her. "You mustn't anger him so."

"I was asleep, Mother. I said something in my sleep I have no idea of and he called me weak. I know I'm not Ajax, not the son he favors, but I can't control my dreams."

Ajax; it was always Ajax. The perfect son, adored by his parents as well as every other person who looked on him. Was he the only one who knew the truth of his brother's harsh, punishing fists and cruel tongue?

His mother brushed a hand over his cheek, her touch soft despite the calluses that covered her fingers. "I know, darling. I know."

This latest beating had been particularly unjust. Asleep one minute, slammed to the wall with his father's hand at his throat the next, Brody hadn't even had a chance to throw his hands up to protect himself in his sleep disorientation.

Throat burning, he wheezed as his father's fingers tightened harder on his windpipe. "Whimpering in your sleep, boy? You sure know how to live up to your name. You really are Brody the Meek."

He tried to gasp out a "no," but the word wouldn't form. There was no air to utter even a sound.

He shook off his mother's hand. "Go rest. He'll be home soon and you'll get none then."

"If he finds me sleeping, he'll give me more work."

He placed a soothing hand on his mother's back. "Shhh. I won't let him. Go rest."

If he'd done nothing else in this life, he'd worked to draw the beatings away from his mother, taking them on himself. When his father's attention seemed to divert to his wife, Brody would do something to pull the ire to himself.

It wasn't much, but in its own way it was as heroic as

*his beloved brother's battle stories. At least he had the sol-
ace of doing the right thing for someone he loved.*

*He slid a glance to her distended stomach. Some bur-
dens, however, he couldn't take from her. "Go, now. Rest."*

*He turned back to the bread, allowing the dough to slide
through his fingers. With frightful precision, he used the soft
matter to slam his fists, over and over, imagining his father's
face, then the perfect visage of his brother's, as he did so.
He was so engrossed in the imaginary beating, he never
heard his father come in.*

*He never saw the fist coming as it boxed him over
the ear, throwing him off balance so he stumbled and fell.*

*"Baking like a girl now, are we? I never should have
left you to your mother's influences."*

*His father threw the wad of dough into the fire, the
large mass falling over the logs in a great, oozing ball.*

*He looked up at his father's large shape looming over
him—broad shoulders, hamlike fists and a large, round belly
from the ale he loved to swill. "She needed help. She is tired
from the babe."*

*A kick landed on his ribs, the pain ricocheting around
his body like fire.*

*He was saved from another kick by knocking and holler-
ing at the door. His father's attention diverted as he moved
across the small cottage, Brody dragged himself to the corner of the room, the walls at his back providing small comfort as he took stock of his latest bruises.*

*Before his father could make it to the door, it slammed
open and three of the villagers streamed into the room. The
one in the lead shouted orders as the other two followed
behind, carrying the large, strapping body of his brother.
An arrow lodged in Ajax's heart and his eyes stared at the
ceiling, sightless.*

The noise had awakened his mother, and she waddled into the room with her hand at her back. At the sight of her eldest son lying dead on her table, she screamed in unison with his father.

"No! Ajax!"

Brody sat in that corner long into the evening. The stench of burned bread flooded the cottage from where the dough had lain in the fire. It mixed with the increasing stench of the open wound on his brother's dead body.

His father hovered over him. "Go fetch the midwife, boy."

"But it's not time."

For his impertinence he received another kick. "Go get her."

In the half hour it took to fetch the Widow Stone from her cottage and return to his mother, the angel of death visited their cottage two more times, taking both the babe and his mother.

Later that night, it came for him, too.

Ava shifted in his arms so she faced him. Her hands reached up, the pads of her fingers smoothing over the bones around his eye before she leaned forward and kissed the path her fingers had traced.

"Oh, Brody."

"My father went after me that night, determined to end my life for all the evilness he believed I caused."

"He wasn't right, Brody. He was broken."

"And he was determined to break me."

She pressed her lips to that same area above his eye, murmuring to him. "But he didn't."

"No. He didn't."

He hadn't thought about those days in so long. Hadn't wanted to remember either his weakness or the days after.

But now, in the telling, he saw it through new eyes, and with a new vision that held more confidence, more objectivity, more self-reliance.

As that new vision replaced the one he'd held for so long, much of the shame receded with it.

He'd survived. Thrived. Flourished. And he lived a life he was proud of. He was no longer Brody the Meek. He was Leo Warrior.

He had strength and power, and he used both for good. He was not his father. He did not beat up on the weak.

He was a *Warrior*.

"Themis found you after that?"

He tightened his hold on her, the warmth of her body seeping into his. "Yes. My father beat me and left me for dead in the fields outside our home. I was nearing my last breath—knew it with each horrible gasp as I tried to fill my lungs. And Themis appeared to me. She offered me a new life. Asked me to take up her battle for justice. I accepted."

He placed a finger under her chin and tilted her face up to look at him. "I had a choice, Ava. We all have choices and I made mine. I wasn't coerced and I certainly didn't have any great faith my life would be that much better. But I had a choice and I made it."

She nodded. "I understand."

"I know."

They lay there in silence, lost in the simple comfort each provided the other. Her voice, scratchy with her crying jag, whispered over his chest. "Why did she pick you? Many, many people live sad lives. Dismal existences."

"She said I was a Chosen One. My inner core of goodness and light made me the right choice to take up her battle."

"She called you that? A Chosen One?"

"Yes, Ava. We're chosen for different things—called to different things—but we're both chosen."

"It's an overwhelming responsibility. I don't even know what it entails, but I already know it's overwhelming. Absolute."

"How do you know that?"

"Why else would someone want the power that comes with it?"

He had to acknowledge her point; acknowledge the truth that where power was sought, great power inevitably existed. "Perhaps it feels like it. The fear of the unknown often makes us feel overwhelmed."

A myriad of emotions ran across her expressive face, captured in the lines of her forehead, the depths of her eyes, the curve of her lips.

Frustration.

Hope.

Fear.

Courage.

He saw them all, marveling at the depths of the woman who sat opposite him.

"Do you really think I'm the Key to the stones? That the prophecy was written about me? About my father?"

"Your reaction to the stones proves it."

"But how?"

He'd puzzled through this ever since reading the prophecy. "There are five stones and five elements of the prophecy."

She nodded, ticking them off on her fingers. "Death, life, love, sexuality and infinity."

"The stone here in New York has to be death. The images you see have been too brutal. Too nightmarish."

"And the London one has to be love."

"Not life?"

She made a good point. All her visions around the London stone revolved around her mother, so it could be life-giving. But as horrible as the deadly images were, they made her feel so safe and so loved. "Maybe, but for now I'm thinking love."

"Personally, I'd like to get my hands on the sex stone. Wonder what those visions are like. How much do you want to bet the French have that one?"

Ava's laughter spilled from her. "You're incorrigible."

He nuzzled her neck. "I try."

As he reveled in the feel of her, the warm, lovely, amazing feel of her, he felt a subtle shift; he felt her drifting away.

"Are my kisses that bad?"

"Hmmm?"

Brody lifted his head. "My kisses. Are they that bad? You're a million miles away."

"I just remembered something I hadn't thought about in years. My father kept journals."

"Of his digs?"

"Yes. I tried reading one as a teenager, but after getting halfway through one I was crying so hard I finally had to give up. It was as if I could hear his voice on the page and this anger just welled up inside of me."

He took a small lock of her golden hair and rubbed it between his fingers. She'd lived through so much and had dealt with such horrors at such an early age.

And she'd done it alone.

"That's understandable."

"Even now, so many years later, I can still remember how angry it made me as I tried to read the first journal.

Why was he taken from me? Why did the other kids at school have their fathers?"

"You had a right to feel that way, you know," Brody said gently, rubbing her back with a small, circular motion.

"I know."

They sat there in silence for a few minutes, both lost in thought. "Do you think you can look at them now?"

"I think so."

"Good."

Ava's gaze locked on his, a small light of mischief replacing the grief he'd seen only moments before. "You'd like to read them, wouldn't you?"

"I'd love to read them."

She smiled and poked him in the ribs. "Dig geek."

"Proud of it."

"I wonder if I have the one from his last dig?"

"It's worth a try."

Ava traced a finger down the curve of his jaw, her mercurial mood shifting yet again as words spilled from her lips. "What if I'm not worthy?"

With slow movements, he took her hand in his big one, pressing a kiss to her palm. "Of course you're worthy. Look at what you've survived. Your mother's death as a small child. Your father's murder. Even these last few days. You've survived everything that's been thrown at you—literally. How can you think you're not worthy? Not strong enough?"

"But because of those things, I've spent the majority of my life actively avoiding everything. I checked out of life, Brody. How can I be worthy of anything?"

"Being chosen is a gift. And like all gifts, we choose if we wish to accept it or not. What came before the choice doesn't matter. It's what comes after."

And as they sat there, the word he'd worked so hard to banish from his mind reared up again, unwilling to be silenced.

Mate.

She was truly his match. He'd spent thousands of years walking the earth. He had met ten times as many women and had always known their presence would be transient. And none of them, not even his sweet first love, fired his blood and filled his soul.

Ava.

His Ava.

Consequences be damned, he could no longer stand not having her, this woman he needed above all others.

So he'd make his choice. And he'd take what he could have. And the glory of being with her could carry him through the rest of his immortal life, long after he walked the earth without her.

"What came before the choice doesn't matter. It's what comes after."

As Brody's words ran round and round in her head, Ava felt each tumbler in the lock around her heart open and fall away. With a deep breath she leaned forward, her lips brushing lightly against his. "Choose me."

It took nothing more than that.

His large hands reached up to cup her face, tilting her head so their mouths met fully; completely. As their breaths mingled and merged, his lush lips played over hers. With purposeful possession, his tongue parted the seam of her lips and met hers in a tangle of warm, wet need.

She gloried in the feel of him as he pulled her closer to sprawl on top of his chest. Without breaking the contact of their mouths, his hands moved over her in light caresses.

From the top of her back to the base of her spine, he ran his fingers in feather-light patterns that teased her nerve endings and shot warm arrows of pleasure under her skin.

Light shivers formed in the patterns he traced over her back, creating sensitive frissons of need she was helpless to stop and responsive trembles that showed him how badly she wanted him.

Shifting, he rolled her onto her back, his fingers roving under her shirt. She'd long since changed out of the beautiful dress she'd worn at the museum. But something—call it women's intuition or just flat-out vanity—had made her leave the sexy bra and barely there panties on when she'd changed back into her Cinderella clothes of jeans and a long-sleeved T-shirt.

"I was hoping to get a look at these." Brody flashed a wicked, wanton smile as his sky blue eyes darkened. He pressed a reverent line of kisses across her stomach as he pushed the cotton material of her shirt higher and higher. She lifted herself up slightly so he could pull the shirt over her head. The jeans quickly followed and then his clothes after that until they were both naked.

Skin to skin. Heart to heart.

Ava lay back as Brody held himself above her, supporting his weight on his arms. "You are so beautiful. I want you, Ava. Body and soul, I want you. I have from the very first moment."

"First moment?"

"I followed you and you wore that horrible gray sweater and I wanted you." He leaned in and nuzzled her neck. "Desperately, I wanted you."

Sheer, feminine power coursed through her veins. He saw her. He saw through her defenses. He even saw through the drab materials she tried to hide herself in. As to sunshine after a rainstorm, she felt herself turn toward the power of the sun.

With a whisper against his ear, she pressed everything in her heart into her words. "Then what are you waiting for?"

And then there was no more waiting as the moment overtook both of them.

Where there was languid pleasure, now there was pulsing need.

Where there was lazy discovery, now there was raging desperation.

Where there was idle enjoyment, now there was a driving, swirling mass of the need to touch, to take, to pleasure.

Brody's mouth moved down her body, his tongue laving over her sensitive skin. He took a nipple into his mouth, his teeth scraping against the sensitive band of her areola, as he pulled on the tip with the hot, wet suction of his mouth. She moaned as the pleasure arced through her body, coalescing into the raging storm of wetness at the apex of her thighs.

Her toes curled against the back of his thighs as his lips and tongue journeyed on, those clever fingers never leaving her breasts as his mouth continued its exploration.

Down over her rib cage. Across the small valley of her belly button. Over the flat surface of her stomach.

Then he dragged his strong, chiseled jaw over the sensitive area of her mons and she nearly came off the bed at the pressure, a long, deep moan dragging from her lips.

"Shhh. Sweet, sweet Ava. You are so hot. So ready for me." She looked down at him, that wicked grin that flipped her heart over in her chest spread clear across his face. "But are you ready for this?"

And then there were no words, only sensations as he grabbed her hips in those large, capable hands and pressed his lips into the wet warmth of her vagina, focused with unerring precision on her clitoris.

She screamed as waves of pleasure coursed through her system, so hard, so sharp, they burned like the sun. Everything that had come before—the joy of every touch, of every single sensation—faltered in comparison to the pleasure he now lavished on her as he made love to her with his mouth.

With long, lapping curls of his tongue he played her body, shooting wave after glorious wave through her nerve endings, driving her up, up, up.

With his lips, he nuzzled the throbbing center of her, controlling the pleasure so that he dragged her to the edge, pulled back, dragged her again and then held her there.

And then with hot suction he tortured the most sensitive part of her body, nearly tearing her apart with the pleasure-pain of it as she bucked underneath his mouth, moaning for release.

Finally, as if he knew she could hold it back no longer, he removed his mouth, then pressed his thumb and forefinger against her cleft.

And let her go.

She screamed as the world burst around her. Mindless from the pleasure, she exploded against his hand, great heaving spasms that wrapped her muscles around his fingers in tight pulses of need.

With his other hand, he reached for hers, their fingers intertwined as she rode the wave.

"You are perfect."

"Actually, after that performance," Ava whispered against his ear, "I think I'm the one who should be giving the compliments."

With a wanton smile, she wiggled out from underneath him, shifting so that she had him on his back, straddling his hips, in one smooth movement.

"And you say I've got some nifty tricks. That was very smooth, Dr. Harrison."

"You ain't seen nothing yet, Dr. Talbot." And then she rained hot kisses on his lips, over his cheeks, down over the rough stubble of his chin.

Farther on to his collarbone, over his chest to his nipples.

With pointed, wet laps of her tongue, she took his nipple into her mouth. Sensation after sensation echoed through his nerve endings at the erotic attention.

He pulled on her arms, trying to drag her up so he could lavish attention on her, but she squirmed out of his reach again, sliding down his body with ease.

"Ava. Come ba—"

The moment was lost as her mouth closed over the long length of him. Long, drugging pulls of suction added to the erotic pressure coursing through his body.

He was desperate for her, his hips moving in unconscious rhythm to the beat she set.

Incoherent thoughts wove through his mind in a pleasured stream of consciousness. He wanted to bury himself in her depths. He never wanted to move under the skillful ministrations of her mouth. He fought to hold on to his seed. He desperately wanted to spill it between her hot, lush lips.

"Ava." He moaned her name as he dragged at her arms again, pulling her off his cock and toward his chest. "Oh, sweet darling, come here. I can't take much more of this."

His hands roamed over her sweat-slick back as she positioned herself over him. As she struggled with his size, he moved his hands, placing them on her hips to glide her down onto him.

"Oh, Brody," she whispered. "You. Feel. Good." She threw her head back, a broad smile spread across her face as her breasts jutted toward him, her nipples erect. Waves of hair rained down her back to brush his knees.

Never had he seen anything sexier.

Never had he wanted a woman more.

"I can't wait for you any longer," she whispered as she began a tentative movement over him. "I need to feel this. Need to feel . . . us."

He wanted to prolong it, to make it last, even as his body screamed for release.

"Want to make this good for you."

She slammed her hips over him, the friction of their bodies drawing desperate moans from both of them.

"It's already good. I want you now."

The long length of her legs straddled his hips as the hot clamp of her sex held him as they moved in unison.

"Fill me, Brody. Please."

It was the "please" that did it—the soft, gentle beauty of the word, whispered between them. After all that had happened in the past week, all the danger that still followed them, this was real.

This was right.

This was completion.

He thrust up into her, slamming his body against hers as she rode him. Like magic, they moved in rhythm, the movements of their bodies driving them both higher and higher toward the summit.

He held out as long as he could, waiting for that telltale moan from her that matched the tightening of her slick channel as she rode his cock.

And the moment he felt her begin, he let go.

As pleasure spun out between them, wrapping their bodies in great lapping waves of it, he felt the world fall away.

With one final thrust, he drove himself up into her warm depths. As she collapsed on top of him, he enfolded her in his arms.

And wished they could stay like that forever.

Chapter Seventeen

"**A**va, do you really think this is a good idea?"

"Other than it's five a.m. and we haven't had the benefit of coffee?" Ava rubbed her eyes and looked around the darkened museum as they stepped off the elevator. Although her surroundings should have felt creepy, walking the cavernous hallways hand in hand with Brody just felt . . . good.

The sound of the doors swishing closed became more and more distant as they headed toward the wing where all the jewels were on display. "I don't know why I didn't think of this sooner."

Brody stood to the side as she punched some codes to the lighting system to give them a bit more to work with beyond the minimal nighttime lights. As she turned back toward him, she was greeted with the most delicious sight.

The mind-numbing appeal of his superior ass.

Oh my. A truly superior posterior.

"Stop looking at my ass, woman, and let's get this over with."

Snapped to attention, her head shot up and, as he spun

around, nearly collided with his chin and the lascivious grin of the eternal charmer who knew exactly what she'd been admiring.

"I'm doing no such thing."

In answer, his smile grew broader. "Kiss me."

A wave of heat shot straight through her body, cutting clean through whatever exhaustion she'd walked into the museum with as his mouth clamped over hers.

Hot and sweet, carnal and reverent.

Brody was everything, as his body pulled wave after wave of response from her. Dizzying heights of pleasure, pounding waves of desire, bone-weakening shots of bliss.

Oh girl, are you in danger here. Serious, serious danger.

"Why are we here again when we could be in bed, working through sequels four, five and six to what we started last night?"

"I want you to be with me in front of the stone to get a sense for what's happening to me. I can't see it. Come on." She reached for his hand. "No one's around and we have the privacy to do this."

"Ava, I don't have a great feeling about this. I've already seen you with the London stone. Why do you want to put yourself through this?"

"The London stone doesn't cause me to go into a nightmarish world of death and destruction. I want to see if you can understand it any better than I can. As an observer."

Much as she wanted to deny it—wanted to run and hide from the truth—these stones did hold power over her. Her best defense against them was to understand what she was up against.

What *they* were up against.

His large fingers threaded through hers, infusing her with warmth. "Are you sure you're ready?"

"Yes. And you'll be with me the entire time."

Something flickered in his eyes as his hand tightened on hers, but quickly gave way to a reassuring smile as he moved in toward her. "I won't let anything happen to you. You have to believe me on that."

He moved in, the warmth of his body arcing toward her as he stepped closer. Warm, glorious heat filled her as he wrapped his arms around her, pulling her close.

"I do believe you."

"I'm not going to let anything happen to you." His lips whispered along the length of her jaw before he shifted, pressing his mouth to hers. Warmth flooded her system, chasing away the lingering cold at the prospect of what she was about to do—to see.

The heat spread out, a languid wanting, as his tongue toyed with hers, filling her mouth and mimicking the joy they found in their bodies.

And as they stood there, mere yards away from the nightmare that had haunted her for decades, she acknowledged what she felt for Brody. Accepted and understood that in the midst of a situation she still couldn't quite believe, she'd found someone who'd finally let her see herself.

The person she *could* be.

The woman she *wanted* to be.

Could it really be possible?

"I won't let anything happen to you." Ava pulled back to stare up at him, his words arrowing straight to her heart. Deep pools of blue stared back at her, willing strength into her with each passing second. "You *can* do this."

"I know. Because you're with me." She took a deep breath. "Let's go."

They moved hand in hand toward the gem room that held the Summoning Stone. She passed her beloved rubies, barely able to make out their shapes in the muted security lighting. Despite her having chosen this course of action, anxiety whipped through her stomach and a bead of sweat did a slow roll between her shoulder blades. Step by step, they moved closer, but the nightmarish images didn't come.

Standing before the glass, Ava stared at the stone. The pulsing sense of evil was there, but the images weren't. She closed her eyes, half relieved, half curious as to why they hadn't come. Her stomach was devoid of food. Her eyelids drooped with the need for sleep after Brody's oh-so-thorough lovemaking. Her nerve endings were ragged with confusion at all she'd learned in the past few days.

But still, the stone simply sat before the glass. The cool blue surface held her gaze with its malevolent force. The smooth edges still seemed to pulse. But beyond that— nothing.

"What do you see, Ava?"

Brody's voice broke through her thoughts. With a confused sigh, she turned to look at him. "I don't feel anything at all."

"The feelings you've had before? They're gone?"

"It's odd. I've never been this close to it before. Never been able to just look at it."

He squeezed her hand. "What do you think of it?"

"I can feel the madness in it."

"How?"

"It pulses. That's the only way I can describe it. It pulses like a heart, nestled there in the velvet. I can still feel that. Can see it, even though I know it's not moving. But beyond that, nothing."

"That's good."

She turned toward him, unable to keep the note of hope

out of her words, and with a small smile, she nodded. "Yes, it's very good."

"Let's get you out of here, then." He dropped her hand, extending his now-free arm to wrap around her.

That simple movement was all it took.

When Brody broke contact, the images flooded her system in a flash, sharp as razors slicing her mind to ribbons. Writhing snakes snapped at her, their fangs sharp in the light of smoke and fire. Their sinuous bodies standing on edge, reaching out for her, hissing before moving in toward her, ready to attack. Bile rose up in her throat and the smell of blood was so strong, the metallic odor translated to her taste buds.

A scream worked its way up her throat, ringing with shrill tones in the depths of her eardrums.

She passed out as two snakes lunged forward, heading for her throat.

"Fuck!" Brody caught her as she fell toward the glass, arms outstretched, fingers curled as if ready to scratch at whatever imagined thing was in front of her.

Panic slid deep into his veins as she struggled in his arms, her screams growing more and more shrill, her arm movements more erratic.

"Ava. Shhh, Ava. You're safe. You're okay."

He tried crooning to her, as he'd done when she'd awoken from the nightmare on the airplane, but it did nothing to calm her; nothing to bring her back.

Every tense inch of her body quivered as screams continued to spill from her throat. Panic glazed her eyes and he could actually smell the fear as it rose off her skin.

His own fear fisted in his stomach as he swept her up in

his arms, moving into a run as soon as he had a firm grip on her. He kept his hold tight, willing his strength into her. Willing an end to the nightmare that held her in its thrall.

They cleared the gem room and continued on. In a blur, they moved past displays of various cultures, then farther on past a special exhibit for children. Her screams died down with each foot he put between them and the stone, but her eyes remained glazed even as her screams faded into helpless whimpers.

Stupid, fucking stupid, thing to do. And yet another miscalculation when it came to Ava and whatever miserable mess was unfolding.

The bright light of an exit sign caught the edge of his vision and he slowed as they hit a stairwell. He took a few steps, dropping to sit on the top step so he could take a quick assessment of their situation.

He glanced down at her huddled form as her fingers dug into the soft material of his T-shirt. Tremors wracked her as if she were in a fever, and he tightened his hold on her.

The fear in his stomach shifted, redirected and coiled in his heart. Tension constricted his chest and he wondered— not for the first time—what it was about this woman that called to him so deeply.

"Ava." He kept his voice soft but firm. "Come on, baby. Look at me."

He squeezed her again, pulling her close in the same movement someone would use to calm a crying baby.

Comfort.

Warmth.

Protection.

"Ava!"

"Brody?" Her chocolate brown eyes cleared as the nightmare receded, coming into focus as she looked up at him.

Stark terror hummed a vicious tune through his body, but he kept his voice light and airy. "You're back with me?"

The screams had dropped her already-husky voice another octave. "Who, me? Sure. I was just practicing my horror-movie tryout. A girl's gotta be prepared for the day she gets discovered, after all."

The fist in his chest eased ever so slightly at her ability to make a joke. "And quite a performance it was. I wasn't sure you were coming back."

She pushed at him, struggling to sit upward. "I wondered the same thing."

"Want to tell me about it?"

She shifted, slid off his lap and moved so that she was sitting upright next to him on the stairs. He kept an arm firmly around her shoulders as the tremors wracking her system faded under the comfort of his touch.

"It's always the same. It starts out where I'm observing a horrible sacrifice, but as I get deeper into it, it's clear that I am the sacrifice."

"Is that all?"

"Snakes and the smell of blood. It's like the worst nightmare you can possibly conjure, ramped up on acid."

"You did acid?"

She shot him a wry smile and the tense knots slipped yet again. "Prim, proper me?"

"You went to college."

"And spent all my time studying. Besides"—she leaned her head against his shoulder—"there are enough unwanted images in my head, I've no desire to add any new ones to them."

His smile faltered at her words and he cursed himself for his insensitivity. Of course someone with her background would avoid anything that smacked of loss of control.

Or anything that suggested mind-altering properties.

"Ava, I'm sorry."

She shifted and looked up at him, her eyes filled with trust. "I know."

She believed in him.

He didn't deserve it and he sure as hell hadn't earned it. But there was no way he was letting go of her.

"Is Enyo always like this?"

"Like what?"

"Well . . . missing."

The lines around Brody's eyes crinkled as he considered her words. "What do you mean by 'missing'?"

"I don't know. Clearly I've never run up against her before, but she's like this mythical thing behind the scenes. These bad dudes of hers come out of nowhere to wreak havoc, then go away. But *she's* missing."

Ava reached for the contraband coffeepot she'd smuggled into her office her first week at the museum. As she refilled her second cup, she marveled at the restorative smell of French roast. Brody was still on his first as he added three more packets of sugar to his half-empty cup.

"You really do have the most horrific eating habits; you know that."

"I consider it the benefit of a supernatural metabolism."

"You can sign me up for one of those," Ava muttered as she took another sip of her black coffee.

"Your metabolism is gorgeous and fine." He took a sip of his coffee, then added, "Seriously, though. You make an interesting point. Something has been off about this op from the start."

"Talk it through with me, then."

"Well, two months ago, on the dig in Egypt, this worker was killed early on—by a messy gunshot wound. So not Enyo's style."

"What is her style?"

"Impatient. Brash. She's a killing machine and that is her core focus. She's a bit weaker on strategy, but her jobs are fast and expedient."

Ava took another sip of her coffee, glad she'd initiated this discussion. She was a woman of learning. Not having thought to learn everything she could about her opponent was a serious misstep. "So tell me about her."

"First, there's the issue of balance between her and us."

"More balance?"

"Consider it my theme. For every battle we fight, the winner gains strength while the loser gets some taken away. She's lost quite a few in a row now, so she has to be hurting pretty bad. We suspected she'd sit back and lick her wounds for a while."

"Maybe it's made her more urgent. More determined."

He cocked his head, that glorious mane of hair framing his face in luscious waves. "Good point."

"What else can you tell me about her?"

"Well, all the Greek gods have something that passes as a moral code, whether it be a basic sense of honor, or even just a greater respect for the higher order of how things work."

"Not Enyo?" she said, guessing.

"Nope. The only gods who rival her are Deimos and Phobos, her freaky nephews."

"Dread and fear?"

"You really do know your mythology."

"So why can't the other gods keep her in check?"

"They do, sort of. I mean, the whole balance issue was designed by Themis and Zeus to keep all of us in line."

"So how does she get around it?"

"She's got one great big ace in the hole. Humanity."

"But she's a Greek god. What does that have to do with human beings?"

Brody poured himself another cup of coffee as he tried to figure out a way to explain what he meant.

In all the years of his life, he'd seen the repeating patterns. The never-ending cycle of aggression and greed. Every century brought new challenges, as they played out the pages of history, but at their core, the stories were all the same.

Humans across the world, in every age, fought for dominance over one another.

And like puppets on a string, in every case where human situations escalated in the worst of ways, there sat Enyo.

She'd whispered visions of power to Alexander the Great.

Promised endless dominance to Napoleon.

Guaranteed absolute supremacy to Hitler.

He and his brothers had won each of those battles, and so many others over the years, but not without cost—not without horrific, soul-rending consequence to the humans caught in the cross fire.

Themis had called it balance. That had been her answer the one time he'd dared ask her—dared to suggest—whether their role as humanity's protectors was a doomed endeavor.

But they'd made a promise and each and every one of them soldiered on, century after century. Brothers forged together in a vow to the goddess of justice. Never, in all that time, had he regretted his vow. Or wished things were different. Or wondered why he'd been called into Themis's service.

Until now.

Even at his lowest moment, when he'd lost his first love, he hadn't questioned his service to Themis.

But if he lost Ava?

There would be no saving him.

Chapter Eighteen

"**Y**ou know, Bill, it is just so hard to see you like this. I have to believe Russell is rolling in his grave, knowing this is what you've come to."

Dr. William Martin stared through the ancient prison bars in the depths of Enyo's lair. His greasy hair lay plastered to his head, and his eyes—usually so bright with intelligent vigor—looked dead and lifeless.

Although Wyatt always hated being down in the subway tunnels, staring at his dead brother's best friend felt so far past creepy, it bordered on a nightmare.

Dr. William Martin lifted a finger, then dropped his hand as if the simple gesture took too much effort. "You killed Russell. I'll maintain it to the end of my days."

"Bill. Come on. My own brother?"

A large, emaciated rat scurried around Martin's feet, weaving in and out. "You might not have pulled the trigger, but you killed him. I know it." Those lifeless eyes lit up with a blaze of fire. "You're a murderer."

Rage flew through Wyatt's body. Pristine little fucker. He'd show him. "Fine. Now cut the crap. I need answers."

"I have nothing. I've told that bitch and I'm telling you."

"Bullshit. You were with Russell in the tomb when he discovered the stones. You know what they can do." Wyatt felt his anger building, that familiar rage that never failed to rear its head at the mere thought of his sainted brother.

"Do? They don't *do* anything."

"Yes, they do. You know they have power."

William shook his head. "You're as crazy as she is. Is this why you have me down here? Those damn stones. Bad luck is all they are. They were bad luck for Russell." Bill looked around the old crumbling stone. "They obviously are for me, too."

"They have power."

"No, Wyatt. You *think* they have power. There's a big difference."

Wyatt looked at Dr. Martin, the man who'd been far closer to Russell than he had. *He* was the older brother. He should have been Russell's mentor. Friend. Confidant.

Instead, this scholarly toady had that role. Bill had been his brother's best friend, there for Russell's crowning accomplishment.

Wyatt tried again, his voice sympathetic. "You really don't think the stones have power?"

Despite the days on end of mental and physical torture, despite the missed meals, despite Enyo's best depravity, the eyes that stared back at Wyatt through the prison bars were clear. "No. I don't. But you do, don't you? You always did. Is that why you killed him? Or has this all been a convenient little excuse to take care of a bigger problem, Wyatt? Does this all go back to how insecure he made you feel? Mommy's little boy. Russell told me all about it."

The words hit Wyatt square in the center of his chest, the implication clear. Even now, all these years later, he remembered Bill and his brother, the archeological team, digging their way to fame and glory.

And what had he had? Jack shit.

A cushy job at a variety of museums until they figured him out. Figured out he had no talent. And Mommy had to bail him out and get him the next job.

"It was you, wasn't it?" Martin whispered. "You're the one who sold me out to that bitch?"

"I believe she was honest and upfront with you from the start. Tell us what you know. Come clean and you are a free man."

"I don't know anything."

"Oh, but I think you do." Wyatt turned and headed for the door, the rage that swam in his veins barely contained as he put one foot in front of the other. Right. Left. Right. Left.

He almost had it under control by the time he reached the doorway. No one appreciated him, but damn it, by the time this was over, they *would* respect him.

All of them.

"I'll let Enyo know she needs to pay you another visit. See if she can jog loose those memories of yours. The truth is in your memories, Bill. Perhaps you just need a bit more persuading to pull them out."

"How can you find anything in there?"

Ava's muffled voice flew back from the inside of her closet. He wanted to help her, but aside from the very real fact they wouldn't both fit in there, he was enjoying the sight of her delectable ass far too much to move.

She backed out of the closet, a triumphant smile plastered on her face and both hands full of leather-bound journals.

"Found them."

"I really don't know how."

She gave him a friendly swat on his shoulder as she settled on the floor next to him.

"He dated them, so we should find out pretty quickly if I have the last journal he wrote in."

"Even if you do have it, do you think he'd have written his true thoughts, for anyone to see?" Brody hated to be the voice of reason, but there was a strong possibility there weren't any answers, only leather-bound memories spread around them on the floor.

"Only one way to find out." Ava brushed at the worn leather cover in her hands, then flipped through the one on top of the stack. "Wrong date."

Brody reached for the next one, quickly coming to the same conclusion.

They were about halfway through the stack when Ava shook her head. "He journaled throughout his professional life. I don't know why I didn't think to look at these earlier. I didn't even think to use passages in the exhibit."

"This is private, Ava. You couldn't have used it for the exhibit. Surely you wouldn't think to put your personal life—and the personal aspects of your father's work—on display."

"No, I guess not."

He leaned over and pressed a kiss to her nose. "I guess not."

Her eyes darted back toward the book in her lap as excitement threaded her voice. "Okay. Wait. Listen to this. It's dated about five days before his death." Her husky voice rose up in the quiet of the room. *"I'm heading home to see my darling Ava today. I know I can't take the stones with me, but I can't bear to be parted from them. The antiquities groups will have my head if they find out, but it's a quick trip and she's my little girl, after all. And I simply must show her, so*

I'll take one. One will be enough for her to see—for her to understand—the great glory that rests in the stones."

"So that's how he showed it to you."

Ava looked up from the journal, her eyes glazed with the distant memories coming to life before her on the page. "What do you mean, that's how he showed it?"

"When you told me the other day about the first time you saw the stone. I couldn't imagine how he managed to get it here—get around the red tape." A broad smile crested his cheeks as a well of bad-boy admiration sprang up in his chest. "That sly dog smuggled it home."

"Fat lot of good it did either of us. That smuggled stone caused problems for my grandmother for years. The authorities frown on removing antiquities before they've been properly analyzed and awarded to the highest bidding museum."

"All she had to do was send it back."

Now it was Ava's turn to smile. "Yeah, well, when she started to argue that it was on his person and that she—or by default, I, when I was of age—should inherit his belongings, she made quite a stink."

Brody mock-shuddered. "She's a scary woman."

"Don't I know it."

Ava buried her head back in the book, a smile on her face as she flipped through the last few pages. "Hey. Wait."

"What?"

"This one. The one he wrote on the day he died. Oh my God, Brody. Read this." She handed him the book and he began to read the last passage.

I never should have brought the stone home. Never should have even looked for it. I regret the discovery and would take every bit of it back if I could.

I nearly hurt my daughter today. I shoved her at the stone. The one I smuggled home. The one that speaks to me.

One minute I was there, in my office with her, and the next I was gone—lost in the lore of the ancients, a willing participant in a ritual blood sacrifice.

I know Ava felt it, too. Felt the power in the stones. The quivering in her body and the sheer terror when I finally let go of her let me know she sees the same things I do.

Maybe even more.

I must destroy the stones. If the rumored prophecy is true, they wield a horrible power.

Why did I ever think to look for them? What folly let me think I could rise above five thousand years of madness and the power of the gods?

What have I done to my child, exposing my beloved Ava to this horror? I must save her.

The stones have power over Ava and I cannot—I will not—give her to them.

Brody lay with Ava's head pillowed against his shoulder, his hands making soothing circles along the curve of her back.

"He was going to give it up for me." Ava still couldn't believe the words in her father's journal. The incredible love and devotion that lived on the page, written in his own hand.

She was more important to him than the stones. More than his job. More than anything.

She had mattered.

"The power you've felt is real. He felt it, too, Ava. Your status as a Chosen One is obviously carried through your bloodline. Your father was chosen, too."

"But we're not Egyptian and we didn't descend from that part of the world. Trust me, Grandmother has traced our ancestry with maniacal precision."

"But it found you. Maybe this was your father's life's work because the stones called to him."

The idea took root, forming in her mind as she thought about it. "As though he was meant to find them?"

"Exactly."

"Do you think that's possible?"

"Yes, I do."

Ava reveled in the warmth of Brody's arms; she felt her spirit soar in the security she found there.

"You know, if this is true, we should be able to use the stones to our advantage."

"Use them? Ava, the power they wield is dangerous. I want to keep you as far away from them as possible."

She scrambled up to sit next to him, pushing the hair out of her face. "Yes, but if I truly am the Key, what if I can use them for good?"

"No way. Absolutely not. Haven't you heard the old adage?"

She pasted on a sickeningly sweet smile and batted her eyelashes. "Day late, dollar short?"

His blue eyes grew dark. "No. Absolute power corrupts absolutely."

Spoilsport. Besides, he was one to talk. "You've got a hell of a lot of power and you're not corrupted."

"I have a great big system of checks and balances on my head, too."

"Themis?"

"Exactly."

"I still think we can use them."

"Use them to do what?"

"Draw Enyo out."

Ava couldn't get the idea out of her head. If they could use the stones to draw Enyo out, they could also find a way to get rid of her. If the Summoning Stones truly had power over all things in the universe, then it would stand to reason it would work on a Greek goddess.

No matter how big a bitch she was.

And if it didn't work? Well then, the stones would lose their appeal to Enyo, too.

Brody stepped back into the bedroom. "Just talked to Kane. We're porting to Paris in a few hours. It'll be morning there and we can retrieve the third stone."

"The sex stone, you mean?"

He shrugged as he moved in close. "I've got a one-in-three shot at being right. I'm taking those odds. It *is* Paris, after all."

"We'll be sure to test it when you get back. I can't imagine what visions that stone will give me."

He pulled her close, his mouth finding hers with unerring precision. "As long as you promise to act them out with me."

She leaned into the kiss, captivated by the mischievous smile that tilted the ends of his lips. "Now, I have another question for you. Are you ready to pay attention?"

"I'm paying attention."

"Then you can tell me if you're ready to use that erection"—she glanced down at the bulge in the front of his jeans—"or if you're going to take it all the way to Paris with you."

And then he made his decision crystal clear as one of

his hands curled in the material of her shirt, while the other one gripped the back of her head, crushing her mouth to his.

Brody smiled through the kiss, the feelings she brought to life in him flaring with white-hot light.

Oh gods, how had he lived his life without her? The mere contact of her mouth was more enticing—more erotic—than anything he'd ever experienced.

The firm crest of her belly cradled his erection as she pulled him toward her bed. As he held on to her, they fell backward on the bed in a tangle of limbs. Brody reached for her, so impatient to remove the barrier of clothing that he dragged her top over her head, catching on the back of her bra and carrying it along. Her pants soon followed his into a large heap on the floor.

Shifting, he lay back on the bed and drew Ava so that she sat astride his hips. Her breasts jutted toward him, her nipples a bright pink in sharp relief on her pale, luminescent skin.

Reverently, he reached up to touch one rosy peak, satisfied when she arched into his touch. With short strokes of his callused fingers, he pulled at her tender flesh, a growl building in the pit of his stomach when the distended tip grew even harder under his questing fingers.

Impatient to have her underneath him, Brody shifted their bodies so the down comforter was at her back. He took one nipple in his mouth while he used his fingers to pluck at the other, feeling it grow hard in his palm. Soft, sweet moans greeted his ears as he laved his tongue over that sensitive peak, drawing on her in deep, sucking waves.

In unconscious rhythm, her hips undulated in sexy circles, the lush scent of her filling the air and driving his already-stretched senses into overdrive. He moved his hand from her breast, running his fingers over her body in tender yet unyielding strokes, over the underside of her breast, past the firm skin of her belly and farther on to the blond curls that hid the core of her femininity.

Another growl escaped him as his fingers met her hot, slick center. A surge of power flooded his veins as she let out a long, low moan when his thumb brushed over her clitoris.

He'd pleasure her until her mind was numb from the sheer bliss of their joining, until she couldn't see for the pleasure, until she was moaning his name and begging him not to stop.

"Brody." He felt her hands on his cheeks before he registered her voice.

"Yes, darling."

"This is about us."

His body was on fire and his ability to conjure a coherent thought was limited, but this he knew. "It's about you."

She held his shoulders—he could feel the light pressure of her palms there and she pressed at him. "No. It's about us. *Both* of us."

When he could only stare at her, she smiled, shifting her weight until she was back on top of him. "Here. Let me show you."

Those long, slender fingers of hers drifted over his chest, her fingernails scraping over his nipples, shooting hot sparks straight through him.

"Ava?"

"Mmmm . . . hmmmm." Her lips followed her fingers as hot suction covered his nipple while her hands ran circles over his stomach muscles.

He tried to fight through the pleasure; he tried to make

her stop, but he was helpless before her as she navigated the length of his body.

And then she shifted, her hands on the full length of his cock, and he nearly came off the bed. A small, triumphant smile crossed her features as she drew one long, low groan from deep in the back of his throat. With torturous movements, she stroked him in one long, tight grip, from base to tip and back again.

His body arched into her touch, her expert strokes pulling wave after wave of pleasure through his body.

"This isn't—," he panted, trying desperately to figure out how to regain the upper hand and desperately wishing he didn't have to. "This isn't how it's supposed to be. This moment is for you. A prop-proper send-off before I leave."

"Oh, but it is, Brody Talbot. This moment is as much about me as it is about you." And then there were no words as her hand fisted around the base and with skillful movements she pumped his flesh. "It's time to shut up and take it, big guy."

He knew it the moment he lost the battle. His head fell back against the pillow and his hips moved to the rhythm she set as he pressed himself into her.

So good.

So hot.

So *necessary*.

Waves of power crashed through his life force as she pumped him—great, glorious waves of pleasure that tightened his body and freed his soul.

Somewhere along the way she managed to shift the position of her body on the bed. And then he figured out why as the position of her hands shifted, too. Opening his eyes, he momentarily forgot the sensual haze she wove around them when he realized she wasn't kneeling next to him.

Then he couldn't think at all as her hot mouth wrapped around his cock, drawing every rational thought from his head. Although her movements weren't nearly as sure with her mouth as they'd been with her hands, the tentative, daring strokes of her tongue slammed sensation after sensation through him in blistering waves. Mind-numbing pleasure crashed into him as her tongue seduced. Enslaved. Enraptured.

Completely helpless and utterly exposed to her, he was powerless to resist her.

Utterly vulnerable and open to her.

Helpless to deny her.

Her tongue was like a brand as she worked it around his cock. Sharp, little darts at the tip were followed by wet suction as she worked her way down over the crown; then lapping waves of pleasure as she caressed down to the base.

Over and over, she drew on him with her hot, wet mouth, driving him more and more deliberately toward his moment of greatest physical defenselessness.

He knew the moment he'd gone around the bend. His already-tight body grew even harder, the urge to spill himself something he couldn't fight any longer.

With determination that matched that of the generous woman before him, he gripped her shoulders, pulling her up. Ignoring her protests, he crashed his mouth to hers. "I can't wait any longer. I have to have you."

Shifting their bodies, he rolled them over, her beautiful nipples hard points as they pressed to his chest.

She reached down and guided him into her body, the mere touch of her hand nearly sending him off. Gritting his teeth, he sank himself into her warm, welcoming wetness, a loud groan coming from him as the tight sheath she made wrapped around him.

Mindless, beyond rational thought, he thrust into her, her movements matched to his as light streamed in the window and over their bodies.

Without knowing how, he held on until he felt the telltale response begin in her very core, the tightening of her muscles as her orgasm began. With a loud, glorious shout, he followed.

As the very essence of himself spilled into her, his life force roared through his veins.

His mouth sought hers and as his tongue took possession, tangled up in hers, he knew he'd never be the same.

Never.

Chapter Nineteen

"You want to do what?" Quinn's rapt expression—eyes fully focused on her and his BlackBerry firmly in his pocket—had a small smile ghosting Ava's lips. So . . . despite his ability to multitask, even the Bull needed to fully focus on things sometimes.

"Brody and Kane need to finish picking up the rest of the stones and then we use them to draw Enyo out."

"Should have just ported immediately after London. Why are we wasting time?" Kane muttered.

Quinn shot him a nasty look and Brody stepped in, narrowly avoiding a fistfight, if Ava wasn't mistaken.

"Even our stubborn and resourceful Bull couldn't get the museums to part with their stones early."

"What a load of bullshit," Quinn added. "Each museum already agreed to being a part of the exhibit. We should be able to damn well move the stones when we want to."

Ava couldn't help the shift into curator mode. "Actually, these items bring in thousands, if not hundreds of thousands, of dollars a day in visitors. Every day the stone isn't in the collection is a day of lost revenue."

Quinn muttered something she couldn't hear as they all turned toward Kane. "How are we going to get Enyo out in the open?"

The Scorpio had arrived at the mansion shortly after her and Brody and had been prowling the halls ever since. Brody had filled her in on what had happened between Kane and the other MI6 agent and, if she wasn't mistaken, there was a raw element to his demeanor that was unmistakable.

Unmistakably, he was in love.

What's this about, Ava Marie? You fall in love and suddenly everyone else has to be, too.

And as the thought crossed her mind, another one followed, sucking the air from her lungs and driving her to sit on the luxurious leather couch in Quinn's study.

Love.

She was in love? With Brody?

One look at him where he stood across the room and she knew. Fighting it was pointless—silly, really. She was so in love with that man, it was amazing it wasn't visibly coming out of her pores.

Correct that. It probably was some wonderful pheromone that told the whole world she was totally, utterly and completely in love with him.

"Earth to Ava. You okay, baby?" Brody sat down next to her on the couch.

"Oh. Sorry. Yeah." She heard the dazed, breathy quality in her voice and fought for focus. "So what we need to do is bring the stones together and then tempt her to them. You do know how to reach Enyo, right?"

Kane and Brody nodded, while Quinn added dryly, "When she feels like being reached."

"How does one go about reaching a goddess?"

"We can get a message to her on Mount Olympus," Brody said, patting her back.

"Where will we meet her?"

"I want the meet on Mount Olympus, too," Quinn interjected. "It's her home turf, but it's also filled to the brim with gods and goddesses. If Ava truly has the power over the stones we think she does, it's not going to sit well with the Pantheon. They'll side against Enyo if they think both the stones, and Ava's power to use them, is a threat to their existence."

"Will they hurt me? The gods and goddesses?" An unexpected sense of dread filled her. "If all that power makes them mad, I mean."

"No one will touch you. I promise," Brody added. "But Quinn's right. Mount Olympus is the best place to deal with the stones."

Kane shifted from foot to foot. "You ready?"

Ava laid a hand on Brody's forearm. "Can I talk to you before you go?"

Kane and Quinn hightailed it out of the room before she could even ask as Brody swooped in and nuzzled her throat. "I think we have time for some other things before I go, too."

"Brody." She giggled, swatting at his shoulders. "Come on, Brody. You need to get there and back. Get this moving."

"I'm building my strength."

"Seeing as how we had a quickie before we left my apartment, I'd say you've got plenty of strength."

He looked up from nuzzling her neck, a broad smile covering his face. "You can't blame a guy for trying."

"No, you can't."

They sat there like that, heartbeats stretching out one after the other until she felt as if she'd burst if she didn't say it; if she didn't tell him exactly what she felt in her heart. "I love you, Brody Talbot."

Brody shifted until they faced each other on the couch, his movements slow and deliberate.

Oh God. Stupid, stupid, stupid, Ava. You never say it first. Never. Ever. Nev—

Brody got to his feet and pulled her up with him. Drawing her close with one arm, he used his free hand to cup her chin and pull up her face. Eyes level, his gaze seared into her, like a brand on her heart. "Say that to me again, Ava."

Fire crawled a blazing path up her throat toward her cheeks. "Brody, come on. Don't embarrass me."

"I'm not embarrassing you. I love you. And I want to hear you say it."

His words echoed through her, soaring through her heart like a bird taking wing. As she took in the warm look in his eyes, she couldn't have held the words back if she tried. "I love you, Brody."

With infinite sweetness he bent his head and laid his lips against hers. With whispered words, he murmured against her mouth, "Then on that we are agreed."

"Tourist. You're supposed to blend in and look like a tourist," Kane hissed at him as they moved through the throngs of people at the Louvre.

"I *am* blending."

"You look like a hit man."

Brody shot him a wry grin. "Takes one to know one."

"And this would be why you don't get put on stealth detail very often. Quit acting like the king of the pride and do the damn job."

Brody growled and continued to push his way through

the throngs of people in one of the museum's most well-visited halls. "You take care of MacIntyre?"

"Yeah, got it covered. Son's being moved to an intensive care facility with specialized treatments, courtesy of MI6. Mother's heading for a rehabilitation facility for a while."

"Ava's worried about her."

Kane grinned at him as they sidestepped a woman with a double stroller. "She already asked me about them."

Brody shook his head. If he weren't so blindingly in love with the woman, it might not make him so damn mad. "The woman held a gun on her *and* tried to turn us over to Destroyers. And Ava's worried about her."

"You don't like it because you don't see the world that way."

"Excuse me?"

"You want to run the show, Leo, king of the jungle. And the moment someone crosses you or tries to do it differently, you get all bent out of shape. We let you work alone for a reason."

Brody came to a halt behind the long line of people waiting for their chance to look at the stone. "You *let* me work alone?"

"It's the reason the guys leave me alone, too. Come on, you don't miss me all the way across the pond, do you?"

"Not like it's hard to find you when we need you."

"Exactly. So in the meantime, you're happy to leave me off on my own."

Brody thought through the rest of his comrades, images of each one snapping in and out of focus. He was part of the North American brotherhood, driven by the skies in that part of the world. They used New York for the anonymity it provided, then maintained rural outposts in Idaho, the Arizona desert and a large ranch in Texas to further conduct business.

Some band of brothers they were.

How often did he see any of them? Either because of his own travels or those of his fellow Warriors?

Grey and Quinn were loners, too, their Ram and Bull tendencies making them increasingly difficult to work with. Kieran and Pierce had each other, biological brothers with their Gemini bond forged in their infancy that empowered them even as it kept them distinctly separate from the rest of the Warriors. Aidan, Rafe, Drake, Gage and Rogan had all been on missions for the better part of a year, taking care of their own leads, using their innate areas of strength to maintain order.

Max was so damn busy building Capricorn Communications, they saw less and less of him as he sought to rule the world of telecommunications. Xander had sunk deeper into his pre-Warrior memories, his search for a killer the driving force of his life.

What had happened to all of them? These men he'd transitioned with, fought with, lived with. What had happened to all of them?

Where they used to be a universe in sync with one another, now they were like separate planets, spinning in their own orbit.

"It's not as though the rest of our little band of merry men are all that well adjusted."

"No, but we've got some predetermined personality traits that don't help. Come on, Brody. We're all pretty fucked up and don't play well with others. As technology has made it easier to stay in touch remotely, those traits have only gotten worse."

He knew the truth of Kane's words—lived it. Hell, he hadn't seen the Scorpio in almost two years prior to this job. He had a basic sense of the man's work for MI6—a broad idea of where he was and how to get a hold of him at any given time—but beyond that, no contact.

"So what? Are you suggesting we need to create a little coffee klatch and visit with one another every week?"

His dropped mouth and wide eyes would have been funny under other circumstances. "Hell no. I'm just saying we need to accept we're all doing our own thing. We pull together when we have to, but when we don't . . ."

The thought hung there, heavy between them as they approached the visitor desk. Was this what Themis wanted? What she'd intended when she made her great arrangement with Zeus? A band of brothers only when it was convenient for all parties involved?

Brody and Kane smiled at the attendant and shared their retrieval papers.

Museum security arrived exactly thirty seconds later, guns drawn.

Brody and Kane made the last port into Sydney, but they already knew what they'd find. Polite chitchat with museum security as they showed their paperwork. A puzzled frown from the museum director as he kindly reminded Brody that he'd *already* picked up the stone. Panicked fury when the museum realized it had been duped.

The stones had been stolen.

"Dr. Talbot, surely you know I need to report this."

Although Brody's anger hadn't diminished one bit, it had changed since his first trip to Paris, then to Alexandria where the situation had grown more clear.

"Trust me, consider it reported. Emerald Security is all over this one."

The debate raged back and forth, with Brody and Kane doing their level best to calm the agitated museum director who now knew a multimillion-dollar piece had just gone missing from his collection.

Three hours later, he and Kane finished in Sydney and ported back to the mansion. Everyone was assembled and waiting for them.

Ava was across the room and in his arms in a heartbeat. "What's wrong?"

"The stones are gone. All of them."

"How?"

Brody gritted his teeth at Quinn's question. Fuck if he knew how. "Apparently my *twin* has done us the great service of retrieving the stones. Cleared security and was a good enough match with my picture and credentials Quinn sent on ahead that no one questioned it."

He felt Ava's calming touch on his forearm, amazed that something that simple could feel so good.

"Your twin?"

Kane brought the rest of them up to speed on what they'd discovered. The paperwork had matched what he and Brody carried. They'd even looked at security footage and seen someone who looked just like Brody coming into each museum and retrieving the stones.

"Is that a power you have?"

"What, Ava?" Quinn was the first to respond, sharp interest in his tone.

"Morphing into another person. Is that a skill you all have?"

Lots of head shaking and a few nos.

"Is it a skill Enyo has?"

Brody looked thoughtful. "Theoretically, if she wanted to, she could try it. But granting a power like that would be a huge drain on her resources."

"But why?"

"It all goes back to the basic laws that govern our bodies. The energy that makes up our life force. Everything lives in our life force. Therefore everything must balance. If Enyo gave that power to someone else, she'd have to give up something of herself."

For the first time since this all started, Ava felt the loss of time as it slipped away.

If they were fighting an enemy who could take the form of anyone, they'd never catch them.

"Well, one thing's clear," said Brody, interrupting her thoughts.

"What is it, Talbot?" Quinn's sharp gaze immediately found Brody.

"We need to get to the museum and get the New York stone under our guard."

Brody ported them into Ava's office. Ava looked around the darkened room, the place she'd spent so many endless hours of her life, and barely recognized it.

It was a part of her old life.

A life she wondered if she'd ever get back to.

Or if she even wanted to.

Without any time to analyze what they were doing, Ava and Brody took off at a run for the gem wing. "I'll know, Brody. I'll know if it isn't real." She shot him a goofy smile. "Clearly, my chosen status can come in handy from time to time."

They ran around a group of schoolchildren, several nannies and their charges, and a businessman or two before they hit the gem wing.

"Take it easy, Ava. It won't do us any good for you to run up to it and pass out. Here. Take my hand. That will mitigate the effects."

As his strong fingers closed around her own, Ava felt a warmth suffuse her. This was real and oh so right. She'd finally come home.

They walked up to the stone, waiting their turn in line. From the corner of her eye, Ava could see Brody's furtive glances as he tried to identify if anyone suspicious was already there waiting for them.

When he gave her a reassuring hand squeeze, she figured they were clear.

Three people to go. Then two. And then she and Brody stood before the case.

Had it only been a matter of hours since she'd last stood here?

"You ready?"

"Yep." She nodded, squeezed his hand one last time and then let go.

Ava waited. Waited for the writhing snakes and the horrible metallic taste of blood, but nothing came.

It was a fake.

"Oh my God, Brody. It's gone."

He nodded, then took her hand and pulled them toward the exit. "Your office. We'll port from there, away from any security cameras."

As Brody practically dragged her the last fifty yards to her office, it didn't register on either of them until they were through the door that they hadn't turned on the lights.

Ava sensed it a moment before she felt it. Dr. Martin had her in a choke hold and had dragged her across the room before she could blink.

Brody watched in helpless frustration as Dr. Martin dragged Ava across the room and out of his range so he couldn't port her to safety. A knife glittered in the doctor's free hand, already wobbling dangerously close to Ava's body as he shoved her across the room.

Shit. Fuck. Damn.

Dr. Martin smiled at Brody. "I can see by the looks on your faces that you've finally figured out we have a problem. Bravo!"

"Who are you?" Ava fought at the arm around her neck, but the slight man held her steady, belying a strength Brody normally wouldn't have associated with a man of Dr. Martin's size.

Brody willed her to be still, even as fiery rage bounced through his system like a caffeine buzz on crack.

Some asshole has his hands on my woman. The thought ran through his head on a loop, driving him into a deeper frenzy with each playback.

Forcing the anger back, Brody tried to take account of what he knew.

The man standing across from him was not Dr. William Martin.

Whoever *was* standing across the room was burning a lot of fuel to keep the appearance of Martin.

The stone wasn't in the room. Ava's lucid features told him that, and the fire in her eyes confirmed it. Instead of the fear and horror he'd seen in her previous exposure to the death stone, now there was only the will to fight and claw her way free.

"Where's the stone?"

Martin shook his head. "I think I'd like to play a different game first. It's a game I like to call guess who."

Brody wasn't going to give him the satisfaction. He'd waited long enough for answers, and he was going to get them, even if he had to puzzle them together. "Were you in Egypt for the discovery of the prophecy?"

"I did spend a bit of time in the Valley of the Kings recently, come to think of it."

"So it was you who killed Ahmet, wasn't it?"

"I don't keep worthless, squealing spies on my payroll. Especially once their family legend about a silly little prophecy is on the verge of discovery."

Brody decided to explore that one, see if he could hit a nerve and get a response. "Enyo's not very fond of anyone who wants to call the shots for her. She knows you were there?"

Brody saw Ava's eye flick downward to the crook of the doctor's arm and realized his diversionary tactics were beginning to work. Dr. Martin's sleeve, over his elbow, was changing colors. The tweed suit he *appeared* to be wearing had started flickering at the elbow—tweed to gray T-shirt material and back to tweed again. "She doesn't control me."

"Of course not. A smart fellow like yourself should be calling the shots." The flickering stopped as the guy's temper returned to normal.

"And what about that attack at the cemetery? Who'd you get to do that job? Those guys couldn't hit the broadside of a fucking barn, their aim was so bad."

The flickering started again, and with it the doctor's pants began to flare between black polyester and jeans.

Hang in there, Talbot. You just need to get him distracted enough for Ava to move. Distract him a little bit longer.

"So tell me, were they your men? On assignment for you? And does Enyo know about that job, too?"

"I told you," the doctor said, gritting his teeth, "I call my own shots."

"Sure you do."

"You know . . . ," the doctor began, his eyes narrowing. With the back of his free hand, he stroked Ava's hair. He still held the knife, wrapped in his palm with the blade pointing down. It barely missed Ava's sleeve each time the doctor stroked downward. "I had a brother once."

Brody barely heard him through the thundering waves of fury roiling through his body.

He had to find a way to get Ava out of here.

"He was younger than I. Weak, too. He never grew as large as I did. Never matched where I was at the same age. My father detested him. Thought he was a little pussy."

"Good for him."

"No, not really. But I suppose that's a story for a different day."

This guy really was nuts. He knew Enyo liked to use the dregs of society, but this little trip down memory lane was a psychiatrist's dream.

"Where's the stone?"

"In a safe place."

Ava's gaze darted around the room as if searching for it. When she'd made a full review of the room, those dark brown orbs narrowed.

Had she found something?

But how could she have? She hadn't shown any reaction to the presence of the stone.

With a blink, Ava caught his attention again. Her lips formed a silent command: *Be ready.*

Before he could give Ava a signal to stay the course, her voice rang out in the room. "Okay, this is boring. The two of you are talking in circles and I really don't give a shit. Can we get on with it?"

The tweed to T-shirt ratio increased as the doctor jerked at Ava's neck. "No one asked you."

"Well, I'm asking. In fact, I have one question in particular. It's been bothering me since you started this. Does it bother you you're such a pussy that you take orders from a woman?"

As a strategy it wasn't the best one, but Brody knew when to take an order. The insult was strong enough and the asshole dropped all pretense of being Dr. William Martin as anger overtook his ability to maintain the disguise.

As his body morphed into an oversized man with a gray T-shirt and jeans, Ava took her shot, shoving at him in the confusion and breaking free.

Brody leaped toward Ava, pulling her into his arms, while he maintained a constant visual on the fake Dr. Martin. As the last glimmer of the doctor's body faded from view, Brody sensed the truth before his brain could process the now-familiar form standing in front of him.

The last thing Brody saw as he and Ava ported from the office was the face of his dead brother, Ajax, staring back at them.

Brody dropped them into the dining room with a heavy thud. The shock of seeing Ajax had nearly broken his concentration and they both felt the impact of a free fall upon landing on the floor.

At least they were away from there.

"Brody! Who was that?"

Ava reached for him, but he pulled out of range, moving to pace the room in long strides. He sucked in a deep breath. "My brother."

"You mean your real brother? But he's dead. You told me." She tried to touch him, but he ripped his arm away and increased the length of his stride.

What was going on here?

"I'd say he's clearly not dead. Didn't you see him? With

your own two eyes. Proof, right. Isn't that what you wanted of me when you questioned my whole life? My entire fucking existence?" Brody's voice rose with each word until his shouts were echoing off the walls, rattling the delicate chandelier above the dining room table.

"What you can see with your own two eyes and make sense of. Isn't that fucking right?"

Ava tried to touch him again; she wanted to reach out and wrap her arms around his waist so they could hold each other.

When he didn't move, she walked closer. Like someone comforting a wild animal, Ava kept her voice low and her movements simple.

"Please come here, Brody. Let me touch you."

When he didn't move, she thought he'd given in. But by the time she reached out her hand for him, all she felt was a rush of air.

Brody ported back to the Natural History Museum before any of them could stop him, the righteous fires of hell at his heels.

His brother?

What had Themis been thinking?

Ajax had been dead. He'd seen it with his own eyes. He had seen his mother killed because of it and he himself had nearly been killed by his father because of it.

The only one who could have brought him back was Themis. Even Enyo didn't have that power, though she'd no doubt dearly love that little benefit. A shudder ran through him at the thought.

Nope, this was Themis. And the bitch had done it without ever telling him.

Talk about manipulation.

Ajax had already left Ava's office, so Brody ported again, into Dr. Martin's office.

And came face-to-face with his brother.

Ajax's features flew through an erratic series of changes, from the face Brody had known well over ten thousand years ago to the face he'd come to know as Dr. William Martin and back again.

"Well, well, Brody the Meek. Does this visit mean you've come back to enjoy a reunion with your big brother?"

"How could you do this?" Brody wanted to leap across the room, arms outstretched and aiming for Ajax's neck. Instead, he could only stare.

How was Ajax alive?

And how could Brody have spent the last ten thousand years not knowing?

The rapidly changing visage calmed until there was only Ajax. His brother. The traitor.

Grief slashed through him, cutting to the bone. His brother? A traitor to their family. To the Warriors. To all of humanity. Regardless of what Brody thought of Themis's motives, she wished to *cure* the ills of humanity, not make them worse.

Clearly she'd been as duped as the rest of them when it came to Ajax.

"You set us up."

"Yes, I did."

"Egypt. The cemetery. The trip to London. It was never Enyo. It was all you."

A lascivious grin flashed across those so-familiar features. "Your girlfriend made it so easy. She's quite a nice piece, by the way."

Brody held himself still, the urge to rip his brother apart

a living, breathing thing under his skin. But he needed information and needed to know what they were up against.

The one thing Ajax had never been able to do was keep his mouth shut.

"Has Enyo done *anything*? Or have you been responsible for all of it?"

"You mean besides torturing the real Dr. Martin?" Ajax snorted. "Hardly. You and your boys are always so quick to blame her for everything. She's not quite the mastermind you'd like to believe."

Ajax leaned forward, his hands spread on the desk warmonger style. "She's quite malleable, actually. Just like you were. Just like Mother and Father. Just like the villagers."

His brother had always had a glib tongue. Flattery came easily to him and, when coupled with his legendary charm and rough-and-tumble features, he was given a far wider berth than most people.

How had he never seen it?

And as soon as he thought it, Brody realized the truth. He hadn't had to see it because he hadn't known. Up until a few hours ago, his brother had been a distant and somewhat painful memory, buried down deep in his past.

And in one blinding flash of awareness and insight, he'd become a nightmarish present.

"Which Warrior were you? I never saw you. In all these years, I've never even seen you. Not once."

"I made sure of it. I didn't want to see you ever again, so I became Asia's Capricorn."

"Which is a perfect fit. Cool and calculating, a Capricorn lets nothing stand in his way."

Ajax grinned, that cold visage twisting Brody's gut into the same knot it had when he was a small boy. "Not that it mattered, since I wasn't a Warrior for that long."

Realization dawned, winking back to one of their earliest battles when Enyo had picked off a few Warriors, turning them to her side. "You were one of the ones Enyo turned."

"I was the first one Enyo turned."

"Always an opportunist, I see."

"Always, little brother." Before Brody followed the shift in conversation—before he could even gather the subtle cues in Ajax's stance—the sharp, pointed edge of an ancient Xiphos went winging through the air to lodge in Brody's chest.

Pain tore through him as the knife set his flesh on fire. Great, violent waves of it coursed through his system.

Ajax smiled again, pure menace emanating off him. "I'm sure by now you realize I added a little something to the edge of the knife? I like to think of it as a little experiment."

Brody fell to his knees, his hands scrambling to hang on to the arms of one of the guest chairs in Dr. Martin's office. "Experiment?" he managed to choke out.

"Oh yes. I'm convinced the head isn't the only way to kill a Warrior. I've been experimenting with a few poisons to prove my point. I do hope you enjoy yourself."

As Ajax swept from the room, Brody reached for the knife, desperate to pull it out. With shaking hands, he got a firm grip on the handle, the sweat beading on his palms causing his fingers to slip.

After three awkward, pain-filled tries, he finally felt movement. He felt the slow, sucking slide as the knife pulled free from where it had lodged in muscle, sinew and bone and he felt the agony of the poison as it began to feast on his blood.

As his vision wavered in front of him, the contents of the room floating on a black, wavy sea, two thoughts consumed him.

He had to get to Themis.

So he could get back to Ava.

* * *

Ajax flipped back into Doc Martin mode just before he entered the hallway. The heavy plastic bag swung from his fingers like a bag lunch. Damn, but he really was a genius.

He wished he could port to the exhibit hall, but the energy required to keep up Doc Martin *and* porting was too much. He hadn't managed to maintain both, even on a full stomach and a dirty bout of sex.

As he walked through the doorway of the exhibit hall, he smiled at the various workmen hovering around the room. They had given him the idea in the first place. No one noticed anything in this room. There was shit everywhere— lunch bags, discarded gum wrappers, sawdust and sawed-off pieces of plasterboard. A small plastic bag stowed under a bench wouldn't draw anyone's attention and it'd give him the extra day he needed.

Sure, it was risky, but worst-case scenario was someone would find it and put it right back in the case, thinking one of the workers wanted to make off with it.

And he'd just go get it again.

But here, hidden away from view, Enyo wouldn't have any fucking idea where to find it. And unless she had all five stones, she didn't have jack shit.

He still held all the cards.

And his hand kept looking better and better.

Chapter Twenty

Enyo watched Ajax preen around the bedroom, a length of chain still wrapped around one wrist. He'd ported in a half hour ago, toppling her to the bed as he landed and inside of her before she could scream.

And then she *had* screamed.

Over and over and over again.

And now she had to put an end to it. For years he'd been an amusement, a diversion.

Now he was a liability.

What was it with men? They always betrayed you. Always thought they knew better when, in reality, they knew nothing.

She had thought sexy, muscle-bound Ajax had been following her orders. But he'd just been trying to double-cross her all along, playing puppet master behind the scenes, chasing Harrison's niece. One step ahead, plotting to get the power of the stones for himself.

To take what was rightfully hers.

Just like her father.

Always believing he knew best. Always ready with a pat on the head and a conciliatory word. Always manipulating.

Fuck it.

She put a little coo in her voice before shooting Ajax a saucy grin. "You're awfully happy today."

"I have much to be happy about, my love. Soon all the power in the world will be ours."

"Ours?"

Ajax slowed his roll around the room, stopping to take a seat opposite her on the bed. "Yes. Ours. I have something for you."

"For me?"

"A present, just for you, lover."

Well, this was interesting. She knew him well. If he was taking this tact and was actually about to show her the stones, he had to have an angle. So what was his game?

The supple leather case he'd arrived with still lay by the door of the bedroom. She watched the long, lean lines of his body as he fetched the oversized leather duffel, then walked back toward the bed.

The loss of such an outstanding sexual partner would be a shame. It was hard to find someone who had her same appetites *and* who was such a fine specimen. And such a willing participant in whatever devious activities she could think up.

But he wasn't her match.

In the dark, muted light of the bedroom, she watched as he opened the bag and withdrew three tightly wrapped bundles.

"There are five stones, Ajax."

Impatience tinged his voice as his gaze remained locked on the stones. "I know. But this is a start."

"A start, maybe, but none of the stones truly means anything without the others. All are required."

With swift fingers, he had the stones unwrapped and laid on the bed before her. "Aren't they beautiful?"

Her gaze ran over them. She supposed so, but she didn't really care. They were a tool, nothing more. She wouldn't look at a hammer and see beauty. This was no different.

The sight of the stones had him breathing hard, just as he'd done earlier when she'd scored marks with her fingernails down the insides of his thighs. He was almost moaning at the sight of the stones where they lay on top of the satin duvet.

And that's when she knew.

Her liability had become a disaster. And there was no waiting for it to happen.

He needed to be dealt with.

With swift movements and not a moment of remorse, her fingers found the jeweled handle of the sword she kept between mattress and box spring. Fast came the light rush of air as she lifted her arm to strike, and then the quick slice of the blade as it met flesh. Ajax's head rolled toward the pillows as his body crumpled backward to the floor.

As she pulled the stones toward her, she marveled that he'd never even looked up.

Brody lay on the floor in the corner of Dr. Martin's office, willing himself to stay conscious. He pictured Themis's cottage on Mount Olympus, but his body refused to cooperate.

Refused to port.

And he'd refused to call Quinn before he'd come back to confront Ajax. Why? He was above backup?

Why had he fought calling for help?

And as he lay there in the corner, hard linoleum under his cheek, Kane's words from the day before came back to him.

"You want to run the show, Leo. And the moment someone crosses you or tries to do it differently, you get all bent out of shape. We let you work alone for a reason."

But he wasn't alone. He had Ava.

And he had his brothers.

With agonizing movements, he dragged his cell from the back pocket of his jeans and dialed Quinn.

"What?"

"Quinn." Brody winced inwardly at the weak-ass voice.

"Where are you?"

"Mar-Martin's off-office."

And then Quinn was in front of him, Ava by his side.

"Why'd you . . . br-bring her?" Gods, he hated the sound of his voice. He hated the vulnerability.

In an instant he was Brody the Meek again. Except now it was so much worse because the woman he loved had to see him fail.

Before he could protest any further that Quinn shouldn't have brought her here, Ava was barking orders. "Themis. We have to get him to her."

With a loud sucking noise, Quinn left them, his body on its way to Mount Olympus.

Brody's gaze roved over Ava. "You shouldn't be here."

"Well, if you hadn't gone haring off like that, neither of us would be here. I was so worried about you." Ava dropped to the ground next to him and, with the most exquisitely gentle fingers, drew his head onto her lap.

"Needed to confront Ajax."

"No, you needed to soothe your wounded pride. There's

a difference." Ava continued running her fingers over his cheek in light, soothing waves.

Although it galled him to admit it, she had a point.

Before he could acknowledge as much, she continued her monologue. "You really are an obnoxious Leo; you know that? Self-centered. Egotistical. Arrogant."

He conjured up a grin. While it wasn't quite up to his usual cocky standards, he did get an answering smile for his efforts. "You're stuck with me." *For as long as I can have you, you glorious woman.*

"I suppose I am. It still doesn't change your need to share things, Brody. With your brothers and certainly with me."

Brody felt another wave of pain wash over him. The physical torment of the poison. The mental torment of Themis's actions. "She never told me."

"She who?"

"Themis. She never told me she turned Ajax."

Themis's voice filled the room. Warm. Knowing. Reasonable. "Well then, maybe we should discuss it."

Brody saw Ava's eyes go wide first, then turned his head to face the goddess.

Themis's robes covered her tall and stately body while a sword hung on a belt at her hip. She rarely traveled outside of Mount Olympus with her scales, but he could see the calculating light in her eyes. He'd often wondered if she simply carried them for effect.

The damn goddess could take everything in with one sweeping gaze.

Themis nodded her head. "Quinn. Ava. Would you leave us, please?"

Quinn moved to the door and waited, sentinel-style for

Ava. Brody watched as Ava leaned down and pressed her lips to his forehead before disengaging him slowly from her lap.

As soon as they were gone from the room, Themis bent down, laying a hand on his chest. Immediately, great healing light filled him.

"What—," he gasped as the tendrils of pain spun out of his body, through his bone marrow, out of his muscles, through his skin.

"Shhh. First things first."

He knew the moment the poison was gone. All pain receded while he regained full use of his thoughts. No longer disjointed from the agony of the poison, he could think through the situation. Muster up his questions.

And damn if he didn't have a lot of them.

"Why did you turn my brother? You had to have known what he was like."

"I was foolish. Drunk on the power of what I'd created, Brody."

He saw the honesty in her eyes and saw the pain that crinkled the corners when she spoke of those days. "But you are incapable of abusing power that way."

A small bark of laughter flew from her lips as she turned away from him to stalk across the small office. "Hardly true. Everyone is capable of abusing power."

"But he was dead."

"Further evidence of my abuse."

"I don't understand. What made you call him in the first place? I know my brother. Justice and compassion aren't exactly his hallmarks."

"I believed I could make him care. Could make him believe in justice and compassion. I believed my work was invincible."

"And then you lied about it."

Her gaze remained level on his. "Yes. I kept the information from you, convinced you'd never know. And in the process I put you in jeopardy."

"You put Ava in jeopardy. I can take care of myself."

He looked down at the ragged stains on his jeans and T-shirt and ran a hand through his hair—still damp at the crown from where he'd sweated through the poison. Well, it might not be entirely true, but it was close. He *could* take care of himself. Had been doing so for thousands of years.

"He has the stones."

"Not all of them. Learn what you can about the one you do have. Draw out the knowledge it holds. Prepare yourselves for the final battle."

"You haven't touched more than three bites of my food." The Warriors' housekeeper, Callie, hovered above her with the largest bowl of mashed potatoes Ava had ever seen.

"I'm not very hungry."

"Which is the exact reason you should eat." Callie added another scoop of mashed potatoes to Ava's plate, even though she hadn't finished the first serving.

Ava smiled as the woman bustled about her. The two of them were alone in the dining room, which had given the Warriors' housekeeper/den mother/cook ample opportunity to fuss over her.

Callie set the overloaded bowl on the table, then dropped into a chair. She looked about twenty-two, her long, dark hair nearly overpowering on her five-foot frame, but Ava suspected Callie, like the rest of the Warriors, had stopped counting birthdays long ago.

Ava had learned two things quickly after she and Quinn had gotten Brody back to the mansion to recuperate.

First, Callie had been at the Warriors' compound in Texas until today. And second, the moment she walked back into the mansion, every one of the Warriors had begun to bow and scrape toward her, proving, without any doubt, who actually ran the show.

Ava was amused to realize this included Quinn.

Brody was resting and Quinn was working through some test parameters for them to run on the one remaining stone in their possession. The love stone, she was sure of it.

So she and Callie were all alone in the dining room. Apparently, the woman was letting her inner cook play diva this evening, if the huge pile of plates covering the table was any indication. The Warriors' housekeeper—if that was even the right term for her—was channeling Paula Deen and Julia Child in a big way.

Callie pointed at the mountain of starch with the serving spoon. "Come on now. Stop picking and eat."

The urge to protest was strong, but the overwhelming feeling of love and safety at being presented with the heaping mass of mashed potatoes had another effect.

She burst into tears.

"Oh, Ava, Ava, Ava. Shush, honey. It's okay." Callie dropped the bowl and spoon on the table and rushed to her. She wrapped her arms around her, surprisingly strong for such a small woman. "Hush now. It's okay. You can tell me what happened."

As Ava took comfort in the warmth of Callie's hug, her thoughts took her back—back to days that were easy and warm and golden. Days where she knew she was loved and protected. Days that were buried so far in her past, she wondered that she could even remember them.

"I was so worried about Brody. What if he hadn't made it? What if Ajax had truly killed him?"

Callie hugged her close. "Shhh, now. Brody's so stubborn and hardheaded, you didn't think a little worm like Ajax could get to him, now, did you?"

"But Callie," Ava half hiccupped, half whispered, into the other woman's shoulder. "It was so bad. So horrible."

"I know. Shhh, now. You're strong. You can handle this. He's fine now."

Ava knew Callie was right. She knew the immediate danger had passed and, no matter how horrible it was, they were all far more prepared because of what Brody had gone through. With that, came another thought: the whispered remembrance of her mother's love as she'd stood near the love stone.

More hot tears rimmed her eyelids and Ava took a hard swallow.

"I saw my mother." At the woman's blank stare, Ava added, "My mother who has been dead for well over twenty-five years."

"Oh my God." Callie shifted back to look at her, made the sign of the cross, then dropped back into an empty chair next to her, taking one of her hands. "Tell me about it."

"The stone. The remaining one we have in our control. Whenever I'm near it, I see my mother. The last time it was with me, I had a conversation with her."

At Callie's puzzled expression, Ava added, "With my dead mother."

Callie made another sign of the cross. "Did she seem the same?"

"Same?"

"As when she was alive."

"I don't remember that well. She died when I was five."

"Yes, but from your memories. Did she seem the same?"

Ava thought back to those moments in Lorna MacIntyre's office. The warmth that filled her at the sight of her mother. The deep well of love that beat under her skin as Marie Harrison spoke to her, encouraged her, offered her words of wisdom.

Offered her love.

"She did. She was my mother, in every sense of the word. In fact, it felt like she was there. Right there with me. What if I see her when we run these tests and she tells me I shouldn't be with Brody?"

Callie reached over and brushed a hair off her forehead. "Why would she do that?"

"We're a danger to each other. Add to that the whole mortal-slash-immortal thing and we're a recipe for disaster, Callie."

"Nonsense. You must stop being afraid. I can see in your face that you hesitate, but you mustn't be afraid."

Ava tried on a smile but knew it didn't reach her eyes. How could she be positive? She was a mortal woman. She was going to age and die, relatively quickly compared to Brody's life span.

How could this ever work?

"But how can we be together?"

"Listen to you. Look at what you've accomplished. Look at how he needed you today."

Ava thought back to Brody's anger, before he ported back to Ajax.

He hadn't shared anything, then. He'd only shut her out.

"Stop this talk. You are afraid. And fear creates bad choices. When we fear, we don't see what's around us—what's right in front of us."

Shame filled Ava at the thought of her own weaknesses.

Her stomach burned with it as more tears pricked the back of her eyes. "The fear is so much a part of me, I don't think I'd know who I was anymore if I weren't afraid."

"Nonsense. You'd still be you, but the veil that covers your eyes would lift. The sun would shine brighter and the night would not seem so dark." Callie leaned in, her brown eyes holding dark secrets in their fathomless depths. "Believe me. I know."

Ava grabbed her napkin and wiped at her tears. She took a deep, cleansing breath and turned toward the older woman. "So what should I do?"

Callie leaned forward and laid her hands on Ava's. The woman's hands were warm, giving. "Only love. That is what you have to give him. And that will be enough.

"Now, there are many ways to give love. I suggest you go try one of them. I'd pick one of the fun ones." Then Callie winked at her before she stood and walked toward the swinging door into the kitchen.

As Ava watched her go, the thought again struck her that Callie appeared far younger—and wiser—than her loving but stern attitude indicated. It was as if she were filled with an inner light that burned deep within. She was yet another dimension to the Warriors' lives, to Brody's life, and Ava was absolutely fascinated.

"Damn it, woman. Would you just run the tests and stop fussing?" Brody muttered after swallowing the last of his lunch sandwich.

Ava turned toward a bank of computer monitors, hollering to Quinn who sat at a matched set in the far opposite corner of the room. She'd specifically chosen this room for its configuration, the long table and even longer room the perfect size for what they needed to do.

Quinn gave her the all clear. "I think we're ready." They were in the museum's subbasement and she had the London stone on the table. With expert movements, Ava played with the calibration on the equipment from the bank of computers she was monitoring.

Although she'd kept to her corner since Quinn had ported back from the house with the stone, she couldn't hide the excitement. Maybe now, they'd have some answers and wouldn't feel as though they were flying blind, without any advantages.

Ava breathed her first sigh of relief as a small kernel of excitement popped in her belly. She loved experiments and the opportunity to learn new things always excited her.

Brody sat behind a lab desk, shoveling a hamburger and fries into his mouth as fast as he could, grumbling again about how long it was taking them to get started. His outburst was exactly what she'd been looking for. It was proof her mother hen routine had finally broken through.

"We should destroy it," Brody mumbled around a mouthful.

"I doubt we could if we tried."

Quinn looked up from a counter of computer monitors on the far side of the room. He had the love stone with him, and the distance seemed to be working for both of them. Other than a few random, stray thoughts of her mother, Ava's mind was sticking to the present.

"Why do you think that, Ava?"

"All five of them work in unison. If—and that's a really big if—they can be destroyed, they'll have to be together."

"So what do we expect to discover with these tests?" Brody tossed his empty paper plate in the garbage and walked over to the large, steel-topped lab table that dominated the center of the room.

"We're going to learn whatever we can. Just as Themis told you to." A breathy laugh escaped her, the first light-hearted moments she'd had since their discovery of Ajax's existence. "I know my being a gemologist makes this a rather stupid question. But, do you really think we'll learn something?"

"Anything we learn is a bonus. Anything that helps point us toward how to destroy the stones is what we're looking for."

"And what about Ajax? He has four stones, Brody. He's got to have some sense of what they're capable of, even if he doesn't know how to use them."

"Then we'll be smarter about them." Brody's smile lit up his face. "If it's you and my brother in a battle of the minds, I'm not going to bet against you."

It was silly, really. Such simple words. Such absolute faith. Tears pricked the backs of her eyes, so she shifted her focus to the computer monitors. And felt a rush of love so strong it nearly brought her to her knees.

Someone who loved her, believed in her, championed her.

"Okay. Let's get started. Ava, come on over here." Brody waited for her at the table, so she moved forward, her feet much lighter than she'd ever have expected. "It's all right, darlin'. I won't let anything happen to you."

"Doesn't mean I want to do this. I like being in control of my own mind. I don't like something being in control of it for me."

Quinn kept his eyes on the monitors, calm concentration threaded through each word. "Ava, I know this is hard. But of all the stones, this one is the easiest for you to handle."

She nodded her head. "The love stone."

"Yep."

For the next two hours, they ran a battery of tests on the stone itself—density, makeup, material of origin. They followed those up by physical tests on Ava as she interacted with it—heart rate, blood pressure, even a few paranormal tests Quinn planned out on his own.

As Ava read the property results on the stone and explained them to Quinn and Brody, the three of them hypothesized about what the results might mean.

One result, however, remained unchanged.

The damn thing was indestructible.

She ran a hand through her hair as she read the same results from three different tests. "How can it be indestructible? It had to *come* from somewhere. Which means it had to be formed into what it is *now*, which would make me think hammer and chisel, but . . ."

Brody picked up the stone, turning it around in his hands. "Nothing's getting through this thing, no matter how big the hammer. It's completely smooth." With a sigh, he settled the stone back on the counter in its carrying case.

"You do realize, if anyone saw me doing this right now, I would be so out of a job."

Ava moved around the lab counter, cleaning up equipment as she went. Quinn had purposely arranged all the equipment at the end of the table so she could pick each piece a clear distance from the stone.

With brisk movements, she replaced each tool in its designated place in the lab. Quinn left them in the subbasement, porting back to the Warriors' mansion with the stone. She and Brody followed a short while later, giving Quinn ample time to store the stone.

As they walked hand in hand toward Brody's room, she ran through the data again. "Inconclusive results, as we expected. But at least I know I can stand to be in the same room with this one. Well, sort of. I can stand to be in the same room with it, but if anyone else wants to spend time with my spaced-out ass, they're going to be disappointed."

"You were amazing."

"Yeah, well amazing will be when we lure Enyo and Ajax out in the open."

"Ava, I don't want you in that situation."

The warm cocoon of love and affection and mutual respect nose-dived as she whirled on him. "You can't leave me out of this now. We have to use the stone to get Enyo's attention. What if she doesn't even know Ajax has the four stones? We might be able to play them off each other. Besides, I'm the only one who can draw on the stone's power."

"I'm immortal. You're not. Remember?"

Ava stepped into the bedroom, shutting the door with a firm click once Brody had cleared it. "I'm the conduit for the stones."

"Which is even more reason why I don't want you out there. Don't you see? That's exactly what they want. Enyo and Ajax, they want to use you, Ava. Whether they're working together or at cross-purposes, both are dangerous."

Frustration beat like a kettledrum in her stomach, the heavy, pumping rhythm a match for the pounding of blood through her veins. She wasn't helpless, damn it.

"We can't fix this—can't solve this problem once and for all—if you don't get me involved. I'm the key in all this, Brody. I know it."

"Well, I'm not ready to go shoving you in any locks and hoping we get a fit. I need you to sit tight and trust me."

"Don't throw trust at me. Anything but that."

He loomed over her, pressing his forehead against hers. "Okay. Fine. I need you to accept that my experience with

Enyo is far longer and deeper than yours. And I'd like you to let my brothers and me use our expertise to fight this battle. We have just a few hours to regroup. Quinn's securing backup from the Warriors and we're plotting our strategy this afternoon. It won't be long before we send up the call to draw Enyo out. Add to that that my real brother's decided to make a return trip from the dead, and I'm just not feeling on firm footing right now."

Even if she had wanted to argue, his last point about Ajax was the clincher. No matter the number of battles Brody and his Warrior brothers had fought against Enyo, Ajax was a wildcard and Brody his clear target. "When you put it that way."

The ringing of her cell phone jarred them out of the moment. Shifting, she hit the speaker button on the handset and answered the call without checking the caller ID.

And regretted it the moment she heard the voice on the other end. "Hello?"

"Ava. It's your grandmother."

When she didn't say anything, her grandmother's voice barked down the phone line.

"Ava Marie, are you there?"

"Grandmother, I'm sorry. I'm, um, at work and I'm not getting very good cell phone reception."

"I need to see you. This evening. I've gotten word from some museum patrons that you've been running around with some archaeologist fellow. We must talk."

Ava shot Brody a wry grimace and wasn't surprised when she got wiggling eyebrows in return, his favorite expression when it came to her grandmother.

"Grandmother, I'd hardly call it running around when that archaeologist fellow is assigned to the exhibit with me."

Oh, and I'm in love with him. And he's saved my life. And he's completely and utterly wonderful.

"Mitzi Boniface said she saw him when she was doing her docent duties and she said he looks like something out of a movie."

"So being attractive is a crime?"

"It is when you run around acting like a common piece of ass."

"Grandmother!" Ava wasn't sure if she was insulted or ready to burst into peals of laughter.

Good Lord, the woman really was losing it. Ava stared at the phone, wondering if she'd mistakenly given belligerence and a haughty attitude far more credence in the mental health department than she should have.

"Now, back to the reason for my call. I need to speak with you."

"Fine, fine, fine. I'll stop by on my way home this evening after work. Will that be soon enough for you?"

"No later than seven. And don't be fresh. I expect you to show me your respect."

"Yes, Grandmother." She wanted to ask about her respect, but she held her tongue. *Ava Marie, ever the dutiful child.* "I'll see you later this evening. Good-bye."

As she hung up, Brody moved in, pulling her into his arms. "Movie star? Piece of ass? Are all your calls like that?"

"Usually. That woman has the timing of a rhino. And is about as stubborn as one, too."

"I don't want you going alone. Enyo or Ajax might attack you there to get the last stone."

She stepped back, but didn't fully pull out of his arms. "Brody, this is my grandmother. It'll take a half hour, at most, to run over and do my duty."

"Need I remind you, yet again, of the family surprise

that awaited me? Nothing is off-limits right now. And at this point, they're going to be desperate to get to the last stone. Neither Enyo nor my brother are ones to sit around and wait for victory to come to them."

"Fair point."

"I'm serious, Ava." Brody took a deep breath. "It's not just Enyo and Ajax. I don't trust your uncle Wyatt."

The vague annoyance of her grandmother's call faded in the light of Brody's comments. "How would you know my uncle?"

"Maybe I should have told you this earlier. I met him on the dig for the prophecy a few months ago. Quinn and Grey ran a few checks on him. Your uncle's up to something, Ava, and we think it's tied to you."

"And you're just telling me now?" Raw fury whipped through her as she stepped out of Brody's arms. How dare he keep this from her.

"I didn't want to worry you. And as long as you're with us, you're safe. Protected."

"You think my uncle—one of the few freaking family members I've got—is a threat to me, and you didn't think it was worth mentioning?" She waited a beat—saw the remorse that ran heavy in his gaze—and pressed harder. "What did you find out about him?"

"He recently had a deposit made to his private bank account for twenty million dollars."

Ava felt the air rush out of her lungs. "Is that all?"

"And he purchased a gun after he arrived in Egypt. And a dig worker was murdered on the site, a few days before Peter Dryson's murder."

Brody and Ava snuck into the museum before heading to her grandmother's. Dr. Martin hadn't been seen or heard from in two days, according to Ava's assistant, Suzy, but Brody wasn't eager to take any chances.

Quinn was out securing backup from the other Warriors, putting everyone in place on Mount Olympus. Although Brody wanted to be with him, running the op, he couldn't leave Ava alone and unguarded.

And they still had unfinished business at the museum.

The great exhibit hall was nearly complete, Ava's efforts around planning and design coming to fruition in the execution.

"I don't believe it."

Brody ran a hand down her back, settling at her waist. "Believe it. This is what a hell of a lot of hard work can create."

"What did you want to see?" She didn't accept the compliment, but she hadn't pulled away from his touch, either, which Brody took as a good sign.

He'd made a serious miscalculation on how he handled the Wyatt situation. And while it chapped his ass to be called on it, he couldn't exactly fault her for her anger.

"I want to look at the prophecy relief again."

"The official translations came in the other day. I picked them up on e-mail. Your translation was flawless."

"Why, thank you."

They moved to the front of the exhibit, where visitors would begin their journey. The relief was already framed up behind bulletproof glass and a freshly created translation hung next to it.

Brody let his gaze scan over both of them, reading the prophecy in both languages.

Once in every age, a Chosen One, selected by the great god Ra, will harness the Great Summoning Stones

of Egypt. The five stones grant the Chosen One do-
minion over everything: death, life, love, sexuality, in-
finity. The Chosen One—the Key—will bind the power
of the stones under its command. The Key will rule
over all the earth and no portal will be immune to its
influence. No god can rule above the Chosen One when
the Chosen One commands the power of the stones.

Though the Key will hold power over all in its
dominion, there is but one force that can magnify its
power tenfold. At the entrance to Heliopolis will the
Key wield its greatest victory.

"Ava. Please pull up your e-mail. Is that last paragraph
in your translation?" A sinking feeling washed over Brody,
the words swimming before his eyes.

Magnify its power tenfold.

Wield its greatest victory.

At the entrance to Heliopolis.

Ava handed him her phone, the e-mail function engaged
and ready for view. Brody scanned the text and saw the last
piece matched.

As his gaze darted over the bottom of the relief, he saw
the hieroglyphics, saw what he had missed—what must have
come to life as the last part of the relief was pulled from the
tomb.

"Brody, what's the matter?"

"Read the bottom part."

"Tenfold? There's even more power in the stones than
we thought?"

"Indestructible power."

Her strangled laugh touched a chord in him as she tried
to be brave. "Times one or times ten, isn't indestructible the
same any way you slice it?"

"Degrees of bad, darling. And this is a very bad thing."

"Right, but where's Heliopolis? Egypt? We still have one stone. Even if Enyo and Ajax have all the others, we're in New York."

"Yes, but the entrance to Heliopolis is right here in Manhattan."

Chapter Twenty-one

"What do you mean, 'right here in Manhattan'?"

Ava scanned the prophecy language again, still not understanding the problem. This wasn't ancient Egypt. Heck, even if these artifacts had remained for all these years, things were different.

Times had changed. Ancient artifacts didn't lie in wait, eager to be unleashed in foreign lands. *Did they?*

"Cleopatra's Needle. In Central Park."

In her mind's eye, Ava saw it immediately, remembered Saturdays in Central Park with her father, picnicking in full view of the monument. "The old obelisk that stands on the back side of the Met?"

"Yep."

"Come on, Brody. I went there as a kid. My father was obsessed with all things Egyptian—how could I have missed it? And in all the times I've been there, I've never felt anything. Not even a hint of anything. It's not like the stones."

"Well, half the prophecy can't be right. It's all or nothing. Besides, it would make sense you didn't feel anything, because the obelisks harness power; they're not the source of power."

"But—" Ava broke off whatever argument she was about to make. If she'd learned anything over the past few days, it was that nothing was quite what she expected.

And nothing was exactly as it seemed.

"Okay. So we need to add yet another dimension to this puzzle."

As Brody turned back toward the prophecy, she left to wander the room, checking out how the various elements were coming together.

Lighting was set up mostly how she'd asked, with very few exceptions. And in those cases, she actually liked the new lighting selection better almost every time.

The glass cases were polished and shined to perfection, just ready and waiting for their first, smudged fingerprints.

Traffic flow was shaping up nicely, as various items were placed to divert the museum-goer into a specific locale, every step of the way.

Immense pride filled her. She had had a hand in this. She owned it.

And it was about time she stood up and owned what was hers.

Following out the rest of the traffic flow, Ava walked the last several yards of the exhibit. The exit would be through a black set of curtains, next to the entrance, but she could see Brody as those hadn't yet been finalized.

Brody smiled at her across the distance as she closed the last forty yards. "Does it meet with your expectations?"

"Does it ever." She eyed a small row of benches that had already been put in place to her specifications.

Who had left a bag lunch sitting there underneath? As she walked toward the bag, a strange taste hit her tongue.

Sharp.

Metallic.

She continued to reach for the bag, unable to stop the pull—the *suggestion*—she needed to pick it up. Hold it. *Own* it.

Don't pick it up, Ava Marie!

Even as she tried to shake it off, Ava recognized the signs for what they were.

Drumbeats pounded as a snake slithered past her ankle, its fangs bared. Another joined it, rearing up before her eyes. It undulated before her, hissing and darting forward in time to the heavy drumbeats stuck in her ears. The smell of fire assaulted her as the large fire pit grew before her eyes.

People screamed as they fought the pull of death.

More snakes slithered toward them to rain down on their bodies.

Brody landed in a heap on the couches in the great room of the mansion. Even Callie's screams couldn't penetrate the wall of fear that gripped him and wouldn't let up. Hard, heavy pressure lay on his heart as he shifted Ava, laying her down on the couch.

"Oh my God! What happened to her?"

"Callie, go get Quinn. Now. Then call Kane and Grey."

For once the woman didn't argue or suggest she knew better. She just left to find the others.

Brody leaned over, incoherent words spilling from his lips as he took in her pale white features and the dark circles that rimmed her eyes. "Baby, baby, baby. Come back to me, Ava. Baby, come back."

Quinn and Kane were on him immediately, while Callie raced back into the room.

"What the fuck is going on, Talbot?"

"She's unconscious. And I don't know why."

Belatedly, Brody realized Quinn had him by the shirt, a huge handful balled up. Without rational thought, he fought at his brother, scratching and kicking as Quinn dragged him away from Ava.

"What did you do?"

His muscles quivered as Brody pushed at the Bull. "Get the fuck off me."

"Brody!"

The urgency in Quinn's voice—and his having dropped his tone to almost a whisper—dragged him from the frenzied need to hover over Ava. "What is in your hand?"

Oh gods.

Brody's hand fisted around what looked like a drugstore bag, the name of a major chain printed on the label. "Ava had it in her hand."

Quinn reached out and took it, walking backward away from Ava as he dug through it. The New York stone.

The death stone.

Where had it come from?

And why hadn't his touch worked?

Quinn ripped the stone from his hand before he could throw it. "Callie, take it. Now. Lock it in the safe in the basement among the papers. We'll deal with it later."

Brody rushed to Ava's side, his heart fisting up again as she screamed and moaned, as if the hounds of hell were snapping at her feet.

"Ava!" He pulled her up, wrapping her flailing body in his arms, absorbing the pressure and weight of her fists and kicking legs as she fought an invisible demon only she could see.

"Ava!" Oh gods, Ava.

*   *   *

Ava looked down at herself, hot panic flooding through her and pushing her heartbeat into overdrive.

Where was Brody? Where were the other Warriors and the mansion? What had happened to her?

That awful, metallic blood taste hit her tongue at the same time the smell hit her nose, and she fought the rising nausea. Fought to keep it down and focus on where she was.

What was this place?

Ignoring the smell of blood, she slowed her breathing into a gentle rhythm, willing a sense of calm through her system.

Focus.

Every time before, she'd allowed her panic to take over. *Use the fear, Ava Marie. Channel it and find out where the hell you are.*

An odd giggle bubbled up.

Maybe it *was* hell.

Focus.

Then the giggles were gone as she opened her eyes and really looked around. Unlike the real-yet-unreal clarity of a dream, this was real. It *felt* real.

She could smell the fire that rose up from strategically positioned pits surrounding the large space.

As her gaze roamed the area, she realized she was outside. And were they on a road? Yes, they were. The road led into the city, two large obelisks framing them on either side.

She could see swaying bodies chanting around her, their screams getting louder the closer they got to the monuments.

Why did those look so familiar? Where had she seen them? And what were they all doing?

Then she saw *him* as she felt herself being methodically pushed forward along the road, toward the obelisks, toward the area lying between them. A long, flowing robe covered his head and shoulders, but the robe had no tie. It hung open down the front of his body, baring a magnificently sculpted chest. The heavy ridge of his penis jutted from the opening, the erect length of him evident even from her distance.

Thutmose's high priest!

Was he chanting? What did he want with her?

Panic scraped her nerve endings as she saw what he held in his hands: the stone. She could only assume it was the death stone—the one her father had showed her all those years ago. How else would she be here?

How else would she see her visions come to life?

With slow, deliberate movements he lifted the stone in rhythm to his chants.

Hot, sharp waves of pain assailed her each time he lifted the stone, like a punch to her midsection.

Lift, chant, punch.

Lift. Chant. Punch.

The scream welled up inside her, dragged from her throat by the sheer pain of it all, by the pure torture of his movements, although he wasn't even touching her.

Lift. Chant. Punch.

Her stomach clenched as another wave of pain assailed her. *Oh my God.* He was killing her, murdering her from the inside out.

Tears streamed down her face as she fought the mind-numbing waves of pain. She watched in horror as he lifted the stone again, bracing herself for what was to come.

Lift.

Chant.

Pu—

Then it stopped. And the room blessedly went black.

* * *

"Hold it steady, Brody. Hold the stone." Callie held tight to Ava's head while Quinn took her feet. Brody stood over her, the love stone in his hands as he ran it over her body.

"Come on, baby. Come on back. Come back to me. Please, baby."

He felt the hot tears falling freely but didn't stop them. Didn't dash them away. Didn't feel a bit of embarrassment or remorse.

With methodical precision, he ran the stone over her body again. Head. Chest. Stomach. Pelvis. Legs. Feet. Over and over, willing the warmth and healing and love he knew she took from the stone into her body.

He willed her to come back from wherever she was and live.

Head bent, Brody laid it on her stomach. "Oh please, Ava. Come back."

"Brody?"

Her throaty greeting was the most glorious thing he'd ever heard.

"Brody, sit down, please. I'm back. I'm here and I'm not broken, and I really don't need to rest in bed."

"To hell with that. You could have died. The power of the stones and their effect on you keeps getting worse with each exposure. It's as if they're reeling you in. What if I couldn't save you this time?"

Ava watched him pace the room—her big, bad Warrior. "It's over. And we've got to take the positive away from it."

"Positive? I fucked up royally, Ava. And it almost cost you your life."

"I'm the one who picked up the stone."

"And I'm your protector. If I can even be called that, seeing as how I did a piss-poor job of actually protecting you."

She reached for his hand, clutching at him and willing him to stand still and stop the agitated pacing. "How did you fuck up? We thought if you held on to me, the stone wouldn't have any power. Guess that only works if you're holding me before I touch it. And besides, Brody, we thought Ajax had stolen it, not hidden it. Why'd he do that?"

"Quinn reviewed the security tapes. He saw him place the bag there under the benches."

"What was the time stamp on it?"

"It was within minutes after he tried to kill me in Dr. Martin's office."

"But why? What is the motivation to hide it? Is he trying to set us up?"

Brody shrugged. "Why does my brother do anything? Ten thousand years without him in my life and it's as if time hasn't ever passed. Clearly he had some twisted reason."

"Well, whatever it was, now we have two stones instead of one. Which means more leverage against Enyo."

Frustration rose in her chest when his attitude didn't get any better. His shoulders held their rigidity, a sure sign he was still blaming himself. *Stubborn, idiotic Leo.* The king of the pride couldn't stand the fact she'd been in danger.

"Brody, look. Now we know even more about the stones. The New York stone is what we suspected—it's the death stone. It portends death and it can be used to kill. I felt its power, Brody."

"Directed at you." When she didn't say anything, he pressed her again. "Tell me all of it again. Exactly what happened. Exactly what you saw."

As she related the story again, he climbed into bed and drew her close. The warmth of his touch and the security in his arms penetrated something so deep inside of her, she didn't know how she'd ever lived without him.

As she lay there in the circle of his arms, the nightmare—or whatever it was she'd lived through—continued to play over and over in her mind. And as she allowed sleep to claim her for a few hours, secure in the knowledge she was safe in Brody's arms, she imagined wielding the same power Thutmose's high priest did.

The power to kill at will.

The power to vanquish enemies.

The power to decide who lived and who died.

When she was a small child, Ava had lived in her imagination. One day she was a duchess, another an astronaut; still another she was an Angel, fighting crime for the mysterious Charlie.

She'd always considered her imagination the one area of her personality that stood out, even after she left childhood dreams behind and progressed into the realm of adult pursuits. Her imagination was unique and vibrant, colorful and active.

And nothing—not one single thought in her entire life—could have prepared her for the surreal experience of sitting through a battle-plan meeting with the Warriors.

As they sat in the basement of the Warriors' magical house, she watched millennia of history and learning and knowledge coalesce into a plan of action.

Quinn pressed the same point he'd been making for a half hour, peppered in between discussions of which weapons to take and the right entrance point into the park. "Brody, we need a triangulation on Enyo's position when she's in New York. We've known forever she's got a lair somewhere. This is our chance to find out where."

"Ava's not doing it."

"She's the only one who can."

"No." Brody's arms crossed against that oh-so-impressive chest of his as his mouth slashed into a grim line. "We focus on the rest of the plan. It's a solid strategy. Besides, the lure of the remaining stones is too great. Enyo'll come to us. She has to come to us if she wants to activate the stones at Cleopatra's Needle."

The one they called Grey looked up from where he was pulling a wicked-looking pile of swords from a case. "Quinn's right, Brody. We need to find Enyo *before* she gets to the needle. We put way more at risk if we let her get that far."

Still, her stubborn Leo wouldn't relent, his mane of hair shaking as he pressed his point. "She'll find us."

Swallowing hard, Ava thought back to those days in her imagination—days of adventure and daring, where she took on the challenges of the mythological worlds she'd created in her mind.

Time to pay up or shut up.

"What's involved, exactly? In getting Enyo where she lives?"

Brody stopped helping Grey with the swords to come stand next to her. "Ava, you're not doing it."

It ate at her to do this, but she dragged her gaze from his and turned toward Quinn. "I want to hear what I have to do."

The Taurus kept his gaze off Brody as well. "You're already going to your grandmother's this evening? Likely your uncle will be there?"

Ava thought back over the ritual and routine of her family. "He usually is."

Quinn nodded. "Good, that makes this easier. We believe Wyatt has some role in the theft of the stones—either directly or indirectly. The way Enyo, Ajax and the Destroyers have narrowed in on you is far too suspicious to assume there wasn't help. Wyatt is the likely choice."

Nausea bubbled in her stomach, but Ava fought it down. She'd never been close to her small family, but to be sold out by one of them?

As her stomach pitched and rolled, Ava felt something spark to life. Something that overtook the sting of nerves, the fear of the unknown. It channeled every emotion in her body into one pounding need.

A desire to *act*.

"Quinn, tell me what I have to do."

"We want you to pin a GPS device on your uncle. I've got a transmitter built in as well so we can monitor his conversations. The moment he goes to see her, we'll move in."

Brody's voice was a low growl, his position on the matter clearly unchanged. "We're not putting her in danger."

"Brody. I'm only in danger if you don't remove the threat of my family. We'll go to my grandmother's. Wyatt will be there and you'll be with me the whole time. I'll drop the GPS, we'll have a quick drink and then I'll be back here. And then it's my turn to worry as you leave me behind with the home fires as you go off to battle."

Kane ran a finger down one of the large battle swords on the table, the blade gleaming in the overhead lights. "It's a good plan, Talbot. It makes sense."

Ava saw the raw fear in Brody's gaze. The love and need and absolute panic that something might happen to her. Reaching up, she ran a finger down his cheek. "Do you really believe my uncle's working with Enyo?"

He nodded, but his gaze remained unchanged.

"Then I need to do this."

Leaning in, Brody laid his forehead against hers. "Why?"

"It's time to stand up for myself. It's time to take my life back."

Ava and Brody arrived at precisely seven o'clock. The butler led them into the house, straight to the drawing room where her uncle Wyatt waited for them.

The moment she saw her uncle, Ava felt her heart trip over. It was one thing to go all Amazon-woman-I-can-handle-anything safe inside the Warriors' cozy, impenetrable house, but it was another thing entirely to act on it. Her stomach muscles jumped with nerves and fear as she fingered the small GPS button Quinn had given her.

Had it really come to this? She'd never been particularly close to her uncle, their relationship framed by a strange formality they both instinctively adhered to. Despite the neutral relationship, she'd never thought him capable of betraying his family.

And now?

Only a fool would ignore the potential threat.

Uncle Wyatt stood by the bar, but he quickly hurried over to give her the requisite familial welcome.

"Ava! So good to see you, child. What a pleasure."

"Uncle Wyatt." She nodded and gave him her cheek. With a pretend twist of her shoe, she made a production of stumbling and caught on to his shirt, dropping the small device into his breast pocket.

"Oh! I'm so clumsy."

"Are you all right, Ava?"

A nervous laugh tittered out and she couldn't help but wonder if she sounded as dumb as she felt. "Sorry. Yes. I'm so worn out from the exhibit. My equilibrium is a bit off."

Wyatt patted her back, the benevolent uncle. "It's to be expected, dear."

The feel of his hand on her shoulder blades nearly sent her into another stumble—this time for real—in her haste to get away from him, but she held her ground.

At his expectant look, she turned toward Brody. "I'd like you to meet my boyfriend, Dr. Brody Talbot."

She didn't miss the look of surprise that washed over her uncle's features before he managed to hide it. *Recognition.*

"Where's Grandmother?"

"She's on her way down. Some trouble with one of the maids." It must have been one hell of a problem for her grandmother to deal with it instead of letting the house manager handle the situation. With a mental shrug, Ava let it go. She had an appearance to make. She'd done her job. It was time to get in and out and not get caught up in the family drama.

Ava took a quick scan of Uncle Wyatt's features as they settled into Grandmother's uncomfortable drawing room seats. They'd had dinner together just a few weeks ago, so she was surprised to realize a lot had changed in him within that short time. His skin had a saggy look and his hair was unkempt, the gray more noticeable than usual.

Had he really deteriorated that much? Was it from the pressure of living such a lie?

Although never a fit man, he'd always had an energy about him. The man who stood before her seemed, well . . . piggish, almost.

"So, how are you?"

"Fine, fine. Fit as a fiddle. So tell me. How are the last-minute touches on the exhibit going?" He poured himself another drink, a broad smile on his face. "Ah, Ava. Just look at you. Your father would be so proud."

"Thank you, Uncle Wyatt. Look, I really don't want to be rude, but the exhibit still needs a few more touches. I'm just going to run up to check on Grandmother and then we do have to be going."

"Ava." Brody followed her into the hallway.

"Brody, I just want to check on my grandmother. I'll be right upstairs. Let me bring her down."

"Why doesn't your uncle Wyatt go check on her?"

Now he was paranoid about her grandmother?

"Brody, I'll be right upstairs."

When he nodded, she hurried from the room, heading for the front staircase. With quick steps, she ran up as she had so many times as a child, straight for her grandmother's room with the big, dark, oversized furniture and heavy, light-killing drapes.

She'd barely cleared the doorway when she heard something from behind.

Whirling, she came face-to-face with a man she didn't recognize in a butler's uniform—two of them, actually. And they had horns.

In unison, they blew a breath at her, the fetid air passing through sharp, pointed teeth.

She passed out before a scream could leave her throat.

Chapter Twenty-two

Ava heard the distinct sounds of Manhattan traffic and struggled to remember where she was. Cracking one eye open, she fought to hold back nausea as the car whirled around her.

Why hadn't she listened to Brody and taken the threat seriously? Oh God, was he hurt in all this? Captured, too?

"Where are you taking us?"

Wyatt faced her across the limo, his back to the driver. A tall, sleek woman rode next to him. Although the woman hadn't introduced herself, Ava had no trouble identifying her.

Enyo.

The thought was completely incongruous with her situation, but she had to admit the goddess looked nothing like she'd expected. Although what she *had* been expecting was a mystery.

All she knew was she hadn't expected a woman who looked like a sleek New Yorker—maybe a high-powered lawyer or a Wall Street executive—dolled up in designer clothes, high-end shoes and enough makeup to walk a runway.

She'd expected . . .

Well . . .

Someone a little more masculine. She was the goddess of war, after all.

Goddess or not, the woman's eyes inspired all the comfort of an ice pick. They bored into you and she could actually feel the blue irises chipping away at her confidence, at her bravado, at her hope.

Keep it together, Ava Marie. You just found a backbone. Might as well try out the merchandise a bit longer.

"What did you do with Brody? And where's Grandmother?"

"I'm sure he's tearing up the house right now, he and his little friends. I made an excuse to use the restroom and he actually allowed me to go."

Grandmother stirred slightly, the movements catching Ava's attention. They'd captured Grandmother, too? For the first time Ava could remember, she thought she saw fear on her grandmother's face.

Where was Brody?

Her head swam with pain, but Ava fought to keep her stomach intact as Enyo grilled her uncle. "You really are a miserable little prick—you know that—to do this to your own mother."

Wyatt held up his stubby little hands. "This wasn't part of the plan."

Enyo gave a wicked little smile as she squeezed Wyatt's knee. "It wasn't part of *your* plan. She's always been part of mine. A little extra insurance, as it were."

Ava watched in disgust as one bloodred nail traced a path across her uncle's inner thigh. "We do know how devoted sons are to their mothers."

Disgust shifted to repulsion when her uncle closed his

eyes, ecstasy stamped on his features as Enyo continued to trace pattern after pattern.

"Enjoying yourself, Ava?"

"No. I'm repulsed."

"Oh well. The night's young." Enyo's attention never wavered, but Ava held her ground, her gaze equally firm and unyielding in return. "I've been waiting to meet you, you know. Ever since I found out about your great prophecy."

"Prophecy?"

"Oh yes. You're the Chosen One."

"What line of bullshit did my uncle feed you? And why ever would you think that about me?"

Wyatt's eyes popped open from his lust-induced coma. "You see visions when you're near the stones. Your father told me."

As a strategy, denial was fairly weak, but she'd take what she could get. "What are you talking about?"

"He told me how upset you were by the stone he smuggled home. And then it was in his journals. Your reaction. How much you hated them. How the stone acted on you."

"How the stone acted on me?" *Play it, Ava. Make it seem real.*

"A vision!" Small beads of spittle formed at Wyatt's lips as he shouted. "Your father told me!"

"Maybe *he* had a vision, but I had nothing."

"Now, now, Wyatt." Enyo patted him on the thigh again, the move even more repulsive the second time. "There's no need for this outrage. We'll find the truth out soon enough. In the meantime, have you told your niece your little secret? I'm sure she'd love to know."

Unwilling to show interest, Ava clamped her mouth shut. She would *not* ask.

"What secret, my Queen?"

Enyo flicked another fingernail down Wyatt's thigh. "That very *big* secret, Wyatt." Leaning over, she whispered in his ear, yet loud enough Ava could hear the entire thing. "You know the one I mean. The secret that you killed your brother."

Ava's vision swayed as the air in the limousine evaporated. Panic exploded in her chest, along with a soul-searing pain that sent shock waves through her nerve endings.

"You didn't?" she whispered.

"Oh, yes." Enyo smiled. "He did. Not all by himself, of course. He hired thugs to do the job, but it was convincing."

Before Ava could digest anything else, the limousine pulled to a stop and two oversized men opened the doors— the butlers from before.

With pointed teeth and horns?

Oh God, what *were* they?

Ava pulled her grandmother to her as one reached in to grab the older woman. When he proved too strong for her, she reluctantly let go of her grandmother's arm.

The second goon grabbed her, dragging her from the car as well.

"Phobos and Deimos, be careful with them. You can't play with your new pets just yet."

The hard pushes on her back grew softer, but they were still awkward. Like puppies who didn't know their own strength, the two of them had a lightness to their step at odds with their large bodies.

Just like Enyo.

The one shoving her along—Deimos, she thought—pressed her toward a set of stairs. Ava swatted at his hand, the overly long fingernails pressing into her back giving her the chills. "Be careful with my grandmother. She's old and she's disoriented."

For one moment, she thought Phobos was going to push

the old woman. Ava let out a great shriek, which was obviously what he wanted. He turned and shot her a wicked grin, then turned to sneer at Deimos.

"I got it first!"

"She didn't scream for herself. She screamed for her grandmother."

"Like it matters."

"You said scream."

"Right. No rules on it. I win."

This continued all the way down the stairs. Phobos and Deimos? The ones Brody told her about?

"What has Wyatt gotten us into?" Grandmother whispered to her as they hit the last step and were dragged down a maze of hallways.

"You wouldn't believe me if I told you."

"Try me."

And then there was no more talking because Deimos and Phobos pulled them up short next to a heavily armed door.

With those large, oversized movements, Phobos unlocked the door, then dragged both of them through it.

One overhead light illuminated the dank room. A line of bars ran along one wall.

A jail cell?

And inside that cell was one lone man.

Then Ava screamed all for herself as she realized whom she was looking at.

Dr. William Martin lay dead in a pile of decaying food. Rats crawled over and around his body as he stared sightlessly up at the ceiling.

Brody stalked around the house, his lion fully extended in his aura, stalking right next to him. The beast hadn't stopped

roaring since they returned home, the echoes of those primal cries ricocheting through the cavernous space of the house.

His brothers came running, Callie bringing up the rear.

"Brody! What is wrong with you?" Quinn's bull reacted
instinctively, escaping from his tattoo form and riding high
in the Warrior's aura, poised to fight with Brody's lion. Only
when Callie screamed and stepped in between them did both
men stand down.

Callie held a firm hand to his chest. "Brody, tell us what
is wrong."

"They've got her! Enyo's got her!"

He walked them through the last few hours, shared what
had happened at Ava's grandmother's house, each second ticking by an agony of missed opportunity.

"Did she get the GPS on Wyatt?"

"I think so." Brody paced, his lion pacing next to him.
"Fuck, fuck, fuck. I never even heard them leave."

Quinn had calmed down, his bull back in his tattoo and
his fingers busy flying over his BlackBerry keys. "That's it."

"What's it?" Callie asked.

Quinn tapped a few more keys and let out a grunt of
satisfaction. "I've been playing with an algorithm focusing
on pockets of energy and electricity, all in an attempt to
triangulate Enyo's position when she's active."

"And?"

"And, there have been two pockets of extra charge that
aren't tied to any ConEd digging or maintenance."

Brody wanted to tear into all of them, the information
coming in frozen dribs and drabs. "Get to the fucking point."

Quinn eyed him head on. "Two areas of higher than usual
electrical readings. I just overlaid the GPS tracker on it."

"Come on, Quinn. I'm aging here," Kane said with a heavy
sigh. "Get to the point."

"We've got two locations. An old abandoned subway and rail tunnel. And Cleopatra's Needle in Central Park. Both have had activity. But the tunnel's my bet for the moment. My GPS reading just matched the location."

"I'm going there first. Quinn, send reinforcements to the needle and give me the coordinates for the tunnel."

The insensate anger driving Brody calmed ever so slightly at the knowledge they had some sense of where they were going.

"Why send additional men to the needle?" Callie demanded.

"There's an added piece of the prophecy. The needle acts as a harness for the power. They feed it back to the users of the stones. If Enyo's already on her way there, I want to make sure we're covered. The needle is her end goal."

"Grandmother," Ava hissed, "are you okay?"

"Other than having my arms and legs bound, yes, I'm fine."

"How's your head?"

"The worst headache I've ever had that didn't involve a martini." Ava heard her grandmother moving around, which she took to be a good sign. When she heard the added grumble of, "The martinis were a hell of a lot more fun, too," she actually felt a smile cross her lips.

Despite the brave front for her grandmother, Ava felt her spirits waning. Did Brody get out of the house? Or was he being held prisoner there? Enyo had to know about killing him by his head.

Ava knew he wasn't dead. He couldn't be. She'd know.

Right?

She'd know if something had happened to him. The bone-chilling numbness in her would feel . . . something.

Right?

Oh God, how were they getting out of this one? And how could she get a message to Brody if he was alive? To his brothers? Did he have any idea how to begin looking for her?

And why the hell had she left to go find Grandmother?

With a sigh, she realized the hows and whys really didn't matter. What mattered was what was.

It was time to figure that out.

"Grandmother. Do you have any idea of where we are?"

"I'm not certain, but I believe it's one of the abandoned subway tunnels."

"But we're on a bed."

"So she must have rigged it up as a waiting area."

She?

What would Grandmother know of Enyo?

Of its own volition, Ava's mind went back to Dr. Martin. She hadn't been able to remove the image of his lifeless body from her mind's eye or erase the evidence of how horrific his last days were. "There aren't jails in the subways."

"She probably rigged that, too."

"Here. Give me your hands and I'll try to work on the knots."

As her grandmother shifted to make her hands more accessible, she kept up a steady stream of quiet chatter. "What does this woman want with you? And what did she want with your boss, the poor man? Is something going on at the museum?"

"Appears so." Ava tugged at the knots, but they were incredibly tight. With a dark sigh, she reset her focus, trying to orient herself by running her fingers over the knots.

Grandmother's voice grew quiet as she held her hands still. "Is my son involved in this?"

"I didn't realize it until last night, but I'm afraid so."

"Oh. Oh no." Grandmother didn't say anything else, but just held herself ramrod straight as Ava worked at the knots.

Ava felt the knots at her grandmother's wrists slip just as the sound of the door lock began to open. "Don't let them know we've got you out."

"Of course." Aha. There was the haughty disdain Ava knew and loved.

Bright overhead lights flipped on as Enyo and Uncle Wyatt moved into the dark, dank room. Wyatt ran immediately to her grandmother's side of the bed. "Mother, are you okay?"

"Of course I'm not okay. I'm tied up."

Wyatt straightened, his focus on Enyo. "Surely you can let my mother go."

Enyo's smile spread out. "Surely not. Your mother is my insurance policy."

"But I'm already helping you!"

"It's not for you, Wyatt. It's for your niece. I want to make sure she's more than willing—eager even—to help me, too."

As Enyo's focus spun around to her, Ava's stomach did a pitch and roll. The only thing for which she could be grateful was that her stomach was empty.

"Insurance for what?"

"Well, now that you've seen how your dear friend spent his last days, surely you will not wish the same thing on your beloved grandmother—the woman who raised you and the only link a poor orphaned girl has to family."

Raw, rank terror like she'd never felt before gripped her insides. Ava clutched at her stomach, clawing at the roiling pain. Partly in terror, partly with remorse, her mind whirled with the reality of her situation.

She was trapped by a crazy goddess with superhuman powers.

She and her grandmother would likely not make it out alive.

She had finally found a life—and someone in it—worth living for and she was about to lose both.

"Now, Dr. Harrison, seeing as how we understand each other, you're going to listen to what I have to tell you. And you're going to follow my directions to the letter. Do you understand?"

Fear choked her throat, but Ava nodded her agreement—as if she had a choice.

The door opened again, Deimos and Phobos bouncing into the room like a couple of psychotic clowns.

"Did she scream yet?" Phobos balanced on the balls of his feet.

Deimos pushed his brother so he lost his balance. "Cried, too? I love it when they cry."

If she wasn't scared out of her mind, Ava realized she actually might be fascinated by the two of them—the sort of fascination one would have for a king cobra, but fascinated all the same.

Enyo shot a benevolent smile in the direction of her nephews, then turned her full focus on Grandmother. "I believe it's time, Patrice. Don't you?"

Patrice? How did Enyo know Grandmother's name?

And why was Grandmother standing up, exposing her wrists?

"*Grandmother!*" she hissed at her. "Sit down."

"No, dear. I don't think I'm going to do that." And then her grandmother dropped the chains at her wrists and smiled—smiled?—at Enyo.

"Grandmother!" Ava hissed again. "Your blue blood won't work on this one."

Her grandmother paid her no mind. Her usual brand of self-belief was in full force.

As though looking at a movie montage that pulled all the pieces together, Ava suddenly saw the truth.

Grandmother continued the walk over to Enyo and stood next to her, like a soldier falling in line with the leader.

Her grandmother smiled broadly. "I told you I'd come through, Enyo."

Ava felt Enyo's gaze laser into hers. Dark, evil currents swirled there, and underlying the mix was pure triumph.

Victory.

With a small pat on the back, Enyo smiled benevolently down at Ava's grandmother. "Yes, Patrice, you were the only one I knew I could count on."

Chapter Twenty-three

Ava couldn't tear her gaze off Enyo and her grandmother.

What the hell?

Of all the things she'd learned over the last week, of all the things she'd had to accept, this really was the bomb of the century.

Impossible.

Her grandmother was in league with the goddess of war?

"Grandmother, what are you doing here with her? With Enyo?"

"Ava, Ava. You really are a disappointment to me. Nothing but a boring scientist after all. No imagination. No spunk. No zest. If only one could choose their bloodlines. Choose their lot in life."

Choose?

"Choose what, Grandmother?"

"The prophecy should have foretold of *me*. Of *my* gifts. Instead, they passed through me! Through me to my son and his useless daughter. It was my gift!"

Wyatt chose that moment to pipe up. He hadn't left his

mother's side since he'd come into the room; he hadn't taken his eyes off her. In fact, if Ava had read the situation correctly, she'd have said he was growing distinctly uneasy about the choices he'd made.

"Ava is the answer to the Great Prophecy, Mother. You told me that years ago. You said we could use her to wield the power of the stones."

Grandmother didn't even turn her head, but just kept her eyes turned on Ava. "And we will, Wyatt."

"How long have you been her partner, Grandmother? Since Daddy died?"

"Even I'm not that crass, Ava. Enyo and I have spent the last few years working on this project. How else did you think you got the curation job? And why else was the dig reopened in Egypt?"

"You did that?"

"Of course I did. All of it. And you were so easy. You've been so easy all along. All I have to do is mention your beloved father and you go into fits of need, desperate to please his memory. What a disappointment you are."

Enyo let out a loud yawn, turning her attention to her nephews. "Deimos. Phobos. Please load up the limousine. I'd like to try out my new toys. *Today.*"

The Bobbsey twins grabbed Ava and Wyatt, while her grandmother was allowed to walk on her own. Now that the visage of frailty was off, Ava saw she had amazing use of her arms and legs, easily walking back up the steps of the old tunnel.

Oh God, where was Brody? Or his brothers? The freaking zodiac cavalry.

Maybe Brody really was hurt. Ava hadn't allowed herself to dwell on that idea, but what if he was dead? Ajax had used the poison on him to great effect—what if Enyo had conjured something like that?

As they marched back up the stairs they'd descended only the evening before, she tried desperately to come up with a plan. Of course, one scan of the broad backs of Deimos and Phobos and Ava had to acknowledge this wasn't the ideal time to make a break.

When that suggestion passed, she found she was dismally empty on any other ideas.

Her gaze continued to roam the inside of the luxury car, desperate for answers—for *something*, for some idea that might help her get out of this.

Brody dropped into the abandoned subway tunnel, his port matched exactly to Quinn's instructions. He found the heavy feel of his drawn sword a comforting weight on his shoulder muscles.

The Xiphos was fine for daily combat, but these were their pride and joy—swords forged on Mount Olympus from the heat of Zeus's thunderbolts. Themis had gifted each of them with one on their turning.

Kane dropped next to him, so quiet Brody nearly missed it.

"You're going to have to teach me how you manage to drop two-twenty in solid muscle with the stealth of a cat."

"Talent," Kane answered with a smirk. The two of them started down a long corridor, the walls of the subway tunnels rising above them in an arch. "At least I've still got something."

"You've still got a lot."

Kane shook his head as they came to a new tunnel entrance. They moved through it, the air darker and damper than the higher level they'd been standing on. "Not if I don't figure out who the bitch was who stung me in London."

"You find any leads?"

"I'm running a few things down."

"You think she's a part of this?"

Kane shook his head, his mouth a grim line, his jaw hard. "Nope. That was personal. I just need to figure out why. What she wanted and why she burned me."

Brody was prevented from saying anything else as a loud noise rumbled down the corridor they'd just left. With barely a second to react, Brody and Kane turned as the Chimera leaped into the tunnel with them. Brody's lion answered in kind, roaring to life and filling up his aura.

The animal raced toward them, its lion head open-throated in a full roar while blood dripped from the mouth of the goat that emerged from the lion's back.

Kane swung his sword in a broad, sweeping motion. "Fuck, even that's bad for Enyo. I thought they'd killed off the last of these."

"Leave it to Enyo to still have one as a pet." Brody leaped in, brandishing his sword in unison with Kane. In mirrored movements, they severed the head of the goat and the lion. As the body fell to the floor, Brody added the death blow to the snake that grew out of the Chimera's tail.

"Come on."

They followed the twists of the tunnel, then saw a set of stairs. Brody beat a path first, Kane's footsteps hot on his heels.

A light beckoned ahead, and Brody could see two matched archways. Even as they moved forward, careful in their footsteps so they wouldn't alert anyone to their presence, Brody knew it was futile.

No one was here.

The air was too still, the subtle hum of another's presence absent.

They rounded the corner of the room, and an empty bed stared back at them, confirming Brody's suspicion. "She's gone."

"The needle?" Kane arched an eyebrow.

"Now!"

Brody walked the perimeter of Cleopatra's Needle, counting off paces, orienting himself with the location. With each step he took—each potential pathway he traced—he thought of the millions of things that could go wrong.

What if this wasn't even the right place?

What if they'd misread Quinn's damn intel?

What if Enyo had already killed her?

"Brody! Over here." He followed the sound of Quinn's voice until he found their Taurus hidden in the trees, a listening device set up in a copse of trees.

"Surely we're not planning on making small talk?"

"I want to get as much information as we possibly can. And, I'm working on a new idea. I want to get a voiceprint of Enyo. See if access to her voice and modulations unlock anything."

"Will that do anything for you?"

Quinn shrugged. "Maybe. Maybe not. It never hurts to be prepared."

"No voiceprint at the risk of Ava's life."

Quinn simply stood there and stared at him. As the moment stretched out, Brody felt an itch at his lower back. "What?"

"You can't seriously be asking me that? I'd lay down my life for that woman, Brody. Surely you know that?"

"You didn't like her at first."

"I didn't know her. Didn't know why you were bringing her into our midst. Didn't know anything. Now I know."

"Sorry."

Quinn blew on the edge of one of his listening devices. "There's something else I know."

"What's that?"

"That woman is your mate. As surely as I'm standing here, she is your woman."

Brody ran a hand through his hair. The blustery fall breeze had whipped his hair around and he'd wished for a cord to hold his hair back more than once since they'd been outside. "My mortal woman."

"Does that matter?"

Did it?

Would immortality make Ava any different? Any more right for him?

"Don't ruin what you have because it's not your version of perfect. Maybe it's perfect just the way it is."

"Quinn. I've been afraid of losing her in sixty years. What if I lose her today?"

One minute he was standing there; the next he was flat on his back, his jaw throbbing from where Quinn's fist had implanted itself.

He took a few deep breaths, willing his lion against his body. "What the hell was that for?"

"How dare you suggest we're going to let something happen to your woman?"

And as Brody continued to stare up at him, Quinn stuck out his hand. With a firm grip, Brody took the offering of friendship, regaining his feet.

"We're not losing her, Brody."

The brief car ride didn't offer any additional illumination of what was going on or where they were going, but it did shed some light on her uncle's role in Enyo's organization. Although she'd suspected since the evening before, his bound hands confirmed it.

He was one hundred percent, wholly disposable.

Even by his mother.

"Shocking, isn't it?" Enyo smiled at her, the bloodred of her lips curling up in mockery.

"No more shocking than anything else that's happened to me in the last week. Hell, my entire life. It's all revolved around those damn stones. Every single thing about my life ties back to those."

"Lucky girl." Enyo pulled out a compact from a small clutch purse hidden in the door of the limousine. "Of course, luck really is a relative term." She dashed powder along the bridge of her nose. "It comes and goes so very, very quickly."

Ignoring Enyo, Ava found her thoughts drifting again to the bleak reality that was her family.

What the hell sort of family had she come from? Was it really possible she'd spent her entire life oblivious to all of them? To their evil natures and greedy ways?

Or had it been the fear? That damnable fear and loathing her grandmother had been more than willing to shove down her throat.

Always present. Never tolerant.

The car came to a halt and Deimos and Phobos immediately began to drag her and Wyatt out of the car. She could hear Wyatt as Phobos held him in what she could only assume was the matched, viselike grip of his brother.

In seconds, Phobos dragged him across a clearing, into what Ava now realized was Central Park. Ava heard her uncle's screams as they moved farther and farther away from the car.

"Where are you taking me?" Panic coated Wyatt's voice

in great, quivering waves. "Why are you asking me to leave my family? I brought her to you!"

Ava watched her grandmother and Enyo as they followed at a distance behind Wyatt. A smile spread across her grandmother's face, the expression so telling—so bereft of motherly love and affection—Ava felt nausea roil in her stomach in great, billowing waves.

Deimos grabbed at her hands, dragging her in everyone's wake. "Time to go, Ava."

As her captor dragged her farther into the park, Ava kept an eye on her surroundings. The heels she'd worn to Grandmother's sank into the damp, autumn earth as they traipsed off the paths. And as they walked, Ava had absolutely no doubt where they were heading.

She'd been there recently, in fact.

In her nightmares with Thutmose's high priest.

The obelisks that had presented the entrance to Thutmose's great city now held places of honor around the globe: one here in Central Park; another in London on the banks of the Thames.

As Cleopatra's Needle came into view, Ava knew. Knew on a soul-deep level that this was where it would happen.

This was where she would change.

This was where she would either die or find new life.

It was all here.

Now.

As Deimos dragged her along, she realized something else, horror dawning brighter and brighter with each step.

A dark shape hung from the top of the ancient obelisk, drawing the eye as it followed the sleek lines toward the sky. And then they were close enough and she knew exactly what it was.

Wyatt lay, impaled on the top of the needle, his body hanging over the top and marring the obelisk's journey to the sky.

Great, agonizing screams flew from her throat as she took in the sight of her uncle, so recently alive, now staring down at them with sightless eyes.

Instinctively, Ava wanted to curl up into herself, close out what was happening and retreat to a small place inside that no one could reach. But not anymore.

She would not be defeated.

As a swirl of wind kicked up, carrying Phobos's and Deimos's laughter toward her, she was helpless to stop the rage that beat inside of her. Helpless to stop the need for vengeance that pulsed to the very depths of her soul.

Brody watched from a distance as one of the demon twins strung up Ava's uncle on the top of Cleopatra's Needle. Despite his loathing for Wyatt Harrison, his honor as a Warrior depended on giving aid to humans in need. If it hadn't been for Kane's quick grab of his ankles, he would have been in the thick of the action before he thought better of it.

And fully exposed as Ava came into the clearing.

Followed by Enyo and . . . Ava's grandmother?

"Brody, stay back. You need to wait on this. See what they're going to do."

Someone prodded Ava from behind. Pure, undiluted rage swam through his veins as he realized it was Deimos and it took sheer force of will to keep his lion against his body.

How dare he touch her?

"Brody. Don't make us hold you back. We need to give them time to set up," Quinn muttered against his ear. "We have to get the lay of the land."

He nodded. He knew the truth of Quinn's words; he knew he needed to wait even as every single fiber of his being cried out to go to her, to save her.

"We need to know what she's capable of."

Brody whirled on Quinn. "You told me you wouldn't let her take unnecessary risks. You told me you'd save her before that happened. That's why we brought the last two stones—for Ava."

"Yes, Brody, for Ava. So if Enyo throws some surprises at us, we can give them to her and see what she can do with all five stones. In the meantime? We need to sit and wait. We have to know how she reacts. What if they cloud her judgment so badly she turns on us? You. Don't. Know."

"Ava won't hurt us."

"Not voluntarily, no. You saw what happened to her with one stone. One. You saw what it can do. Don't tell me you've conveniently forgotten?"

Of course he hadn't forgotten. But surely she would do better with all the stones. They'd balance one another so she could use them.

You. Don't. Know.

Quinn's fucking words pounded in his head.

And then Enyo appeared in the clearing, at the base of the obelisk. Her arms were raised and great beams of light exploded from her fingertips. Within the beams, Enyo balanced a clear pouch that looked as delicate as jellyfish skin.

Even from this distance, Brody felt the coiled power hover in the air. Like the threat of a thunderstorm, the heavy air grew, expanded and oppressed everything in its path.

Ava tried not to look at Uncle Wyatt. She tried to keep her eyes averted, but it was hard—nearly impossible not to feel some sense of remorse for what he had become.

For what her whole family had become.

Was this the result of her father's life's work? Was this all it meant?

Enyo lifted her hands higher, the gossamer bag opening at the top. With her gaze focused on some point in the distance Ava assumed only the goddess of war could see, the woman began to laugh.

Then she lowered the clear, translucent bag, reached in and pulled out—

Oh my God.

Bile rose immediately in Ava's throat as her stomach cramped. A human head—or what was formerly human; it was Brody's brother, Ajax.

"Now, Dr. Talbot!" Enyo screamed in the direction of the needle. "I suggest you come out from wherever it is you're hiding. You can claim your brother's body. I believe he's really dead this time. And you can try and save your girlfriend while you're at it."

Brody?

Hope burst through her chest, a rainbow in the midst of this emotional hurricane.

And then he was there. And he was looking at her. And his blue eyes locked with hers, his gaze giving her strength she never knew she had.

With deliberate movements, he moved into the clearing, taunting Enyo the whole way. "You just can't stand anyone who tries to get in your way. On this one, however, you miscalculated. Do you really think I give a shit about my brother's body? I haven't missed him for the last ten thousand years. I'm certainly not about to start now."

Enyo tossed Ajax's head in Brody's direction, sheer rage in her movements. "I'd say things went down a bit differently than that. I got in *his* way. And clearly"—Enyo shot a nasty sneer in the direction of Brody's late brother—"I call the shots."

Brody stood, tossing his Xiphos with lightning-quick movements from hand to hand. He was magnificent. Her Warrior.

Her man.

The gossamer pouch Enyo held dangled from her hand, the top still open. As Ava watched the fight unfold between the two of them, the air around them began to change, like the building fervor of a team of horses or the increasing crash of waves as a hurricane blew into shore.

Images of the last few weeks—the renewed memories of her mother and father, the freshly made memories with Brody, the horrors of the past night as she learned the truth about her family—all began to coalesce around her, drawing on the deep power of her emotions.

Unable to hold herself still, Ava stretched out her arms, amazed when three stones floated from the pouch Enyo held to hover above them all in the clearing.

"Ava!" Quinn hollered from behind her as he stepped into the clearing. "Catch!" With that, he tossed the two remaining stones up, where they got caught in the vortex, hovering along with the other three.

The five reunited stones spun in the air of their own accord, a frenzy of activity on the wind.

Hands up, her hair whipping in the wind, Ava drew power from the air around her. Like her innate ability to breathe, the power beat through her very essence.

Natural.

Real.

Raw.

She drew the power from the stones, pulling it into her

hands and then reflecting it back. Bright, beautiful waves of light, matching the color of each stone.

Deep indigo, bloodred crimson, yellow ochre, emerald green, incandescent white; they all swirled around her.

What was happening to her?

Great magnetic waves of force pummeled her body, even as she stood straight and tall in the clearing. From the moment Enyo stepped in front of the needle and opened the satchel, Ava felt her body operate independently of her own thoughts.

Great, gusting waves of power washed over her, in her, *through* her.

She felt it fill her up—nerve and sinew; flesh and bone. Her entire body was filled with power—with the sheer joy of it, like a thousand orgasms, released all at once.

She. Was. Incredible.

The stones spun around her head. Curious at what she could do with them, she extended her hands toward her uncle's body. With deliberate movements, she lifted him off the top of the needle and gently moved him through the air to lay him at Grandmother's feet.

When the woman didn't move—didn't even deign to look at her son—Ava felt a small short circuit in the currents around her, a break in the power coursing through her as she stopped to stare at her grandmother.

Who was this woman? She'd lived her entire life as a lie—a polite facade designed to fool the world.

She should be punished.

"Come here, Ava. Come closer to me." Enyo had her own arms outstretched, pulling her closer. "You feel it, don't you? The beauty of power. The strength in it." She was close enough that Enyo closed the distance between them to whisper in her ear. "The way it makes you feel. You are no longer nothing. You have nothing to fear. All power is yours."

As Enyo's voice washed over her, Ava knew it was fake. She knew the goddess told lies.

But, oh God, did the power feel good. Great, huge, coursing waves of it.

She'd never be afraid. Ever again.

Never run from any situation.

Never . . .

Brody stepped out of the clearing, his arms outstretched as Enyo's had been.

"My Ava. Don't do this. Don't give in to her. Her promises are empty."

The stones faltered in her hands as she moved them. Then, she pulled back.

"And yours aren't?"

"No, my darling. They are full of love for you."

And then Enyo was in her other ear, hissing like a snake. "He's a man. They make promises that are handy. Promises to get what they want. Look at what my father did to me. Themis and Zeus's great bargain, eh? Where was my choice? My decision in all this?"

She didn't want what Enyo offered; she knew she didn't.

Brody didn't offer empty promises.

He offered love.

As she turned toward him, a loud scream broke through the field as Deimos and Phobos headed straight for Brody.

With a feral war cry of his own, Brody charged back at them, his lion at full throttle next to him.

Ava watched the colors of the stones dance before her eyes. Somewhere, reason clawed at her, trying to tell her something.

Trying to break through.

"Kill them," Enyo whispered in her ear as Quinn and Kane launched themselves into the fray, the Warriors and the demons locked in battle.

"It's so easy, Ava. You can kill my nephews. Just reach out and take it."

As if suspended in time, Ava watched the battle play out. The stones continued to whirl around her, infusing her with power. Enyo remained at her perch, whispering in her ear. She whispered for her to reach out and take—to own—the power she held in her hands.

And still, Ava didn't move.

She just let the power swirl around her.

"Some prophecy you are!" Enyo screamed in her ear as those blood-tipped fingers clamped over her hands. "You will not take this from me!"

The air swirled around them.

The skirmish raged in front of them.

But the real battle was the one inside of her.

Who do you want to be, Ava Marie? Who do you believe you already are?

And then she saw Brody as he struggled for his own life, fighting for her.

With nothing but his own strength, he fought for her.

For *her*.

Slowly, she lowered her arms, pressing all her might against Enyo's superhuman strength.

She was desperate to flush the power from her system.

Frantic to prove she was worthy of Brody.

Determined to prove to herself that she was a woman of value.

Ava had nearly lowered the stones entirely when Enyo threw a last burst of strength, pulling up on her arms. Power lasered through the clearing, the colors of the stones coalescing into a streaming rainbow of continuously changing color.

And then Ava took control again, twisting her arms so the power of the stones fed back on the two of them.

She felt the power shoot up her arms and into her heart.

Felt the power of it throw Enyo off her back.

And as the stones flew from her hands, Ava felt herself fly through the air to land at the base of Cleopatra's Needle.

Chapter Twenty-four

A va opened her eyes, instantly aware and instantly alert. "Brody? Is he okay?"

"He's fine. Vanquished his enemies in another fine show of valor."

Brody was okay. He'd *survived*. Ava looked around. "Where am I?"

Smooth, tender fingers brushed the hair off her temples. "Mount Olympus."

Ava looked up at the sweet woman with the tender face and sad eyes. "Themis?"

"Yes, my sweet child?"

"Why am I here?" Ava heard herself, and her voice sounded all scratchy. "Did I die?"

"In a way."

"In a way?" Ava struggled to sit up. "What way?"

"Shhh. Conserve your strength. You were very brave today, Ava. You made a great choice."

"Choices again." Ava thought she'd said those words inside her head, but Themis's soft laughter suggested otherwise.

"Yes. Choices. Life is full of them, isn't it?"

She had a point there. "What great choice are you referring to?"

"You discarded the very essence of power when you discarded the stones."

"Discarded them? All I remember was throwing them as hard as I could."

"It was that act—that simple act of denial—that destroyed them. They disintegrated before they even hit the ground."

"I needed to be worthy of Brody. He doesn't abuse *his* power. Had I used the stones, I'd be no better than Enyo; no better than my grandmother."

"And what about before Brody? You had a good life and you discarded it, living your life in fear. Is that not giving in to a dominating power?"

Shame burned her skin like a sunburn. "Yes. I lived that way."

"Are you prepared to discard that way, too?"

She wanted to scream a great, big, sobbing yes, but something held her back.

Did she have it in her to give full trust to another?

An image of Brody's face as he fought Deimos and Phobos for her rose to life in her mind's eye.

Loving meant trusting.

Loving meant everything.

With firm resolve, she looked at Themis as she made her vow. "No, I don't want to live that way any longer, either."

"Then I think this is a most special day, Ava. Today you made a decision that will set the course of the rest of your life."

"What life? I'm dead, aren't I?" Ava felt the telltale pricks at the back of her eyes, then felt the tears well up and spill in one great, hot rush.

Good grief, even in death she was a waterworks.

"Come. I want you to look at something with me."

With barely a thought, Ava went from a bed to a standing position next to Themis, a large viewing screen in front of them.

"Stand before my Mirror of Truth and tell me what you see."

As the screen came to life, she saw Brody, cradling her body at the base of Cleopatra's Needle. Tears streamed down his cheeks. His fellow Warriors stood guard around him as his body convulsed in great heaving sobs over her.

"So I did die, then."

"As I said, in a way. Your mortal body died in that clearing in Central Park."

"Then how can I be here? How can we be having this conversation?"

"You denied the power in the Summoning Stones. For that, I can give you something equally unselfish. Something of equal measure."

As Themis turned toward her, the reality of her words crashed into Ava.

There was a way.

Themis had found a way.

"Brody. Only Brody and an immortal life with him."

"Then go, my sweet Warrior. I give you life with your beloved."

Brody would not let her go. His brothers and Callie urged him on, to allow her spirit to begin its journey, but still, he held on.

"I can't leave you, my love." He squeezed her tighter as he pressed his forehead to hers. Great, heaving sobs wracked his body as hot tears bathed her face. "I can't leave you."

"Then don't, my love. Don't leave me—ever."

What?

With frantic movements, he sat back, lifting her body to bring her face close to his. "Ava?"

A small smile hovered about her lips as that gorgeous brown gaze locked with his. "Yes, my love."

"How?"

"We have someone wonderful on our side." At his blank stare, Ava smiled up at him. "Themis."

"How did Themis do this? Her agreement with Zeus. No more Warriors. And then her bad experience with my brother, bringing him back to life."

"Apparently she found a loophole. I gave up something so selflessly, she could grant me something I wanted with my whole heart."

"Life."

She reached up and framed his face with her hand. "You. Only you. Forever."

Hope whispered under his skin, floating through his veins to fill his heart. "You're immortal."

"She called me a Warrior as she sent me on my way."

"A female Warrior?"

"You got a problem with that?"

His smile rivaled the sun. "Absolutely not." He shifted her so that she was cradled in his lap, his mouth nuzzling her neck. "But let me get this straight. She made you a Warrior? As in a What's-your-sign Warrior?"

"Well, we didn't talk about that part. How about if we're partners on the hunt for ancient artifacts? Clearly I have a knack for them."

Brody pulled her close. "Clearly you do."

"Of course," Ava added, "I'd like a more romantic job description, too."

"Name it."

"I'll be the moon in your ascendant and we'll call it a life."

"When you put it like that."

Brody knew they'd figure out Themis's true motives soon enough. For now, it was enough that he had Ava in his arms and a future with the woman he loved.

Epilogue

"Ava, you have to keep your eyes open when you port; otherwise you can't see the landing."

She giggled, the light sound filling Brody's heart with pure, unadulterated joy. "I always forget that part."

He rubbed his lower back as he shot her the gimlet eye. "Which is why I keep landing on my ass."

She leaned over to make a quick inspection. "And an incredibly fine ass, it is. It's a good thing I keep landing us in bed."

"I guess it is."

They lay there quietly, the only sound their breathing, in sync with each other. Ava spoke first. "I feel like I'm getting used to it."

Brody couldn't argue with her there. Ava had embraced her role as a new Warrior of Themis with dedication and devotion. They'd already been to Alexandria to inspect some Greek artifacts said to date from Alexander the Great's time and on a trip to inspect some ancient Babylonian scrolls.

The scrolls had turned out to be nothing more than ancient grocery lists, but they were heading back to Greece in a few weeks to make sure the Greek government disposed of Alexander's staff as promised.

"Do you miss your old life?"

"No." Ava shook her head against his chest.

Brody lifted himself up on an elbow. "Really?"

"Really. I found you. And that's all I need."

She rolled toward him and planted her soft lips against his. The fire that raged between them grew and expanded, heated and burned, as the kiss stretched out.

Long. Languorous. Needful.

Shifting, Ava climbed on top of him, a broad smile stretched across her face. "Besides, you're way more fun than Sunday dinner at Grandmother's house."

"That's no way to speak of the dead, darling."

Her eyes darkened momentarily. "Yes, well, I haven't hit the point where I feel very sorry for her."

"I wouldn't waste a single second of thought on the matter."

"I won't." She reached down and grabbed fistfuls of his T-shirt. He lifted himself slightly so she could slide it over his head. "My thoughts of late have been filled with other things."

Brody lifted her blouse, the soft globes of her breasts a welcome treat where they spilled over the lace of her bra. "Well then, why don't you tell me about it, Mrs. Talbot?"

Ava leaned forward to plant a kiss against his throat. "I've got an even better idea, my love. Why don't I show you?"

GEMINI/LEO STAR CHART

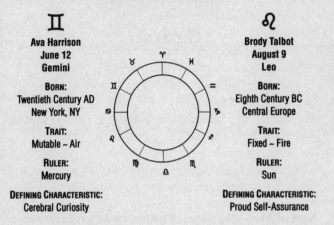

♊

Ava Harrison
June 12
Gemini

BORN:
Twentieth Century AD
New York, NY

TRAIT:
Mutable ~ Air

RULER:
Mercury

DEFINING CHARACTERISTIC:
Cerebral Curiosity

♌

Brody Talbot
August 9
Leo

BORN:
Eighth Century BC
Central Europe

TRAIT:
Fixed ~ Fire

RULER:
Sun

DEFINING CHARACTERISTIC:
Proud Self-Assurance

Opposites attract when airy Gemini meets fiery Leo.

Although the Gemini woman might initially chafe at her Leo's self-assured intensity, the Lion is exceptionally loyal, especially to the woman he chooses as his mate.

Always seeking answers to her questions, the Gemini woman hungers for a man who can keep her constantly interested and engaged. Leo, with his fierce pride and love of action, will ensure her seeking nature always finds something interesting in his flair for the dramatic.

Our brave Leo seeks a woman who can tame the beast. A natural leader, a woman who can be a true partner—a mate worthy of equal respect—will win his heart and his lifelong loyalty.

If Ava and Brody can prove they are worthy of Themis's respect, the stars promise a long and prosperous life for both of them—and for their descendents. . . .

GLOSSARY

Ages of Man—the stages of human existence, as identified by the Greek writer Hesiod. Most often associated with metals, the ages—Gold, Silver, Bronze, Heroic and Iron—reflect the increasing toil and drudgery humans live in. The world only thinks the ages are myth. . . .

Cardinal—a sign *quality*, Cardinal signs (Aries, Cancer, Libra, Capricorn) mark the start of each season. Those born under Cardinal signs are considered dynamic and, like each season, forceful in their beginnings. Cardinal Warriors are equally dynamic, forcing change with their impatient natures and independent spirits.

Chimera—With the body and head of a lion, the tail of a snake and the head of a goat extending from the center of its back, the Chimera is one of the eleven monsters of Mount Olympus. It is created by the goddess Echidna, the Mother of all Monsters, whose menagerie is a favorite resource of terror for Deimos and Phobos.

Deimos—The god of dread, Deimos is the son of Ares and Aphrodite, and the brother of Phobos.

Destroyer—a soulless creature created by Enyo from an emotionally damaged human. Destroyers take on the appearance of men, but their bodies are nothing but husks, filled with a superconductive life force. They can be slowed and hurt, but quickly recover. The only way to kill a Destroyer is by removing his head. Each Destroyer Enyo creates takes some of her power, preserving an innate balance agreed to during the creation of the Great Agreement.

Element—Just as all signs are Cardinal, Fixed or Mutable, each sign also possesses an elemental quality of Fire, Earth, Air or Water. Each Warrior has an elemental nature to his sign, allowing for additional powers for those who have learned to develop them. These elemental qualities exist beyond those granted to all Warriors—immortality, the ability to port, rapid healing and above-average strength—and have begun to express themselves as the Warriors have grown more comfortable in their abilities and better understand the full range of their skills.

Enyo—Daughter of Zeus and Hera, Enyo is the goddess of war, equipped with the ability to create anarchy and death wherever she goes. Zeus offered Enyo up to Themis for their Great Agreement. Before Zeus allowed Themis to create the Sons of the Zodiac, she had to agree to a counterbalance to the Warriors' power. Enyo provides the balance, at constant war with Themis's Warriors. For each battle Enyo wins, her power grows; for each she loses, her power diminishes.

Equinox—a nightclub owned by Grey Bennett, Aries Warrior. Each Warrior has a role within the whole, and Grey's is to keep an eye on the underbelly of New York for Enyo's likely crop of new Destroyers. None of the Warriors knows, however, that Grey carries a secret—one that will lead him to his destiny or to his doom. . . .

Fixed—A sign *quality*, Fixed signs (Taurus, Leo, Scorpio, Aquarius) mark the middle of each season. Those born under Fixed signs are considered quite stubborn and persistent. Fixed Warriors are equally stubborn and persistent, unwilling to yield to their enemies.

Great Agreement—an agreement entered into during the Iron Age (the Fifth Age of Man) by Zeus and Themis. Fearful that her beloved humans had no protection from the trials of life, Themis entered into an agreement with Zeus that created the Sons of the Zodiac. The Sons of the Zodiac are Warriors modeled after the circular perfection of the heavens, and each Warrior carries the immutable qualities of his sign. Under the Great Agreement, the immortal Warriors will battle Zeus's daughter Enyo, the goddess of war, for the ultimate protection, quality and survival of humanity.

Hera—wife of Zeus and mother of Enyo.

Iron Age—the Fifth Age of Man, generally thought to be about ten thousand years ago, where humans toil in abject misery. Brothers fight brothers, children turn against their fathers and anarchy is the rule of the land. During this age the gods have forsaken humanity. It is during this time that Themis—desperate to alter the course of human existence—goes to Zeus and enters into the Great Agreement. The Sons of the Zodiac are created during this age.

Mutable—A sign *quality*, Mutable signs (Gemini, Virgo, Sagittarius, Pisces) mark the end of each season. Those born under Mutable signs are the most comfortable with change, making them easily adaptable and resourceful. Mutable Warriors are the first to see the big picture, able to adapt and shift their battle plans at a moment's notice. Their ability to see issues from multiple angles make them strong Warriors and a comfort to have watching one's back.

Phobos—The god of fear, Phobos is the son of Ares and Aphrodite, and the brother of Deimos.

Port—the shortened form of teleport. Warriors and Destroyers have the ability to move through space and time at will. Porting diminishes power.

Prophecy of Thutmose III—Carved on the walls of Thutmose III's tomb and not discovered until the early twenty-first century, the prophecy outlines the power of the Summoning Stones of Egypt, for those who are chosen by them.

Sons of the Zodiac—created by Themis, the goddess of justice, upon her Great Agreement with Zeus. The Great Agreement stipulates that a race of Warriors—156 in total—will have the traits of their zodiac sign. Tasked with protecting humanity, they are at war with Enyo. A Warrior is immortal, although he may be killed with a death blow to the neck that decapitates him, this being the only way to kill him. His strength may be reduced from extended time in battle, multiple ports and little food, and his strength may be replenished with food, sleep or sexual orgasm. Each Warrior has a tattoo of added protection that lives within his aura.

Summoning Stones of Egypt—The five Summoning Stones of Egypt were crafted during the reign of Thutmose III. For those who are chosen—there is a Chosen One in each age—the stones give the user the power to control the universe. Each of the five stones represents a different element—death, life, love, sexuality and infinity.

Tartarus—a prisonlike pit below the Underworld. Zeus's father, Cronus, is housed in Tartarus at Zeus's hand.

Themis—One of the twelve Titans, Themis is the goddess of justice. Disheartened that her beloved humans toiled in misery and abject drudgery, she petitioned Zeus to allow her to intercede. With Zeus she entered into the Great Agreement, which provided for the creation of the Sons of the Zodiac, 156 Warriors embodied with the traits of their signs. Originally she envisioned twelve of twelve, but upon reaching her agreement with Zeus, gained an additional twelve Warriors so Gemini might have his twin. Themis's Warriors live around the globe, battling Enyo and keeping humanity safe.

Titans—the original twelve children born of Uranus (Father Sky) and Gaia (Earth). Themis is one of the Titans, as is Cronus, Zeus's father.

Warrior's Tattoo—The Warrior's Tattoo is inked on his body, generally on his upper-right or -left shoulder blade. The tattoo lives within the Warrior's aura and, when the Warrior is in danger, the tattoo will expand as an additional form of protection. The tattoo is never separate; rather, it provides additional protection through the Warrior's life force.

Xiphos—An ancient Greek weapon, the Xiphos is a double-edged blade less than a foot long. Each Warrior carries one strapped on his calf. Although a Warrior may use any Xiphos—or any weapon—when necessary, each Warrior is granted a Xiphos at his turning. A Warrior may deliver a death blow to a Destroyer's neck when at close range, but the Xiphos provides an additional tool in battle. Although the Xiphos is nothing more than metal, many Warriors find a personal connection with their Xiphos because it accompanies them through many years of battle.

Zeus—King of the gods and ruler over Mount Olympus, Zeus is married to Hera. Zeus's first wife was Themis, the goddess of justice and one of the Titans. Zeus entered the Great Agreement with Themis, which resulted in the Sons of the Zodiac, the protectors of humanity.

Turn the page for a preview of the
next book in Addison Fox's powerful
Sons of the Zodiac series,

WARRIOR AVENGED

Coming from Signet Eclipse in September 2010

The poison coiled, a living, writhing beast that skipped through his veins on spiked heels. The venom was an unmerciful taskmaster, lying in wait for the one day each year when it could dominate. Control. Kill.

Even now, silky threads of it wove through his bloodstream—expanding, growing, pulsing with life.

Kane Montague, Scorpio Warrior of the great goddess of justice, Themis, ignored it. Ignored the whip-quick lashes that slammed through him from the inside out, as if his very organs were being rent in half. Ignored the brutal assault on his muscle fibers that felt like the stinging prick of a million wasps. Ignored the wicked, boiling sensation that filled his bloodstream like a flowing river of lava.

If you pretended for long enough that something didn't exist, you could almost convince yourself that it didn't exist. *Almost.*

He continued to bench-press, his rhythm even and easy, his breathing focused and controlled. Arms up, breath out. Arms down, breath in.

This cold-blooded, laser-sharp focus had been the hallmark of his life, even before he made his life-changing agreement with Themis. The selection as one of her Scorps only sealed the deal.

Nothing got in the way of his militant focus and there was nothing that could pull him from his goals.

Not his Warrior brothers.

Not the poison.

And sure as fuck not a luscious brunette with endless legs and a gorgeous rack.

So why did she still dominate his thoughts six months later? The woman had gone by the name Ilsa. The double agent who had managed to seduce him, fuck him brainless and drug him so she could make her escape.

"You keep driving yourself like this and the poison won't need until the end of the month to kick your ass to the curb."

Kane grunted on an exhale and didn't even bother to turn toward their Taurus and self-appointed leader as he walked across the weight room. "Get out of here, Quinn. I don't need a babysitter."

"Since when don't you want a workout partner?"

Kane ignored the Bull, although in his peripheral vision he could see Quinn Tanner's hulking form move closer. "Since you've taken it upon yourself to treat me as if I'm still in diapers."

Quinn dropped to a nearby weight bench and began lifting his own set of metal. "Concern, buddy. Nothing more."

With a loud thud, Kane slammed the heavy bar onto its rack and slipped off the bench. He'd be damned if he was going to sit around and listen to this shit as if he were some invalid. He ignored the sharp stabs in his gut as the poison twisted his intestines like rows of tangled Christmas lights, and headed for the exit.

A rush of air greeted him as Quinn's large body took shape in front of him in less than a second, as the Bull's port from his own weight bench was instantaneous. "You've got two weeks, Kane. And you're pushing too hard. Give it a rest. Stay strong, and once you beat it back, you can go after her again."

Whether it was his own anger or added aggression from the poison, Kane wasn't quite sure—nor did he care. He launched himself at Quinn, knocking the Taurus to the ground, where they fell into a heap of grunting, groaning testosterone.

Where Quinn's body was broad, beefy muscle, Kane's was long and lean, his muscles more sinew than heft. He knew they must not look very well matched from a distance, but his leaner form allowed him fuller range of motion and the ability to squeeze out of Quinn's hold.

Of course, it also meant he took a sizable hit from Quinn's meaty fists when the larger man finally laid one on him.

A satisfying zing ran up Kane's arm as he planted his own fist in the middle of Quinn's baby-faced mug. The satisfaction was short-lived, as he felt strong hands latch on to his shoulders and pull him from behind. The black silk shirt covering his captor's forearm gave away the man's identity before Kane even saw his face.

"Get off me, Grey. I don't need your help."

The strength of the hold persisted, but Grey's voice held sly amusement. "What you need is an ass kicking from both of us, but you're not worth the risk to my new Brioni slacks."

The hold loosened, followed immediately by an open-palmed smack to the side of Kane's head. Before Kane could react, Grey was already leaning down to extend a hand to Quinn, whose mouth was on overdrive, as usual. "Ignore him, Grey. The Scorp's wardrobe is even flashier than yours."

"Hardly." Grey dusted a hand over those black slacks he was so proud of. "Seeing how I didn't actually come here to break up a dogfight, you want to hear me out?"

Kane still felt pissy, but his curiosity quickly won out. "Fine. What's going on?"

"I think I got a line on that brunette you've been after."

A renewed flare of anger flooded his system, but this time it had nothing to do with the poison living underneath his skin. "How do you know it's Ilsa?"

"She's been paying an awful lot of attention to my club lately. Couple that with several jaunts up and down the front of this place that were captured on the cameras—they're a match with the photo of her that Quinn turned up. I think we've got her."

Kane's stomach tightened again. He didn't want there to be any *we* in Ilsa's capture. He wanted to take her down himself. Shaking his head, he pressed through the selfish desires he had no business having. "She's clearly a highly trained agent. There's no way she'd be so stupid as to get caught like that."

Grey shrugged. "Maybe she's not as savvy as you think."

"She knocked me on my ass, Grey. She knew what she was doing."

Quinn rubbed at his jaw as he added his input to their little coffee klatch. "Grey's got a point, Kane. Something's always rung false for me, like how you've done nothing to make yourself a target. Hell, from the files I've hacked into, you're seen as an incredible asset within MI6. What would be the incentive to get rid of you?"

Kane had asked himself the very same question for the last six months. Banging his head against concrete would have produced better answers than what he'd managed to come up with.

Grey held out his cell phone, a surprisingly clear image covering its glass face. "Is this her?"

Kane knew it before he'd even focused on the screen. It was clear as he took in the shape of her jaw and the aristocratic line of her neck. A blond wig couldn't disguise the essence of her face. "It's her."

Grey was already in motion. "Then let's go. She's been outside Equinox the past three nights. If she follows suit tonight, we'll intercept her outside the club."

Kane stopped Grey before the Aries hit the doorway. "She's mine, Grey."

"Don't worry, Monte. None of us are dumb enough to get in your way."

There were serious benefits to being a Greek goddess. Immortality, permanent youth and a blessed lack of self-doubt all rode quite high on the list.

So when had she become so intent on second-guessing herself?

The goddess known as Nemesis hotfooted it down the New York sidewalk, which was growing increasingly full of humans as she neared her destination. When had she become a sniveling bore like the rest of them? And why in the name of Hades would she risk herself with these stupid jaunts past the Warriors' club?

Even the name she'd selected was stupid. Ilsa. As in Ilsa and Rick from *Casablanca*.

It had seemed like such a great idea at the time, a cheeky wink at the Fates. Of course, somehow in her rush to make a joke of her original encounter with Kane, she'd forgotten one small fact: She'd watched that movie over and over, weeping each and every time for the ill-fated lovers.

And now she knew exactly how Ilsa had felt. Torn between bone-deep attraction for one man and duty to another. Suddenly trapped inside a life she didn't actually want. Full of a love that drove you nearly mad.

So why, then, had that cold rock of a heart she'd ignored for millennia suddenly decided to come alive with a vengeance?

Kane, her conscience whispered.

Ilsa remembered the first time she'd laid eyes on him. Her contact inside MI6 had arranged for the two of them to attend a state dinner to ferret out as much information as they could from a well-connected scientist. Or at least that was what Kane had thought they were doing. Her real job was to keep an eye on the Warrior, searching him for weakness.

Vulnerability.

Something—anything—that might give her an advantage.

In retrospect, Ilsa knew her first glimpse of him should have set off her instincts. They should have warned her somehow. Her only defense, when she'd thought about it later, was that there was simply no way anyone could have been prepared for the image of Kane Montague in a designer tuxedo. The suit jacket molded to his broad shoulders, descending in a vee toward the whipcord-slim hips that sat atop long legs. Legs that she now knew from a later viewing were all sculpted muscle.

She could still remember the feel of the silken fabric of his tuxedo jacket under her fingertips as he'd maneuvered her across the dance floor. She treasured the memory of his bold onyx eyes, their endless depths fathoms darker than the black cashmere of his tux, and the almost-harsh planes of his body as he pressed her against him.

No, there was nothing vulnerable about the man.

Nothing.

Ilsa snapped back to attention at the loud squeal of a silly girl dressed in a nearly nonexistent miniskirt as she sidestepped a puddle of rainwater. What was she even doing here? Especially since she had a big job tonight and should already have been on her way to it. Duty called, and all that responsibility nonsense. Yet here she was, doe-eyed and obsessive, walking past this stupid club. Again.

Why are you here? He's not worth it. Not worth what you'll have to sacrifice.

Ignoring the mental bullshit, Ilsa had barely cleared the back side of the club when a harsh line of static burned a fiery path down her spinal cord. Although she was not fully immune to pain, very little could deter her immortal body.

But this? The intensity of the heat was so jarring that she fell to her knees in a puddle, rain running in rivulets down her back and neck, over the exposed line of her cleavage. Pushing the pain aside, willing the stinging heat away, she attempted to regain her footing. Surprise—and was that panic?—shot through her as a heavy weight bore down on her back, holding her in place as large arms wrapped her in a bear hug.

Vaguely, a shout registered through the adrenaline lighting up her system and the heavy rush of blood in her ears. "Do you have her yet?"

A vile stench filled the air as wet lips rubbed against her ear, breath coming heavy against her face. "Got her."

Forcing strength through her slight frame, she rammed her head back toward the heavy weight, trying to dislodge the asshole who thought he'd have his way with her. Just as she made contact—a deep, satisfying thud—another wave of heat assaulted her, wrapping her nerve endings in liquid fire. Her neck, extended from the reverse head butt, swam with pain as she choked in breath, desperate for air.

Real panic flared, and with it, a wave of resolute anger filled her. She'd vowed the day Zeus abandoned her that she would never be weak again. Would never surrender to another. Would *never* be beaten back.

With grim determination, Ilsa forged renewed strength in the fire of the pain. Straightening inch by inch, she pressed against the immense weight at her back. She felt it—*knew it*—the moment she had him. As her captor's resistance slipped, she used one final burst of strength to dislodge him.

Stumbling forward, she whirled around to finish the job and take the asshole down. No sooner did she have him in her sights—a large brute of a man with scars crisscrossing his face and a spiderweb tattoo covering his neck—then his head went spiraling off his body.

Ilsa blinked through the pouring rain. *What the . . . ?*

Kane Montague stood over the rapidly disintegrating corpse, his wolfish smile broad and easily visible through the torrents of rain. He held an ancient sword aloft in his firm grip. "Hello, Ilsa."

She nodded and bit back an actual gulp. "Kane."

"I guess there's really only one thing to say."

Her gaze drank him in as he stood before her. Rain poured off the short length of his hair, down over the gray T-shirt that now molded itself to every delicious inch of his torso. Ilsa heard her voice come out on a breathy moan. "What's that?"

"Of all the gin joints . . ."

JESSICA ANDERSEN

NIGHTKEEPERS

A NOVEL OF
THE FINAL PROPHECY

*First in the acclaimed series that
combines Mayan astronomy and lore with
modern, sexy characters.*

In the first century A.D., Mayan astronomers predicted
the world would end on December 21, 2012. In these
final years before the End Times, demon creatures of
the Mayan underworld have come to earth to trigger
the apocalypse. But the descendants of the Mayan
warrior-priests have decided to fight back.

**"Raw passion, dark romance, and seat-of-
your-pants suspense, all set in an
astounding paranormal world."**
—#1 *New York Times* bestselling author J. R. Ward

Also Available
Dawnkeepers
Skykeepers
Demonkeepers

**Available wherever books are sold or at
penguin.com**